A Tender Reed

A Tender Reed

Teresa D. Slack

Tsaba House
Reedley, California

Cover design by Bookwrights Design
Interior Design by Pete Masterson, Æonix Publishing Group
Senior Editor, Jodie Nazaroff
Author Photo by Andrea Schwagerl

First Edition: 2005

Library of Congress Cataloging-in-Publication

Slack, Teresa D., 1964-
    A tender reed / Teresa D. Slack.-- 1st ed.
        p. cm.
    ISBN-13: 978-0-9725486-3-2 (pbk. : alk. paper)
    ISBN-10: 0-9725486-3-7 (pbk. : alk. paper)
1. Abandoned children--Fiction. 2. Rejection (Psychology)--Fiction. 3. Women farmers--Fiction. 4. Family farms--Fiction.
5. Aunts--Fiction. I. Title.
    PS3619.L33T46 2005
    813'.6--dc22

                                        2005014926

Published by
Tsaba House
2252 12th Street, Reedley
California 93654

Visit our website at: www.TsabaHouse.com

Printed in the United States of America

Acknowledgements

The outpouring of enthusiasm and support I received after the publication of my first book continues to be such a blessing to me. I want to express my gratitude to all the library staffers and bookstore owners, who hosted an author discussion/book signing in my honor. Many of you provided door prizes and snacks, took pictures, alerted the media, and went above and beyond what was expected to make the event fun for everyone.

Thank you to all the readers who attended these events in support of an unknown writer. Some of you were old friends, and others I met for the first time while autographing a book for you. I hope you had as much fun as I did. A special thanks to Brett Nutt, a sixth grader from Seaman, Ohio, who arrived at my signing before I did and waited most of the afternoon to meet me.

Thank you to my church family at the Hillsboro Church of God in Hillsboro, Ohio. Your ongoing support and prayers make all the difference.

A special thank you to Wayne and Angel Wilburn who answered questions concerning Michelle's nursing career and came up with good reasons when the story dictated that she work late or go in early.

I want to thank my family and friends, whose love and support continues to overwhelm me. Thanks to my dad who bought several copies of my book even after I offered them to him for free.

My undying love and devotion goes to my husband, Ralph, who attended nearly every writing event with me and stood in the back of the room, directing readers to my table, and generally bragging me up to anyone who would listen.

I want to close with a prayer of thanks to my Heavenly Father for opening doors so that my writing might touch hearts. Jesus said; "If my name be lifted up, I will draw all men unto me." May that continue to be the purpose behind every word I write.

In memory of my dog, Reiley, whose early morning barking was the jumping point that inspired this book.

Chapter One

I awoke to the sound of Gypsy barking like a wild thing. She had spent the night outside on the front porch like she often did when the weather was nice. Leaving her outside overnight was not a problem. The farmhouse was two miles down a back road, off another back road, off a minor highway; and the nearest neighbors on either side were kin to me. Every now and then Gypsy would wake me up barking at another dog a couple of miles away with a combination bark/howl sequence, depending on how put out she was, to let anyone who cared know she was on duty and not to go getting any ideas. Normally I'd roll over and go back to sleep. She wasn't the watchdog she'd been a few years ago. I assume she finally realized nothing much happened around here that warranted losing a night's sleep. Unless someone was standing over me with a chain saw, she didn't raise her hackles. Even then I had my doubts.

I rolled over and looked at the clock: six-fifteen, and on my weekend off. I had planned to sleep in, which for me was about seven. I stuffed the pillow around my ears and tried to ignore her.

The barking continued, unabated. It wasn't her usual "there's-a-squirrel-in-the-tree" announcement, or "here-comes-the-meter-reader-and-I-haven't-got-anything-better-to-do" barking. She wasn't stopping. I could either stay where I was as the racket wore on my every nerve, or get out of bed.

Ugh, that dog! One of these days…

I threw the sheet off my damp body. For a moment the change in temperature, or maybe just the breeze from the sheet, cooled my skin, but then I was hot again. It was going to be another scorcher, like every other August day in northern Arkansas.

I sat up and swung my legs over the edge of the queen-sized bed, the linoleum cool and delicious under my bare feet. I went to the window and hit the pane with the heel of my hand to loosen the swollen wood. Someday I would install vinyl windows. It sure would be nice to have windows that slid smoothly up and down, and didn't have to be propped open with a stick of wood. I had dialed the flashing number at the bottom of the screen during one of those TV commercials last fall, and the guy offered me a discount if I agreed to replace every window in the old farmhouse. Only two-twenty per, installed. That was big of him. This house had thirty windows if it had one.

I stuck my head out the screen-less window to see what had Gypsy stirred up. She was on the front porch directly below me. I couldn't see her through the porch roof, but I could tell by her infernal barking she was standing next to the left roof support, above the top step, her usual post. I listened for any other noises that may have disturbed her. Could it be another dog barking; Uncle DeWitt doing some early morning tinkering down the road; a masked gunman breaking through the front door? All was quiet, except for Gypsy.

"Gypsy!" I hollered in my early morning croak. It was a good thing for me there was only family within a half-mile radius. If my melodious voice reached them through the leafy trees and other morning sounds, they wouldn't be alarmed. "Knock off that barking."

She paused for a half second before going right back at it. She wasn't going to listen to any commands from me as long as she knew I wasn't serious enough to come downstairs to correct her.

With an aggravated huff, I left the window and flopped down on the edge of the bed. I stepped into the pair of cotton shorts I'd stepped out of the night before, pulled them up over the tail of my thin nightgown, and padded down the stairs in my bare feet.

If she was carrying on over a dead snake she'd dragged onto the porch, I was going to really let her have it. The other night, she'd dug a mole out of the yard and then barked at the blind, confused creature and knocked it around every time it struggled to get back underground. She wouldn't kill it; she just tortured it for her own pleasure. My beloved Australian Shepard-Beagle-Collie mix was a Nazi.

I finally had to kill the mole with a shovel and throw its body over the fence. If I had to get that up close and personal with a snake, Gypsy was going to be in hot water.

I yanked the front door open with enough force to demonstrate my irritation at getting woke up so early. I stepped out onto the porch and set my fists on my hips to drive home my point. Gypsy stopped barking long enough to glance at me over her shoulder before turning back toward the road and starting in again.

Well, the posturing hadn't worked. It was time to get serious. "Gypsy, for crying out loud, is this necessary? Do you think the neighbors appreciate hearing your mouth at six o'clock in the morning?"

Gypsy and I lived alone on what remained of my family's farm. Consequently, I had taken to talking to her like she was a person instead of a dog from the first day I brought her home. I enjoyed her company above any other living creature on the earth, so I figured she deserved the respect. I also believed she understood more that came out of my mouth than the usual "Sit" and "Stay." In fact, those were the words she chose not to understand.

Rather than heed the irritation in my voice and stature, she leaped off the porch, bypassing the steps in one bound, and landed deftly on the worn dirt path. She headed to the opening in the white picket fence, some fifty feet away, where the path met the road. She dashed through the opening where a gate once stood and made a right turn toward the mailbox on the other side of a thirty-year-old lilac bush. The white gate that I passed through every day on my way to and from the school bus had been missing for years. Even back then the gate was loose, one hinge rusted and squeaky, the other completely gone. Uncle Jeb was never handy around the house, regardless of how he talked. I couldn't remember exactly when the gate disappeared for good, but I think it was around the time I started applying for scholarships, when I had a personal reason for checking the mail. I still painted the wooden fence every other year so it remained white and crisp against the lilac and forsythia bushes, but I never gave a thought to the missing gate—until now.

I could see Gypsy's hindquarters sticking out from behind the lilac bush. Her fluffy tail was erect, the tip twitching ever so slightly. She barked once more for effect, and then got quiet. While she still felt the need to proceed with caution to whatever was on the other side of the fence, she was no longer threatened. At least I could dismiss the notion of someone waiting for me with a chainsaw; I hoped.

I wished now I'd taken the time to slip into a pair of shoes before hurrying out the door. The dirt under my feet was cold and wet. I'd track mud into the house when I went back inside if I didn't spray them off with the garden hose around back. I winced as a pebble dug into the ball of my foot. That blasted dog, one of these days I was going to wring her neck. Whatever she was carrying on about had better be worth all this trouble if she knew what was good for her.

I stepped through the garden gate and turned right. The dirt path ended and I stepped into the dew-covered grass. Gooseflesh rose on my bare legs. "Gypsy, what's all the…" I began as I rounded the lilac bush.

Gypsy looked at me over her shoulder and then sat back on her haunches, barely missing my foot. She turned back to her discovery.

I followed her gaze. My breath caught in my throat. Gypsy sensed my reaction and jumped forward, I suppose, to assure me there was no cause for alarm.

She put her nose against the trembling little boy, circled him and the little girl huddled next to him in the cold grass, and then looked back at me. *"I told you it was important,"* her reproving gaze told me. *"Now what are you going to do about it?"*

I forced myself out of my trance and moved gingerly forward, so not to startle the wide-eyed children staring up at me.

That's when I recognized them. "Jonah? Emma?"

Neither of the children's expression changed.

Gypsy nudged closer, apparently satisfied that all was well. She put her nose against the little boy's neck and sniffed. He turned his head toward her and his lips twitched into a smile. A tiny hand reached out and disappeared into her thick, dark red coat. It was all the encouragement Gypsy needed. She shoved against him and nuzzled his neck. Then she reached across him to inspect his sister, knocking him over with her broad body in the process.

I stepped forward. "Gypsy, stop."

I heard a muffled giggle.

I took hold of Gypsy's collar and pulled her back. The little boy lay on his back in the grass, his knees pulled up to his chest where Gypsy had upended him. At the sight of me towering over him, the giggling ended abruptly and his face sobered.

"Are you okay?" I asked.

He stared up at me. After a moment, he pulled himself upright and asked in a tiny voice, "Are you my Aunt Shell?"

"Shell," that's what my kid sister, Nicole used to call me before she could pronounce Michelle. Someone must have told him where he was going and who to expect. He never would have recognized me on his own. The last time I saw him, nearly two years ago, he was still a baby. I wouldn't have recognized him either had I seen him somewhere else, under different circumstances.

At the sound of the little boy's voice, Gypsy lunged forward and broke free from my grasp on her collar. She loved everyone, but children were her favorite. She inspected the little boy's face with her wet nose, before straddling him to get to his sister again. Emma shrank away from the big dog's face, apparently not as sure of her intent as Jonah.

I moved forward again and took hold of her collar once more. "Gypsy, that's enough," I said sternly. I gave her collar a firm jerk. She reluctantly complied and sat down at my feet, never taking her eyes off the children.

"Yes, I'm your Aunt Michelle. You must be Jonah and Emma." I leaned forward and held my arms out to him. He paused for only a moment before reaching willingly for me. From what I remembered, he had been a shy baby, but the wet grass and fear of spending—who knows how long—out here by the gate, drove him into my arms.

Gypsy whimpered and looked like she was about to pounce again, but a growled "stay" command from me kept her in her place.

I took Jonah in my arms and straightened. He wrapped his legs around me. His bare feet chilled me through my thin nightgown. How long had they been sitting out here? Not too long since Gypsy had just started barking, but long enough that he shivered in the morning air.

I shifted Jonah to my right hip and reached out my free hand to his sister. Emma looked from my hand to Jonah and back again before reaching out to take it. She stood up on shaky legs. Her feet were also bare. She was dressed in a pair of cotton shorts and a baggy tee shirt that looked like she'd slept in it. She gave Gypsy a nervous look. Gypsy stood up and returned the stare, eager, waiting. Cautiously, Emma reached out with her other hand and took hold of Gypsy's collar.

When our bedraggled group stepped away from the lilac bush, I noticed a frayed book bag in the grass. I presumed it contained their belongings. I would come back for it later, after I got them into the house, into something warm and dry, and put some food in their bellies. It looked like they could use it. I headed up the dirt path, no longer concerned about the mud that would be tracked across my relatively clean floors.

Jonah bounced on my hip, his cold feet snuggling intentionally against my warmth. Emma's hand trembled in mine. I still hadn't heard a peep out of her. Gypsy, who wasn't that big of a dog, came nearly to the little girl's shoulder. She strode beside Emma, her head and tail erect, the only one in our raggedy group apparently happy with the situation.

I was a registered nurse; trained to take care of the situation first, fix what was wrong, make everyone as comfortable as possible, and ask questions later. I didn't need to worry right now about how they came to be under my lilac bush. I didn't want to think of them sitting alone outside, just inches from the road where anyone could have come by in the early morning light and run them over.

And I certainly didn't want to worry about Nicole. As my mind conjured up questions, I resolutely pushed them aside. There was too much else to worry about now. I couldn't think about what terrible thing may have befallen my sister to cause her to leave her two young children in my front yard without a word of explanation. Or worse, that nothing had happened and she just plain abandoned them.

Chapter Two

I was nearly ten-years-old and happily relegated to the status of only child when my parents saw fit to present me with a little sister. It turned out they were full of surprises. When I was eleven and Nicole, fifteen-months, Dad took off. One day he was just gone. Mom never told us where he went, what possessed him to go, or even if she saw it coming. The whole situation makes no more sense to me now then it did then. We held out as long as we could in our little apartment in Memphis, Tennessee, but Mom wasn't one of "those step-up-to-the-plate, when-life-gives-you-lemons-make-lemonade" personalities. She was a good woman, but she lacked the fortitude to raise Nicole and me on her own.

We packed everything we had, that the bank didn't own, into our battered Ford Maverick, and moved back to the family farm where Mom and her sisters and brothers were raised. Grandma Catherine still lived in the big farmhouse. Grandpa was some twenty years older than Grandma, and had been dead for a number of years. By this time the farm had been divided into several portions to accommodate members of the family who felt no inclination to move away. Mom's brother, DeWitt, a crusty old bachelor, lived in a simple shotgun house he'd built himself in 1964. It was a half-mile east of the original farmhouse, and he farmed eighty acres there. No improvements had been made in the ensuing forty-plus years. The trees he planted in the yard had grown into massive, looming pines, successfully concealing the house from the road, which was what he intended. No one ever saw much of Uncle DeWitt.

Aunt Wanda and her husband, Jeb Rowe, a retired state highway worker, farmed and raised cattle on the forty acres to the west. The rest of the family used their good common sense and high tailed it out of the county as soon as the ink was dry on their high school diplomas. Uncle Jeb tore down the little house on his portion of the property and built Aunt Wanda a modern brick split-level about the same time Nicole, Mom and I were moving in on Grandma. I was often envious of Aunt Wanda's modern kitchen, ample closet space, and full basement that didn't flood after every spring rain, but not enough to sink any real money into Grandma's old farmhouse.

Aunt Wanda and Uncle Jeb had one child, a sickly, whiny, spoiled girl named Violet. She was nearly a year older than me, but we were in the same grade at Jessup Elementary in Winona, the tiny town five miles east of the farm. Since the small school only had two homerooms per grade, I spent a lot of time in Violet's company.

I hated the school, the depressingly outdated farmhouse, and most of all, simpering Violet, who got off the bus every day at the farm with me. Even after Mom moved home with Nicole and me, Aunt Wanda finished her housework every morning by ten and came over to spend the rest of the day with Grandma. Supposedly, it was to help out. According to Grandma, she couldn't get by without Wanda. It seemed to me that Grandma just liked a sympathetic ear for her constant complaining, and Wanda liked to remind Mom that her own husband hadn't taken off, leaving her high and dry with two kids to raise alone.

Considering Uncle Jeb's options, I never understood what kept him around.

Whatever Aunt Wanda's motivation, much of my afternoons were spent entertaining Violet when I would rather have been reading, walking in the woods behind the house, playing with Baby Nikki, or composing letters to my missing father; letters I would never send since Mom wouldn't, or couldn't, tell me where he'd gone.

I missed Dad and could think of little else. My grades at my old school had always been at the top of the class. After moving to

Winona, about a hundred miles east of Memphis, my grades plummeted and continued their downward spiral well into high school. I couldn't get over Dad's leaving. I didn't understand any of it. I thought our family was happy and stable. Why did he leave? I didn't know such things as "other women" or "disenchantment with life" existed; and if I had, I would certainly have thought that they didn't apply to my father. He was my rock, and at the time I loved him more than anything. I thought he loved me back.

Had I been able to see past my own misery, I might have noticed what a toll our new circumstances were taking on Mom. I should've known she couldn't last. Grandma Catherine was a faultfinder, in me, Mom, Baby Nikki, Uncle Jeb, even her dead husband, Grandpa Walt, whom I'd never met. Mom didn't have it in her to stand up to anyone, especially someone as headstrong as Grandma. She took a job in town that she hated because Grandma told her to. She stood quietly and listened to Aunt Wanda's unwelcome advice even though she resented it deeply. She didn't have it in her to tell them to mind their own business. Then again, how could she when she needed them so badly?

I didn't pay much attention the first time I saw her taking a sip from a narrow bottle she kept in her underwear drawer. Mom and Dad had always been what they called "social drinkers." It didn't take me long to realize there was nothing social about her behavior. I did her share of the housework when she was hung over. I shushed Baby Nikki and tried to keep her out from underfoot when Mom was sleeping in. I didn't want to give Grandma another reason to scold her as if she were a child. I was secretly pleased to know I wasn't the only one suffering from Dad's absence. Our pain became a badge we shared.

I was absolutely devastated when she left.

Instantly, it was only Nicole and me who were the outsiders. The ones here, not by invitation, but because of a curse sent by God to punish Grandma for some sin she had unknowingly committed. At least that's the impression I got. I was fourteen by this time. Nicole was nearly four, precocious, darling, and too energetic to be tolerated by Grandma. She had no recollection of Dad, whom I was also beginning to forget, and her memories of Mom soon became blurred.

"Does your dog bite?"

The sound of Jonah's voice snapped me out of my reverie. I climbed the three porch steps and opened the front door. "No, she loves everybody." I let go of Emma's hand to trip the latch on the screen door, and held it open with my hip while Gypsy led Emma in ahead of Jonah and me.

"She barked at us," Jonah told me.

"Yes, I heard her," I said. "I hope she didn't scare you."

"She scared Emma a little."

I stepped inside and lowered Jonah to the floor. The screen door banged shut behind us. I looked at Emma. She seemed to have gotten over her fright. Her hand still clung to Gypsy's collar.

"I'm sorry she scared you, Emma."

Emma patted Gypsy's head with her free hand. A tiny smile curved the corners of her mouth. She looked like Nicole at that age; sunny blonde hair that cascaded in long, loose curls down her back, delicate features, an upturned nose, and the bluest eyes this side of heaven, fringed by long blonde lashes.

I straightened and put my hand at the small of my back. For such a little guy, Jonah sure got heavy between the lilac bushes and the front door. His blonde hair was darker than Emma's, the kind that would go brown before he got much older. His eyes were brown and the shape of his face was angular where hers was soft. If I didn't know Emma was the oldest, it would be hard to tell. They were almost exactly the same height and build, and Jonah was definitely the more outgoing of the two. I counted backwards in my head. He was born in 2001 on March thirtieth, no the thirty-first. That made him three and a half. Emma's birthday was February fourteenth, 2000. She was the sweetheart baby. That's what Nicole always called her. Too bad the sweetheart who helped produce her didn't hang around after the stick from the drugstore test turned blue.

What in the world was I going to do with two preschoolers? This happened to be the start of one of my rare weekends off, but I had to go back to work Monday. I worked long hours. I didn't have time to baby-sit two tiny children while my irresponsible kid sister was off finding herself or sleeping one off.

When I got my hands on her...

The two of them were staring expectantly up at me. "You must be starving," I said.

Jonah nodded. Emma put her head against Gypsy and hugged her neck. I mentally went over the contents of my pantry. Slim pickings if I remembered correctly. I didn't cook. When I wasn't working, which wasn't often, I grabbed whatever was easy and convenient: low fat yogurt, Lean Cuisine, or a bag of microwave popcorn. I completely relied on multi-vitamins to balance out my irregular diet.

"Do you like pancakes?" I asked in as cheery a voice as I could muster. Surely I had the necessary ingredients to whip up a batch, if I remembered how.

Jonah nodded again. Emma tightened her arms around Gypsy and buried her face in the dog's long hair. "Emma likes pancakes too," Jonah said, to be helpful.

"Great." I took Jonah's hand in mine and reached for Emma's with the other. As soon as I made physical contact, she began to wail. She let go of Gypsy's neck and dropped to the floor on her hands and knees. She buried her face in her hands and bent forward until her forehead rested against the cool wood floor.

I jumped back like I'd been scalded. Now what? I worked in the cardiac care unit at the University Hospital in the next county. I could handle any emergency that arose with my adult patients with grace and a cool head. This was different. I avoided children as much as possible, especially loud ones.

Jonah slipped his hand out of mine and squatted on the floor beside his big sister. "It's okay, Emmy," he said soothingly. "She'll come back. She always does." He patted her back and pulled her long hair away from her face.

Even Gypsy seemed to know what to do. She slumped on the floor next to the crying child with a loud sigh and laid her head in her paws. Emma rose up enough to put one arm around Gypsy and the other around Jonah. Then she continued to cry into her lap.

I stood there, just inside the door of the old farmhouse, and watched the drama at my feet. In my thirteen years of nursing, I'd seen families weep as I explained a Do Not Resuscitate Order for their terminally ill parents. I stood within reach to provide a comforting shoulder, or someone to scream at, when parents received the news that their child had died from the head trauma sustained in a traffic accident. My entire adult life had been spent taking care of people in their time of need.

Now as my own niece and nephew sat on my floor and bawled their eyes out over their missing mother, I was helpless. Even if I could think of an appropriate platitude that would explain to a child why she and her little brother had been abandoned in a virtual stranger's yard in the middle of the night, the words wouldn't have gotten past my own thickened throat.

"*It's okay, Emma, she'll come back. She always does.*" What did that mean? What had these two little kids been through in their short time on this earth? More importantly, where was Nicole? What was she thinking?

Why had she done this to me?

Chapter Three

Icouldn't remember the last time I made pancakes. Since Grandma passed away six years ago, I'd become a stranger to the kitchen. It turned out I hadn't lost my touch, at least not with pancakes. They turned out perfectly. Neither Emma nor Jonah had much appetite.

Emma stopped crying long enough to move the pancakes around on her plate in a puddle of syrup. Jonah ate a little better. He also had better luck at keeping his tears in check, but just barely. Neither one looked up or spoke while they ate. I stayed close to the stove, fearful of saying too much or intruding on their suffering, lest the tears start flowing again.

After they finished breakfast, I ushered them into the living room, sat them in front of my miserable nineteen-inch television set, and flipped around for cartoons or something that would interest them. I didn't have cable, and the set was a throw back from Grandma Catherine's days. I personally didn't have time or the inclination for television and got by just fine with an occasional dose of the evening news.

I found something animated, although it didn't look anything like the Bugs and Daffy cartoons I'd grown up on. Emma and Jonah stared at the fuzzy picture and exchanged glances. I backed out of the room and fled to the telephone in the hallway. I took the handset from the base and retreated to a secluded corner where I wouldn't be overheard.

It was nearly eight A.M. by now. I knew Aunt Wanda and Uncle

Jeb would be up and about, working on their second pot of coffee. Aunt Wanda answered on the second ring.

"Can you come over here?" I said without pretense. "It's Nicole. She's gone and done it this time, and I don't know what to do."

"Oh, dear," Aunt Wanda said. "Is she all right?"

"I'm not sure. I woke up this morning and found the kids outside under the lilac bushes."

"Emma and Jonah, you're kidding? You don't suppose something's happened to her, do you?"

"I don't think so, at least I hope not. Jonah told Emma not to cry, that she always comes back."

"Oh, dear," she said again, "Those poor, babies. I'll be right over."

It was sad that I didn't need to convince her I was telling the truth and not over-reacting. The whole family was accustomed to Nicole and her antics by now. By the time she was sixteen, embroiled in her third or fourth serious love affair, this time with a married man, we all realized there was no scandalous behavior beneath her.

Aunt Wanda burst through the back door five minutes later. Her garishly unnatural blonde hair stood out away from her head in a fuzzy mess. Years of overuse of harsh hair coloring products and home perms, coupled with an incredibly dated hairstyle, added years to her appearance. I had never seen her outside of her house, even to go to the mailbox, without that hair being teased and sprayed within an inch of its life. Uncle Jeb always said if she were ever in an accident, her hair would save her from head injuries. Only her hair belied the fact that her morning routine had been interrupted.

"Where are they?"

I jabbed my thumb toward the kitchen doorway. "They're in the living room watching TV."

"Well, what did Nicole say?"

"Nothing, I didn't see her. Gypsy woke me up barking, and when I went out, I found them huddled outside the gate next to the road."

"Oh, this is rich," Aunt Wanda fumed, "Even for Nicole." She crept to the doorway and peered into the living room. She turned and looked back at me. "Did she leave a note or anything? Did the kids say where she is?"

I shook my head. "I don't think they know anymore than we do. They're upset, of course, but I don't think they're terribly surprised."

She shook her head and clicked her tongue.

Suddenly I remembered the book bag under the lilac bush. "They did have a bag with them. Maybe there's something in it." I stepped into the mudroom and took a pair of garden shoes out of the wicker basket by the door. "I'll be right back."

When I got back, the battered book bag in tow, Aunt Wanda was no longer in the kitchen. I looked into the living room and saw her sitting in Grandma Catherine's easy chair, watching the kids watch TV. Only they weren't watching anymore. They were cowering together in the center of the sofa, Gypsy leaning protectively against their legs, staring at Aunt Wanda.

All three looked up when I walked in.

I held up the book bag and smiled. "Look what I found outside. Does this belong to anyone?"

"That's ours," Jonah offered. "Dean brought it."

Dean. I vaguely remembered the name from a previous telephone conversation with Nicole; it was one of our typical "can you send me a few bucks, I'm in a real bind?" conversations. Without going into particulars, Dean had apparently messed up her face in a drunken fight and forced her to lose her hostess job at Denny's. When I tried to talk her into coming home until she could get her life together, we'd ended up having a fight of our own.

She didn't come home. I sent a check.

"Is Dean the one who brought you here?" Aunt Wanda asked.

Emma and Jonah exchanged nervous glances. I wondered if they'd been warned against telling anyone how they ended up outside my gate.

"May I look in here and see what you brought?" I asked.

They exchanged glances again, but the fear in their eyes subsided. Jonah nodded. Emma had yet to speak, or even maintain eye contact with me.

I sat down on the chair opposite them and set the book bag on my knees. "What a nice book bag," I said conversationally. "It's so big, and it's heavy too. You must have lots of cool stuff in here."

Jonah gave me a half-smile. Emma slid onto the floor and wrapped her arms around Gypsy's neck.

I had the bag halfway unzipped before I wondered if this was such a good idea. What if there was something inside the children shouldn't see? Jonah said Dean was the one who brought the bag. It occurred to me that Dean could have done something to Nicole. My stomach lurched. What if Nicole was hurt somewhere and totally unaware of what Dean had done with her kids? Even if she had left the kids before, it didn't necessarily mean she had willingly done so this time.

I scooped the bag into my arms and stood up. "Oh, my, I think I forgot to turn off the stove."

Aunt Wanda gave me a strange look and jumped up from her chair. She followed me into the kitchen. I deposited the bag on the table and turned to look at her.

"What's going on?" She knew I hadn't left the stove on. She stared at me, and then the bag.

I glanced toward the door to make sure no little ears were within hearing distance and finished unzipping the bag. "I was afraid this might contain something the kids shouldn't see."

"Oh, you're right." Aunt Wanda pulled a chair out from under the table and sat down in front of the bag.

I reached inside and pulled out a sheaf of papers. Underneath were hastily packed clothes; tee shirts, shorts, two pairs of jeans, a pair of boys' jockeys, and girls' panties. No socks, no shoes, or jackets or sweaters.

I exhaled with relief. "They apparently aren't going to be here long. This is only enough stuff to last a day or two."

"Or it could've been packed by a man who wouldn't know what children would need," Aunt Wanda pointed out. She reached for the sheaf of papers. Her brow furrowed in confusion. "Now, what is all this about?" She held the papers up for me to see. "Here's both the kids' birth certificates and their shot records."

"Why in the world…" I snatched the papers out of her hand and scanned over them. "Why would she think to bring their shot records and birth certificates, but not a simple pair of shoes? What is she thinking?"

Aunt Wanda stood up and looked at the papers over my shoulder. "I don't know, Michelle, but I really don't think this Dean the kids were talking about would think to include a birth certificate if he brought them here without Nicole knowing about it."

I suddenly had a pounding headache. I forgot to be relieved that Dean apparently hadn't done anything to my sister. "So you think Nicole is planning to leave the kids here…indefinitely." I gazed at her hopefully, silently begging her to tell me I was wrong. Nicole wouldn't do that. She just needed me for a few days. She was probably between jobs and in a bind. I'd keep an eye on the kids for a couple of days, a few weeks at the most, and then she'd be back, and my life could go back to normal.

"Well, she knows you go to work every day. If you have her kids, you're going to need daycare. You can't put a kid anywhere these days without this stuff. She's apparently put some thought into this."

I refused to accept what seemed to be happening. I sank into a kitchen chair and stared despondently at the papers. "But this doesn't make any sense. Nicole is a piece of work, but she loves her kids. I know she does. She wouldn't just leave them here, especially without telling me what she's doing."

Aunt Wanda continued to stare at the rumpled pile of clothes on the table neither confirming nor denying my rambling thoughts.

This wasn't making any sense. Sure, Nicole was flighty. She wasn't even a great mother. She lived here until Emma was a few months old. Barely out of high school and between boyfriends and jobs, she claimed she wanted to get her life straightened out. Unfortunately she had no patience for a needy, demanding baby when she was practically one herself. Her hairpin temper snapped frequently over colic, messy diaper changes, and Emma just being a baby.

I found myself getting up in the middle of the night more and more often for feedings. I couldn't stand listening to Nicole's cussing and grumbling through the thin walls as she demanded Emma hurry up and eat so she could get back to bed. Or worse, the way she ignored her altogether.

When she decided to move with Emma to the city where she could look for work, I refused to dwell on what life would be like for the baby. Parenting was difficult and stressful for anyone, especially a single girl. I hoped against hope Nicole would mature and the two of them would get along fine.

I didn't hear anything about the next boyfriend, some long-haired loser named Bones, who played in a band, until after Nicole called and said she was carrying Jonah. It didn't take much math skills on my part to realize she had become pregnant while living here on the farm with me, thus letting Bones, whom she'd just met, off the hook.

For the life of me, I couldn't imagine how Nicole had let another unplanned pregnancy occur when Emma was still waking her up in the night. She went out a few times to a club in town with a couple of girlfriends while living here, leaving me home to baby sit Emma. She never mentioned meeting someone. I could never make myself believe she was the type of person who could meet a guy in a club and let herself get pregnant, practically on the same day. But apparently, that was exactly what happened.

"I do know Nicole's situation," I said to Aunt Wanda, "and there's no way she would just leave her kids without a word of explanation."

"Maybe that's not what happened," she said hopefully. "We can only pray that Nicole is planning on this being a temporary arrangement."

"Of course it is. Nicole will be back soon and straighten this whole thing out."

"When was the last time you talked to her?"

"It's been awhile. The end of last year, I think." As soon as I said it out loud, I realized how bad it sounded. I continued, a little ashamed of myself. "I sent the kids some stuff for Christmas."

"Goodness, Michelle. This is August. That was eight months ago."

"I know. She was living in Memphis, but I think she's moved since then. I don't even know where to look for her."

We sat at the table, staring at the papers in front of us. My mind was whirling. I didn't even want to think about how this would affect my life. I didn't have time for children. I had a job; a very demanding, job; two jobs actually. Besides putting in forty hours a week in the I.C.U. unit at University Hospital, I worked weekends on contingency in the surgery prep unit at the county hospital in Geneva. It was a rare thing for me to take a weekend off. I had planned to get some stuff around the farm done while the weather cooperated, now this! What was I supposed to do with Emma and Jonah when I went to work on Monday? There weren't enough clothes in the bag to last the kids through the weekend. What was I supposed to do about that? I didn't even have anything in the house to eat; nothing children would want anyway.

Aunt Wanda must have been thinking the same thing. She got up and went to the refrigerator. She looked inside and sighed in dismay at the meager contents. She slammed the door shut with her elbow. "I can see I need to go to the store if you plan on feeding those two anytime soon."

"That's what I was thinking," I said. "I was totally unprepared for two mouths to feed, especially ones so young."

She crossed her arms over her chest and leaned against the refrigerator. "So, what are you going to do with them?"

I rested my chin in my hand. "I have no idea. At least I have the weekend to figure it out."

"They haven't said a word about where Nicole might've took off to, or what she's up to?"

I shook my head. "I can't get more than a word or two at a time out of Jonah, and Emma's not talking at all. Since Dean brought the bag that means Nicole isn't alone. I don't know if that's good or bad."

"That girl's never been without a man for more than a week at a stretch. I've never seen anything like it." Aunt Wanda sat down again. "What a mess. What an absolute mess. Leave it to Nicole to take off without even thinking of her responsibilities. How typical. She has no more business with two kids than a submarine has with a screen door."

The last thing I wanted to hear was a list of my sister's shortcomings, especially with her two abandoned children comforting one another less then twenty feet away. "She surely wasn't thinking," I agreed, and then hastened to add. "But regardless of what Nicole's done, I don't want those two in there thinking any of this is their fault."

"No one said it was, Michelle. We all know how selfish Nicole is. She's only thought of herself since God saw fit to put her on this earth. How would she have felt if you hadn't been home this weekend? What if you were out of town, she left them here, and they weren't found for three or four days? What a situation to put your own children in."

"She knows I never go anywhere," I said in Nicole's defense, although she certainly didn't deserve it.

"How does Nicole know anything? She hasn't been home in at least two years. Why, you could've up and joined the circus by now."

"I agree. This is her most irresponsible stunt to date. When I see her again, I'll personally wring her neck. Until then, I've got to decide what to do with Emma and Jonah."

"From where I sit, the decision's been made for you. Nicole's made a mess of things, but she is family." Aunt Wanda's earlier irritation had softened into resignation. She shrugged. "You do for family, period. And even if they weren't kin, Michelle, it's plain Christian charity. You're duty bound."

My jaw tightened. Not Christian charity again. I'd heard that from Grandma my whole life. The only reason she allowed Mom to move in with Nicole and me after Dad left, and the only reason she kept us on after Mom disappeared, was Christian charity. She never let us forget that we were living under her roof, eating her food, and sleeping under her warm blankets because she was a good Christian. If not for her generous spirit, the Lord only knew what would have become of us.

I had enough Christian charity to last me a lifetime.

"Maybe this is for the best," Aunt Wanda went on.

"How can this be for the best?" I snapped. We both glanced at the kitchen door. When I resumed talking, I held my voice in check. "I'm sorry, Aunt Wanda. I didn't mean to raise my voice. But this is not for the best. I don't know anything about kids. I work sixty hours a week. I'm barely home long enough to take care of Gypsy, let alone two kids I didn't bring into the world."

The more I talked, the madder I got. How dare Nicole! If she wanted to mess up her own life, that was her business, but now she'd gone and messed up mine. I was ticked.

Aunt Wanda reached over and patted my hand. "I know this isn't fair, Michelle. But have you stopped to think this may be just what Emma and Jonah need?"

No, I hadn't thought about it, and I didn't want to.

"None of us knows a thing about kids until we become a parent for the first time," Aunt Wanda continued, "Even those so-called experts who write those child-rearing books. Let me tell you, you can spot the non-parents a mile away. They don't know a thing about what they're writing. The only way to learn is to have kids and figure it out as you go."

I looked in the direction of the living room one more time. I leaned toward Aunt Wanda and whispered, "But I don't want kids. Not now, not ever. I don't particularly like them. I don't want a husband. I don't like those either. I'm perfectly happy here on the farm with Gypsy. I don't need or want anything else."

Aunt Wanda actually had the nerve to laugh. If she kept it up, she was going to find herself on the receiving end of the wrath I currently felt for Nicole.

She got up and pulled open a kitchen drawer. "Have you got any paper in here?" she asked, rifling through it. "We'll make a grocery list and I'll go shopping for you."

As usual, she wasn't paying attention to the words coming out of my mouth. She thought I was being funny. What did I have to do for someone to take me seriously?

"I can do it," I said, jumping to my feet. I took the paper and stub of a pencil out of her hand. I needed to get out of here, at least for a few minutes. And, I sure didn't want Aunt Wanda spouting Nicole's and my business all over town. "It would really help me out if you stayed here with the kids."

She sighed. "I suppose I could. I'll make lunch with something out of these cabinets." She opened one door, and then another, working her way down the wall. "You don't have much, do you?"

"I don't cook."

"I can see that."

"I'll explain to the kids where I'm going," I said on my way to the living room.

"Michelle."

I stopped in the doorway and looked back.

"It will all work out," Aunt Wanda assured me. "You may just find this is the best thing that's ever happened to you."

I tried to smile like I thought she could be right, but my lips stuck to my teeth. No, this was definitely not the best thing that ever happened to me. I was not one of those women who oohed and ahhed over babies at the grocery store. They leaked, they smelled, and were downright inconvenient.

Emma and Jonah weren't babies. So far, I hadn't seen them leak or smell, but I could almost bet they would prove to be inconvenient. I didn't want my life to change. I liked things just the way they were. I wanted to go to work Monday morning like always, and not worry about two little people who were suddenly dependent on me.

Chapter Four

When I got home two hours later with enough frozen and pre-packaged food for an army of little people, Emma and Jonah were fast asleep on the living room rug, their arms around Gypsy. Gypsy raised her head off the floor and looked at me when I came in, but didn't get up, a first. I guess I'd been replaced as far as she was concerned. I reminded myself not to take it personally. Gypsy sensed who needed her most. Still, I couldn't help wondering what their presence in the house would rob me of next.

I followed the sound of pots and pans rattling in the kitchen, and found Aunt Wanda on her hands and knees, rearranging the bottom cabinet shelves.

She paused in her rattling to explain that it was no wonder I didn't cook with the lack of organization in my kitchen. "Now that you've got little ones here," her voice rang out from the dark recesses of the kitchen cabinets, "you're going to have to learn to run a tighter ship."

I didn't want to run a tight ship. I wanted everything to stay the way it had been for as long as I cared to remember. I was thirty-three years old. I earned a decent wage doing something I loved. I kept the farmhouse's old roof from caving in on my head. Gypsy's shots were up to date. I didn't owe anyone money I couldn't pay back in an acceptable amount of time. No tighter ship could anyone expect of me.

I turned and left the kitchen without a word and went back to the car for the next load of groceries. This was the first time since Grandma

Catherine died that I couldn't carry all the groceries into the house in one trip. Things were already changing and I didn't like it.

I ran into Sandy Cline at Kroger's. She eyed my grocery cart suspiciously and asked if I was expecting company. Anyone with the slightest observation skills could figure out their neighbor's business by looking at what they bought at the grocery store, especially in Winona. You couldn't develop diabetes, adopt a kitten, or confirm a suspected pregnancy in private, unless you shopped in the next county.

I had smiled at Sandy and said I was expecting my sister any day, which I was…sort of. When she asked where Nicole was keeping herself these days; that no one around here had seen her in a month of Sundays, I smiled brightly and pushed my cart with the squeaky front wheel toward produce, telling her over my shoulder that I would tell Nicole she had asked about her.

Ah, the joys of small town life.

I started putting away groceries as Aunt Wanda backed out of the cabinet and slowly climbed to her feet. She slapped at the knees of her slacks. I braced myself for the lecture on the condition of my floors, which I knew was forthcoming as sure as I was standing there, and tried to recall what possessed me to buy yogurt in a tube. Couldn't kids eat yogurt with a spoon anymore? Did everything have to come out of a squeezable, convenient, overpriced tube these days?

"Did you stop by Children's Services?" she asked in lieu of the lecture.

I stared. "Children's Services, Why would I do that?"

Aunt Wanda set her hands on her hips and leaned her backside against the counter. "Michelle," she said, in that mildly irritating, condescending way of hers I'd learned to ignore over the past twenty-some years, "Nicole has disappeared. The police aren't going to go looking for her, since technically she isn't missing. Personally I don't think anything's happened to her that a swift kick in the rear wouldn't cure. But in the meantime, you've got her kids. What if she isn't coming back—ever? Does your insurance cover them if they get sick? Do you have the authority to even have them treated? What are you going to do about childcare? I doubt a birth certificate will be enough for you to enroll them in daycare. They barely have more than the clothes on their backs. All this is going to cost money; who's going to pay for all of it, you?"

I closed my eyes and massaged my temple. She had obviously done a lot of thinking while I was out. This was adding up to more than just a simple weekend's worth of inconvenience.

I opened my eyes and looked at her. "There's no need to bring the county authorities into our business." The last thing I wanted was for everyone in Harrison County to know my irresponsible sister had abandoned her kids in my front yard. "Emma and Jonah might not even be here that long. Besides, it's Saturday. All the public offices are closed."

Aunt Wanda continued, ignoring that minor setback. "You don't have a choice, missy. Things like this aren't as simple as they used to be."

I knew she was remembering how Mom just up and vanished, leaving her burdens behind for Grandma to take care of.

"I'm sure Nicole foresaw all those things you were talking about: childcare, doctor visits. That's why she left what she did. She was covering all the bases, and she'll be back when she gets whatever's going on in her life right now, straightened out."

Aunt Wanda arched her eyebrows. "You're kidding, right? This is Nicole we're talking about. If she was only leaving them with you for a week or two, she wouldn't have done a single thing to make things easier on you, and you know it. She wouldn't have thought far enough ahead to consider one of them getting sick. She would've assumed you could use a few vacation days you've got stored up to baby sit while she did whatever it is she's doing."

She was right. Nicole never put herself out if she could avoid it. But I wasn't ready to accept the fact that her kids were here and I was the one responsible for their care. I had a full-time, very demanding job. I drove a Mazda RX8 that the dealer had ordered especially for me the week the new model was launched. I never cooked and sometimes forgot to change the sheets on my bed. Now to have two kids for an indefinite period of time; no, that couldn't happen! My life was set. I loved my niece and nephew, I guess I did, considering I didn't really know them, but I had no room in my life for children.

"If I haven't heard from Nicole by tomorrow night, I'll call

Children's Services first thing Monday morning and see what all this means."

That gave my sister thirty-six hours to remember she had two small children in need of her.

⅋

Uncle Jeb came over to see how we were getting along just as I was getting the kids out of the bathtub. I heard his heavy tread on the stairs long before he appeared in the bathroom doorway. I was sopping up water off the floor with a towel, and Emma and Jonah were struggling to get their still-damp bodies to slide into their resisting nightclothes. The nightclothes consisted of tee shirts and shorts since neither Nicole nor Dean had thought to pack pajamas.

"Well, would you lookie here?" Uncle Jeb's amiable voice boomed. He grinned at Emma. "If I didn't know better, I'd think little Nicole was back in the flesh. You're the spittin' image of your mama, little lady."

Emma stuck her finger in her mouth and took a half step behind me. I smiled reassuringly at her as I straightened up.

"She's a beauty, isn't she?" I said to Uncle Jeb. I dropped the towel on the floor and put one hand on her shoulder and the other on Jonah's. "Kids, this is your Uncle Jeb. He's married to Aunt Wanda, the lady who fixed you lunch. He lives on the next farm."

"Yep," Uncle Jeb said to the silent, staring children, "Got a real nice pond on my farm, just perfect for fishin'." He focused on Jonah. "Don't guess you know anybody who'd be interested in fishin', now do ya?"

Jonah's eyes grew wide with delight and a smile crept across his features. He nodded. "Me."

Uncle Jeb jerked his head back in mock surprise. "You? You like to fish? Well, don't that beat all?"

Jonah nodded faster. "I do. I do like to fish."

"Now, ain't that somethin'? I was just telling' Wanda the other night, 'Wanda', I said, 'What I need me is a fishin' buddy. Somebody to sit on the bank with, and drink soda pop, and tell me stories to keep me from fallin' asleep and fallin' into the water.'"

Jonah's face flushed with excitement. "I will. I can do it. I love to fish."

"He ain't never been fishing."

I jerked my head around to stare at Emma, who was still partially concealed behind me. It was the first words I'd heard out of her mouth.

"Have to," Jonah countered.

Emma must have realized Uncle Jeb and I were staring at her. "Nuh-uh," she said, with less assurance this time, then stuck her finger back in her mouth and focused on the floor.

"Well, now, ain't this just dandy?" Uncle Jeb said. "I bet I could get me two fishin' buddies. What do you say, Michelle? I came here lookin' for one, and found two! Ain't that dandy?"

Jonah stepped over the wet towel he had dropped on the floor and stood in front of Uncle Jeb. "I can go fishin' anytime; whenever you want."

"Now, that's good to hear." Uncle Jeb took Jonah's hand and reached for Emma's. "Why don't the three of us go downstairs and let Aunt Michelle straighten up this bathroom."

Emma studied his calloused, outstretched hand for a moment, before deciding it was okay to take it. As the three of them started out of the bathroom, Gypsy jumped up from her position between the tub and commode and crowded in close. Emma took hold of Gypsy's collar with her free hand and followed Uncle Jeb and Jonah down the narrow staircase.

Uncle Jeb introduced himself again on the way downstairs in case the kids hadn't been listening when I'd done it. Jonah offered his name eagerly, and after a moment's silence, introduced his sister. I rinsed out the bathtub and laid the wet towels over the side to dry. I washed the toothpaste out of the sink. Jonah and Emma had shared an extra toothbrush given to me during my last trip to the dentist, since I had forgotten to buy them one at the grocery store and there was none to be found in the frayed backpack. We definitely needed a trip to Wal-Mart if the kids were going to be here any length of time. I made a mental list of other things I needed if I was going to have children in the house: chewable aspirin, underwear, pajamas, socks, and most definitely shoes. How could Nicole have left them without anything on their feet? Did she know how dangerous it was to let children run around without shoes? A farm contained all sorts of hazards for barefoot children, from sharp rocks and rusty nails to bees.

When I joined them in the living room, I found Jonah perched atop Uncle Jeb's knobby knees, a place I'd seen Nicole many times in years gone by. Violet and I were too big for lap sitting by the time I moved to the farm, but Uncle Jeb attracted children wherever he went. I had a sudden remembrance of him carrying other people's toddlers around the church building before and after services. With his booming voice and infectious laugh, they automatically went to him. Even the shyest ones sensed in him a loving, patient spirit. It didn't hurt that he kept his pockets full of candy. While Grandma and Aunt Wanda were dry and aloof, especially with little ones, Uncle Jeb was fun.

I sat down in Grandma Catherine's old recliner and watched him flipping through a magazine, pointing out objects of interest to Jonah. Emma sat a few feet away with Gypsy at her side, feigning disinterest, but I saw that she was studying the magazine out of the corner of her eye.

"Climb up there, too, Emma," I wanted to say out loud. *"Don't be afraid to let someone love you."*

The random thought brought to mind the last time I talked with Nicole. It was a few days after Christmas. She had called to thank me for the gifts I'd sent the kids. "I don't know what we'd do without you, Michelle," she'd said, seemingly appreciative, though experience made me doubt her sincerity. Whenever she called I was immediately suspicious. No matter what she said or how she said it, I always figured she was buttering me up for something.

I was not a naturally suspicious person.

"I feel so bad," she went on. "The kids wouldn't've had a Christmas at all if it weren't for you."

"I'm sure things aren't that bad," I'd said, hoping she would leave me blissfully in the dark.

"Yes, they are. I got fired from my last job because I overslept a few times," she whined. "People without kids don't understand how it is. It's hard to sit up all night with a sick kid and then be to work on time."

I didn't believe for a minute she overslept because she sat up all night with Emma or Jonah, and I wasn't feeling particularly generous. "Is the woman beater still with you?" I asked.

"Michelle, how can you be so cold" she snapped, the sugar gone from her voice. "If you mean Dean, yes, he's still here. He isn't going anywhere. I love him."

"Even after the last time," I said, referring to the beating he'd given her a few months earlier that resulted in the lost job at Denny's.

"You don't understand anything, Michelle," she said. "Sometimes people lose their tempers and do things without thinking."

"I understand all too well. I work in a hospital, remember? I see women like you every other night with their noses broken or their jaws wired because someone lost his temper."

"I wish for once you'd talk about something you knew a little bit about. Dean's changed. He's not like he used to be. He isn't drinking as much, and when he's sober, he's a little lamb."

"That's good to hear. Has the little lamb got a job?"

She snorted her disgust into the phone. "I don't know why I bother to call you. You are so hateful. Just because you don't need anyone in your life, doesn't mean the rest of us can live like that. I want a man, Michelle. I want someone to tell me I'm beautiful, that I'm needed. I'm sorry I'm not as cold and self-sufficient as you are. No, wait a minute I don't mean that. I'm not sorry. I'm thrilled that I have feelings; that I'm not made of ice. I couldn't bear to live like you."

"You mean in a house that's paid for, with a real job, and a car that's not falling apart?"

"Thanks for the gifts," she spat. "The kids loved the toys, and the coat fits Emma perfectly. She really needed it."

"I'm sorry, Nicole," I said, softening, wishing I didn't need to voice every thought that flitted across my mind. "I don't mean to be so hard on you. I just want to see you—"

"I know what you want, Michelle," she cut in. "You want me to be like you. Well, I can't. I'm a living, breathing human being with needs, whether you understand them or not. *Merry Christmas!*"

I hadn't heard from her since.

"A living, breathing human being with needs...." I was a living, breathing human being. I had needs. I just didn't need a Neanderthal with a mean right hook to fulfill them.

I looked again at Emma, sitting close enough to Uncle Jeb and

Jonah to see the pictures in the magazine, but far enough away to protect herself from possible harm or worse, rejection. Is that how it started with me? Is that what turned me into the woman I was today, a workaholic who hadn't had a real relationship since high school? My stomach tightened as I thought back to that relationship. I thought I had been in love. When Kyle Swann joined the Air Force I thought I'd never recover, but I had. And everything turned out fine. There was nothing wrong with me. I wasn't lonely. I didn't need a man to prove my worth. My worth came from a meaningful career and a loving heart.

Well…I had a meaningful career.

I shouldn't let anything Nicole said bother me. I pushed aside all thoughts of her, and Kyle Swann. I didn't have to apologize for paying my bills on time and being a responsible member of society.

Jonah yawned widely. I looked at the clock over the fireplace. It was nearly nine o'clock. They'd had a long day, as I had. Jonah begged Uncle Jeb to go upstairs with us as I put them to bed. Uncle Jeb looked questioningly at Gypsy who settled among the covers between them. I knew what he was thinking; "*If Catherine Barker was alive to see a dog livin' in her house, let alone sleepin' in a bed…*"

I agreed with the part about sleeping on the furniture. Gypsy had never slept in a people bed in her life, but I couldn't bear to separate her from Emma, even for tonight. I wanted to get a little sleep myself.

"So, what are ya plannin' to do, Peanut?" Uncle Jeb asked when we were back downstairs.

I shrugged. He hadn't called me by my childhood nickname in more years than I could count. I was always Peanut, and Nicole, Ladybug. Violet had several, chiefly Daffodil, Tadpole, or Snapdragon.

"I don't know," I said. "It doesn't look like there's much I can do."

"Wanda says you're goin' to Children's Services."

I nodded. "I guess I don't have a choice. I just hate to involve anyone else when this will probably end up not amounting to anything."

"I sure hope you're right." He looked away and rubbed his rough hand across his chin. "But with Nicole, it's hard to say. I don't want to think she's up and abandoned her kids anymore than you do, but ya gotta admit that's what it looks like. If she was drunk or somethin' and some man decided to bring the kids here without her permission, well, first off, he probably wouldn't even know where to find ya. And second, no man would think about birth certificates and shot records. Nicole knows what she's doin', she just didn't bother to let the rest of us in on it."

I nodded in agreement, though my heart sank. All day I'd been holding out hope that Nicole was hung over somewhere, and as soon as she slept it off, she'd come and collect her kids. The last thing I wanted was to do her parenting for her.

Uncle Jeb leveled a hard stare at me. "I just wonder what'll happen to Jonah and Emma if ya send 'em back to Nicole, that is, if she can be found. If ya took 'em back to 'er tomorrow, or let's say next week, what do ya suppose'll happen to 'em then?" He didn't give me time to think up an answer before he continued. "She'll find somebody who'll take 'em, probably somebody not as reliable as you. Or she'll keep 'em herself. Either way, those kids deserve better."

The conversation had taken a turn I didn't like. I opened my mouth to defend myself. Nicole needed to face her own responsibilities. I wanted to point out that she couldn't keep messing things up and then expecting everyone else to fix them for her.

My arguments were valid. I had every right to live my life the way I chose. But my independence didn't matter to Uncle Jeb, and it apparently didn't matter to the two children upstairs in Nicole's old bedroom.

"It'd be hard on Wanda," Uncle Jeb said, looking out the window, thinking out loud. "Neither of us is as young as we used to be. But I suppose we could take those two little 'uns in before we'd send 'em back to Nicole."

"Oh, no, Uncle Jeb," I cried. "You couldn't do that. At your age, you've got to consider your health."

"My health don't matter, if I know they're not bein' taken care of." He stood up. "You do what ya need to do, Michelle. I know you're busy with the hospital and all. I'm not playin' games with ya, tryin' to guilt ya into anything. We all have our choices to make. I've made mine."

He leaned over and kissed me on the cheek. "We'd love to see ya in church tomorrow. It's the best place for kids."

I nodded absently, without accepting his invitation.

"Bring the kids over tomorrow afternoon," he said on his way to the door. "I'll take 'em up to the pond."

"We need to go to Wal-Mart first," I said. "They don't even have shoes."

"So I hear." He put his hand on his hip pocket. "Ya need any money. I'd like to help out."

I quickly shook my head. "No, no, I've got it covered."

I sat in the gathering darkness after he left, thinking about what he had said. Yes, he was right. I hadn't thought about what it would be like if Nicole actually did come back to get them. They were better off away from her if she was unstable enough to leave them in my front yard. They needed a home, but did it have to be my home? Of course I didn't want them raised by strangers. I wanted what was best for them. Couldn't the best be that their mother get her act together and grow up?

Was that too much to ask?

As the room grew darker and my heart grew heavier, Grandma's words rang in my head. "You do for family, Michelle. Whether you want to or not, it's your Christian duty."

I wasn't a Christian and didn't claim to be. I guess that left me in the clear.

Chapter Five

If I never learned anything else about children, the following morning I discovered that a trip to Wal-Mart with an aunt in possession of an ATM card could bring even the most bashful child out of her shell.

I stopped at the convenience store in Winona and bought two pairs of flip-flops before heading on to the county seat of Geneva. Even at an eastern Arkansas Wal-Mart, it was; no shoes, no shirt, no service. We headed straight for the shoe department. *"This'll be easy,"* I told myself, feeling so superior to those parents I often saw coaxing little Junior back into the cart so they could head for the check-out. *"I'll be in and out of here in thirty minutes."* I was so naïve!

It was August, so sandals were on clearance. Score one for Wal-Mart. Judging from Emma's reaction every Hurley woman had an extra gene that kicked in a rush of endorphins at the sight of a shoe sale. The white ones, with a little daisy on top and hard soles that clicked smartly against the floor when she walked, were marked down to three dollars. Then an iridescent-striped pair, also on sale, caught both Emma's and my eyes. How could I go wrong? They joined the others in the cart. Emma actually squealed with delight when she spotted a pair of black slip-ons with a dangerously high, chunky heel. They weren't on sale, but they were adorable. Into the cart they went. The whole point of the trip was tennis shoes, so we found a pair of simple canvas ones with a zipper closure for a paltry five dollars. I would have liked a pair for myself, had they come in my size.

Fortunately for my pocketbook, the gene that made us ga-ga over shoes had missed Jonah. After picking out a pair of black and red, horribly ugly running shoes, he lost interest. I found another suitable pair in his size in case I ever needed to dress him up a little, and added them to the cart while he crawled up and down the aisle, making faces at himself in the foot mirrors.

I had never spent more than twenty minutes at a stretch in Wal-Mart before, the checkout lanes notwithstanding, but now I was shopping with children. It was lunchtime by the time we exited the store. My shopping cart was so loaded down I almost lost control of it going across the parking lot. I even had to pull up to the front of the store where a disinterested young man in a blue vest waited with two new booster car seats that would surely gouge the leather on the back seat of my beautiful car. But the kids were set. I couldn't think of one thing they didn't now own.

I watched their smiling faces as I unloaded the cart. Emma swung her feet to admire her new sandals. Through their new "shades," they both stared at the balloons I had bought, which, of course were strategically placed in the checkout lane. They also cracked bubble gum, another checkout lane purchase, while making a horrible racket with toys I already regretted buying. I felt buoyant myself. They were happy; really smiling for the first time since I'd found them under the lilac bushes. I was pleased.

So this is how it felt to make a child happy. It didn't really take much; a little attention, a little cash, and lunch at McDonald's. I tried not to judge Nicole. No one could afford to do this on a consistent basis. But still, if she only made better choices in men, or realized she didn't need one at all, and put a little more thought into her future, her children might not be in the sad state they were today. If I thought about it long enough, I could almost strangle her for letting them get used to such deprivation in the first place. But not right now. Now I wasn't going to think about Nicole. I wasn't going to wonder where she was and what she was thinking. I was simply going to enjoy the good mood brought on by the rapture on my niece and nephew's faces.

After lunch at McDonald's, I drove home and sent the kids outside to play with their new toys. I thought of the little TV with the grainy picture and considered investing in a new one with cable. This was costing me a fortune, and they'd only been here one full day. No! I wasn't buying a new TV or cable. They needed shoes and car seats. The toys and sunglasses had been no big deal. But I would not allow them to take over my life; not anymore than they already had. They would be leaving any day.

Things would settle down once I got back to work at the hospital. I could think rationally about the situation. I would make as few changes as possible and wait for Nicole to call and tell me she didn't know what she was thinking, that she'd made a mistake and was on her way. Surely it would happen any minute. These were her kids. No matter what her shortcomings, she would at least call to make sure I'd found them and brought them into the house before they wandered off.

I called the hospital to take Monday off as a personal day. Meg, who worked the switch board evenings and weekends, sounded surprised. I had never used a personal day in all my years of working there. Instead, I always took the pay at the end of the year. Not because I needed the money for gambling debts or because I was a workaholic; it was much simpler than that—I had no personal life. Everyone at the hospital knew it. I was the one they approached when they wanted to switch holidays or maneuver a long weekend out of the schedule. They knew I didn't have anything better to do than collect the triple-time pay that came from working holidays in I.C.U. They had wives, husbands, visiting in-laws, kids with soccer games and dentist appointments. I had Gypsy. She didn't complain when she spent Christmas Day alone or if I didn't take her out of town for the Labor Day weekend.

When I first graduated from nursing school, back when I actually fantasized about having a life, I resented how they all made a beeline to my locker when the holidays approached. I knew ahead of time who to expect just by looking at the schedule. Bev had a husband in law school who worked a night job, so her early mornings were better spent at home. Dennis would sell a kidney for a three-day weekend so he and his wife could work on the nineteenth century house they were renovating. Deb's four kids were born during her five years between high school and nursing school. How she managed, I couldn't imagine. Because she got on my nerves the least, she usually got first dibs on my Christmas mornings.

Still I resented how they assumed I had nothing better to do with my long weekends and holidays than trade with those of a lesser schedule. I did have a family, of sorts. Back then Aunt Wanda always came over early to get a jump start on the holiday dinner preparations with Grandma. Why should my coworkers assume I would rather pull a double shift in the pouring rain, in my underwear, with a migraine and cramps, than stay home in the bosom of my loving family?

The first Christmas after Grandma passed away, I drew the preferred schedule. Just to throw them for a loop, I held onto my hours. "No," I said, mysteriously. "I have plans." They didn't press for details and I didn't offer.

Christmas Eve, after pulling twelve hours, I loaded an overnight bag and Gypsy into the car and headed south. We spent two days in a virtually abandoned family resort village, walking the trails and keeping the minimal staff company. I hated it. Even Gypsy seemed depressed. I missed the hospital. I missed smiling and talking with the lonely patients who would rather be anywhere but in a hospital over the holidays. I missed the lame Christmas party food we all brought from home to share in the break room during quiet hours. I missed everyone's stories of misery over being away from their families, and the funny ones of Christmases past. Come payday, I missed the check that was several hundred dollars short because of the missing holiday pay.

More surprisingly, I missed Grandma Catherine keeping a plate of turkey warm for me in the oven for when I stumbled home from work at seven-thirty. I missed Aunt Wanda's bellyaching over doing all the cooking herself. I missed watching the parades with Uncle Jeb.

After that year, I stopped resenting my coworkers assuming I had nothing better to do on holidays and weekends than work. I didn't. Why pretend my life was something more than it was?

Poor Meg at the switchboard would think I had totally cracked when I called my supervisor Monday morning and took Tuesday and Wednesday as vacation days if Nicole hadn't appeared by then. That was another thing I seldom did. Every spring I took a week off to put out my garden. It was something Grandma insisted on when I first got a regular job with vacation days, and a habit I hadn't been able to break.

Late summer, I took another week to harvest what we'd grown. That week coincided with the county fair where Grandma entered a quilt, some pies, jams, tomatoes, late flowers, and any other category she qualified for. She'd been gone six years now, and I still took those two weeks. I loved working the soil, getting my hands dirty with mindless work that left my back aching and hands blistered. I even enjoyed the week at the fair. It was now I that entered produce from the garden I no longer needed to raise, and volunteered my time in the Band Boosters booth. It gave curious townspeople a chance to see me when they weren't under the influence of anesthesia. It also quelled the rumors for another year among the town's young that I hid a forked tail under my scrubs.

Besides those two weeks and an occasional day for yearly doctor checkups and dental exams, I collected the pay for my unused vacation days along with the personal days at the end of the year. On the way to the bank to deposit my yearly gains, I bought Gypsy a toy and myself a new sweater or something else I didn't really need.

A person living alone with no family on whom to spend her money, becomes one of two things; miserly or a rabid Bingo player. Since I didn't smoke and couldn't hold my breath for the three hours it took to play Bingo at the crowded Elks' Lodge, I leaned toward miserly. I preferred to think of it as thrifty. I had few needs. My wardrobe for work was decided for me. A leisure wardrobe consisted of comfortable "lying around" clothes, or old shorts and jeans for working what remained of Grandma's garden. I had a nice pair of jeans and a few decent sweaters for running errands in town. I didn't collect anything. I didn't give to charities, take vacations, or eat in expensive restaurants...or cheap ones, come to think of it.

I made no improvements to the house or farm, except what was vital for human habitation. It was only Gypsy and me, and our tastes and expectations were simple. I had no future generations breathing down my neck, demanding I keep the place up for their sakes. So what if the front fence had no gate, the driveway needed paving, one or two upstairs windows were missing shutters and screens? My life was at work. That's where I thrived.

So, my savings account grew steadily and I made the maximum contributions to my 401K. What I was saving for, I didn't worry about. "*Retirement*," I told myself. A retirement that everyone in town, including myself, knew would never come.

✤

When the unexpected ringing woke me, I jerked my head up to look at the alarm clock. I wasn't going to work today. Why in the world was it ringing in my ear—at two-sixteen A.M. no less? Then I realized it wasn't the alarm, it was the phone. I sat up farther and leaned over the alarm to reach the phone.

"Hullo?" I was too groggy with sleep even to sound irritated.

"Michelle, it's me."

"Nicole?" I should have known. I was instantly wide awake. "Where are you? Are you all right?"

"Oh, I'm fine, I guess. As good as I can expect to be." Her voice carried the appropriate amount of self-pity and despair.

Now that I knew she wasn't dead, I was mad. "Where are you?" I repeated.

She let out a long, belabored sigh. "I'm all right, Michelle. Don't worry. I know you're probably really mad at me and I'm sorry—""Nicole," I interjected, "where are you? What's going on?"

"I told you, everything's fine. I'm sorry but it couldn't be helped."

"What couldn't be helped? What are you talking about?"

"If you'd give me a chance to say two words without interrupting, I would tell you." She was not too irritated to maintain the whine in her voice. "It's a long story so I won't bore you with details."

I wanted details more than anything, but I wouldn't interrupt again.

"I just can't keep the kids right now. I don't know how long it's going to take, but I need you to keep them for me. I have some things to sort out in my life, and I just can't do that and be Mommy at the same time."

I was never good at keeping my mouth shut when I had something I thought needed said. There was so much I wanted to yell at

Nicole right now. So much I could say. With great resolve, I clamped my teeth over the anger bubbling up inside of me and waited.

"I don't know when I'll be back, Michelle, but don't worry. No one is forcing me to do anything I don't want to do. As soon as I get my head straightened out, I'll be back."

I wanted to tell her not to bother. She was the most selfish creature God ever put on the earth; she had no business with two great kids like Emma and Jonah. But of course, I didn't say that. I wanted her to come back, desperately. They were her kids. They weren't my problem. Why should she be allowed to shirk her responsibilities while she got her head straightened out, when every other mother on the planet had to stay home and play "Mommy" whether they felt like it or not? I didn't say that either.

"Michelle? Are you still there?"

"Yeah, I'm here. I'm trying not to interrupt."

"Well, I wanted to tell you thanks, Michelle. I really appreciate this. You don't know how much. I knew I could count on you."

Nicole paused for a moment and I heard a voice in the background; a man. That figured. It was always a man. Nicole couldn't live one day without some loser in her life. I wondered if it was the same one Jonah said had dropped them off in my front yard. She put her hand over the receiver and said something I couldn't make out. Then she came back to me. "Well, I gotta go. I'll talk to you soon."

With a click, the connection was broken.

I sat there in the dark, holding the dead phone in my hand, trying to figure out what had just happened. Not only did my darling kid sister thank me for something I never agreed to do, she hadn't asked one word about how her kids were doing.

I called Children's Services first thing Monday morning. The young woman on the other end of the line promised to have someone to the house by the end of the day. She sounded harried, overworked, and genuinely distressed that two children had been left in someone's front yard, even if that someone was a family member.

At one-thirty that afternoon, a small car pulled into the driveway and a young woman with her hair pulled back in what she must have thought was a businesslike, practical style, stepped out. From inside the front door, I watched her gaze around the property, sizing up my life with a critical eye. I thought of the missing gate, the drafty windows, the lack of air conditioning, the barn that leaned dangerously due south, and all the outlets that didn't have covers. I immediately resented the invasion of privacy. I had to impress this woman just so my worthless sister's kids could live here until she saw fit to come back.

From the looks of things, I could tell the young woman hadn't been on the job for long. She found my story duly pathetic. I didn't think at first she even believed me. Her eyes said she thought I found them in a parked car at the Piggly Wiggly. At least I had their birth certificates and shot records to back up my story. That seemed to make things go smoother. How thoughtful of Nicole to leave them in the back pack, *"Yeah, thoughtful."*

I expressed my concerns that I wasn't exactly a mothering type; I had a demanding job, a small car, and basically no room in my life for kids, although I didn't say it in so many words.

She nodded patiently before telling me as far as the law was concerned, I was under no obligation to provide for another woman's children. All I had to do was sign a few papers verifying that my sister's children had been abandoned with me. They would take the children into custody where they would be put into foster care, thus relieving me of the burden.

Even though it was exactly what I wanted to hear, watching the words form on her lips made me feel like an utter heel for even bringing it up.

"Ideally, in cases such as this, the best place for the children is with other family members," she added. "Foster homes in this county, as in every county in the United States, are extremely hard to come by. We screen our foster parents, but it is always better that the children remain in the home of a loved one where they feel at least a modicum of security. I am sure you wouldn't be comfortable turning your niece and nephew over to strangers when they don't even know where their mother is."

I sank lower in my chair.

"I'm not suggesting that you've done anything wrong. I just want you to be aware that what you decide to do could cause irrevocable damage to your family. Your sister brought her children to you for a reason. She could have taken them to the agency in her county, but she didn't. She saw fit to bring them to you. She trusts you. She feels confident that your home is the best place for her children at this time. You need to carefully consider what you want to do before you alienate your sister and her children. A rift like this among family members may never be repaired." She smiled warmly and slid a stack of papers across the kitchen table at me.

"Go ahead and fill out this paperwork. It's just an order for temporary custody. Like you said, your sister could walk through the door by bedtime and all this will have been for nothing; but if she doesn't, don't you feel better knowing for the present time, the children are in good hands? When you're finished, we'll go over a few things and you'll be all set. You can enroll them in daycare so you won't have to miss any more work than necessary. In a few weeks, if the kids are still here, I'll come back for a more thorough visit."

She opened the fridge to make sure it worked and contained some sort of food. I showed her the bathrooms, which were thankfully relatively clean, and where the kids would sleep. She smiled like I'd just won the lottery and announced I was awarded custody of my niece and nephew. She made her exit, promising she'd see me again in about a week.

I watched her walk back to her older model car with Gypsy sniffing her shoes the whole way. I couldn't believe my simple no nonsense life had been reduced to convincing some government agency that I was fit to provide a home for my own niece and nephew. How had things come to this? All I wanted was to go to work tomorrow, leave the world to its own devices, and keep it out of mine. Was I such a terrible person because I didn't want to solve everyone's problems? The longer I thought about it, the less I cared about what the Children's Services woman thought about me. I didn't want to raise Nicole's kids, even if they were my own flesh and blood. Of course, I couldn't let them go into some foster home, but I didn't have to like it that they had intruded into my life.

Chapter Six

Even though I had basically sworn off religion and church for myself, it seemed like a good idea to enroll Emma and Jonah in a church affiliated facility. If nothing else, they would learn respect and manners. I supposed memorizing a few Bible verses and singing a few Bible songs wouldn't give them any twisted ideas or make me a hypocrite.

There were two such places in Geneva. I didn't even call the one run by my old church. Just reading their ad in the telephone book brought back all the hurtful memories of Grandma and her Christian charity. I hadn't darkened the door of that church since Grandma's funeral. My adult rationale told me not to blame the church for Grandma's warped sense of Christian love and compassion, but I couldn't help doing exactly that. I wanted nothing to do with religion, especially that particular church. And I didn't want them getting their hands on Emma and Jonah.

I listened to the slightly deranged sounding administrator of the second preschool explain their program and agreed to meet her Tuesday morning to fill out the appropriate enrollment paperwork. Could anyone really be that happy? She had the answers to all my questions, not that I knew exactly what a person should ask in these situations, and the daycare center was located in the heart of Geneva, right on my way to work; a perfect fit. If all went well, I hoped to leave the children for a half day. That should be enough to get them used to it, so

I could work my usual weekend at the county hospital. Janet, in charge of scheduling, had already called to see if I could work. Without going into details, I told her I hoped so.

An impressive brick and wood building stood before me when I pulled into the parking lot of the Abundant Life Fellowship on Tuesday morning, Emma and Jonah in tow. The church had apparently begun as one building with a new addition added a few years later. The construction appeared recent, but you couldn't prove it by me. Everyone says they are creatures of habit, but I truly am. The farm was located a few miles from Winona, a town of about 1800 residents. To get to the University Hospital in the neighboring county where I worked, I had to drive through Geneva, which was considerably larger. I traveled the same roads whether going to work, the bank, the grocery, or the county library—every time I left the farm. My route never deviated. If they decided to build a nuclear power plant one street over from the one I drove every day, I'd never know unless they rerouted traffic.

I parked my Mazda between a minivan and a SUV, both outfitted with multiple car seats, near a pair of double doors on one of the main building's many outcroppings. What happened to the little clapboard churches with the spire shooting heavenward parked at a country crossroads like the ones they printed on postcards and calendars? Churches nowadays were more like businesses with pastors who resembled CEO's and deacons who looked like board members.

Before getting out of the car, I glanced into the back seat through the rearview mirror and saw two terrified faces staring back at me. This was going to be fun. I pasted a smile on my face and climbed out.

"Okay, guys, we're here."

My Mazda was equipped with freestyle doors that looked great but which I never thought I'd use. Now, with both driver side doors wide open, I was able to lean in to unbuckle Jonah's car seat. I stretched farther inside the cramped interior to unhook Emma from her vinyl prison and a shooting pain went up my back. She would have to get out herself. There was no way my hips were going to squeeze any farther into the car to help her.

"You're going to have so much fun today," I said in a singsong voice. I immediately recognized the tone. It was same as the woman I spoke to on the phone, an occupational hazard from spending one's days in the company of children. "You'll make all kinds of new friends."

"Will we be together?" Jonah asked. His brown eyes, so unlike his sister's blue ones, were wide with terror.

I swallowed hard. I wouldn't lie to the child, but I hadn't thought to ask the administrator how that would be worked out. "I don't know, sweetheart. I'll ask the lady." I couldn't remember her name. I imagined real parents would never leave their children with someone whose name they hadn't even bothered to remember.

The parking lot with its bustling parents and assorted, squealing children was intimidating enough, but did nothing to prepare me for inside. We marched up the walk and into a vestibule. The walls were lined with hip level coat hooks and cubby boxes stenciled in colorful block letters; KENDALL, PRESTON, TANNER, MONTGOMERY. Didn't they allow the children to use their first names? How confusing for children with siblings. Maybe they had to share personal space. That didn't seem fair.

An attractive brunette bustled forward. She gave me a brief smile before ignoring me completely and squatting down so that she was eye level with the kids. "You must be Jonah and Emma," she squealed with the enthusiasm of a TV infomercial hawker. I immediately recognized her as the woman I'd talked to on the phone yesterday. Her long curly hair was held away from her face by a wide, functional barrette. She wore minimal make-up and wash-and-wear clothes. I imagined our jobs weren't too different.

"I'm Miss Billie," she was saying. "I'm so pleased you could be with us today. We are going to have so much fun," she said, repeating my earlier predictions. She squeezed their hands and straightened. Her smile remained fixed in place. I doubted she could relax her cheek muscles if she tried. "Ms. Hurley, I presume. I'm Billie Kirk, the school administrator. We spoke on the phone. Please, come into my office."

She took a step back, and nearly fell over a little boy who appeared out of nowhere. "Jordan!" With one quick hand on his chest and the other on his back, she artfully brought his full-tilt sprint to a standstill. "It's so good to see you this morning. Please, don't run to the play area. We would hate for you to get hurt. Then you couldn't play with your friends."

"Okay, Miss Billie." The little boy grinned adoringly up at her and then walked sedately through the vestibule into a large, corralled area to our left teaming with children of all shapes and sizes. At least some wise individual had the foresight to fence the little angels in. I was impressed that a few soft-spoken words from the administrator could curtail the little boy's breakneck enthusiasm. Maybe there was more skill involved in doing this job well than a bubbly personality and low IQ.

I followed her into a tiny office opposite the play area, followed directly by Emma and Jonah. She motioned us to the chairs across from her desk. I lowered myself into one. Instead of taking the other chair, Emma and Jonah leaned against my legs. It was the first physical contact we'd shared since I carried Jonah into the house Saturday morning.

"We are so pleased you've chosen Noah's Ark Preschool," the administrator said. "After you fill out the paperwork, I'll give you a tour of the facilities. We didn't discuss it yesterday, but I'm sure you want to see everything."

Not really. It hadn't occurred to me to doubt a word she said on the telephone. Boy, I was not cut out for parenting!

I took my copies of the paperwork the woman from Children's Services had given me along with the kid's medical records out of my purse and handed them across the desk. Miss Billie got up to make copies on the machine behind her. "Have you been to preschool before?" she asked Emma and Jonah.

Emma shrank against my leg and stuck her finger into her mouth. Jonah stared at the administrator and said nothing.

"I don't think so," I answered for them. "Like I said yesterday on the phone, I haven't had much contact with them since they were born. They were pretty anxious about the whole idea of coming here, so I don't think they have any daycare experience."

Miss Billie pulled the copies out of the tray and handed the originals back to me. She took her seat at the desk. "Okay," she said, smiling brightly. "I think we have everything here to get started."

She went through the run-through of the preschool's program. Everything sounded simple enough; payment due every Friday for the following week. The amount gave me a bit of a shock, but this was just a temporary arrangement until Nicole returned. I could afford it for a month or two. Miss Billie said something about a monthly Sunday morning program which they encouraged participation from all the children and parents. The kids got up in front of the whole church and sang some songs and recited memory verses they'd learned that month in preschool. The idea of getting roped into attending church just for bringing your kids here for daycare seemed a bit presumptuous. Leave it to a church to come up with such a scheme. But I didn't figure it would affect me anyway. Nicole would be back any day and I'd be off the hook. Even if she didn't come back by the next Sunday morning program, this was still America; these people couldn't force me to attend.

I smiled and nodded until she clasped her hands in front of her and asked if I had any further questions.

"Yes," I said. "The children are concerned about being separated. Because of the circumstances, I wonder if it would be possible to keep them together, at least in the beginning. I'm not even sure if it's a good idea for me to leave them here today."

"Oh, that won't be a problem at all," Miss Billie said, through her big smile, directing her words at Jonah and Emma. "A new place can be scary when you don't know anyone. But I have a feeling you're going to just love it here at Noah's Ark. You'll make friends in no time at all." She stood up and looked back at me. "They're close enough in age to go into the same class, just to see how everything goes. Hopefully, it won't be long before they want to separate into their own classes. If you like, I can show Jonah and Emma the play area and introduce them to the teachers while you fill out your paperwork. Afterwards, I can give you a tour of the facilities while the children have breakfast. By then they'll probably be more than ready to spend the rest of the morning here."

She held her hands out to them.

"Oh, um…" I looked from Emma to Jonah. They were staring at Miss Billie's outstretched hands. "I suppose that would be…if they want to…" I couldn't explain the tiny nugget of betrayal when they reached out and took her hands. She led them from the room, talking a mile a minute about all the fun stuff that went on at the preschool, with not a backwards glance at me from any of them.

I bent my head over the stapled forms in front of me and went to work. Food allergies, Medical history, Sleeping patterns; I filled in as many blanks as I could while trying to block out the din coming from over my shoulder through the open door.

Someone hurried into the office. "Billie, have you seen the—"came a masculine voice, "Oh, sorry."

I looked up to see a rugged-looking man dressed in khakis and a blue Henley shirt standing in the doorway, his large hand on the doorjamb. "I was looking for Billie," he explained. In an instant, his expression changed from rushed to recognition. "Michelle? Michelle Hurley? I don't believe it!"

I gasped and jumped to my feet. Of all the people I ever expected to see again, especially here, in a church on a Tuesday morning, with a hundred screaming kids providing background noise, Kyle Swann wasn't among them. In high school, he had been my one and only serious boyfriend.

Until this very moment, I thought I was over him.

For a split second I was torn between a handshake and the hug I wanted, and then he stepped toward me and pulled me into his arms for a regrettably chaste embrace. I ran my tongue over my teeth and prayed I didn't have bad breath. "Kyle. Hi. It's good to see you."

I hoped my voice belied the condition of my insides. Kyle was more handsome than he'd been in school, if that was possible. His shoulders had widened, his brown hair darkened, and the gaze from his deep blue eyes had intensified. Too bad I looked exactly the same except for an additional fifteen pounds and the beginning of crow's feet.

"Wow, Michelle, you look great."

I see he had learned to lie in the past fifteen years.

"I didn't know you had kids," he said and turned to face the doorway. "Which ones are yours?"

"Oh, uh, they're not mine. I mean I don't..."

He turned back slowly and studied me with those deep blue eyes I remembered so well. After all these years, looking into them still left me weak in the knees. I looked past his broad frame to search the crowd for Jonah and Emma. He'd gained weight too, but all athletic muscle from the looks of things. The kids were standing in the middle of the play area, apparently invisible to every other kid in the place. Emma's finger was still in the corner of her mouth. Jonah was studying his shoes.

I pointed them out. "They're my sister's kids. They are...um, staying with me for awhile." The hint of cologne I smelled on him made it difficult to concentrate; spicy, woodsy, with a hint of musk. It smelled familiar, yet different. I was instantly fifteen-years-old again; flat-chested, knobby-kneed, and unsure of what to say in front of a boy. Kyle was sure of himself, even back then. I remembered standing next to my locker the first day of my freshman year, trying to get the lock to open when he came up behind me.

"Here. Sometimes, they have a mind of their own," he said. He grabbed the lock and gave it a quick twist. "Now try it."

It worked. The heat rose up in my cheeks. I knew all the freckles on my face were standing out against my pale skin. "Thanks," I mumbled, peering inside the locker.

"Sure," he said with a nod, and then spun on his heel and disappeared down the hallway.

My first encounter with Kyle Swann—burned indelibly on my brain.

"You mean little Nicole? Those two are your sister Nicole's kids?"

I nodded.

"Well, that's great. It doesn't seem possible that Nicole's old enough to have kids."

"She's not," I blurted before I knew what I was saying. "I mean, she is old enough, obviously. She's twenty-three. She just acts immature sometimes."

"Oh, I didn't mean to imply that," he explained. "I just meant it's amazing how quickly time flies. The last time I saw Nicole she was like...what, eight-years-old? I think it was at our high school graduation. Do you remember that?"

Of course, I remembered it. It was the last time he'd seen me too—the day after our big break-up. He'd told me he had enlisted in the Air Force and was leaving for San Antonio in two weeks. I hadn't considered how things would change after graduation, even though I was going to Nursing School and didn't expect him to keep working at his uncle's gas station. His announcement took me totally by surprise. In retrospect, I could see I didn't exactly handle the situation with grace and dignity. More like screaming and name-calling.

But Kyle wasn't talking about us. I could tell by the look on his face, he was still thinking of eight-year-old Nicole and how it didn't seem possible that she was old enough to have kids of her own.

"Yes, I remember," I said, returning his smile. "Nicole was a corker. I'm afraid she hasn't changed a bit."

He nodded and laughed. I laughed too, trying not to think about the Nicole who couldn't stay sober, or keep a man or a job for more than six months.

"So, what have you been doing with yourself, Michelle? Do you still live in Winona?"

I couldn't believe he didn't know. Everybody knew what became of me; absolutely nothing. I attended the local college, lived much like I had during high school, except with double the responsibilities, and went to work as soon as I had enough training—the girl most likely to turn into a radish. "Yes, I still live on my Grandma Catherine's farm."

It wasn't Grandma's farm anymore. I'd held the deed ever since she died. I paid the insurance and property taxes every year, but I felt like a squatter. As long as I lived, the farm would always seem like "Grandma's farm."

"I'm a nurse in the Cardiac Care Unit at University Hospital," I continued. "I also work on contingency at the county hospital here in Geneva on weekends."

"Sounds like you're keeping busy, but then, you always did. I remember how you wanted to go to Nursing School. You were always good to have around when someone needed something."

When someone needed something; well, not exactly. My ears burned with shame at the way I'd resented Emma and Jonah's abrupt arrival into my life.

I motioned through the open office door. "So, which ones are yours, Kyle?" I asked to change the subject. For some reason, I didn't like the idea of him having children. If he'd gotten fat or lost his hair, it would've been easier. "I didn't think you'd be living around here. I thought after joining the Air Force and seeing what the world had to offer, you'd be in some exotic location by now."

"Oh," he grinned, the corners of his mouth turning upwards in that mischievous manner I remembered; the one that made all the girls in school stop breathing whenever he walked past. "I don't have children. I never married."

I managed to control the exultant smile that threatened to take over my entire face.

"Then...what are you doing here?"

His grin broadened. "I work here. Not at the preschool, although this is where I start most of my days. My office is in the main part of the building. I come up here on the days I'm in the building to listen to the children recite their pledges before classes start; the pledge to the American flag, the Christian flag, and the Bible. Then I lead them in prayer. I'm the church pastor. I transferred here in March."

He could have knocked me over with a feather, Kyle, a pastor? I never would've guessed it in a million years—playing in the NFL, maybe, a construction worker, or even a schoolteacher. He had always cared about people and he got along with everyone. Even a therapist was within reason—but a pastor?

"A pastor?" I said, "I had no idea."

"Yeah, I received my calling while living in Japan in the Air Force. I had planned on making a career out of it, but God had other plans."

"Um," I said, nodding my head, like everyone I knew let God choose their careers for them. "So, where did you transfer from?" I managed to ask conversationally.

"Tahlequah, Oklahoma. That was my first church. I pastored there for eight years. But I guess Harrison County will always be home to me."

I nodded again like I knew what leaving home was like, and turned my eyes back to the play area. It was strange talking to my only serious boyfriend from high school as if there had never been anything between us. But stranger by far was that he was the pastor of the very church I chose out of the phone book to bring Nicole's kids to for preschool. If there truly was a God in Heaven, he was having a grand old time at my expense right now.

We watched together as Miss Billie cheerfully settled a dispute over a baby doll between two little girls. She found Jonah and Emma in the crowd, said something to them, and headed back to the office alone. "Oh, good morning, Kyle. How are you coming with the paperwork, Ms. Hurley?"

I glanced guiltily at the pile of unfinished papers on her desk.

"She was interrupted," Kyle volunteered. "We're old friends," he said easily. "We were catching up on old times."

"Oh, how nice," she smiled at both of us and then focused her attention on me. "It's almost time for breakfast, so I can give you the tour of the preschool, Ms. Hurley, if that's all right. Kyle, did you need something first?"

"I just came in for last month's attendance roster."

"Oh, I'm sorry. I haven't had time to take it to your office."

While she went around her desk and shuffled through her out box, Kyle said to me, "It was good seeing you, Michelle. We'll have to get together and talk over old times one of these days." He took the paper Miss Billie held out to him and raised his free hand in a half wave. "Have a nice day, ladies."

I turned back to the administrator and tried to get the image of Kyle Swann out of my head.

A pastor, it still blew me away. How did that happen?

The administrator was looking over what I had filled in on my forms. I saw by the arched eyebrows, she couldn't understand why I didn't know more about the personal habits of my niece and nephew. How to explain? Rather than commenting, Miss Billie handed me a list of articles each child would need, pencil box with crayons, kiddy scissors, glue, a box of Kleenex, etc. Another trip to Wal-Mart; my checkbook groaned inside my purse. I would also need a photo of each child to put on their cubby boxes. Obviously each kid got his or her own.

"It helps to teach name recognition," she explained. She continued to flip pages and study the lines I'd left blank.

I cleared my throat and scratched an itch on the back of my head. "I'm sorry I couldn't fill in more on the forms. Like I told you yesterday, my sister, she sort of left the children with me unexpectedly. I haven't seen them in over a year. Actually, it's been longer than that. Jonah was practically a baby then." I didn't understand my anxiety. The administrator was smiling benignly. In this day and age,

I imagined she came across more hard luck stories perpetrated on children then I did in my work.

She looked down at her folded hands and nodded politely.

"Nicole, their mother, could waltz in here tomorrow and take them back," I explained. "I almost feel guilty asking you to do all this paperwork when it may be for nothing."

Her smile stiffened for the first time since I'd walked through the door. "Do you think that's wise?" she asked.

"What do you mean? Don't you have to do the paperwork regardless of how long they stay?"

The patient long suffering smile returned to her face. "No, I don't mean that." She studied her hands again before looking at me. "I mean about the children." She gestured with her head at Jonah and Emma, who were sluggishly getting into line with the rest of the children. "Is it in their best interest for their mother to waltz in here and take them away from you, like you said?"

"Um, I, um, I don't have any right to keep her from doing whatever she wants. I mean, she is their mother. Like I said, I haven't had any real contact with her since last Christmas. I don't really know her situation, except that she needs me to keep them for a while. I couldn't keep her from them if she came back." I realized I was defending Nicole and myself much too vehemently and clamped my lips shut.

Miss Billie leaned forward and rested her elbows on the desk blotter. "I understand completely. It is difficult to decide what's best for children when there are family ties involved. You don't want to hurt anyone's feelings."

"Oh, it isn't that," I said quickly.

"Personally, I don't believe it would be fair to you or the children for Nicole to feel like she can breeze in and out of your lives whenever the mood strikes her. You won't know, and certainly the children will have no idea, when this behavior is going to repeat itself. Children need security, structure. They need to know who is in charge and when and if a situation may change. I imagine they are much better off with you for the time being. You obviously care a great deal for them. You've gone to all this trouble, setting them up here, paying, taking care of everything before you go back to work. I'm not trying to tell you what to do. I know you don't have children of your own and this is a huge adjustment for everyone. I just think it might be a good idea for you to seriously consider what you will do when, and if, Nicole comes back."

I sat across the desk from this sweet diminutive woman, stunned. The chance of Nicole not coming back had been a nagging fear in the back of my mind since I picked Jonah up off the dew covered grass and took him and Emma inside. But I kept telling myself she would come back and my life would go right back to the way it had been since Grandma Catherine died; back to the point where I was in charge of something. No more at the mercy of the choices made by my absent parents. No more hearing what a strain my and Nicole's mere existence had been on Grandma. I was finally free. Not that I was relieved when Grandma died, but my newfound freedom was something I clutched tightly to my breast.

What would happen when Nicole came back? What then? How could I, as a self-respecting human being, thrust those innocent children back into her care? How could I sleep at night knowing the next time they might end up in the front yard of someone other than me?

I did watch the news. I worked in a hospital. Even in the sheltered little world of my own making, I was too aware of the evils that could befall children in today's society. But I didn't want children. No one seemed to understand that. Emma and Jonah weren't better off with me. They would have been better off born to a family who actually wanted them and cared for them. Preferably two parents with a minivan, a dog and a mortgage they couldn't afford; not Nicole, and certainly not me.I wasn't the person for this job. I was selfish. I wanted my life back. Nothing would change my mind. I didn't ask for this job and as soon as Nicole showed her pretty face she could take her kids and go. Go where… I wouldn't concern myself with. That was her business. I didn't have any problem stepping in to help for a while so she could get her life straightened out, but the sooner she did, the happier I'd be.

Chapter Seven

Aunt Shell."

The tiny voice behind me startled me out of my reverie as I prepared another supper, courtesy of Betty Crocker and Kraft. Ever since this morning, my thoughts had flitted from what Miss Billie said about the kids to Kyle Swann. Why had he appeared out of nowhere after fifteen years? And why did I even care that he was once again living in Harrison County and pastoring a church? It was his life; he could do whatever he wanted with it. But I couldn't get over it. More importantly, I couldn't still the fluttering in my chest every time his deep blue eyes came to mind. I set the box of dry macaroni on the counter and turned around. Jonah stood directly behind me his neck tilted all the way back so he could stare up at me.

After my tour of the preschool, I'd left the kids there for three hours while I ran errands and tried to gather my thoughts. When I picked them up right before lunch, they seemed none the worse for wear. Jonah shrugged when I asked how his morning went. But later he did mention someone named Ben whom he played with. Emma said even less. Her answers were simple "yes" and "no" answers, with an occasional nod. At least they hadn't screamed and shrank away in terror from any of the teachers. I took that as a good sign. We would stick with the half-day plan for the rest of the week, and hopefully I could go back to work on Monday. I wasn't sure what I'd do about the preschool closing at five-thirty and me not getting off work until seven on Mondays and Wednesdays when I pulled twelve hours.

I hoped Aunt Wanda and Uncle Jeb could pick the kids up for me and keep them till I got home.

"What is it, Jonah?" I asked, sounding more compassionate than I felt.

"Emma's crying."

A rush of annoyance washed over me. Again? What was it this time? That girl cried continuously it seemed. What was I supposed to do about it? This wasn't my field of expertise. If she was a fifty-eight year old chain smoker who'd had his chest cracked open the day before, I'd know exactly how to handle his pain and frustration. I was good at that. In that situation I knew what I was doing, but not here. What Emma needed, I couldn't give her. I couldn't make her mother materialize in front of her. I couldn't wiggle my nose and make all her problems disappear. If I could, I would.

I took a deep breath and reminded myself to be patient. She had a right to cry under the circumstances. The poor thing was only four. Her whole world had disappeared in front of her very eyes. She goes to bed one night in her own bed, presumably, and wakes up under a stranger's lilac bushes. What a nightmare for anyone—at any age.

"Why is she crying, Jonah?" A dumb question, but it bore asking.

"She wants Carrie."

My jaw dropped and I forced it shut again. I turned the heat off under the pan of water that was heating for the macaroni noodles, and squatted down in the narrow space between Jonah and the stove. I gazed into his concerned face. "Who's Carrie?"

"Our neighbor; she takes care of us when Mommy's sick…or with Dean."

Dean again—boy, what I wouldn't give to meet this character. But I would worry about wringing his neck later. Right now, I needed to focus on getting as much information out of Jonah as possible. This was the first tidbit about their lives either of them had thrown me since they got here.

"Where does Carrie live?" I asked carefully.

"Across the hall; she's real nice. She reads to us and she makes peanut butter and jelly sandwiches and lets us sit on the couch with her and watch TV."

Once again my heart ached for the simple pleasures my niece and nephew obviously lacked. "Oh, my, that sounds wonderful," I said around the lump in my throat. "How long have you lived across the hall from Carrie?"

He shrugged. "Long time."

"As long as you can remember?" I asked hopefully.

He shrugged his thin shoulders again.

"Is she old like me, or old like Aunt Wanda?"

He pursed his lips thoughtfully and tilted his head to study my face. I braced myself for the insult about my age that was surely on its way.

He touched his finger to my forehead and drew a line. "She's got lines on her face like you, but they're bigger." That was good to hear. He put both hands on either side of my mouth and drew more lines. "She's got lots of lines here," he touched the corners of my eyes, "Lots more than you. And her hair's brown and white."

Okay, so she was definitely closer to Aunt Wanda's age.

Jonah giggled. "And she's got a big belly. It's real soft and squishy. I put my head there sometimes when I'm watching TV and I can hear thump-thump." His smile suddenly faded and his eyes misted. "I miss Carrie too. Do you think you could take us to her apartment?"

I straightened up. My knees were beginning to lock in the squatted position, and I wanted to get away from those big puppy-dog eyes. I put my hand on his head and tousled his hair in what I hoped was a comforting manner. "Well, Jonah, I don't even know where Carrie lives."

"I told you," he said, his voice raising an octave. "She lives across the hall from us."

How could I make him understand I didn't even know what town Nicole was living in now? I presumed Memphis, but had nothing solid to base my assumption on. "Does Carrie have a telephone?"

His reply was a blank stare.

"Do you know her other name, her last name?"

This time I got a definite shake of the head. What was I going to do? I didn't know where Nicole lived. The last phone number she'd given me had long since been disconnected. Why didn't I pay closer attention to her when I had the chance? Why was I so satisfied with keeping her totally out of my life? Even if I knew for sure she was living in Memphis, probably in a low rent part of town, that wouldn't get me any closer to finding Carrie or my sister. I was going to have to figure this out on my own with no help from anyone and no one with whom the kids were close to, to comfort them when I couldn't.

I reached out and took Jonah by the hand. "Let's go see if we can make Emma feel better." He looked as doubtful as I felt.

"Oh, Nicole," I groaned inwardly, *"How does it make you feel that your children are crying for another woman and have yet to mention your name?"*

꙳

I had never sat idle in my entire life; having two small children in the house wouldn't change that. I wasn't due back to work till Monday, five whole days away. I planned to make good use of my mornings while the kids got used to preschool. After dropping them off Wednesday morning, I planned a trip to the local Sherwin Williams to pick up some paint for Nicole's old bedroom, the one her children now shared. The room hadn't been painted as far back as I could remember. If the drab, faded eggshell walls depressed me, I could only imagine what they did to Emma and Jonah.

Dressed in my old gardening pants with the ripped knees and bleach stain on the right leg, and a stretched out tee shirt, I made the drive to Geneva to drop the kids off. My fine honey blonde hair was pulled back in a non-flattering ponytail and my face was void of make-up. No one had ever accused me of being a fashion plate, especially when there was work in my immediate future.

This morning while concentrating on getting the kids dressed and out the door, I hadn't thought anything about my own appearance. I had painting on my mind and nothing else. It never occurred to me until I pulled into the church parking lot that I may run into someone other than Miss Billie at the preschool or the old guy who mixed paint at Sherwin Williams.

I was still struggling with the release on Emma's booster car seat, blissfully unaware of my appearance, when I saw a shiny, new black pickup pull into the parking lot at the edge of my peripheral vision.

I didn't bother looking up. Another parent I didn't need to impress, nor had any intention of making friends with.

The lock finally released after causing irreparable damage to my thumbnail. Emma shrugged out of the restraints. I shoved a tendril of hair that had escaped my ponytail out of my face and backed out of the car.

"Good morning, Michelle."

Kyle!

I should have known. I spun around, one hand fiddling with my ponytail that wasn't even centered on the back of my head, and the other assisting Emma out of the car. "Kyle, hey," I said, "Fancy meeting you here. And just when I got all prettied up."

He didn't even raise an eyebrow as he surveyed the mess that was me. "How did the kids like their first day of preschool?"

"Fine, just fine." Why wouldn't that strand of hair stay behind my ear?

"That's good." He looked at Emma, and then Jonah who waited for us at the curb. "You're going to have a lot of fun here," he said.

Emma stuck her finger in her mouth and ran over to where Jonah stood. Kyle turned back to me.

"I'm sorry," I said. "They're shy around new people."

"Yes, I can imagine, after everything they've been through." He said.

Miss Billie sure didn't miss a second airing my family's dirty laundry all over the place. Every teacher in the preschool probably knew too, what a terrible injustice had been done to sweet little Emma and Jonah by their irresponsible mother.

"Praise God for watching over them and sending them to you," Kyle said.

I wanted to tell him that if God were watching over them at all, He would have given Nicole a righteous kick in her thinking place so she would accept responsibility for raising her own kids. Instead a soft "humph" sound escaped.

This time, the eyebrows went up. "They're blessed to have you, Michelle," he reiterated.

"I really don't want to discuss this in front of the kids," I said softly so only he would hear me. "They've been through enough without hearing my opinion of my sister, or a God who would give her two beautiful children to neglect."

Kyle's eyebrows practically met in the middle of his forehead. "I see."

I glanced pointedly at my watch. "I've got tons of things to do this morning before I pick them back up at eleven-thirty."

"Oh, certainly," he said. He reached around me and shut the car door and followed me onto the sidewalk. I walked slowly, giving him plenty of opportunity to go his own direction. He didn't. Instead, he picked up his pace and got to the door two strides ahead of me. He held it open for us to walk through.

"Any time you need to talk, Michelle, my door's always open," he offered graciously. "I know this is quite an adjustment for you."

I nodded in response and bent my head over the sign-in sheet. He took the hint and walked away. I showed the kids to the play area and then beat my retreat, just in case Kyle or any other do-gooders were waiting in ambush with more meaningless platitudes about a merciful God watching over my niece and nephew. That was the last thing I needed to hear. Nicole was lazy, irresponsible, immature, and self-serving—period. She had answered no divine call when she dumped her kids in my front yard. As usual, she was thinking only of herself, and not about how her actions would affect anyone else. God, if he even existed, had not blessed Emma and Jonah by sending them to me, or vice versa, if that's what Kyle was implying. My life had been totally turned upside down, Emma and Jonah were devastated, and Nicole, who knew about her? She was probably lying somewhere, passed out drunk at this very minute. How could God be in any of it?

It wasn't until I buckled my seatbelt and caught sight of myself in the rearview mirror, that I remembered what a horrible mess I was. I no longer cared. Hopefully Kyle Swann had been scared off for good by my appearance. I suddenly had enough complications in my life.

Chapter Eight

Aunt Wanda was waiting on the front porch when I got home. I groaned inwardly but pasted a smile on my face for her benefit. I was already going to have barely enough time this morning to move furniture, take the pictures down, and wash the walls before time to go back to the preschool to pick the kids up. I didn't have time for company.

"Morning," I called out as I went around to the trunk to retrieve the paint and supplies I'd bought at Sherwin Williams.

"Good morning," she called back and started down the path toward me. "I see you have a project this morning." She reached into the trunk and took out a gallon of paint. "Oh my, what a pretty shade of blue."

I smiled my thanks at the compliment. "I'm painting Nicole's old room." I lifted two more cans out of the trunk. "I've got a soft yellow for the walls. I thought I'd tack up some trim a foot or so from the ceiling and paint the top area blue."

"Sounds pretty. You always had such an eye for colors."

I wondered where all the compliments were coming from. I'd never designed anything in my life and could barely coordinate my socks with my slacks. The only time I painted was out of sheer necessity. My one attempt at hanging wallpaper had ended in upside down roses so I never tried that again. "Not really. I stole the idea from TV."

She followed me in the back door and set the gallon of paint next to mine in the mudroom. "Does this mean you've decided to keep Emma and Jonah?" she asked gently.

Aha, her true purpose for being here. Uncle Jeb had obviously told her about our conversation the other night. She was afraid she was going to get stuck with Nicole's kids.

I went into the kitchen and headed for the coffee pot. "Well, it doesn't look like I have much choice at this point. And I've been meaning to do some sprucing up around this place anyway, nows as good a time as any. You want some coffee?"

"Oh, you know me. I always have room for coffee." Never one to settle into the role of guest, Aunt Wanda headed straight for the sink and the dishes I'd left from breakfast.

"I'll get to those later," I began.

Too late. The sink was already filling with lemon-scented bubbles. "I don't mind," she said cheerily. "There's only a few."

I flipped the switch on the coffee maker and started straightening the kitchen table. Now that I no longer lived alone, my table was suddenly used for eating. I stacked the magazines and bills into orderly piles and slid them to the far end of the large table. I straightened the place mats and refolded the napkins to slide into the napkin rings. At some point long ago, I went out and bought beautiful place settings to display on the table to fit the motif of a country kitchen. I kept up the façade for close to a week before my typical disorganization crept back over the table. Soon the placemats were stained and wrinkled, and usually hidden under a mountain of whatnots that couldn't seem to make it to where they belonged. Someday I'd put away the magazines, maybe cancel a few subscriptions, file the bills, and take back my kitchen table—someday.

Aunt Wanda wrung the dishrag out and brought it over to wipe the child sized fingerprints off the cleared end of the table. "Jeb and I have been talking, and we think it's best this way. This is probably the first chance those two little ones have had at a normal life."

She was right. She was absolutely right. Miss Billie was right. Even Kyle was right. But why did I have to be the one doing all the work?

"It was kind of pitiful," I told her. "Their reaction, I mean, when I took them to Wal-Mart Sunday. I could tell they are totally unaccustomed to getting anything new. Emma was crying again yesterday, but it wasn't for Nicole. She wanted someone named Carrie."

"How terrible," Aunt Wanda shook her head and went back to the sink. "Those poor little darlings."

"This Carrie, whoever she is, is probably worried sick about the kids too. I wish I had some way of getting in touch with her and letting her know they're all right."

"Neither of them know her last name?"

I shook my head, but realized Aunt Wanda had her back to me and couldn't see. "No, they don't know her phone number or even their own address. She lived in the apartment across the hall from them, but I'm not even sure it was in Memphis. The last time I talked to Nicole, she was the one who called me and she didn't offer a number."

Aunt Wanda's head wagged back and forth. "Those poor darlings," she repeated, though I figured she was thinking out loud. "What a blessing they have you."

Not that again.

"Nicole was about Emma's age when your Mom took off outta here." Aunt Wanda pulled the stopper from the sink and tore a paper towel from the roll on the holder to dry her hands. "You would think she remembered what it was like. It's beyond me how someone can do something to someone else when they know firsthand how horrible it is." She tossed the paper towel in the wastebasket at the end of the counter and turned to face me. She crossed her arms over her chest and wagged her head again. "No one thinks about anyone else anymore."

I went to the pile of magazines at the far end of the table and picked up the first one. It was the November issue. I either had to find a drawer for all this junk or start throwing stuff out. I sat down and started putting them into chronological order. I didn't want to think about when Mom left.

Aunt Wanda, on the other hand, was all ready to reminisce. "My, my, how that poor little thing carried on, Nicole, I mean. Do you remember that, Michelle? Of course, you do. You were what, about fourteen? I thought she'd never stop crying and hollering for Ruth. And Mom never had any patience for tears. She used to threaten to whip her if she didn't stop crying, but Nicole wouldn't stop. I guess she couldn't."

"Of course, she couldn't stop," I snapped, enraged at the memory of Grandma Catherine's injustice. "She was four. All she wanted was her mother. She didn't understand what was going on."

"I know, Michelle. Don't get upset with me. I'm the one who calmed Mom down every time Nicole started in. You think that bawling didn't grate on my nerves, too? It was all I could do to keep Mom from beating her half to death when she took to carrying on."

"I'll be sure and have Nicole thank you the next time she sees you."

"There's no need to get all up in arms at me," Aunt Wanda cried. "None of it was my fault. I sure didn't have nothing to do with your momma taking off the way she did. Her place was with you girls. We all wanted her here, but she quit listening to us years before. If we'd 'a had our druthers, she never would 'a married that worthless Hurley in the first place. It was all his doing. She was a practical, responsible young woman, just like you, until he got his claws into her, that is."

I'd heard all this before, more times than I cared to count. Grandma used to have this conversation with anyone who'd sit still long enough to listen. Aunt Wanda was usually willing to lend an ear when Grandma got into one of her griping moods. Back then the two women were interchangeable in my book. If Grandma wasn't reminding me of the yoke my parents had tied around her neck by taking off with no thought of her age or failing health, then Aunt Wanda was telling Uncle Jeb loud enough for me to hear, how unfair it was of Ruthie and that worthless Hurley to impose on Grandma the way they did.

"He wasn't worthless," I snapped, putting all the indignation I bore as a child into my voice. "For ten years he was a wonderful father. He and Mom just had their differences. It happens to a lot of couples."

Aunt Wanda snorted derisively. "Ten years does not get a kid raised. It takes a lifetime. If a person doesn't have a lifetime to give, then they have no business bringing children into the world."

I took a deep, cleansing breath. There was nothing to be gained by debating my father's parenting skills with her. Besides, on this point, she was right. "I agree. In a perfect world, adults would never consider bringing children into the world until they were able to handle the job. Dad made mistakes. He still is, obviously, since we haven't heard from him since he left twenty-three years ago. Mom made mistakes, too. She should've been strong enough to handle Dad's leaving. But she and Dad weren't the only ones who made mistakes. Grandma never should've made Nicole and me feel like we were a burden to her, although now I can see how much we were. It wasn't our fault our parents dumped us on her, but she made us feel like it was—every single day. Maybe that had something to do with the way Nicole turned out."

"Mom did the best she could," Aunt Wanda defended her, though meekly. "She was an old woman. Your parents had no business forcing you girls on her."

I nodded. "Oh, I know. She told me so all the time. I heard time and time again, that if she wasn't such a good, Christian lady, I'd be in an orphanage somewhere, while Nicole would be adopted by a nice family who wanted a pretty little girl. People didn't adopt girls like me, she always said. I'd be stuck in that orphanage working in the kitchen like a galley slave. I needed to be grateful for having it as good as I did."

Aunt Wanda's face softened. She dropped her arms to her sides. "She shouldn't have told you that," she said softly.

I let out my breath. It wasn't right that I take out my pent up anger at Grandma Catherine on Wanda. I was too old to hold onto anger at an old woman who said insensitive things. And Aunt Wanda was only defending her mother's memory. Things had been different then. People had different attitudes. Children were way down on the food chain. No one worried about hurting their feelings, at least not in my family where it was assumed they didn't have any.

Shamefully, I realized I'd been having basically the same thoughts about Emma and Jonah ever since they showed up under the lilac bushes. Like Grandma Catherine, all I thought about was how their being here affected me. They kept me from work, cost me money, and wrecked my routine.

Nicole and I had been a burden to Grandma, and were reminded of it everyday. Now the shoe was on the other foot. I was the beleaguered one and Emma and Jonah, the crosses to bear. While I hadn't said anything to make them feel unwelcome, my actions and attitudes spoke volumes. Like Aunt Wanda pointed out about Nicole, I knew firsthand how it felt to be abandoned by the ones who were supposed to love you more than anything, and left with someone who saw you as nothing but a yoke about the neck.

My attitude needed to change. Like it or not, Emma and Jonah were here for the foreseeable future. I couldn't expect Aunt Wanda and Uncle Jeb to do anymore than they already had. I couldn't expect Nicole's eventual return to solve everyone's problems. What if like Mom and Dad, God forbid, she never came back? Or if she did come back, how could I in all good conscious let her take the kids as if nothing had happened?

Chapter Nine

Thursday morning I awoke determined to get an early start on painting the remainder of Nicole's old room. Yesterday after the kids got home from preschool, I took them upstairs with me. I poured a small amount of yellow paint into two old bowls and let them paint along the bottom of the wall. With the drop cloths and newspapers I spread over the floors, messes were minimal. I had to leave the windows open for ventilation, so by the time we finished we were dripping with sweat. But it had been fun. The kids giggled and talked while they painted. I mostly listened. I found amusement in their observations about preschool and arguments over which one was the better painter. They soon forgot I was in the room and talked more candidly and openly than they would had I opened my mouth.

This morning I was going to concentrate on getting finished. All I had left to do was the trim around the doors and windows and the crown molding; two hours maximum if I got right on it. I'd be finished before time to go back to the preschool or the sun got around to that side of the house, making it too hot to work. I was hoping I could get Uncle Jeb to come by this weekend to help hang the chair rail I bought at Home Depot.

I woke the kids up a half hour earlier than usual.

"Are we going back to that school today?" Jonah asked, sitting up in bed and rubbing the sleep from his eyes.

I reached inside a drawer for a clean shirt and shorts. "Yes. Remember, you're going every morning this week? Then next week, you'll go everyday for the whole day while I'm at work; except for Friday. I don't work on Fridays."

Emma swung her legs over the side of the bed. Jonah scooted over next to her and they both stared up at me, their faces forlorn.

"You like the preschool, don't you?"

Jonah shrugged. Tears formed in Emma's eyes. Impatience welled up inside me. I didn't have time for this. The minutes ticked away on the clock beside the bed and the sun climbed higher in the sky with each passing minute.

"What's the matter?" I asked a little too brusquely. With great effort, I softened my voice and began again. "I thought you had fun yesterday. Didn't you like all the toys they had there?"

An almost imperceptible nod moved Emma's head. I went on, encouraged. "Well, see there. You'll have friends in no time. And you'll be learning all kinds of things there, too."

"We want to stay here with you and paint," Jonah said.

I tossed an outfit on the bed for each of them, determined. "Not today. I'm painting on the ladder and neither of you can reach. If there's any paint leftover when I'm finished, maybe we can paint the back side of the barn after you get home."

They brightened immediately.

"Then we'll go into town for ice cream."

This had them bouncing on the bed. "Yea!" they both squealed.

I smiled to myself. I was brilliant. This parenting stuff wasn't so complicated. Keep them busy. Feed them ice cream. Never let them smell fear or indecision.

"Can we get some Play-doh when we go to town?" Jonah asked.

I grimaced inwardly. Wasn't that stuff messy? "Play-doh?"

"Yeah, they have it at school, but we haven't got to play with it yet."

I looked from one expectant face to the other. Play-doh in my house, on my rugs; Ice cream, I could do; I could even stand in the blazing sun this afternoon and supervise while the kids splashed leftover paint on the back side of the barn—but Play-doh— that meant I'd have to put an old sheet on the floor. I'd probably have to pull the table apart afterwards and clean out the Play-doh that got down in the cracks. I'd have to keep an eye on Gypsy and make sure she didn't eat any of it. For that matter, Jonah and Emma might eat it. Could the human body digest Play-doh?

Emma turned to Jonah. "Mommy says Play-doh's too messy," she stated. "Remember? That's why we can't have it."

Three whole sentences out of Emma's mouth, one right after the other. It didn't register for a moment what she said; I was too surprised that she had spoken at all. Was this some kind of breakthrough, or was she simply preparing her little brother for the inevitable refusal she knew was forthcoming? They couldn't have Play-doh because it was too messy, too much of a bother for Mommy to fool with. That figured.

And I was about to give them the same excuse.

"Yes, it is messy," I agreed, giving them a solemn look. "But, I have an idea. We'll buy some Play-doh after school and save it for rainy days when we can't play outside."

The light in their eyes was worth whatever inconvenience this would cost me. "But you have to promise to be careful and not get any on the floor," I said in a stern reminder.

"Yea!" they chorused, pumping the air with their fists.

"And we gotta put the lids back on so it won't dry out."

"Right; we mustn't let it dry out," I admonished.

The two of them leaped off the bed and started slinging arms through sleeves. I stole a surreptitious glance at them on my way downstairs to let Gypsy outside for her morning exploration. Jonah and Emma still weren't as animated as even I knew children could be, but they were making progress. The threat of tears was gone. They were actually talking between themselves; probably about the Play-doh and all the fun they'd have at preschool today.

I wondered briefly if I'd been duped into buying the Play-doh by the mention of Mommy saying no. I didn't think so. Neither of them seemed to have a manipulative bone in their bodies. And it wasn't because I was a totally selfless person that I gave in so easily. I was beginning to like the way their eyes lit up and the infectious giggle that escaped their mouths when something made them happy. My heart swelled when I saw the simple delight in their eyes at the prospect of painting the barn or getting new shoes at Wal-Mart. Yes, I was making them happy, but in return, they brought joy into my life, too. A joy I'd forgotten.

Emma and Jonah weren't my first go at motherhood. Grandma Catherine was less than enthusiastic about getting stuck raising Nicole after Mom disappeared. Dealing with me was one thing; I could see to my own needs and even came in handy around the house. Nicole, on the other hand, was high maintenance. She was a coquettish child, and while Grandma seemed to like her, though she never admitted as much, she had no intention of tending to a four-year-old twenty-four hours a day so Nicole's rearing fell naturally on my shoulders.

At fourteen, I had seen my share of hard times and injustice. I didn't bat an eye when it became apparent who was expected to care for Nicole. Other than school where the law required I make an appearance, I was expected to be home where I could keep an eye on her. Nicole was lovable and, though precocious, hard to refuse. She learned quickly how to get her way. She knew exactly what worked with whom she might be dealing with at the time. Even Uncle DeWitt, who seldom made a facial expression, was wrapped around her little finger. Telling her no became impossible for even the most hard-hearted among us.

During my high school years while most girls were dating and whispering in the hallways about boys they liked, I hurried home to take care of my little sister. I attended few dances or ball games, and with the exception of Kyle Swann whose infinite patience convinced me we would someday marry, I had no social life.

I got my nursing degree from a local college, having never spent a night away from home. For me, college was no different than high school, other than I was now expected to hold down a fulltime job while attending to pay for added expenses. As Nicole grew older, she became wilder and harder to control. I did what I could to rein her in, but I was busy and sleepy and struggling to absorb information that I feared was beyond my comprehension.

Grandma couldn't do anything with her. I gave up trying. Nicole was seventeen when Grandma Catherine passed away. I was twenty-seven and totally accustomed to Grandma ruling the roost. Little changed after her passing; her ways had become my ways without my even noticing it. I woke up every morning and went to work. I had no expenses other than the taxes and insurance on the farm, which I had assumed responsibility for as soon as I got my first paying job. After all, I had to do something to begin repaying my debt to Grandma for her Christian charity. My social life was still nonexistent.

Grandma had been sick the last few years of her life. I developed my habits of working overtime and most of her care fell to Aunt Wanda. Nicole, who already had a wild streak a mile wide, was set totally adrift. Any reins I tried to put on her were strained past the point of my control. I couldn't do anything with her, and I really didn't want to. I'd done what I could to raise my kid sister. By that time, I was thoroughly sick of her. She wasn't my responsibility. Where were her parents? Didn't they have to account for anything?

After Grandma died I turned a blind eye to Nicole's indiscretions. What could be done about them now? I had done what I could to turn her into a responsible young lady, but somehow my plans went awry. She wasn't responsible. She wasn't even a lady. She had a reputation around our small community that was less than favorable. She was popular, to say the least; an embarrassment to the family.

Since I couldn't do anything with my sister, I went out and got a dog; something I could train; something that would listen when I spoke—most of the time.

Nicole left high school halfway through her senior year. She saw no point in finishing. She already had a job at the candle factory and school was keeping her from getting more hours. Nothing I said could dissuade her. Nothing anyone said or did could change Nicole once she made her mind up about something. She reminded me of Dad in that respect. A total stranger could talk Mom into shaving her head within five minutes of meeting her on the street, but the same person couldn't convince Dad to leave a burning building. Nicole was no different.

Working at the factory fulltime was the worst thing Nicole could have done. The high school boys who gave her attention and told her what she wanted to hear were replaced by men; men who knew how to prey on a young girl's naiveté. Suddenly, the ones calling the house and stopping by at all hours weren't teenagers; they were in their thirties. Many of them married. Nicole didn't care. She loved being the center of attention, the object of desire. It didn't matter how many times I pointed out that they were using her, she laughed and said, no, she was using them.

I didn't realize she was pregnant until I walked in on her in the bathroom one day when she was wearing only her bra and panties. What bothered me almost as much as her obvious pregnancy was that I hadn't noticed earlier. How could I have missed it? She was at least five months along. I was a registered nurse. I dealt with young women at work all the time that had gotten themselves into similar predicaments. I listened to their excuses and logic, and shook my head in dismay that in this day and age a young woman could allow such a thing to happen to her. All it took to prevent pregnancy was a trip to the school nurse. Now it was my own sister. I wanted to wring her neck.

She continued working at the factory until an eight hour shift became too great a strain on her back and feet. She quit work and came home to sulk full time. Her boyfriends stopped calling. She ranted to me how she would expose the one who did this to her. She would make him regret the day he'd ever been born. He would support her and her baby; she didn't care if he did have a wife and kids at home. She wasn't anyone's fool, she cried over and over again, as her middle increased and the hormones raged.

But she never named anyone. The welfare claimed they wouldn't pay her a dime unless she gave them the name of the father, someone to go after for support. So she made someone up. He was passing through town, she said. She only spent one night with him. He probably used a fake name. She refused any paternity tests because there was no man to go after. She wouldn't subject her baby to such humiliation, she said. She talked big. She did nothing except sit on the couch in front of the TV, fuming, blustering, and waiting.

Emma was born on Valentine's Day with me assisting in the delivery. All my irritation at Nicole for allowing this to happen in the first place, melted away as I cut the umbilical cord connecting the red, wrinkled, mewling creature to her mother.

Emma's presence did nothing to dampen Nicole's social life. Within two weeks, she poured herself into her size four jeans and headed into town. She smoked, drank, and stayed out all night, as if she didn't have a baby at home who needed her.

I'd get home from work at seven-thirty and Nicole would be gone by eight. I tried to stay out of her life. Everything I said ended up in a fight. I was tired of arguing, tired of sitting up half the night with a colicky baby, tired of listening to Nicole blaming everyone she ever met for the mess that had suddenly become her life. When Emma was a few months old, Nicole decided her prospects were better in the city. So she loaded up her battered car with everything she owned, Emma included, and headed to Memphis. By bits and pieces, I learned about Bones, the guy in the band, and their subsequent breakup. I heard of one job after another, another man and discovered there was another baby on the way.

Chapter Ten

I left the windows in Nicole's room open a crack for ventilation, but drew the blinds to keep out the brunt of the sun's rays; mid-August, relentless heat, little rain. It was the same story every year, yet people still gathered in general stores throughout the state and tried to remember a summer that had been so miserable.

"Let me think, oh, I remember—last summer!" I wanted to scream every time the topic came up within my hearing.

I drove to the school with the AC on high. It was Emma and Jonah's last half day. Next week, I was back to my regular routine at work, which meant they'd stay at the preschool until three-thirty on Tuesdays and Thursdays. Mondays and Wednesdays I worked seven to seven. On those days I'd ask Uncle Jeb, whom they'd taken an instant liking to, to pick them up for me until I found a sitter. What if she didn't drive? That would stink. It was too late in the year to hire a teenager; they'd be going back to school in two weeks themselves.

It was too hot to play outside. Inside the fellowship hall, the preschool staff was trying to keep seventy-five preschoolers from raising the roof off the church with their pent up energy. They had been divided into playgroups; I assumed that helped keep them under control. Nonetheless, the fillings in my teeth vibrated from the noise.

Miss Mary, Emma and Jonah's teacher, approached. A smile lit up her round, warm face. She seemed unaffected by the chaos pulsating around her. I wondered if the State had considered issuing the teachers ear protection. "Did you get your painting done?" she asked.

I smiled and scratched at a smear of paint on my forearm I had missed during cleaning up. "All finished, until I get another creative urge."

She chuckled and then her face sobered.

Uh, oh. I braced myself. Which one, Emma or Jonah? I had my suspicions.

She clasped her hands in front of her and announced, "This was our first tear-free day."

I exhaled. "Thank goodness."

She took my arm and steered me a few feet away. "Emma talked a little today. It's the first time she's done that. If she speaks at all, it's usually through Jonah. We try to discourage that."

"I know. I'm sorry."

"Don't be, it's fine. She's a wonderful little girl. She's even started playing with one of the other little girls."

"Wow! That's encouraging."

"Yes, it is. Jonah spent his first morning here stuck to Emma like glue, but then he started moving around the room, feeling out the other boys and finding a place for himself."

I wasn't surprised. Jonah was already the type who would get along anywhere; it was Emma who concerned me. My heart broke for her.

"Most of this morning, Emma stayed close to me like she always does, not talking or anything, just sitting next to me, watching what I was doing," Mary explained. "Every chance I get, I talk to her about anything I can think of. Usually she doesn't say anything back, she just keeps watching my hands if I'm cutting or preparing the next day's lesson. Then today, out of the blue, she told me she and Jonah painted yesterday."

I had to swallow the lump in my throat before I could answer. "Yes, I'm painting the room they're sleeping in. I let them help. They seemed to enjoy it."

"You don't know how much. While she talked, she positively glowed. You're doing a good job with them. I know it's hard on you, but you're doing fine. It's showing."

I wasn't sure how to react to her praise. I wanted the kids to be happy and adjust to the situation. I wanted them to be comfortable at my house and feel secure. I wanted Emma to make friends and start speaking for herself. I just wasn't sure I wanted to get good at this mothering thing. It wasn't my job. Nicole would come back someday. I knew she would. Just when the kids got used to me and I got used to them, she'd stroll in like nothing was out of the ordinary and resume her place as authority figure in their lives. No matter how I questioned her parenting skills, she was still their mother.

Wasn't it best that I hold the kids at arm's length until then?

I already knew the older woman's answer to that question, so I didn't ask. "Thank you," I said instead. "It's a learning process for all of us."

"After telling me about the painting," Mary continued, "I saw her studying another little girl in the room who tends to play on the edge of the crowd, too. I got a brainstorm and called Caitlyn over to where we were working. I asked her to hand me something. Then she looked at Emma, Emma looked at her, and the rest is history." Miss Mary's eyes scanned the playgroups. "There they are," she said pointing. "They've been together ever since."

I followed her pointing finger and saw two heads bent over what looked like a wooden puzzle. One was fair, the other carrot-top red. "Now I won't feel so bad about the kids staying all day next week."

Miss Mary patted my arm. "Oh, don't you worry about that for one minute. They'll get along just fine."

I smiled appreciatively before starting toward the two little girls working on the puzzle. Mary put her hand back on my arm. "Don't forget. This Sunday is our Sunday morning program. All the children gather in Miss Jennifer's classroom fifteen minutes before morning worship."

My reply was a blank stare.

"It's been posted all week," she said.

I didn't need to tell her I didn't bother reading the notices posted next to the sign-in sheet. It was written all over my face. "I'm sure Miss Billie mentioned it when you enrolled Emma and Jonah," she went on.

I still had no idea what she was talking about. I had a ton of things to do today and needed to get going.

"Once a month we have the children from the preschool come in and sing a few songs and say the memory verses they've been working on for that month to the church. It is a wonderful experience for everyone. Many of our preschoolers don't have a home church, and it gives the church members a chance to see what goes on in the preschool all month."

"Sounds wonderful, but I'm working this weekend," I told her, my face a picture of regret. I hadn't planned to work at the county hospital, but that could be changed with one simple phone call. They always needed the manpower on weekends.

"Oh, that's too bad, maybe next month. Emma and Jonah have been practicing the songs with the other children. Jonah loves to sing, don't you know?"

No, I didn't.

"Maybe there's someone else in the family who could bring them Sunday morning," Miss Mary said hopefully. "Or even a babysitter would be fine. That way they could meet more people from the church and the preschool. It may help them get used to things quicker. I guarantee everyone who attends will be blessed."

"They're staying with my aunt and uncle for now on the weekends I work," I said. "They're Presbyterians, but I'll ask them."

"We don't want to keep anyone from their home church," Miss Mary was quick to assure me. "If they prefer, they could stay for the program and then leave. Some of our parents do that."

"I'll ask them," I said again.

I gathered the kids and the papers they'd made that day and exited the preschool as quickly as I could. What a racket. Trap parents into attending the church with the promise of seeing their little songbird performing on stage. Crafty, I had to admit. I wondered who came up with it, the benign Miss Billie or Kyle himself. I looked over at his usual parking spot in front of the doors that led to the main building. His truck wasn't there. A worm of disappointment worked its way into my belly. I don't know why. I wasn't even sure why I bothered to look in the first place. Maybe so I could tell him how disgusted I was with his scheme to lure new people to church. Was he such a poor preacher, he had to trick unsuspecting people to get them through the door?

I considered my appearance and was glad I wouldn't run into him today. I looked a fright. My clothes were paint spattered, and I doubted I smelled very good. My fine hair was falling from the confines of its sweaty ponytail. I was naturally fair haired and fair skinned like Emma, so my complexion was red and splotchy on the best of days, especially when I got overheated. Most women with my coloring covered it up with makeup. I seldom bothered. It was bad enough I came out in public at all, but I'd promised to let the kids paint with the leftover paint, so what was the point of showering before I left the house?

Kyle was nothing more than an old boyfriend from high school; hardly a boyfriend really. We dated some, spent a lot of time together and even talked about the future. But who didn't do that in high school with at least one other person? It never amounted to anything. Before the ink had even dried on our diplomas, we both went our separate ways; me to college, and Kyle to the Air Force. I wondered again about his alleged "call to preach" as he called it. From what I remembered, he wasn't religious back then. His parents dragged him to church every Sunday like everybody else's. Including Grandma Catherine.

"In this family, we go to church," she chanted every time I complained.

"Why?" I would demand. "What good does it do?"

"Don't sass, young lady," came the inevitable reply. I never did get an answer to my question.

I was true to my word. The kids had already eaten lunch at the preschool before I picked them up, so we headed straight to Wal-Mart. "No toys," I warned as I pulled the car into the parking lot. "Except for the Play-doh," I added quickly at the look of dismay that flashed across both their faces. I doubted they would complain if I suddenly broke my promise. They seemed used to disappointment.

Inside the store, they didn't ask for a thing. Besides helping me choose the right colors of Play-doh, they didn't make a peep. I almost caved and let them buy a toy, just because they were so good and obedient, but stopped myself in time. I wouldn't spoil them. There were already enough whining, disrespectful, irritating brats, reared by lazy parents, whom the rest of us were forced to tolerate, without me adding two more to the equation.

I didn't mention the Play-doh castle or ice cream parlor I noticed sitting nearby on the shelf. One or both would be a nice surprise some other time, if they stayed around that long. I picked up a few other things we were running low on around the house and headed toward the bank of cash registers. It's amazing how two tiny people could change the entire simplistic way a house ran in a matter of days.

Emma and Jonah sat cross-legged in the cart, holding onto the two packages of Play-doh. They studied the writing on the packages as if they could tell what the words meant and occasionally smiled at each other. A wordless communication passed between them. They had been privy to each other's sufferings for as long as they'd lived. Now they were almost like one. When one hurt, they both hurt. When one rejoiced, the other experienced the same joy. Sharing the Play-doh, like the paint, the ice cream, and the new shoes, delighted both because it delighted the other. I almost envied their bond until I reminded myself why it was so strong. If not faced with such despair and loneliness on a regular basis, they would never be so close.

The weight of their bodies at the front of the cart made it cumbersome and difficult to manage. I seldom required a cart when I shopped. I found it slowed me down, especially with sixty-five pounds worth of preschoolers in the front end. I rounded a corner too fast and had to hold back hard on the handle to keep from careening into a man suddenly in my path. I moved my eyes upward and realized with a sinking heart it was Kyle.

He put his hands out defensively and caught hold of the front of the cart. I couldn't help noticing the strength in his hands and wondering what in his job description required he be so tanned and strong. "Whoa, now," he said, his face open and friendly. Then he looked up and recognized me. He grinned and managed to scowl playfully at the children at the same time. "Are you trying to run me over?"

Emma giggled and gazed up at him through lowered lashes.

Jonah got onto his knees and proudly held up his four pack of primary colored Play-doh. Emma had chosen the pastels. "Look what we got, Pastor Kyle," he said eagerly.

"Pastor Kyle." I would never get used to that, it didn't describe the Kyle I remembered. It was too holy, too reverent. It made me think of

a much older, more rounded man in robes, swinging incense decanters, not sporting jeans, a polo shirt, and carrying a pack of strawberry licorice in his calloused hands.

Kyle's eyes widened at the sight of the Play-doh. "Wow! Play-doh; I love playing with that. Looks like you're going to have some fun."

"Not today," Jonah said in his serious tone. "We've got to paint. The Play-doh's for when it rains."

Kyle nodded like it all made perfect sense. He looked at me and smiled, before turning his attention back to the children. "That's a good idea." He reached out and tousled Jonah's hair. He smiled gently at Emma, who beamed discreetly under his perusal. How did he know she wasn't ready for the easy manner of her brother?

"What are you painting?" Kyle's question was directed at me.

"The kid's room." I realized with a start it was the first time I'd referred to it as their room instead of "Nicole's old room."

Kyle noticed something in my eyes. What, acceptance? "I guess you know how well they're doing at preschool," he said in more of a statement than a question.

I nodded. "I talked with Mary about that very thing today."

"We're glad to have them."

I nodded. Was he expecting me to say I was too?

When the silence lengthened, he looked down at the children. "I'll see you two at school Monday." He glanced back at me, "Unless you're coming to the preschool program at church Sunday morning."

Emma and Jonah turned to me, expectant and hopeful.

I resented being put on the spot like that. "I don't think so," I said, looking past the kids, straight at Kyle. I thought about telling him I had to work like I'd told Miss Mary, but I had already decided there was no need to lie. I was a grown woman. I didn't need to make excuses. My life had changed enough without adding church attendance to the list of things I was required to do now that I was in charge of two small children. I ignored Uncle Jeb's advice from the other night telling me that church was where children belonged. Grandma Catherine made sure Nicole and I went every Sunday we lived under her roof and it hadn't made our situation one bit better.

Emma and Jonah looked disappointed. I ignored them. I wasn't a fairy godmother who could make them happy just by waving my magic wand. I was who I was, and had changed enough in the past week to accommodate them. I had to stand up for myself somewhere.

Kyle smiled, first at me, then the kids. "All right, but the invitation is always open for any Sunday. You have fun with that Play-doh," he said to the kids. "Don't get it all over the floor."

"We won't," Jonah assured him cheerily as he moved past our cart in the narrow aisle.

With one more wave to encompass all of us, Kyle disappeared. I pushed the cart toward the cash registers. Emma and Jonah watched warily as I put my things on the belt to be rung up. Something was bothering Aunt Michelle, that much they could see, they just weren't sure what. To tell the truth, neither was I. I'd been invited to church countless times since Grandma passed away. For a while, a group of ladies from her church visited me to see if I was all right and if there was anything they could do for me. They were sure it was my despondency over losing Grandma that kept me from appearing every time the church doors were open. On their last visit I finally admitted to the pastor and his henchmen that I only went to church as a courtesy to my grandmother since I lived rent-free in her house. Now that she was gone, I was no longer under that obligation. While shocked and dismayed at my candor, my confession did the trick. They never came back.

Even though I presently lacked the nerve to say the same thing to Kyle, I wasn't going to let him use Emma and Jonah to guilt me into anything.

Chapter Eleven

G ypsy, the traitor!

For the past six years, barring the occasional night spent out on the porch, she had slept on a discarded quilt I left crumpled on the floor next to my bed. After Grandma Catherine passed away, I let it be known I was in the market for a dog. A woman at work had a neighbor who owned an Australian Shepard who found herself in trouble by a handsome stranger of questionable lineage. The handsome stranger was part Border Collie, part Beagle, with a little Lab thrown in. The mix didn't bother me since all I wanted was a companion, an alarm system, and another warm body in the house. Owning a dog had always been an off limits subject with Grandma, who viewed most living creatures as a thorn in her flesh.

I drove an hour away to see the man with the wayward Australian Shepard, and fell in love with Gypsy at first sight. I trained her rigorously for the first six months and shaped her into what I wanted in a pet.

She lived up to my expectations and beyond. She was my best friend and I was hers. She hung on my every word, and in return, I chased her around the yard, pretending to want the soggy tennis ball she had clamped in her jaws. She was the last thing I saw every night when I laid down to sleep, and the first thing I tripped over every morning when I stumbled out of bed—until the night the kids came.

Now she slept every night sprawled across the foot of the double bed in Nicole's old room. I wasn't thrilled with a dog on the furniture;

I guess it was the Grandma Catherine in me, but I didn't have her mettle. There was no way after everything the kids had been through, I could tell them dogs belonged on the floor, or better still, out in the back yard attached to a dog house.

Gypsy wouldn't understand either. She knew where she was needed. I loved her. I kept her clean and groomed and healthy. I filled her dog dish, but it was Emma and Jonah who needed her more than I ever would. Gypsy knew it. I knew it. The kids knew it.

Grandma Catherine's garden had completely gone to rot and ruin in the two weeks since the kids showed up under the lilac bushes. The weeds had overtaken the tomato plants, and the cucumber vines had wrapped themselves mercilessly around the green peppers. The weekend before I told the administrator I wouldn't be working for the next few weekends. Uncle Jeb and Aunt Wanda were babysitting for me on weekends and it didn't seem fair. They were already doing enough by picking the kids up at preschool the afternoons I worked at University and keeping them until I got home after seven. Besides, I had things to do around the house. Saturday morning, before the dew had a chance to burn off the plants, I dressed in my old work clothes, stopped outside Nicole's old bedroom door, motioned for Gypsy to join me, and made my way to the garden.

I was a little surprised to hear Gypsy actually padding along behind me. It was the first time she'd been out of the kids' sight in two weeks. I knew it was only because they were still asleep, but I appreciated the company regardless. I grabbed a hoe from the shed and started to work on the east end of the garden, the end where the sun was already beating down. By the time it got unbearably hot and I was good and tired, I'd be in the shade and the work wouldn't seem so arduous. Gypsy plopped down in the dew-covered grass in the shade of the hydrangea hedge to watch, one ear turned toward the house, just in case a little pair of tiny feet hit the hardwood floor upstairs.

I smiled at the dog and attacked the weeds with vigor. For all its tedium, I enjoyed working the garden. Things had certainly changed from when I was young. I hated working out here when Grandma was the one giving orders. Not only was she unreasonably particular about her garden, no dirt clods, rows perfectly straight, cucumbers to the east, carrots and radishes to the west, and of course, the weeds went without saying, she had the uncanny ability to suck the pleasure out of any project.

I became adept at blocking Grandma's presence, whether physical or implied, from my mind. I was determined not to become like her. While she seemed to rejoice in searching for the bad in any situation, I decided I would do the opposite. I would make a game out of everything, whether canning beans, snapping peas, or scrubbing the living room floor. I closed myself into my own little world where everything was fun, mysterious or an adventure.

It wasn't just for my benefit. Regardless of my chores, I was still required to keep an eye on Nicole. When working in the garden, I would sit her at the end of the row, close to where Gypsy currently lay, and tell her a story about a fairy princess held captive in a tower or a beautiful young girl waiting for her beau to return from battle. Of course there was always countless obstacles that kept the beau from returning or the princess locked in the tower.

The favorite story for both of us was the one in which I convinced Nicole she was a princess left in the care of me, her Royal Guardian. Her parents, the king and queen, had lost their kingdom to an evil knight, and had gone home to try and regain it. Princess Nicole had to wait at the end of each garden row and never take her eyes off me. If she did, the evil knight, who could be hiding anywhere, might jump out of the bushes and get me. Then she would have no one to protect her until the handsome prince, who was out slaying dragons at the time, could come to rescue both of us. Every now and then, to keep things interesting, I'd drop my hoe in the dirt and growl and yell, and run at her, pretending the evil knight had tricked her by pretending to be the Royal Guardian. She always squealed and leaped to her feet and ran a few times around the garden until I caught her or she dropped into the grass in gales of laughter, pretending to be scared.

Every summer, we added more details and characters to our stories, until they often overlapped, which only added to the fantasy. I always thought of writing them down after my chores were done for the day, when Nicole and I were relaxing on the couch or the front porch. Somehow I never got around to it.

It was a long time before we stopped playing our games and making up stories. I couldn't remember exactly when. I imagined around the time I started college. I became an instant adult in Grandma's eyes; still responsible for whatever could possibly go wrong around the farm, whether I was present or not.

And things started to go wrong fast. I sure didn't have time to put any stories down in a notebook.

I whacked angrily at a weed to get my mind off Grandma. Here I was, thirty-three years old, and could still get my dander up thinking about the old woman. It hadn't done any good then, and it sure wouldn't do any good now.

Grandma had never liked me, not from the very beginning. Anyone could see it. Mom tried to make light of it, though she wouldn't insult me by denying it. "That's just how she is, Michelle," she'd say. "She's an old woman, set in her ways. Don't take it personally."

I didn't. I didn't take anything personally. If I had been the delicate sort like my cousin Violet, I wouldn't have made it past eleven.

Still, living with Grandma Catherine's Christian charity waxed sore on even the strongest of constitutions. She didn't want me to forget what a burden I was. "It's not your fault, girl," she'd say after a good scolding over some infraction I'd committed. "It's that worthless daddy of yours."

Like, I wanted to hear that.

"He's the one that took off and left your mama with no choices," Grandma continued. She'd click her tongue and stare out the window, her gnarled fingers flexing and relaxing around the ends of her rocker arms. I knew she was imagining wrapping her hands around my missing daddy's neck and squeezing as tight as she was able. "I told Ruthie he was no good the first time she brought him home."

I always stopped listening whenever Grandma got tuned up like that, knowing full well how the story turned out—at least Grandma's version.

"Your daddy always was a smooth talker." She always called him "your daddy" to Nicole and me, or "that man of yours" to Mom, unless she was really angry and threw in a few less than charitable adjectives. I never once in my life heard her call him by his given name. He was Bobby, Rob, or Robert to everyone but Grandma.

"I remember tellin' your Grandpa—" she'd continue, as she pushed her rocking chair back and forth, faster and faster with her spindly legs. The madder she was, the faster that rocking chair would rock. "He'll be nothin' but trouble. I said, Gib, that boy'll be nothing but trouble. He's worthless. Too pretty for his own good. A man shouldn't be that hand-some, it always leads to trouble, sure as I'm sittin' here. Yes indeedy."

I never understood how good looks automatically overrode any good quality a person might have as far as Grandma was concerned.

"When your daddy was workin' steady, things went okay. I have to admit he took pretty good care of you and Ruthie. But I knew it was just a matter of time before he'd mess things up and leave my poor Ruthie high and dry. After the plant shut down, that's when it hap-pened. It takes a strong man to stare adversity in the face and bounce back. But your daddy, oh no, he wasn't the bouncin' back kind."

I whacked at another weed and decapitated a carrot top instead. "Watch what you're doing, dummy," I hissed out loud.

Where had I heard that before?

Grandma Catherine was correct that our tiny family's downward spiral began when the plant Dad worked at for five years shut down. I had to give her that. The event also coincided with Nicole's birth. For Mom's sake, I tried to be surprised when he left. Deep down, I couldn't help wondering why Mom was so shocked. She holed up in her room for a week, leaving me in charge of Baby Nicole.

I empathized with her pain, and at the same time, resented her weakness. If her life was such a wreck, why didn't she do something about it? She could have gone after Dad, force him to do the right thing and return to his family, or start her life over without him. It seemed so cut and dried to my eleven-year-old mind.

Mom handled things the only way she knew how. She sank deeper and deeper into depression and the bottle. She wasn't strong enough to take care of Nicole and me…and herself. Within a couple of weeks the cupboards were bare, the rent was due. At least she had the decen-cy to wait until the last day of school. I came home with that sense of freedom and an incredibly long three months stretching ahead of me, to find our belongings sitting on the sidewalk outside our apartment building. Nicole was playing on the sidewalk and Mom was loading boxes into the back of our old Maverick.

It wasn't the first time I met Grandma Catherine I was later told, but I didn't remember the white-haired, pinched faced woman standing before me. We stood nearly nose–to-nose. The top of my head came to her chin. She was narrow and small, she reminded me of a white crow, sitting on a fence post, alarmed and paranoid, her head darting back and forth, her beady eyes taking everything in. She didn't smile or pull me into her arms like I thought a grandmother would. She sized me up in one severe, intimidating glance, made a derisive comment about how much Nicole cried, turned on her heel, and went back into the house. We had no choice but to follow.

For years after, I wondered if Dad was aware of how his leaving had put us at Grandma's mercy. Had he known, he would've come back. I was sure of it. He wouldn't do that to his family. But how could he not know? Surely he realized his wife would end up back home with her family in Winona. He knew she couldn't survive in the world without him. The three of us would be forced to put up with a hateful, old woman he couldn't bring himself to visit since I was little.

Why had he done it? Hating us was one thing. Leaving a wife he no longer loved was another. But forcing us onto Grandma when he knew she wouldn't turn us out, which would have been the kindest thing she ever did to a person, was beyond cruel on his part. How could he do it?

I put my hand on the small of my back and stretched. I hadn't let myself dwell on all this baggage in years. After Grandma died, I decided it took too much effort to harbor bad feelings toward her, Dad, Mom, or anyone else. I planned to move on with my life, get serious about saving for retirement, take some courses, move ahead in my field, and leave my family's problems in the past where they belonged.

In a move that surprised me more than anyone else, Grandma left the farm to me with the provision that I never sell without first offering it to Uncle DeWitt, Aunt Wanda, their descendents, and then the rest of the family, in that order. I couldn't hate her. Somewhere deep inside her, she must have seen something in me that made up for my kinship to that Hurley man she hated so. Maybe she even realized I deserved the farm after putting up with her and doing her bidding for sixteen years. Or, maybe she loved me. I could never quite believe that possibility; she had taken too much pleasure in causing Nicole and me pain. I stared at her pictures many times after the reading of the will and tried to see something behind those hollow, blue eyes that hinted at what was going on in her head. Why had she done the things she did; said the things she said? Had all those years of pointing out my faults, and everyone else's, been her warped way of training me to be a better person?

Whatever her reasons, the farm was mine.

I made an effort to get my mind off its dark path and plan breakfast instead.

Waffles were always a popular choice. The kids loved them. Emma wouldn't eat until she'd filled each little hole with syrup. Jonah tried but he wasn't as patient. He'd use half a bottle before my impatience would get the better of me and I'd snatch the bottle away from him and do it myself. The syrup never went to waste though. He licked up every drop, no matter how big the puddle. Life was too short to worry about going through a bottle of Golden Griddle a week.

I'd gained three pounds in the two weeks since Emma and Jonah arrived. I didn't have the figure of a woman who could afford three pounds here and three pounds there. If Nicole didn't come back soon, I wasn't going to fit into my scrubs, which were already less than figure flattering. After Grandma died and I could live the way I wanted, I became a toast and coffee person. Dinner was often a bag of microwave popcorn in front of the television, a Lean Cuisine, or skipped altogether. Not anymore! The frequent stops at McDonald's, the fish sticks and macaroni and cheese, were all catching up with my hips. More gardening, less waffles, I told myself as I worked my way into the shade.

Chapter Twelve

Uncle Jeb showed up at the back door just as we were restoring order to the kitchen after a late breakfast of waffles and cantaloupe. "What's all the ruckus in here?" he demanded in his fake gruff voice. He glowered down at the kids from his six-foot height, but the gleam in his eye was evident to all, even Emma. "I could hear you all the way up the road."

"Uncle Jeb!" Jonah squealed. He ran forward and hugged him around his long legs. Uncle Jeb was one of those people old dogs and children automatically took to, but still I felt a pang of envy that the kids hadn't reacted to my presence with that kind of enthusiasm. Of course, I wasn't as open to them as Uncle Jeb. Kids had a sixth sense. They knew who was comfortable around them and who wasn't, just like old dogs. "Are we going fishin' today?" Jonah wanted to know.

Emma stayed near the safety of the table, but watched his face, just as eager to hear his response.

I jumped to Uncle Jeb's rescue. "Come on, you two. Uncle Jeb has taken you fishing three times already. Maybe he has other things to do."

Uncle Jeb winked at me and looked back down at Emma and Jonah, his bushy gray eyebrows furrowed together in a frown. "As a matter of fact, I've got a million things that need takin' care of today and don't have time for no pesterin' kids. I've got to bush hog around the pond. Then I gotta put the horses into the north field. After that,

Wanda wants me to clean out the barn and the field next to the house so maybe we can have a barbecue tonight."

Jonah and Emma exchanged glances. "A barbecue?" Jonah asked. "Do we get to come?"

Uncle Jeb rubbed his chin and chewed his bottom lip. "Well, I expected Wanda'd be callin' here in a little bit to see if ya wanna come, but I told her, no, there's too much work that needs to be done around here first."

"We can help you, Uncle Jeb," Jonah offered.

Emma took a brave step forward and nodded emphatically.

Uncle Jeb dismissed him with a wave of his hand. "Nah. You wouldn't want to ride around on that old hot tractor all day; and I know ya don't like 'em horses."

"Yes, we do! Yes, we do!" Jonah assured him, jumping from one foot to the other.

"How 'bout it, Emma?" Uncle Jeb said. "Is that so?"

She nodded again and said in a small voice, "We like the horses."

Uncle Jeb pulled his mouth into a bow as if he was considering the validity of their words. "Well, I guess if you're sure."

"We are. We are!"

"Okay, then. Michelle, how about I put these two little whipper snappers to work today? Then, if they work really hard, they can go into town with me to get some steaks and hotdogs and whatever else we'll need for a barbecue."

Emma and Jonah turned pleading eyes to me.

"Well, I don't know," I said, playing along. "Neither one of them look big enough to be much good on the tractor."

"Yes, we are," Jonah, said. "I'm strong, so's Emma."

"Oh, all right," I said. "Go upstairs and put on some long pants. I don't want you getting eaten up by critters while you're bush hogging."

"Yea!" They tore out of the kitchen, waving their hands in the air.

"Don't forget, you're comin' to work," Uncle Jeb called after them. "Like the Good Book says; ya don't work, ya don't eat."

"'Kay, Uncle Jeb," they called back as they thumped their way up the stairs, although I was sure his Bible reference was lost on them.

I turned to my uncle. His face was lit up with a thousand stars.

"You know you don't have to do this, Uncle Jeb. You and Aunt Wanda fool with them enough during the week. I'm sure you'd appreciate some time to yourselves."

"That's all we've got, Peanut, time to ourselves. It don't look like me and Wanda's goin' to have grandkids anytime soon, and if we do, they'll be all the way in Texarkana. I love having the kids around. Doc's always tellin' me I need a little recreation. Those two kids are better than any blood pressure medicine."

I arched my eyebrows and said, "I don't know about that."

He smiled. "Trust me, they are. We have a high old time together."

"Are you sure about them on the tractor?"

"Don't you remember you and Violet riding all over the farm by yourselves on that thing? And while you were at school, Nicole sat right up there beside me while I got my work done."

"But we were used to it. Emma's awfully bashful. What if she forgets to hold on, you have to scold her, and she starts crying?"

Uncle Jeb smiled. "If I didn't know better, I'd think ya sound just like a worryin' mama."

"No, no, I'm not worried…" My voice trailed off and I felt my cheeks heat up. "If you're sure…"

"I'm sure." He put his hand on the screen door. "Send 'em over to the house with Gypsy. I'll be putterin' around somewhere. Don't be a stranger. I'll light the fire for supper sometime around six."

"Sounds good, I'll be there. Thanks, Uncle Jeb. You've made those kids' day."

"No problem." He was halfway out the door when he turned back. "Michelle, you could return the favor and make my day tomorrow by bringin' the kids to church with your Aunt Wanda and me."

So, his good deed came with a price.

"Now, Uncle Jeb, I don't go to church. You know that…"

He waved his arm dismissively. "Yeah, I know. But you may want to reconsider, for the kids' sake. It ain't just you anymore."

I checked the irritation welling up inside me. Uncle Jeb didn't mean to use the kids as a way to get me to do what he wanted. He cared about me, and the condition of my soul, although he worried needlessly. I had no intention of attending church no matter how many times he or Kyle invited me. I was taking good enough care of the kids without dressing them up and forcing them to church every week. I set as good an example as any church-going aunt. It wasn't like I was sitting around snorting coke or breaking into banks on my way home from work. They weren't picking up any bad habits from me.

"You know how I feel about church," I said simply. "I had enough of do-good Christians growing up."

"Now, Michelle, you mustn't let a few bad experiences sour you on the Lord. You're right, the church ain't perfect. That's because it has people in it. But regardless of the way His children sometimes behave, there's still only one way to the throne; through His son Jesus Christ, who shed his blood on the cross for saints and sinners alike."

"I don't know if I believe in a merciful God who sent His only son as a way to redeem sinners to Him. If there is a God and there is a Heaven, it has to be a very empty place. I haven't met one single person who lives according to what I remember from the Bible. The people going to church every Sunday are just like me. We all work and pay our bills and don't break any laws, but the only difference is, I'm not fooling myself into thinking I'm better than everybody else."

I didn't miss the hurt on his face. I hadn't meant to put my foot so far into my mouth, but I really believed what I said.

"I'm sorry ya feel that way, Michelle," he said. "I'm even more sorry that ya can't see God's light shinin' through me. I serve Him the best way I can, and I'm doin' Him a great disservice if my own niece don't see my witness."

"No, no, I didn't mean you," I said quickly. "You're not a bad person. I just meant most people—"

"I know what you meant. My Christianity is who I am, and if it ain't apparent to the people I come across in my daily walk, well, then, I need to reexamine myself. 'Study to show thyself approved, rightly dividing the word of truth'. Don't forget, dinner'll be around six."

He backed out the door and stepped off the back porch. I watched him head across the field that separated our properties. I wanted to yell to him and tell him I was sorry. I didn't mean to insult him. He was a good man, and if anyone were going to heaven, he would surely be among the very few there. But it was too late. He would know

I was apologizing because I hurt his feelings, not because I didn't mean what I said.

I thought of Kyle Swann. Would my thoughts insult him too, if I said them aloud to him as I had Uncle Jeb? Were all Christians so sensitive about their calling, or did Uncle Jeb just take the whole witnessing business more seriously than most? I know Grandma never worried about what anyone thought about her and her attitudes. If I'd said half the things to her that I said to Uncle Jeb, she'd have screamed at the top of her lungs that in her day, fresh-mouthed kids knew better than to pop off to their elders like that. She'd say I had a lot of nerve. If her father were alive right now, why, he'd slap me right across my smug little mouth. It wouldn't have occurred to Grandma to step back and examine the witness she was showing to the world that had made me say such a thing in the first place.

Kyle was a pastor, probably more sensitive than Uncle Jeb. He would be furious if I called him a hypocrite. Maybe he wasn't; him and people like Uncle Jeb. If they didn't know they were doing wrong, that they were kidding themselves with their pointless faith, then it wasn't really sin. Wasn't that what the Bible said? He who knows to do wrong and does it, to him it is sin. They were good men, simply misguided. But if their faith brought them comfort, I was wrong to blow holes in the whole theory.

I wasn't an atheist. I knew too much about science to believe every living organism was the result of a huge cosmic accident. It took more faith to believe that theory than Creationism in my book. It was like saying the Empire State Building was the result of an explosion in a steel mill. My logical mind knew there had to be some truth to the whole Creator God idea. My problem came with the thought of a benevolent Father figure in heaven looking down on all of us, solving our problems and listening to our prayers. A merciful, benevolent God wouldn't allow some children to be born into loving homes with loving parents while others were born in bathroom stalls and thrown into dumpsters. If God was up there, why wasn't He watching over Emma and Jonah and kids like them? Why did he allow the Nicole's of this world to treat them like puppies they'd grown tired of?

Emma and Jonah scampered back into the kitchen. Their faces fell when they saw only me. "Where's Uncle Jeb?"

"He headed home. He's waiting for you to catch up."

They darted for the back door. Gypsy plowed out from under the kitchen table, her toenails scraping on the linoleum in an attempt to gain traction.

"Take Gypsy with you," I said unnecessarily. They couldn't roll over in bed without that dog right there beside them.

"We will," Jonah said over his shoulder as he disappeared out the door with Gypsy at his heels.

"We will," Emma echoed, hurrying to catch up. I watched as they hurried off in the same direction Uncle Jeb had gone. I could see the top of his John Deere hat just disappearing over the rise. I needed to do something to fix the hurt I'd caused by my careless words. Why couldn't I have just said no thanks to his church invitation and left it at that? I turned toward the cabinets. If I had the ingredients, I'd make the German chocolate pie he loved so much, the one he wasn't supposed to eat. Wouldn't he be surprised when it showed up on a day other than Thanksgiving?

ᏅChapter Thirteen

Ms. Hurley."

I was instantly suspicious of the look on the preschool administrator's face when she approached me Monday morning. I pasted a smile on my own face, albeit a pale imitation of hers, and waited. Were the children being asked to leave? Was Emma crying all the time or not participating? Was it Jonah? Had he bitten someone? I knew children under stress did that sometimes. A few weeks ago, a five-year-old showed up in the emergency room during one of my weekend stints, with a bite size hunk missing from his cheek where his little sister decided she'd had enough of his bullying.

"Yes?" I said calmly when she was within speaking distance, though my heart was racing.

"I wanted to make sure you saw our sign up sheet," she said and nodded benignly toward the table just inside the vestibule that held the sign-in roster, a lost and found box full of small toys, sunglasses, and miscellaneous children's wear, and sign up sheets for field trips or calls for volunteers.

It was then I noticed the paper taped on the table next to the clipboard where I had just signed Emma and Jonah's names. She had probably already figured out I was one of those clients who rushed in and out every day, in too much of a hurry to notice anything other than what demanded my immediate attention. I wondered what else I'd missed in the past two weeks.

"We're taking the children to the park on Friday," she went on to explain. I feigned interest by looking down at the paper and nodding. Across the top was written; Field trip to City Park on Friday. Was I really as dumb as I looked?

"Each child needs to bring a sack lunch. I know you're usually off on Fridays and don't bring the kids in, but I thought they might enjoy it. If you decide to bring them, you need to sign here, and here," she said as she pointed to a blank line, "First the child's name, yours, and today's date. That lets us know you're aware of the trip. There will be permission slips on Friday with each child's name for you to sign that day, too."

I nodded again. "Sounds like fun," I said noncommittally.

"And since you're off that day, we're always looking for volunteers." She clasped her hands in front of her and beamed. "Any time we leave the facility, we try to have as many adult volunteers as possible. It's always a lot of fun," she added in response to the look of panic that swept across my face. "And it gives you a chance to meet the other parents."

"Well…I'm sure Emma and Jonah would love to go," I mumbled.

"Wonderful!" she squealed. "Does that mean you're volunteering?"

"I—I don't know. What exactly would I have to do?"

"Oh, nothing really; we just need plenty of warm bodies to give the illusion that the adults are in charge. And you're a nurse. You'll be the stabilizer for all the other parents. I'm sure nothing upsets you."

"I used to think so."

She laughed, delighted at my wit. She put her hand on my arm. "Don't forget to pack a lunch for yourself. We're leaving the school at 9:30."

I walked out of the church, feeling like I'd just been tricked into doing something I would definitely regret.

❧

I had not seen Kyle since I almost ran into him with my cart at Wal-Mart the day the kids and I painted Nicole's old room. I felt bad for insulting Uncle Jeb over his invitation to church. I didn't want to put myself in the same situation with Kyle. I successfully put him out of my mind until I saw him climbing behind the wheel of one of the eighteen-passenger vans at church Friday morning. It never occurred to me that he might go on the field trip to the park with us. In all the confusion of assigning seats, holding hands, making sure everybody went to the bathroom first and was in the right group, I barely had time to look up, let alone notice what was happening around me. Besides the teachers and staff, whose names I couldn't keep straight, there were three mothers, one dad, and somebody's teenage sister, helping to get the kids wrangled together into some mass of organization. Over all of us, reigned Miss Billie, whom I had yet to see lose control.

For a moment I imagined life in Miss Billie's house. Did she smile incessantly at her husband, even in the midst of a brawl over an un-balanced checkbook? Did she cock her head, arch her perfectly sym-metrical eyebrows, and say, "Now, Paul, we mustn't raise our voices that way. It doesn't help get your point across, and it only makes me sad. Don't you wish you'd used your indoor voice?"

Poor Paul.

Each child was told to choose a partner with whom to hold hands while crossing the parking lot. From there the partners would ride to the park together in either the church vans, one of the minivans of the parents, or the teacher's vehicle to whom they were assigned. Mine was the only sports car in the parking lot. I felt like a fish out of water. At least it got me out of driving duty.

Jonah joined hands with the little boy he'd been sitting next to all morning, who I'd learned earlier was his friend, Ben. Poor Emma, how would she react when she learned her beloved brother paired up with someone else? I scanned the crowd and saw her standing against the wall, whispering and holding hands with the lovely red-haired girl I'd seen her playing with the day we painted. I think her name was Caitlyn. I exhaled gratefully.

Miss Mary witnessed my reaction. "Emma has certainly blos-somed in the past two weeks," she said. "She's quiet, but that's just her nature. She doesn't give me a moment's trouble. She and Caitlyn do everything together. They're like two peas in a pod."

"I'm so glad," I said sincerely. "She's opening up more at home too. She had me worried there for awhile."

"No need for that. She's a bright little girl, and very resilient. She'll be just fine."

We watched a few moments as Emma and her friend leaned on the wall, whispering and smiling at each other, while they waited for the call to line up. A sense of pride surged through me. *"Where are you, Nicole? Are you enjoying yourself? I hope whatever you're doing is worth everything you're missing here."*

Miss Billie came into the large room where we waited; still referred to as the library, and announced it was time to leave. The church library had been moved to the new part of the building shortly after construction. The remaining bookshelves were mostly empty except for the TV and VCR. Each teacher called her class forward. The parents stepped forward too, and shadowed the teacher to whom they'd been assigned. In front of the double doors leading to the parking lot, the children were divided into smaller groups. The children who rode in car seats went outside to be loaded first while the rest of us waited in our crooked noisy lines.

The only Dad in the group looked at me and smiled. "Is this your first field trip?"

"Oh, no, is it that obvious?"

He grinned. "Yeah, you've got that deer in the headlights look. But don't worry, you'll be an old hand at this in no time."

I didn't bother to tell him I was hoping their mother would return long before the next field trip. Almost as if they had a will of their own, my eyes sought out his hands. I hated it when single women did that. No wedding band. Was he divorced or a deadbeat? I was relatively certain deadbeat Dads didn't go on field trips with preschoolers. He was average looking with rust colored hair that was beginning to recede. Faded freckles graced his wide nose and when he smiled, which seemed to be pretty often, he exposed white, even teeth. He wouldn't stand out in a crowd, nor would he scare away children.

"I'm Barry Schilling," he said, extending his hand. He glanced across the tops of the children's heads milling around us and motioned to the only redhead in the crowd. "That one's mine, Caitlyn."

"Oh, you're kidding. The blonde with her is mine," I said. "I mean, she's my niece, Emma. Jonah is around here somewhere."

I thought I should explain why I, their lowly aunt, had volunteered for the field trip instead of their mother, but then I figured it would take too long, and he probably didn't care anyway. Families nowadays were made up of all kinds of mixes, and he had probably heard it all, just like the teachers. But I didn't want him thinking I was misrepresenting myself, that I had volunteered while their mother was at work or something, when really she was God only knew where, doing God only knew what, and had left them with me, with no explanation whatsoever. But then, the line started to move forward and my chance to say anything vanished.

I tensed. Where was Emma? I couldn't even see Jonah in the sea of milling children. What group was he in? I couldn't remember. He had been moved out of Miss Mary's class last week and put into…whose? I couldn't even remember his teacher's name, and she was supposed to be in charge of him today. The children were pushing forward, anticipation reaching a fever pitch. I rested my hands on the shoulders of the two children closest to me and tried to look like I wasn't freaking out. What if someone ran under the wheels of a minivan? What if they didn't stay in line? What if one of them ran away or was kidnapped?

"Things will settle down once we get everybody buckled into the van," Barry said, reading the terror in my face. "It's just getting them ready to go that's hectic."

"I'm ordinarily very calm," I said. "Believe it or not, I'm a nurse. I'm trained to handle emergencies. It's just with kids, it's different."

"Especially when they're your own," he chuckled, and moved forward to hold the door open.

When we got the kids buckled safe and sound into the van, I would tell him again the kids weren't mine; I was just their aunt, and leave it at that. That's all he needed to know. Now that they were outside, the orderly lines fanned out as children crowded forward to get in the vans. Kyle stood at the open side door of the first van, lifting children inside.

"Stay with your partners," the teachers called out over and over.

"Fasten your seat belts."

"Austin, stop kicking the back of the seat."

"Kali, sit on your bottom."

The parents who were driving had already loaded their charges into their minivans and waited in a caravan behind the church vans with their engines running.

What an undertaking, I thought, just to drive three miles to a park.

There were two empty spaces left in the recesses of the van Kyle was driving after the children were loaded. "Michelle?" Kyle said when I stepped forward to climb inside. "So that was your name on the sign up sheet. I thought it was a typo."

"Ha, ha, very funny." I put my foot on the step and held my hand out toward him. "Are you going to help me up or not? I think they make these vans taller than they used to."

"Yeah, I'm sure that's it." He took my outstretched hand to steady me as I heaved myself up and inside the cramped space between the seats.

With my body nearly bent in two, I lurched to the rear of the van, a rookie mistake. I was careful not to fall on anyone, and finally buckled myself between the boy who had been kicking the back of the seat and his equally ornery looking counterpart. Barry climbed in after me and took a seat two rows ahead of me. He turned around in the seat and smiled. "You going to be all right back there?"

"Yes, I can handle it. They're strapped down now. What could possibly go wrong?"

He arched his eyebrows and the lines around his mouth crinkled into a mischievous grin. "You'll find out," he said as he turned to face forward.

I glanced up and saw Kyle watching the exchange in the rearview mirror. When he caught my eye, he looked away and started the ignition. I stared at the back of his head as he put the van into gear and pulled out of the parking lot. He didn't look up again. I wondered why he had in the first place. Did he have a problem with me talking to Barry? Did he know something about the guy I didn't? Was he jealous? I smiled to myself at the thought then immediately banished it from my head. Kyle had no reason to be jealous of me and a man I had just met. And I had no reason to want him to be. He was only watching me because he found it amusing that I chose the back seat. I could already tell it was a big mistake. The van swayed, the noise level was deafening, exhaust fumes were making me nauseous, and dear little Austin was kicking the back of the seat again.

I concentrated on breathing through my mouth and tried to ignore the swaying and the kicking. It was only three miles. I couldn't stop thinking about Kyle and what his look could have meant.

The morning flew by at a hectic pace. I spent my time running from swing to swing pushing little ones who soon learned I couldn't say no, and helping others to the bathroom, where it turned out they preferred playing in the sink over actually doing what they'd come to do. Through no intention on my part, I ended up sitting across the picnic table from Barry during lunch. For a moment I allowed myself to be flattered that he'd planned the whole thing. I wasn't exactly a bad catch. In the right clothes, a little bit of make-up, and a decent haircut, I could hold my own. I'd had a date or two in my time and more than one opportunity that I turned down. But I was too busy for men and relationships. Eventually they stopped asking, or else I stopped putting myself into a position to be asked. I think I sent off a vibe, if anyone said vibe anymore; but somehow men knew. Maybe they discussed it at the meetings. Don't approach. Waste of time.

All work and no play had definitely made Michelle a dull girl.

It took quite a bit of opening juice boxes, unwrapping sandwiches, and peeling back the stubborn films over ready-to-eat lunches before I lowered my posterior onto the seat board of our picnic table. Even after eleven hours on surgery prep duty, it never felt as good to sit down as it did right now.

"I never caught your name," Barry said, the first time I glanced up from my sack lunch.

"Oh, I'm sorry. I'm Michelle Hurley. You've met Emma and Jonah." I nodded at Emma, who sat four children down on my side. Jonah was at a different table, surrounded by a group of rowdy boys who couldn't be bothered with boring aunts.

"I hear about Emma all the time. I guess you haven't had them at the preschool long."

"No," I said. "Just about two weeks. Since my sister…" Oh, I hadn't wanted to get into that right now. "Well, they're staying with me for awhile. But they're warming up to the whole preschool thing. I hear a lot about your Caitlyn, too."

He chuckled. "I'm glad. She doesn't make friends easily. She's always been shy—like her daddy."

"Oh, please," I said, smiling.

"Well, a long time ago. I guess I got over it."

We nibbled at our sack lunches. In between rising up and down from the seats to assist little hands, Barry managed to tell me he worked nights. It worked out well with Caitlyn. He was free to attend many of the morning field trips and help out on special days. He shared custody with his ex-wife who kept the little girl at night while he worked.

I couldn't help wondering why he was telling me so much about his personal arrangements with his wife when we'd just met. Did he want me to know there would be no jealous ex knocking my door down if something happened beyond this? Was he killing time until we headed back to the school? Was he just an easy talker who didn't know a stranger?

I didn't say much about myself. There was nothing to tell besides why Emma and Jonah were living with me in the first place, and I sure didn't want to go into that.

I looked around in a subtle attempt to spot Kyle. I found him sitting at the table directly behind me with Miss Billie and a few of the teachers. I couldn't exactly see him without turning completely around in my seat or giving myself a neck ache. But I could hear him. The people at the table behind me often erupted into laughter. His was the only adult male voice, deep and resonating. Just like I remembered, he always had a sense of humor. He could even make Grandma Catherine laugh, which was no easy feat. I wished I knew what they were talking about. It sounded like they were having so much fun. I wished I had paid closer attention when I chose my seat.

What was I thinking? I didn't want to sit next to Kyle, the pastor. What a nightmare *that* would turn out to be! I could imagine all the terrible sins of mine he could point out for the good teachers to avoid. No, thanks!

After a lunch that ended all too quickly, the adults cleared the picnic tables while the kids charged back to the playground. Kyle moved continuously through the crowd, playing games with the kids, pushing swings, being one end of the teeter-totter while two little boys perched on the other and squealed with delight. Everyone seemed to love him.

"How are you holding up?" he asked pleasantly the one time we got within speaking distance.

I smiled broadly. After all, I was having a marvelous time in spite of myself. I was finally beginning to tell a few of the kids apart, I participated in a popular shark game where I was the shark and fifteen squealing kids the bait, and I pushed swings for a solid twenty minutes. "I'm hanging in there." I stopped pushing a swing long enough to tuck hair behind my ears. Next time, I'd wear a ponytail.

"I hope we haven't scared you out of volunteering again."

"Oh, no, I'm enjoying myself, although I am wondering when's naptime."

"Not soon enough."

"I can see how they roped me into volunteering for a field trip," I said, "but what about you? Couldn't you come up with some kind of excuse?"

He chuckled and gave the swing another push. "To tell you the truth, I don't mind at all. I seldom have a free day, and when I do, I enjoy spending it with the kids and getting to know some of the parents better."

I nodded like it all made perfect sense, when really I wondered if his personal life could possibly be as pathetic as mine. Just then a whistle shrilled through the heady August heat. Kyle brought his swing and rider to a halt. "Okay," he shouted. "Time to load up."

The little boy on the swing I was pushing leaped off before I could bring it to a safe stop and took off running toward the van. "Not a moment too soon," I said. But Kyle had already moved away and was herding the kids into groups.

As soon as we got back to the preschool, I climbed into my steaming Mazda long enough to start the engine, crank the AC, and jump out again. The interior of the car was at least 115 degrees. I could just imagine what those car seats would feel like against bare skin.

I headed into the building to tell Miss Billie I was leaving and to collect Emma and Jonah. They could nap at home. I met Barry coming out with Caitlyn in tow. "Nice meeting you, Michelle," he said, holding the door for me.

"You too, Barry—and you, Caitlyn."

She shrank against her father's leg and smiled up at me.

"Maybe we could get together sometime," he said. "Plan a play day for the kids… or something."

His eyes twinkled at the "or something."

This was not what I needed. Not now. Barry was friendly and not bad looking and obviously a caring father. But the Big D was a major consideration. I had never dated a divorced man, but I ran into plenty of them at the hospital. They knew before they even met you what they were looking for. It all depended on what point they were at in their lives. They either wanted a mother for their children, a mother for themselves, or something warm for a night. They were never looking for a wife, until they came to the eventual realization that it was easier to fulfill all three roles in one fell swoop. Their radar told them immediately which role you could fulfill.

They were always in a hurry; a hurry to strike up a conversation, a hurry to get you to dinner, a hurry to let you know how miserably they'd been treated by their ex's, a hurry to get you out of the restaurant to see if the rest of the evening would go as they hoped. Divorced men were about as high maintenance as you could get.

My life was complicated enough.

"We'll see, Barry," I said as gently as I could. "I've got a lot going on right now with the kids, work, and everything."

Understanding registered in his eyes, followed by disappointment. "Sure, me too. Well, I'll see you around; maybe at the next field trip."

I went inside, hating myself for being so cold, and hating society more for putting me in this situation in the first place. Barry didn't seem like the typical divorced man. If he had been out for one thing, he would have tried to cajole me out of my rejection. All the way home and for the rest of the evening, I agonized over giving him the brush off. Maybe I should have given him a chance. When would I learn that all men weren't alike? There had to be some out there with redeemable qualities, right; even divorced ones? Just before tucking the kids into bed, I realized what was bothering me so much about the whole thing. If Kyle had been the one to ask to get together, I would've jumped at the chance.

Chapter Fourteen

Miss Billie gave me the number of a woman from her church who did daycare in her home. I couldn't keep taking advantage of Uncle Jeb and Aunt Wanda who were going above and beyond what they should be doing at their age to help out. The woman sounded stable and responsible over the phone, accepted second and third shifts, and had two openings. She agreed to pick Emma and Jonah up from the preschool at four o'clock on Mondays and Wednesdays, the days I worked twelve hours. She would also watch them on weekends when the county hospital couldn't do without me. I promised her I wouldn't work more than two weekends a month although I dreaded losing out on the money. Barring any criminal record, she was hired as far as I was concerned. While we talked I did the math in my head, and was staggered by the amount it was going to cost to hire this woman and continue paying full-time rates at the preschool. My IRA and mutual fund contributions were going out the window, I could plainly see. So were the frequent trips to Wal-Mart for shoes and toys, and meals at McDonald's.

Angie Burkheimer, the stay-at-home-mom, had two girls of her own, one in first grade and the other in kindergarten. When Jonah, Emma, and I arrived for our interview, I saw two babies in playpens and two little boys, about the size of Jonah, playing in her daycare room. Jonah was immediately satisfied with the arrangement. I figured Emma would enjoy playing with the babies. I was right.

As soon as I saw Angie, I recognized her from high school. She was a year or two behind me, but I still remembered her. Winona High School only had about five hundred students between seventh and twelfth grades so we all shared at least one elective or a study hall. The Burkheimer part of her identity was new. She'd married a man she met during the two quarters she spent in college, she told me while we caught up on old times. His family was originally from Northeast Arkansas so the two of them moved back after serving six years in the military.

Angie's little girls were beautiful. They looked just like Angie and, as I was happy to see, seemed well behaved. I didn't want Emma and Jonah picking up any annoying habits I'd begun noticing in other children.

Angie had converted the large attached family room off her kitchen into a daycare area. We left the kids to play and settled ourselves at the kitchen table where we were still within sight and earshot to go over details. "So, how is Nicole these days?" she asked discreetly.

I was getting used to explaining to people why I was keeping my sister's kids while skipping over most of the embarrassing details. I hated for every person in the county to know what a flake my sister had become. Angie, on the other hand, should hear the whole story since she would be spending so much time with the kids.

After I finished explaining the last three weeks of my life, she took a sip of her coffee and sighed. "I didn't know Nicole that well. She was a lot younger than me. But I know of her. I'm sorry to hear things haven't worked out better for her."

I nodded in agreement. There was no need to deny it or feel embarrassed. Most people around here knew *of* Nicole, even if they'd never met her. She hadn't lived in Winona for more than three years, but her memory lived on. I guess I was partly to blame for the mistakes she made, but there was no use apologizing now. If I had done a better job teaching her the difference in what was right and what was wrong, if I hadn't given into her so easily, if I hadn't sheltered her so much from Grandma Catherine and had let her face some of the consequences for her decisions, maybe she would be stronger today, better equipped to deal with life's trials and disappointments.

Now I was paying for the slipshod job I'd done. This was my penance; raising her kids so she could learn to be an adult on her own. I just hoped she got it over with quickly so I could go back to my life.

"I saw in the church bulletin that the sixteenth is the next preschool Sunday," Angie told me. "Are you bringing Emma and Jonah?"

Another preschool Sunday coming up already, where did the time go? I went over my work schedule in my head. I could easily get that weekend off since working at the county hospital was on a contingency basis and totally up to me. They would understand if I never worked another weekend as long as the kids were staying with me. I could lie to Angie and say it was because of work or I could come clean and she wouldn't be hounding me about going to church for every preschool Sunday.

"I haven't really thought about it," I answered truthfully.

"We'd love to have you. The preschoolers are always such a blessing."

A blessing—it seemed everyone at that church found blessings in all the simple things the rest of the world ignored.

"I don't know. I'm not really into church. I haven't gone since Grandma Catherine passed away."

Angie took another sip of her coffee. I studied her face for condemnation but found none. "That's a shame," she said. "It's hard enough for a person to get through life with no anchor in the Lord, let alone when there are children involved. I don't know how I would navigate these waters of motherhood without my Heavenly Father for guidance."

She sounded like one of those commercials on TV. "Well, fortunately for me," I said flippantly, "I don't have children. I'm just filling in while Nicole's doing whatever it is she's doing."

Angie's eyes widened for a brief instant. She set her cup into the delicate matching saucer and smoothed the edges of the tablecloth. "Oh, I thought," she motioned with her head at Jonah and Emma playing on her family room floor and looked back at me. "I thought since you had custody...I'm sorry. I mean, I knew they were Nicole's kids, but since they're living with you, I thought it was more permanent."

I remembered the first day I took the kids to the preschool. Miss Billie had tried to make me feel guilty for not taking some sort of permanent action to get custody of Emma and Jonah. Neither she nor

Angie could possibly understand how difficult this was for me. "No, no, this is definitely a temporary arrangement. I mean, I care for Emma and Jonah, but I never wanted to be anybody's mother. Nicole will be back anytime, and my life will go back to the way it was."

She raised her hand in front of me. "No, it's my mistake, Michelle." She took a sip of her coffee and gazed at me over the rim of her cup. "Are you sure that's what you want, though? For life to go back to the way it was?"

I wasn't sure what she was asking. "Sure, I'm sure. Hey, I'm just helping my sister out of a jam, but the sooner things go back to the way they were, the better."

For the remaining twenty minutes of our visit, we chatted some more about the passage of years. I even got the nerve up to ask her what she thought of Kyle as a pastor. Angie didn't say anything more about making my arrangement with Emma and Jonah permanent, or a Heavenly Father who would be willing to help me through this trying time if I only asked him.

❧

I wasn't sure what woke me in the middle of the night. I sat up in bed and strained to see through the gloom shadowing my room. The bottom half of the window that faced the security light next to the barn was blocked by a window air conditioner six months out of the year. What little light filtered through the shades didn't do much to illuminate the room. I listened for whatever it was that might have woke me out of a sound sleep. Silence—probably Gypsy moving about. Had it been anything more than the usual night sounds of an old house, she would be barking and carrying on. Suddenly I remembered the kids. Though three weeks had passed since their arrival, their presence still eluded me in the early waking hours.

I swung my legs over the side of the bed and headed across the hall. I stopped outside their bedroom door and peered inside. The moon shone on this side of the house and I could make out a few details. All seemed quiet. A lump at the foot of the bed that looked like Gypsy, shifted, sighed, and then repositioned itself. I continued down the hall, stumbled into the bathroom, and groped blindly in the top drawer on the left of the vanity for the eye drops. I found myself relying on them more and more with each year beyond thirty.

I rummaged around until I found the tiny bottle and unscrewed the cap. I knew the danger of putting something into my eyes before reading the label. One night back in my E.R. duty days, a woman brought her husband in, nearly blinded from putting acrylic fingernail glue in his eyes. Like me at the time, he worked nights and woke up at eleven P.M. to get ready for work. Like every other night, the first thing he did upon getting out of bed was shuffle to the bathroom to apply eye drops. Only this night he got hold of his wife's nail glue instead.

Two drops later and he was yanking out the contact lens that ultimately saved his sight. Had the nail glue landed on the cornea instead of the disposable contact lens he slept in, he would be in much more trouble than he was already. His optometrist met him at the E.R. and irrigated the eye. He called an ophthalmologist friend from the city who called in a steroid prescription for the poor guy. I watched the doctor work on the guy who had no eyelashes left on his right eye; they had been yanked out along with the glue and the ruined contact lens, and thought I'd never do anything that stupid. I didn't even keep acrylic glue in the house. Still I grew careless. Nail glue wasn't the only dangerous thing people kept in their medicine cabinet, yet I never took the time to look. I did think of that guy every time I applied eye drops though.

Trails of overflow slid down each cheek as I blinked in the bathroom. Then I heard the noise again, the noise that had presumably woke me in the first place; a muffled thump and shuffling coming from Nicole's old bedroom. I listened for a pronouncement of danger from Gypsy. As long as she wasn't alarmed, there was no need that I be.

Fully trusting my dog's judgment, I used the bathroom and washed my hands before heading back down the hall. As I drew closer to the door I heard more shuffling and whispering. Someone was awake, probably both of them. I gently rapped my knuckles on the doorframe and stuck my head inside.

"Is everybody okay in here?" I asked into the darkness. I could make out shapes on the bed, snuggled among the pillows and blankets. I could see Gypsy clearly now that the moon had shifted. She lay at the foot of the bed, her dark red coat standing out against the light covered chenille spread.

The shuffling and whispering came to an immediate halt.

"Emma, Jonah, are you awake?"

The blankets shifted and Jonah's head appeared against the white pillow. I stepped into the room and closer to the bed until I could distinguish his tiny face. The blanket shifted again and Emma appeared beside him. Her long hair was standing up from the static electricity, clinging to her soft face. She pushed her hair away with her hand and stared solemnly up at me.

I sat down on Jonah's side of the bed. My weight displaced them and they shifted toward me. Gypsy got up impatiently, resituated herself, dropped down again, and heaved a loud sigh. I rested my left hand on the other side of Emma, a sort of embrace encompassing both of the kids. "Is everything okay? Can't you sleep?"

Emma stuck two fingers in her mouth. Jonah glanced at her before turning to me, the spokesman for the two of them. "When's Mommy coming to get us?"

There. The question I most dreaded. They'd been here three weeks and it was the first time either used the dreaded M word. I knew it had to happen eventually.

I reached out and smoothed the hair away from his face and smiled at both of them. "I don't know," I replied. "Soon, I'm sure." Why did I go and say that? I had no idea when Nicole would show her face—maybe never. Hadn't that been exactly what Dad and Mom did? They took off. I watched for them for years, expecting them to appear at the end of the driveway any day. They never had, either of them. I always wondered if they met up somewhere far away from Winona, Grandma Catherine, all their responsibilities—smiled, joined hands and went back to whatever it was they were doing before they got burdened down with kids and bills and the lousy redundant things that make a person wake up one morning and wonder why they were ever put on this earth. I imagined Dad turning to Mom and saying, "Ruthie, what took you so long?" She'd clasp his hand and smile and say, "Oh, you know how it is, Bobby, first one thing and then another. But I'm here now, that's all that matters."

Apparently that isn't exactly what happened since we did hear from Mom from time to time. She even showed up on the farm on a few occasions. She didn't come to Grandma's funeral though. No one knew where she was living at the time to notify her. By the time she called again, Grandma had been dead for over a year. Mom already knew about it; I never asked her how she knew or where she'd been keeping herself. I was too mad at her by that point to care.

"Are we going to live with her again?" Jonah asked, his brown eyes round saucers in the pale moonlight squeezing in through the curtains.

"Well, I don't know," I said, inwardly struggling. Which would be better, kinder? An outright lie that Mommy would be fine someday and they'd live like all the other kids at the preschool, with a Mommy, a Daddy, a maw-maw and paw-paw who loved them and took care of them and didn't disappear without notice or should I give them the facts now? *"Hey, listen, kids, you're old enough to hear the truth. You see, the thing is, your Mommy's a flake. Nobody even knows who your daddies are, or for that matter, where they are. Your Mommy might come back, but then again, there's a good chance she won't. See, long before you were born, her Mommy and daddy did the same thing to her, so she grew up all messed up. She doesn't know how to be a Mommy because the only person she had to teach her was your Aunt Michelle, and we all know Aunt Michelle is no better equipped to be your Mommy than...well, than Gypsy here. So, you see, I don't know what to tell you. I don't know when your Mommy's coming back, but if I were you, I wouldn't hold my breath or anything."*

"I know she loves you and wants to be with you," I said, taking the diplomatic approach. Always answer the question with a bunch of nice sounding rigmarole and conjecture that makes the questioner forget what they wanted to know. "But for now me, your Aunt Wanda, and Uncle Jeb think it would be best if you just stayed here."

They turned their heads and looked at each other. I couldn't see their expressions well enough in the darkness to tell what they were thinking. I prayed Emma wouldn't start crying. I could feel a headache developing between my eyes. I needed to get back to bed.

"If she does come back," Jonah said, catching me off guard by using *if,* and not *when,* "can you tell her we want to stay here?"

My mouth dropped open. I clamped it shut as quickly as I gained control of myself. I couldn't believe my ears. They actually preferred living here on this dreadful farm with me rather than with their own mother? "Well, um, sure. I'll tell her."

"Do you think she'll be sad?" Emma asked in a quavering voice.

That was their concern. They didn't want to go back to Nicole, but they didn't want to hurt her feelings or make her mad at them.

"No," I said confidently. I smoothed her hair away from her face as I had done Jonah's a moment ago. "She'll be glad you're here where Uncle Jeb can take you fishing and you can go to preschool with your friends."

They looked at each other again, the tension visibly eased. "You sure?" Jonah asked.

"Yes, I'm sure. I'll tell her myself about all the fun we're having and all the stuff we get to do. Don't worry about it. Now, why don't you two go to sleep?" I leaned forward and kissed their foreheads. I stood up and moved to the foot of the bed. "You go to sleep, too, Gypsy." I took her head in my hands and kissed her on the furry spot between her eyes. Jonah and Emma giggled. "Night, everybody, see you in the morning."

"G'night, Aunt Shell," I heard as I headed back to my room. I couldn't believe it. They didn't want to go back home, wherever that was. They wanted to stay here. They would rather live with a crotchety old aunt they barely knew who took them to Wal-Mart and McDonald's than with their own mother. Was it because here they got what they wanted and had Gypsy to play with and sleep with? Or because they knew when they woke up in the morning, they would be in the same bed they went to sleep in the night before?

Poor Nicole; couldn't she see what she was doing to her own children? Did she even care? I don't know how long I lay in the dark, staring up at the ceiling before I finally drifted off to sleep. In no time, the alarm was going off in my ear and it was time to face another day, another day with children. I had told Angie I didn't want to be anybody's mother. I could walk away any time. I knew now that wasn't entirely true. I still wasn't crazy about having my life suddenly overtaken with the responsibilities of parenthood, but I knew there was no walking away from it.

Chapter Fifteen

J ust because the preschool had roped me into attending church with their monthly Sunday morning program didn't mean I had to subject myself to Sunday School. With Miss Billie reminding me every morning when I dropped the kids off and Emma and Jonah singing their Bible songs and reciting memory verses all over the house, I couldn't find an excuse not to attend. I arrived at the church with Emma and Jonah in tow at precisely fifteen minutes before the regular morning service was due to begin. I told the man at the door why I was here and was ushered through the relatively quiet fellowship hall and down the hallway to the classrooms. Most of the doors were closed since Sunday School was still in progress. I could hear faint murmurings of conversation coming from the main sanctuary where I assumed the adults were gathered for their class. I wondered if Kyle was teaching—probably not. For Sunday School, he was just another student, often called upon when the subject matter or questions became too difficult for the Sunday School teacher to answer. I thought of the adult classes I had endured after I outgrew the teen class. At least in the teen class, the discussion was lively and fun. Our teacher at the time, a relatively young and hip guy named Rick, directed the discussions toward topics that pertained to us. The adult class was about as interesting as a root canal; no discussions, no pertinence to everyday life. Not as far as I could see anyway. Sunday after Sunday, I sat rigidly in the pew next to Grandma and listened to the doddering old man's voice intone endlessly, as I cast copious glances at the clock every chance I got. At home that afternoon, Grandma always made some reference to our lesson, usually condemning, and I would nod and pretend I knew what she was talking about. Unlike her, I never paid enough attention to criticize or comment on the teacher or one of my fellow classmates.

Halfway down the hall, we could hear the excited voices of pre-schoolers coming from one of the classrooms. Emma and Jonah quickened their pace. Jonah turned back and grabbed my hand. "In here, Aunt Shell."

He led me inside the room, where nearly every teacher from the preschool, dressed in their Sunday finery, presided over about twenty children. What a relief! From my estimations, about eighty kids attended the preschool on a regular basis. Apparently I wasn't the only parent/guardian who didn't participate in preschool Sunday. At our arrival, the buzz from the children intensified as they descended on Emma and Jonah. Jonah dropped my hand and was immediately absorbed into the crowd of boys dressed in an assortment of apparel sold for little lads: everything from suspenders, clip-on neckties, and smart miniature vests, to shorts and tee shirts. The girls' clothing was more consistent with traditional church wear. All of them were in dresses, most of which were covered from bodice to hemline with rows of ruffles, frills, and ribbons. Almost every female in the room under three feet tall had their hair teased, curled, braided, and/or tied back with an elaborate bow that complimented the outfit. Even the patent leather shoes and ruffled socks, in every color of the rainbow, matched the outfit. I felt like an old maid in a potato sack. At least Emma wasn't overdressed, as I had first feared. When Aunt Wanda first heard about the preschool Sundays, she insisted on taking the children shopping and returned with a wardrobe befitting any little princess or prince attending church.

Miss Billie greeted Emma and Jonah first, before approaching me. Everyone at the preschool believed above all else each child should feel special, important, loved, and a necessary part of any situation. "Michelle," we had since graduated to first names, "I'm so glad you were able to come this morning. Jonah has talked about this all week. I'm afraid you've got quite the little performer on your hands. You'll see what I mean when he gets onstage."

I smiled, though I wanted to remind her he wasn't on *my hands*. I was just filling in. Was that so hard to remember?

"You can go on to the sanctuary and find a seat," she said, putting a hand on my elbow and steering me toward the door. "We'll get the children ready to go out at eleven. It usually goes smoother if there are no nervous parents around to watch."

I hesitated. "Um, I won't interrupt class if I go in before church starts?"

"Oh, no," she assured me. "It's nearly over anyway, and they're used to late arrivals. Go on in and make yourself at home." She pushed me through the open door into the hallway. "Enjoy."

I dragged my feet down the hall toward the double doors leading to the sanctuary. I wasn't sure what was holding me back. I wasn't by nature a shy person. My life in the hospital had taught me the hazards of hanging back. Better to rush in and take charge than let things happen of their own accord. Many of these people I would recognize from the community or work. There was nothing to be nervous about. They would welcome me with open arms in the love of Christ, right?

That was precisely what I dreaded most.

I took a right turn at the end of the hallway and went into the ladies' room instead. I managed to kill four or five minutes and another thirty seconds at the drinking fountain. For lack of any more detours or delays, I moved to the heavy, double glass doors of the sanctuary and reached out.

A beaming deacon or usher or whatever title this church gave such men, saw me coming and pushed the door open for me before I could pull from my side. "Praise the Lord, sister," he exalted in a hushed tone. "Come right in."

I smiled back, though not as broad, and squeezed past him. A balding man in an off-the-rack gray sports coat and black Dockers stood at the front of the room, not on the elevated stage, but in front of the pulpit, an open Bible in one hand, the other gesturing toward the crowd, obviously driving home a point. He looked up at me, his lips turned upward in a welcoming smile, but he didn't miss a beat in his oratory. I smiled back, even though his eyes were already again scanning the congregation. I headed for a side pew. Much to my relief, I spotted Aunt Wanda and Uncle Jeb seated a few rows up from the back. I made my way toward them, trying to avoid calling attention to myself. They had chosen to miss their own service at the Presbyterian Church to be here for Emma and Jonah's stage debut. Aunt Wanda had to see for herself how Emma was received in all her dressed up glory. I knew she'd disapprove when she saw the simple fashion in which I'd secured Emma's hair. But I wasn't a hairdresser, especially to a little girl who couldn't hold her head still for more than a minute at a stretch. At least I'd used the hunter green hair bow with the trailing streamers that flowed halfway down Emma's back and looked gorgeous against her pale blonde hair. That would make up for my lack of hair fashion.

Aunt Wanda saw me coming and wiggled her fingers in greeting. I smiled and slid into the pew. "Are the kids excited?" she whispered, her face aglow.

"Jonah is," I whispered back. "Emma isn't saying much."

It took another twenty minutes for the typical opening hymn, announcements, an over-long prayer by Brother So-and-So, and collection of tithes and offerings: I dropped a tightly folded five into the collection plate so I wouldn't look like a complete jerk. Finally a line of nearly thirty preschoolers filed up the center aisle and took their place on a waiting set of risers on the stage. They burst into a hearty rendition of "This Little Light of Mine," followed by two songs I'd never heard, and then a recital of a memory verse from the book of Joshua. Aunt Wanda dabbed her damp eyes with a tissue from her purse. Even Uncle Jeb's eyes were shining. I couldn't believe the lump in my own throat. Jonah sang with a hearty gusto that amazed all of us. Anyone with eyes in their head could see he was the most talented one up there. I reminded myself neither he nor Emma belonged to me so I needn't get puffed up, but I couldn't help myself.

After the ten-minute performance, the children left the stage and joined their parents; or guardian, in my case. They sat quietly at my side while the choir led the rest of us in a few choruses, and then Kyle took his place behind the pulpit.

I had spent the last few days since the field trip putting Kyle out of my mind. The last thing I needed right now was for my heart to get used to the idea of renewing an old flame. That wasn't going to happen. Kyle wasn't interested in me; I didn't know if I was even interested in him. He was a pastor—one of "those people"! But when he took his place behind the pulpit, I had a hard time separating the man in the dark suit expounding the necessity of living a Godly life from the boy I dated in high school. Could this be the same Kyle: popular, funny, and handsome, at ease in any situation?

His sense of humor remained after all these years; he elicited chuckles from the congregation several times as he drove home a point, but always respectfully of his position and message. While I lacked his conviction, I enjoyed the sermon for its unapologetic message of the need for holiness and its forceful delivery.

The shallow, fleshly side of me especially enjoyed watching the trim, athletic young pastor as he moved from one side of the pulpit to the other, occasionally descending the stairs and moving across the front of the sanctuary as he spoke. I wondered how many other young women in the church were distracted from the message by the messenger. Why wasn't he married? I found myself pondering, before forcing my mind back to the words he spoke. That was none of my concern. People often wondered the same thing about me; I knew because they sometimes came right out and asked.

Maybe, like me, Kyle was crotchety, set in his ways, and liked his independence. Maybe the right person had never come along. Maybe he was stingy with a dollar and abhorred the thought of supporting a wife. Pastors didn't make much money, or at least that's what they liked the rest of us to believe.

After the service, we shook a few hands and joined the throng making its way toward the exit. I waited in the slow moving line, wishing it could move faster, with Emma and Jonah glued to my pantyhose. Aunt Wanda and Uncle Jeb were greeting old friends and having the time of their lives. All I wanted to do was shake hands with the pastor and make my escape. I nodded and smiled at a few familiar faces, mostly other parents and teachers from the preschool. A familiar voice sounded behind me.

"Morning, Michelle." I turned and saw Barry Schilling behind me. He glanced at his watch and laughingly corrected himself. "I guess I should say 'good afternoon'. Sometimes the message goes a little long and it's after twelve before we get out of here."

"I didn't know you attended church here," I said, ignoring the lightly spoken insult directed at Kyle. I looked down at the copper-haired Caitlyn, glued to her father's pant leg. She was studying Emma, who was studying her in return. Emma's first two fingers were planted firmly in her mouth. Caitlyn worried the fabric of Barry's trousers. Though best friends at preschool, the two girls were struck dumb in the strange and crowded surroundings of the church sanctuary.

"We don't come as regularly as we should," Barry was saying. "Usually only when Caitlyn is spending the weekend with me. She loves Sunday School, especially since Miss Gail is her teacher."

"Oh, yeah? I didn't realize some of the preschool teachers teach Sunday School too. If I come again for another preschool Sunday, maybe I'll come early enough for Sunday School. I'm sure the kids would like it if they recognized a few faces."

Barry smiled. "Yeah, I saw you sneaking in at the end of class. Neat trick."

"I wasn't sneaking in," I assured him, even though that's exactly what I had been doing. I changed the subject. "The preschool program was great. I probably will come the next time. Too bad more parents don't give it a chance."

Barry shrugged. "Everybody's busy."

I nodded agreeably although I was of the mindset that people always found time for what they thought was important. I caught hold of Aunt Wanda's sleeve and turned her toward Barry and me. I made the necessary introductions, which included Uncle Jeb even though he had left the line to chat with another farmer he knew.

"Nice to meet you, Barry," Aunt Wanda said. "What a little doll you have there. I've heard so much about Caitlyn from our Emma."

Barry beamed at the praise. "Well, rest assured, I hear plenty about Emma. Two peas in a pod, those girls are."

Someone spoke from the crowd to Barry and he gave his regrets for leaving our company. After he moved away, Aunt Wanda leaned toward me. "What a nice gentleman," she whispered.

"Yes, he is," I agreed. "I've never seen a more dedicated father."

By all accounts, Barry appeared to be the gentleman, and I wasn't exaggerating about the dedicated father part, but something about him didn't sit well with me. I wasn't sure if it was my aversion to di-vorced men, his comment about the length of the service, or the fact that he wasn't Kyle Swann.

Kyle groped at his chest in mock disbelief when our turn at the front of the line finally came.

"Very funny," I said at his reaction.

He reverted to the sober man of God image and clasped my hand. "I thought that was you. I nearly fell out of the pulpit."

Aunt Wanda laughed behind me.

"You are hysterical," I said with a mischievous smile. This was the Kyle I remembered—and missed, I realized with a start. "Too bad you can't bring some of that wit to the pulpit with you. You wouldn't have so many parishioners falling asleep on you."

"Michelle!" Aunt Wanda hissed, scandalized.

Kyle dropped my hand and grabbed hers. "Don't worry. Michelle and I go way back. There's nothing she can say that'll shock me. Be-lieve me, she's tried." He kept hold of Aunt Wanda's hand but turned his eyes on me. "She always did think she had a lightning wit."

"Well, as long as you know how to take her," Aunt Wanda said uncertainly.

Kyle released Aunt Wanda's hand and gave me his full attention. "What did you think of the sermon?"

"Not bad, though I was kind of disappointed at the lack of fire and brimstone," I quipped. "I always enjoy a good roof-raiser."

Kyle slapped me on the shoulder. "You keep coming back. I guar-antee you'll hear one the next time the Lord lays it in my spirit."

I wasn't sure if he was serious or not. With Kyle, it was always hard to tell. The way he talked left me a little unsettled; he talked al-most…spiritual, as if he and God had some kind of easy rapport. But at the same time, his dry wit bordered on irreverence based on my memories of "church men." I could honestly say he didn't remind me of the ministers from Grandma Catherine's church. His youth prob-ably explained it. He would undoubtedly grow stodgy and boring like them someday. Of that I was certain.

Chapter Sixteen

The phone rang that evening. I sat on the front porch swing with my nose in a romance novel that had been lying around the house forever. I was finding it hard to concentrate. I couldn't stop peeking over the top of the book every few minutes to watch Emma and Jonah at play with a hodge-podge village of Army men, Barbie dolls, and Lego characters they'd constructed on the porch floor. Gypsy lay nearby; her nose on her paws, apparently asleep, but always on the alert in case plans changed and the kids took off to do something else. She didn't stir when I jumped off the porch swing to answer the phone. I swept aside a pile of villagers with my foot and hurried inside.

"Hello, Michelle? It's me, Barry."

With great determination, I ignored the flutter of disappointment in my stomach. Whom would I have preferred on the other end?

"Oh, hi, Barry, how are you?"

"Great. Hey, I was just sitting here and I couldn't help thinking of you."

I suppose he meant to flatter me. Instead, my disappointment changed to apprehension, "Oh, yeah?"

"Yeah, I know I mentioned it before and it wasn't a good time, but I was thinking it might be fun to get the kids together for a picnic or something. Anytime would be fine with me. I know your schedule changes a lot, but I have Caitlyn every other weekend. I thought maybe some weekend while the weather's still nice, we could take the kids out to the lake or something."

He paused. I could hear the gears turning in his head, going over his invitation, wondering if he'd pled his case adequately, or if he needed to add anything to sweeten the deal. Aunt Wanda was right; he was a gentleman. I knew the kids would have fun. I could too if I'd let myself relax. I did almost miss male company, not that I'd had any for more years than I cared to count. So what if he was divorced—who wasn't these days? It was only an invitation to a picnic. It wasn't like he'd proposed or anything. It would do us all good to get out of the house and spend some time with someone who wasn't related through work or family ties. The thoughts rushed through my head in less than the blink of an eye.

"Sure, that would be fun," I said and meant it. "As a matter of fact, I work next Saturday, but I'm off Sunday."

"Great. How about I pick you all up around one? Unless you'd rather we go to church together and drive out to the lake afterwards."

"No, that's all right. I'm not much of a church-goer."

"No problem."

I could tell by his voice it really wasn't. Since everyone I came in contact with lately was preaching to me about how I needed to get the kids in church, it was almost unsettling to find someone who wasn't concerned with the condition of my soul. I'd tell anyone who asked that I was a non-believer. Barry didn't seem like much more of a Christian than I was, but still, it seemed odd that he wasn't trying to save me.

"Caitlyn and I will see you at your house, then, around one," he continued. "I'm an all right cook, but I'm not so great with sweets, so how about I bring everything but dessert?"

"You don't have to do all that. I can bring something else, too."

"No, I want to," he replied. "This was my idea. See you next Sunday."

I replaced the cordless phone on its base and went back outside. I decided to tell the kids about the invitation later, just in case something came up and we couldn't go. For some reason, I couldn't seem to work up much enthusiasm.

❧

It rained nearly all week and I started thinking our picnic at the lake would be canceled. But on Saturday afternoon the rain tapered off to a fine drizzle and by Sunday, the sun sat high in the sky, offering a gorgeous day to sit on the water's edge.

Emma and Jonah were beside themselves with happiness. They'd talked of nothing else the night before and even woke me up a little after seven to ask if it was time for the picnic. Emma was beginning to treat me with some of the familiarity she showed Uncle Jeb. She didn't squirm or stick her finger in her mouth whenever I came into the room. She still showed signs of anxiety if I pinned her down with a direct question, so I tried to avoid doing that. Anytime I had something to say, I talked to the kids together so she wouldn't feel singled out.

Jonah still did most of the talking. Last night, sitting on the floor in front of Grandma Catherine's grainy television set, I saw Emma whisper in Jonah's ear. Then he turned to me and asked if we had any ice cream. *"I need to break that habit, if Emma is ever going to stand on her own two feet,"* I decided,

I looked directly at her and asked, "Emma, do you want ice cream?"

Her finger went into her mouth. She started to nod, but I purposefully turned my head so I wouldn't see her response. Out of the corner of my eye, I saw them exchange glances. After a moment, she said, "Yes, I want ice cream."

I jumped off the couch enthusiastically. "Well, then, let's get some ice cream."

Emma, Jonah, and Caitlyn were relatively quiet, considering their ages and excitement level, as we drove to the lake in Barry's car. While the girls whispered back and forth and covered their giggles with their hands, Jonah managed to make his presence known. Barry and I exchanged smiles and continued to steal surreptitious glances to the back seat.

"Can we go feed the ducks?" Jonah asked before he was halfway finished with his chicken drumstick. It was the third or fourth time he'd asked, the first time being before Barry even cut off the engine.

"Finish your lunch first," I said. "All of it."

He took a huge bite of the drumstick and commenced chewing.

"Don't choke yourself there," Barry said. "We've got all day. Those ducks aren't going anywhere."

Jonah chewed faster. He cast a dubious glance toward the water to see if Barry knew what he was talking about. I smiled at Barry over the top of Jonah's head. The man was definitely patient and understanding with children. He had gone out of his way to make the day fun for the kids. I didn't appear to be his top priority, which suited me fine.

Was he trying to woo me with reverse psychology, or was this day for Caitlyn's benefit, and he knew he couldn't invite Emma without Jonah and me tagging along? Either way, I was enjoying myself. I studied Barry out of the corner of my eye. He wasn't bad looking. While not traffic stopping handsome, he was growing on me. He obviously loved his daughter and would do anything for her. In all my years at the hospital, I ran into more men than I cared to count who did not share his commitment. I wondered if he'd be interested in me after Emma and Jonah went back to Nicole. Did I want him to be? Before the kids came, I was perfectly happy with the notion of remaining single and independent the rest of my life. I didn't need a man for financial support. I was capable of taking care of my own lawn and car. Why else would a seemingly intelligent, capable woman fetter herself to a man? A month ago I couldn't have thought of a single reason but now, with the kids suddenly in my life, I was looking at things differently.

Nicole needed to come home, and come home quickly, or I was going to find myself married, barefoot, and pregnant. Perish the thought!

I tore a crust of bread off my sandwich and stuck it in my mouth. Marriage was not in the cards for me. Children hadn't been either until my irresponsible sister thrust them upon me. Fortunately, the situation was temporary. It would be remedied as soon as Nicole came back.

Emma and Caitlyn were also finishing up. They were as anxious as Jonah to get near the water to see the ducks. I stood up and started stuffing empty sandwich bags into the picnic basket Barry had so carefully packed. He stood up on the other side of the picnic table to help. Within moments, all evidence of our picnic was gone and the children were scampering toward the water. Barry and I hurried to catch up.

"I knew this was a good idea," he said as we watched the kids tear apart pieces of bread to throw into the water for the gathering ducks.

I nodded and put my hands into the pockets of my Capri pants for something to do with my hands. "They are having fun." The silence lengthened between us. It had been so long since I'd been in the company of a man who was neither a doctor barking orders, a technician accepting them, or a patient doing both, I was completely out of practice. I had an uncontrollable urge to fill the silence, but couldn't think of a single intelligent thing to say.

"So am I."

I turned to look at him, wondering if he meant what I thought he meant. He smiled back, leaving no doubts of his meaning in my mind. I felt the corners of my mouth turn up in a bashful smile. I was flattered, but at the same time, a little nervous. I thought back to the last date I'd been on. As I recalled, it had ended disastrously, with the man mumbling something about he would call, while we both knew he'd rather eat barbed wire.

Barry took my smile as encouragement. "I don't often meet women I feel so comfortable with," he said. "In fact, I haven't dated anyone since my divorce."

Just what I was looking for, a rebound relationship, I thought to myself.

"We aren't dating, are we?" I detected a hint of panic in my voice.

He grinned, obviously amused by my reaction. "Not yet."

I looked back at the kids playing by the water. At that moment, Jonah's foot slipped out from under him and he stumbled. While not anywhere close to harm since he was still several feet from the water's edge and it was only about a foot deep, I dove onto the distraction from our conversation.

"Careful, Jonah, not so close."

"'Kay," he called over his shoulder, not taking his eyes off the ducks.

I wasn't ready for dating. I wasn't ready for Barry to think about dating. I wasn't ready for anything resembling a relationship. I was barely getting used to the idea of having two little people dependent on me. I didn't know a thing about Barry and he didn't know a thing about me. I couldn't even remember what he did for a living. I shouldn't have come. I should've taken the kids fishing in Uncle Jeb's pond and ignored Barry from here to eternity. But he was such a sweet guy. How could I tell him what a mistake this was without hurting his feelings?

Why did I care? I was a trained professional. I was paid to administer pain. I could do this.

I took a deep breath and opened my mouth.

"Daddy, we're out of bread." Caitlyn held up the empty bread bag and waved it in the air. All three children came running at us.

They all looked imploringly at Barry. "We need more bread," Jonah said, stating the obvious.

Barry held his hands out in front of him. "Sorry, that's all we brought."

"Can we go get some more?"

"The ducks are still hungry."

"We need more. Pleeeze!"

Barry looked helplessly at me and shrugged. I was just thrilled the shortage of bread got me off the hook. "Why don't we walk one of the trails," I suggested.

"But what about the ducks?" Emma asked, her eyes wide with concern.

I put my hand on her shoulder. "They'll be fine. Now that they've had their bread, they can go fishing for bugs."

Emma and Caitlyn squealed in disgust.

"Cool," said Jonah.

Barry stuffed the empty bread bag in his hip pocket and we set off in the direction of the closest walking trail, the plight of the ducks forgotten. I kept busy for the next thirty minutes, explaining what kinds of bugs ducks preferred, what kinds of trees and grass we were passing, why snakes didn't have legs, and how come the lake looked brown when everybody knew water was supposed to be blue. Only Barry didn't ask questions. I was glad. His were always more difficult to answer.

Chapter Seventeen

Almost without my realizing it, the weeks passed with comfortable regularity. After one home visit, I didn't see anything more of my caseworker. She was busy, overworked, and I'm sure, thrilled that a relative had been close at hand to take Emma and Jonah in, thus relieving her office of the burden. She called me once at work to "chat," and as I later discovered, had checked up on me with Miss Billie and Angie. Everything was fine. The kids were blossoming. They were clean and well fed. She could move on to more pressing matters.

Our lives on the farm settled into a dull routine. My mornings were punctuated with mad scrambles for shoes, socks, and misplaced personal objects that just couldn't be left behind. I didn't bother to cook breakfast. I woke the kids thirty minutes before we had to run out the door; they dressed, brushed teeth, and lolled on the floor with Gypsy until the last minute before I started stressing out. At work, I found my thoughts turning to the kids more and more. A teacher would tell me some little bit of progress that Emma had made or about something funny Jonah said or did, and I would think about it as I went about my day. I wondered if they were having something they liked for lunch; I worried if one of them seemed lethargic that morning; I started paying attention to interest rates for new cars. No, I told myself over and over, it would never come to that. I did not need a larger vehicle. My Mazda would work out fine for the short amount of time

Emma and Jonah were staying with me. Nicole would be back soon. There was no sense in trading in my car for something that would better suit our needs. Soon enough, it would be just me again, like the old days. No trade-ins, no minivan, or even a sedan; I had worked too hard for that sporty, Titanium grey contraption in my parking spot. I wasn't getting rid of it.

My trash output went from one bag every week at the end of the driveway to four. I couldn't believe two tiny people who didn't even make up one of me could cause so much damage to the environment. In all honesty, it was my fault. I had developed a disposable lifestyle. Prepackaged food had become the staple of our diet, sodium, starch, and grease, our three basic food groups. Chicken nuggets, pop tarts, frozen pizza, a hundred items I'd never looked at before now graced my pantry shelves. I was even developing a taste for the high salt, low nutritional content fare.

I couldn't put it off any longer; I had to learn to cook or at least buy more fresh fruit and vegetables. A half a banana with sweetened cereal a couple times a week could not undo the damage to my checkbook and the kids' intestines my prepackaged cooking was doing.

The kids attended preschool four days a week. On Fridays when I didn't work, they slept in, and then spent their day on the front porch with Gypsy or bugging me to take them across the field to see Uncle Jeb. Mondays and Wednesdays were my twelve-hour shifts and Angie picked them up from the preschool at four and kept them until I got into town at seven-thirty. They loved Angie and the preschool, so I never had trouble out of them for anything. We got along great. Emma was beginning to come out of her shell. She still relayed many of her requests through Jonah, but not as often. I engaged her in conversation occasionally, albeit short ones. We were making headway.

It distressed me sometimes that they were getting along so well without Nicole. Other than a time or two early on when Emma cried for Carrie, neither of them mentioned anything pertaining to their life before moving in with me. I wondered if they needed to see a therapist. I'd heard good things about a juvenile specialist who worked at the county hospital's clinic. I was confident he wasn't a crackpot, but would talking to him make their living arrangement that much more apparently dysfunctional to them? Everything seemed fine. The old adage *"If it ain't broke, don't fix it,"* kept me from asking him about the kids' plight. If they suffered inwardly, they were keeping their pain to themselves, and I was hesitant to bring it up.

Barry called one Tuesday evening in early October as we were sitting down to dinner; chicken nuggets, macaroni and cheese, yum, nutritious. "Michelle, hey, it's Barry."

I glanced at the kitchen table where Emma and Jonah were dipping their nuggets into great pools of ketchup and turned halfway around to face the wall. "Oh, hi, how are you?"

"Great. And you?"

"Fine," I nodded imperceptibly as if he could see me through the miles of wire separating us. I couldn't think of much else to say.

"How was work?"

"Good. Busy."

"Yeah, me too."

I wondered if he was having the same sense of a drowning man as I was?

"So, Michelle, I was thinking, maybe we could do something this weekend, just the two of us. You know, no kids this time."

"Oh, I'm…"

He jumped in to fill my lapse. "I thought we could see a movie or something; or maybe try out that Italian restaurant in Geneva. I've never been there before, but I hear good things."

I hadn't been there either. I never saw the point in getting dressed up to go to a restaurant by myself before the kids came, and these days it was Mickey D's or Burger King. "I don't know, Barry. I've been working a lot and I feel guilty leaving the kids with the sitter so much."

"Oh, yeah, I see." Did he really? "I just really enjoyed our picnic last month and I've been thinking about you a lot. Maybe I should…I'll give you some time. It's just that, well, with Caitlyn and all…"

"Barry?"

He was relieved at the interruption, "Yeah?"

"I know it's been awhile since we got together but everything in my life is moving so fast right now. These changes, well, there's quite a few of them and I think I need to get my bearings."

"Yeah, sure, I understand. Well, hey, you have my number. Whenever you want to try out that Italian place, just call; the invitation's open."

"Thanks, Barry. I appreciate it."

"Okay, then. See ya."

I hung up and took my place at the table. My chicken nuggets lay limp and greasy on my plate. I couldn't believe I'd actually thought about eating them. I was too old for such a diet. I pushed one absently around on my plate. What was wrong with me? Barry was a great guy. He could... could what? What need did I suddenly have for a man in my life, just because I now had children to care for? And what was behind his comment about Caitlyn? Was that his motivation for pursuing me—if that's what he was doing? Did he want a mother for his daughter, knowing I could also benefit from having a man around the place? I sure didn't want to become another little girl's surrogate mother.

Good grief, when did things get so complicated? All I knew for sure was I didn't want to date Barry, or anyone. Nicole would be home any day and my life would return to normal. She could come in right now.

I glanced at the back door as though expecting her to appear; nothing. I sighed and got up to return the chicken nuggets to the metal baking dish. I wasn't hungry.

"We played with the parachutes at preschool today," Jonah said.

"You did?" I was glad for the change of subject. "Was it fun?"

The kids were off and running. Even Emma had a comment or two. I pushed every other thought aside and gave them my full attention, thankful that I no longer had to worry about Barry and my nonexistent feelings toward him.

※

Uncle Jeb drove the tractor across the field Saturday to bush hog. Emma and Jonah heard the old tractor coming and ran outside to meet him. By the time I got to the porch, he was hoisting them up beside him to perch on the tractor fenders.

I went out into the yard and gave him a grave look. "Uncle Jeb," I called over the roar of the motor. "Are you sure this is such a good idea?"

He waved dismissively. "They know how to hold on. Now get on back inside and enjoy the time to yourself. This won't take long, it's supposed to rain later."

I shrugged in defeat, waved at Emma and Jonah, who waved back exuberantly, and turned back to the house. A free Saturday; I'd be a fool not to take advantage of it.

I breezed through the pantry and jotted down a grocery list on the back of a store receipt. I had noticed a trip alone to the grocery store did less damage to my checking account than when two little darlings tagged along. I got in and out a lot quicker too, with exactly what I needed and not an item more.

I grabbed my purse and my car keys and headed out the back door. I waited until Uncle Jeb made another pass on the tractor, and then held up my keys and jingled them, a questioning look on my face. He nodded and waved. The kids waved too, their faces aglow. I headed for the car.

I dashed through Winn Dixie, not wanting to take advantage of Uncle Jeb's kindness, even though I knew he loved spending time with the kids. It made him feel young again; I could see it in his eyes. A crash of thunder announced that the rain Uncle Jeb predicted had arrived. Within moments, a heavy torrent beat down on the roof above my head. The lights flickered once, casting the store into total darkness for a brief instant. A chorus of dismay went up among the shoppers. Several of us joked amongst each other that it was going to be a treat getting from the front of the store to our dry cars. Back outside, a rushing torrent raged through the parking lot, flooding the storm drains, the backwash coming up to the fenders of the cars that braved their way through it. Several shoppers huddled under the store awning waiting for the rain to subside. I squeezed my cart in among them and waited. Usually storms that came on suddenly and ferociously, passed just as quickly. I only hoped Uncle Jeb got the kids off the tractor and inside before it hit. Of course he had. I needn't worry.

"I don't think this is going to let up anytime soon," an elderly woman spoke up.

"Well, we always need the rain," someone answered.

A young man told his wife to wait for him and he dashed into the squall to fetch their car. We watched him run as fast as he could across the wet pavement, his cotton shirt instantly plastered to his back.

"Here goes nothing," another man said. He hunched his shoulders, gripped the handle of his cart, and took off. Several others did the same, while many of us lone women were left stranded to watch the rain come down.

"I'm going for it," one woman said. "I've got to get home."

We laughed and wished her well. By the time, she reached her car with her cart of soggy groceries she was soaked to the skin.

"I think I'll wait it out," the elderly lady said.

I nodded, still undecided myself. I wasn't thrilled about braving the onslaught of rain, nor did I want to spend my afternoon in front of the Winn Dixie. But I had a twenty-minute drive home and there was ice cream in my cart. I couldn't stand here thinking about it much longer. A bolt of lightning lit up the sky over the Burger King. Rain was one thing, but lightning. I'd wait another minute or two.

A young man came running toward the store. His shoulders were hunched against the rain and he held onto the bill of a baseball cap, pulling it low over his face while still making it possible to see where he was going. He looked familiar, and when he got close enough, I saw it was Kyle. It amazed me that in the six months he'd been the pastor at the Abundant Life Felllowship, I managed to miss seeing him around town at all. Now that I took the kids to the preschool, I ran into him everywhere. "Do you think it'll rain?" I joked.

He took off his cap and shook the rain out of his hair, showering my cart. "Michelle. What are you doing out in weather like this?"

"It wasn't raining when I left the house."

"Yeah, me either. Are you stuck?"

"Sort of, if it doesn't slack off in another minute or two, I'm going to go for it. Uncle Jeb's watching the kids, and I really need to be getting back."

He turned and scanned the parking lot. "Where're you parked?"

I pointed toward my Titanium gray Mazda, near the far end of the parked cars. I never parked near the store entrance, even when the kids were along; I didn't want my car getting dinged by careless car doors or lazy people who wouldn't return their carts to the bays provided by the store. The extra exercise wouldn't kill me either. Today I longed for one of those handicapped signs so I could park right up front.

Kyle heaved an exaggerated sigh. "That figures." He held out his hand. "Here, give me your keys. I'll get your car for you."

The lightning struck again, a jagged bolt slicing through the ashen sky. "Oh, no, I couldn't let you do that."

"Oh, come on," he said. "I promise I can't get any wetter."

"It's all right, I can wait."

More and more shoppers were exiting the Winn Dixie while cars pulled along the front to let out others. Before long I'd be crowded out from under the awning. Some were braving the storm and going for their cars, but I couldn't let someone else do my dirty work for me.

Kyle stuck out his hand impatiently. "Michelle…"

"Okay." Reluctantly, I handed over my keys. A boom of thunder crashed over our heads and echoed against the stone walls of the building. I flinched. "But be careful." Kyle arched his eyebrows at me like we were playing a game, ducked his head, and headed into the rain.

I watched and held my breath as he dodged other cars and ankle deep puddles on his way to my car. I flinched again at another flash of lightning. The Mazda's parking lights blinked once, indicating he had unlocked the doors on the run. I exhaled with relief when he slid inside the car and started the engine. When he drove over a storm drain the water came up to the car doors. I grimaced. I'd have to take it easy on the drive home. The car had a tendency to hydroplane on wet roads.

Kyle waited for another car to load up and then pulled up in front of me. I dashed out from under the awning and headed for the back of the car. Kyle and I threw in grocery bags with abandon, not overly concerned if bags overturned or the cookies were under the orange juice. We laughed as both of us reached for the same bag, our hands getting tangled up in each other.

Finally the job was finished and I ran to the front of the car and climbed in. "Thanks, Kyle," I said breathlessly, before shutting the door. "I don't know what I'd've done without you."

He smiled, exposing those toothpaste commercial teeth and lifted his hand in acknowledgement. He took the cart and headed for the front of the store and his own shopping. I honked and edged the nose of the car into traffic. He was still watching me through the rear view mirror so I threw up my hand and waved. He waved back from under the protection of the awning, a wide smile on his face, his dark hair plastered to his head. I checked my own image in the mirror and groaned. After taking the brunt of the downpour in my behalf, Kyle looked rugged and desirable, while I was an absolute fright. My hastily applied mascara had left black puddles under my eyes. Tufts of hair had dried stiff from the hairspray I'd applied this morning. My tee shirt was plastered to my body, and my old lady support bra was evident through the fabric. How attractive was that.

Kyle... I hadn't been rescued by a knight in shining armor in a long time. I could get used to it. I thought of Barry. He actually showed interest in me as a woman. On more than one occasion, he had sought out my company. If I allowed it, things could actually progress further between us. Kyle was only being polite, a decent person who wouldn't leave a woman to retrieve her own car in a lightning storm. Barry would have done the same thing had he pulled into the Winn Dixie ten minutes ago and saw me stranded under the awning; he was a gentleman through and through. But somehow, it meant a lot more that Kyle was the one to do it.

Chapter Eighteen

I stopped in Emma's doorway, trying to fit my earring into the hole in my lobe. Why, after all these years, could I still not do this without a mirror? Emma sat on the bed, dressed in the new outfit we'd bought the other day, but still with no shoes or socks. "Hurry up, sweet cheeks, or we're going to be late for the party." This was the first birthday party Emma and Jonah had ever attended; they told me when they proudly presented two invitations from preschool last week. Some courageous and questionably off in the head mother had decided to invite every single child from the preschool to a party in honor of her darling's big "Number Five" at Chuck E. Cheese's. Miss Billie assured me it wasn't that big of a deal since at least half of the invitees never showed up to these things. Regardless, the thought of thirty-plus preschoolers at a birthday party—Saints, preserve us!

I displayed the proper amount of enthusiasm over the invitations and decided Emma and Jonah would be counted among the half who wouldn't show up. They could go fishing with Uncle Jeb that day, or maybe a walk in the woods, and they'd forget all about the party. Neither of them knew the concept of time nor one day of the week from another, unless I reminded them. They were easily distracted when I played my cards right. They'd get over any pang of disappointment they might experience the instant I waved an ice cream sandwich under their noses.

My plans didn't change when Jonah said they'd never been to Chuck E. Cheese's before. They'd seen the commercials and drove past the one at the shopping center near their apartment in Memphis but had never been inside. My resolve faltered a bit until I reminded myself that there were children all over the world who never went to Chuck E. Cheese's to play in the contaminated ball pit or hit randomly appearing moles on top the head with a mallet for sport, yet still managed to grow up and lead productive lives. They didn't even have places where parents could drop a couple hundred bucks in one afternoon eating stale pizza and exchanging dollars for tokens to games that were never satisfied when I was growing up, and I turned out okay.

Then Emma asked if there would be a cake at the birthday party.

When I told her every birthday party had a cake, she and Jonah exchanged wide-eyed glances. It was then they informed me they'd never been to a birthday party, and the closest they'd come to a real live birthday cake was looking through the glass at the ones in the display case at the grocery store.

That cinched it. Never attending a birthday party—who could imagine such a thing? Surely Nicole could have at least given them a party at home for their own birthdays. That wouldn't have been too much for her to pull off. When had she become so selfish? She wasn't brought up that way. Well, maybe she had been. Hadn't I done what I could to spare her from as much hurt as possible? Hadn't I absorbed the brunt of Grandma Catherine's treatment to spare her any pain? But to turn around and deny her own children the simple pleasure of a birthday party, it was beyond me.

We would go to that party. I'd spend twenty bucks on a gift for a child who most certainly didn't need it. I'd join the other adults at the parents' table, whose sole purpose was to buy tokens for overpriced, lopsided games, eat bad food, smile a lot, and engage in anal conversation about preschool policies, work and the potty training habits of younger brothers and sisters.

I went the rest of the way into Emma's room and bent down to look at myself in the child-sized mirror over the dresser. Emma had moved into my old room two weeks ago. I had moved my things into Grandma Catherine's room shortly after learning I had inherited the farm. As the new homeowner, I had no qualms about claiming the biggest bedroom for my own. I was currently in the process of redecorating my old room to suit a little girl, nearly five-years-old. Jonah now had Nicole's old room all to himself. So far things were working out well; no tears, no bad dreams. Everyone seemed to be adjusting to the living arrangements, even me.

Emma cocked her head to one side and gazed up at me through the mirror's reflection. "What'd you call me?"

I wiggled the earring post into the hole in my earlobe. It took a second to realize what she was talking about. Oh, yes, "Sweet Cheeks." Had I hurt her feelings with the harmless nickname? Uncle Jeb was always calling her something silly like "Cricket" or "Emmy Doodle," and she seemed to like it. Then I noticed the glint in her eyes. I secured the earring, straightened up, and turned around to face her. I set my hands on my hips. "I called you sweet cheeks. Hasn't anyone ever told you what sweet cheeks you have?"

She shook her head from side to side as a pink blush crept up her cheeks. Her sapphire eyes glittered.

I leaned forward, twisted my fingers into claws, and started toward her. She shrank into the pillows and grinned up at me. Her blush deepened. "You've got the sweetest cheeks I've ever seen," I said in a cackling voice. I sank to my knees in front of her where she crouched on the bed, and put my hands on either side of her face. "I could just eat 'em with a spoon." I put my face against hers and nibbled at her cheeks and tickled her neck. "I'm going to eat you up," I said over and over, my voice growing louder and more maniacal all the time.

Emma squealed with delight. Her childish laughter pierced my eardrums. I kept tickling. She kept wiggling and giggling and pretending to hate it. Finally I collapsed on the bed beside her, both of us out of breath.

She shoved the pillows aside, propped herself up on one elbow, and studied me for a moment. Then she bent over and kissed my cheek. "Aunt Shell, you're pretty," she said.

I was so shocked I couldn't respond. Emma wasn't a cuddly, demonstrative child. No matter how used to each other we'd become, she still only spoke when absolutely necessary. I had to watch for clues to determine if she was happy or distressed. She only truly opened up with Jonah or Uncle Jeb, and only when she thought I wasn't watching.

If Aunt Wanda, another adult, or I were in the room, she remained tense and on guard. I had given up on trying to make her relax, knowing it only made her more self-conscious. I figured she'd come around when she was ready.

I rolled off the bed, feeling awkward. I leaned over to smooth out the wrinkles on the lavender and white candy-striped duvet. "You're pretty too, sweet cheeks," I said, barely looking at her. I turned around and headed for the door. "I'm going to go light a fire under your brother. Get your shoes on so we can leave in a few minutes."

"Okay." She slid off the bed and dropped to her knees to retrieve her shoes from under the bed.

Her voice stopped me at the door. "Aunt Shell?" I turned back to look at her.

"I love you."

I swallowed hard. "I love you, too, Jelly Bean."

The sound of those words coming out of my own mouth was more unsettling than hearing them from Emma's. It was true. I did love her, and Jonah too. When had this happened? Nothing good could come from this. I was just setting myself up for heartache. When Nicole came back, and she would come back someday, to take them away, I'd never see them again. Then what? Why did I have to go and let myself fall in love with them?

Unaware of my inner turmoil, Emma stuck her head and shoulders under the bed, her rump in the air, and dug underneath for the pink canvas sneakers that matched her outfit. My heart continued doing all sorts of weird things inside my chest. I wanted my house back. I wanted to work weekends without paying an arm and a leg for childcare. I wanted to sleep late and work in my garden and eat microwave popcorn for breakfast if I chose to do so. I didn't want to be awakened in the middle of the night by a child with bad dreams or a wet mattress. Was that so much to ask? If there was a God in heaven, why was He doing this to me? I never bothered anyone. I was a good person. I respected my elders. I always dropped dollar bills into the Salvation Army buckets outside every store in town at Christmastime. Didn't my being a nurse count for something? I gave more of myself in one day than most people did in a month.

I shook my head to clear it and headed across the hall where I could hear Jonah talking to his plastic action figures. I could almost guarantee he wasn't ready for the party either. But instead of my customary aggravation, all I could think was, *"The one thing greater in the world than a child's laughter in my ear is being loved by that same child."*

The first face I recognized upon entering the loud, crowded, confused location for the party belonged to Barry. Before I could even think about losing myself in the crowd, he spotted us and cut across the restaurant to greet us. Then I realized he was actually following Caitlyn, who was making a beeline for Emma. *"So much for being irresistible to the opposite sex,"* I thought. Still, he seemed pleased to see me. We hadn't seen each other since our picnic at the lake. I was busy, I told myself every time I started feeling like I owed him a phone call. I wasn't intentionally avoiding him; I just couldn't think of a thing I'd say once he picked up on the other end.

"You decided to brave the birthday party too, I see," he said when we met in the middle of the floor.

I nodded and raised my voice to be heard above the din. "The kids have never been here before," I explained. He didn't need to know it was also their first birthday party ever. I smiled and added, "Neither have I."

"Then you're in for a treat. Here, let me help." He took the oversized gift bag out of my hand and led us toward the rear of the restaurant, if this type of place constituted a restaurant.

I looked around and down for Emma, Jonah, and Caitlyn. Satisfied that they were all within sight and easy reach, I started walking. I was suddenly paranoid about losing them. Didn't all sorts of kooks who preyed on small children hang out in places like this? I did watch the news. I heard the reports of missing kids and warnings about teaching them not to talk to strangers or go off unsupervised. Jonah's eyes were roaming everywhere at once. He veered slightly to the left and I grabbed hold of his shoulder and brought him back on course. *"Oh, no, buddy, you're not getting out of my sight,"* I thought.

The birthday girl's mother had gotten here early and moved tables and chairs around and covered them with paper table cloths so it looked like several incredibly long tables. Barry set the gift bag on an overloaded table against the wall and motioned me toward two empty seats in the middle of a long table occupied by adults and a few little brothers and sisters who were too shy or too small to play with the older kids.

I wasn't sure I wanted to spend the duration of the party seated next to Barry. He seemed like a great guy. I couldn't imagine many other fathers who would be willing to give up a Saturday afternoon to escort his four-year-old daughter to a birthday party, unless forced into it by a wife. Barry loved Caitlyn; he'd obviously do anything for her. He was moderately intelligent and not the least interesting person I'd ever talked to. But…I couldn't explain my lack of interest in him even to myself without sounding petty, ungrateful, or snobbish.

Emma bounded after Caitlyn to a group of little girls surrounding the guest of honor. Someone called out Jonah's name and he headed in that direction. I followed him with my eyes, forgetting all about Barry. I smiled when a little boy grabbed his hand and pulled him down onto the floor where five or six little boys were playing. He was popular; all the boys liked him, and even most of the girls from what I could tell. He had adjusted to this situation better than I could have hoped.

Barry pulled out a chair for me and lowered himself into the one beside it.

I smiled my thanks, sat down, and turned my eyes back to the kids. The entire party was almost more stress than I could take. Anyone looking at me could tell I was new to this parenting thing. My eyes flitted around in my head like a pinball machine, determined to keep my eyes on Jonah and Emma at all times. When they got up to play games, I followed them from one to the next. When I finally relented to Jonah's begging and let him go off to play with a friend outside my line of vision, in the company of the little boy's father, I warned all of them to stay together. The little boy's father resisted the urge to roll his eyes as he assured me he never let his child go off unsupervised.

After they disappeared into the crowd, the mother put a placating hand on my arm. "I know how it is, honey, but don't worry. Ryan is really careful with the kids. Just let the boys have fun."

That was easy for her to say. She didn't have to do this on her own.

Dear responsible Ryan was here to help, not like the losers Nicole had chosen to father her kids.

During the eating of the dry cake and bland ice cream and unwrapping gifts, I relaxed enough to almost enjoy myself, or at least enjoy the sheer rapture in Jonah and Emma's eyes as the birthday girl unwrapped her gifts. I fantasized about the elaborate parties I'd throw when their birthdays rolled around. The guest list was formed in my head before I realized what I was doing. Surely Nicole would come to get them by Valentine's Day, which was Emma's fifth birthday. I almost resented her disrupting my plans. I wasn't so lazy as to deny Emma a birthday party she deserved. She deserved to be fussed over. A voice came over the loudspeaker and wished a happy fifth birthday to Amelia. The little girl clasped her hands over her mouth with excitement. All the children clapped and said, "Amelia, that's you. They said your name."

My eyes sought out Emma. She was standing on a booth seat with four other little girls trying to see the gifts as the birthday girl unwrapped them. She didn't look envious, just happy to be with her friends. But I was envious. She'd get her party, that is, if Nicole didn't come back and spoil everything.

At the end of the party, we gathered our things together. The entire afternoon had been confusion, but now it was amplified. Tired, cranky kids whined about leaving. Parents exposed frayed nerves. I was nearly sick from too much pizza.

"Can I go home with Robbie?" Jonah asked, pulling on my shirt-sleeve.

"No, you've been with Robbie all day. You'll see him Monday at school."

Jonah stomped his foot and pulled harder, nearly making me drop my purse. "I wanna go. I never get to do anything."

I had never seen this side of the child and wasn't in the mood for it now. He was too young for a sleepover, and he'd be well off learning this was not the way to talk me into something. I refused to be bullied by someone under three feet tall. "No," I snapped. "We're going home. Where's your sister?"

"Too much soda," Barry explained at my side. "Don't let it get to you."

"I don't know about that," I said. "Kids seldom need artificial stimuli to turn into brats." I turned to face him and realized I had barely spoken two words to him all afternoon. It was not really my fault considering the hectic afternoon, but I felt a little rotten for ignoring him. He always went out of his way to be polite.

"It isn't all Jonah's fault," I conceded, softening. "I am a little short tempered and headachy."

"Yeah, me too, but you'll get used to it."

"I don't know if I want to," I said before thinking.

His eyes widened in surprise. "Don't want to what?"

Barry still didn't know the complete circumstances of how I ended up with Nicole's kids. I wasn't sure I wanted him to. For some reason I couldn't explain, it just didn't feel right to let him get too close to me.

I gave him a half smile. "I just mean I don't know if I'm up for any more parties, at least not one on so grand a scale."

"Oh. Well, I see what you mean. I'm glad you came to this one though. It gives me someone to talk to."

I smiled again. We hadn't really talked this afternoon, but now wasn't the time to point it out. "I'd better get these kids rounded up," I said. "See you around, Barry. Come on, kids. Bye, Caitlyn."

I extracted Jonah from his shrinking group of friends and led him and Emma from the restaurant before Barry had a chance for further conversation. Yes, he was a great guy. I just didn't want to spend a lot of time with him. Hanging around him gave me the idea he was looking for something I wasn't ready to offer.

Chapter Nineteen

I couldn't remember a more enjoyable holiday season. In the past, the period from Halloween until New Year's Day was marked by an increased number of patients in the emergency room, overtime, and coworkers bugging me to switch holiday hours. Not this year. Besides shopping for the children, I took them out to purchase some gifts of their own. We bought small gifts for each member of the preschool staff, with something extra for their own teachers and Angie, their babysitter. They both had their own ideas of what to get Uncle Jeb and couldn't reach a compromise. Consequently he ended up with twice what anyone else got. One entire afternoon was dedicated to the shopping, and I had great fun. Besides shopping, there was a tree to decorate, not the puny four-foot artificial one I usually set up in front of the living room window. There were lights to string on the bushes outside, and parts to learn for the preschool Christmas program which would be held at the church the Wednesday night before Christmas. The unending Christmas carols sung around the house the entire month of December in tiny, high-pitched timbre was enough to put anyone in the Christmas spirit; or drive you out of your mind.

This time I denied Aunt Wanda the pleasure of buying a dress for Emma to wear to the Christmas program. One day after work, I stayed in the city and went to the mall. I'd driven past the exit for the past five years but never felt the inclination to actually stop, until now. The incredible selection in the Little Girls' Department made for an agonizing decision, but I eventually settled on a midnight blue velvet number, to bring out the shine in Emma's eyes, complete with white piping, starched organza collar, and faux pearl buttons. In the Boys' Department, I found a dashing blue velvet vest and matching bow tie. I bought new black trousers with the most darling cuffs and pleats I'd ever seen, for Jonah to wear with the white button down shirt he already owned.

I left the store via the Women's Department. I never had a need for dress clothes before, but I was tired of showing up for preschool Sundays in the only black skirt I owned. I chose two pretty but practical dresses I didn't think would go out of style for at least a decade. I chastised myself for spending money on clothes I would probably never wear after Nicole came for the kids, but in the back of my head, I secretly loved choosing the dresses. And it was beginning to look like Nicole was in no hurry to come back. I wasn't sure how I felt about that.

The Monday morning before the Christmas program, Jonah's teacher, Miss Jennifer, met us at the door as we marched in. "Morning, Jonah, morning, Emma. Did you have a nice weekend?" She listened attentively to their responses before turning to me. "Michelle, hi, I've been meaning to talk to you." Her smile was so effervescent that I knew there was nothing wrong with Jonah's performance at preschool, so I relaxed. "It's about the program Wednesday night."

"Oh? I hope you're not thinking of asking me to make any shepherd or angel costumes."

"Oh, my, no," she squealed, giving my arm a playful slap, "Something much simpler than that. We teachers are looking for a few parent volunteers from each class to help get the kids lined up in the hallway before we enter the sanctuary. I promise you'll have plenty of time to get inside and in your seat before it begins so you won't miss anything. It's really no big deal. Not a lot of work. It's just helpful to have a few level heads present. It can get a little frantic." She put her hand on my arm again and leaned toward me conspiratorially. "We only ask certain parents. We'd rather not have any stage mothers helping, or the ones who manage to get their own kids crying, if you know what I mean?"

I knew exactly what she meant. "Sure, I don't mind helping out."

Aunt Wanda could hold my seat until I got back into the sanctuary. We'd already decided to arrive early and get seats as near the front as possible. Uncle Jeb was on camcorder duty that night, and we were all excited about the whole thing.

She squeezed my arm one last time. "Great. I really appreciate it. Jonah is so excited about his part. He does it flawlessly during rehearsal."

"He does it all the time at home, too." I smiled down at him and Emma, who were showing no interest in our conversation. They finished hanging their coats on the hooks and headed toward the play area. "Hey, wait a minute," I called after them. "Didn't you forget something?"

"Oops."

"Sorry."

Two little faces turned up to me, lips puckered. I put my hands on either side of Emma's face and planted a kiss, and then Jonah's. "Have a good day. Be good." The same admonishment every day followed by the same reply.

"We will. Bye."

They were gone. I smiled a farewell to Jennifer, signed them in, and headed for the door. The air outside was cold and blustery. My hair immediately flew across my face, momentarily blinding me. I pushed it aside, barely noticing. A familiar Christmas carol was pealing from the church bell tower, totally appropriate for the bite in the air and the song in my heart. It was going to be a perfect Christmas. I didn't realize until later that I couldn't remember the last one.

Emma, Jonah, and I arrived much too early for the Christmas program. When we got to the designated classroom, half the teachers hadn't even shown up yet. There were only a handful of children present. But they were already keyed up. I didn't know how the teachers would get them calmed down in time for the program to begin. I wished I hadn't arrived so early. Now Emma and Jonah would have too much time before the play started to get bored and antsy. But I couldn't have stayed home any longer if I tried. I was totally caught up in the moment. Aunt Wanda had picked up the kids from preschool early while I was still at work so she could set Emma's hair in hot rollers, something I didn't know still existed in this day and age.

Two hours later, about the same time I arrived home, the curlers came out and the hair ribbons went in. Thank heavens for Emma's patience. Her hair was a masterpiece. I couldn't remember Cousin Violet's hair ever looking so marvelous. When I said the same to Aunt Wanda, she shrugged. "Violet got her fine, limp hair from Jeb's side of the family. I never could do anything with it. Emma's, on the other hand, you can put a comb in it and it will stay there." She proceeded to demonstrate.

After helping get the kids in semi-orderly fashion outside the sanctuary doors, I sneaked inside and up a side aisle to where Aunt Wanda and Uncle Jeb were seated. Next to them sat Uncle DeWitt. I smiled in surprise and squeezed in next to them. Uncle DeWitt seldom left the farm except for errands he couldn't avoid. I hadn't noticed any particular interest on his part in Nicole's kids, yet here he was. On the outside at least, he was as crotchety and cantankerous as I was. Was it all a ruse to get people to leave him alone? It sure hadn't worked for me.

I barely settled into my seat when the double doors opened. A rustle went through the crowd as four hundred parents, grandparents, siblings, and church members turned as one to face the back of the sanctuary. Uncle Jeb pressed the record button on the camcorder and my nose unexpectedly tickled with unshed tears.

Music started and two lines of forty children deep filed into the church. Each child carried a small bell. Most of them were ringing the bells in the manner in which they'd been taught. Some like Emma were clasping their bells in front of them like a shield, shoulders rigid, and their eyes wide with terror. The more rambunctious ones were ringing the life right out of those bells. I feared that any minute, the insides would go flying and put out someone's eye. Cameras flashed and red blinking lights captured the moment for eternity. People shifted in their seats and elbowed for a better view as their own youngster came into view. Two or three actually stood up, blocking the view of the parents behind them.

While my heart practically ached at the sweetness of the moment,

I almost felt sorry for Nicole. Where was she? Did she have any idea what she was missing? Was she so self-absorbed, so hardened, that even this moment wasn't worth experiencing? Even gruff Uncle De-Witt, who never left his farm dressed in anything other than bibs and a flannel shirt, had known what was important.

Over and over the chorus was sung until all the children had filed through the sanctuary and formed four long rows across the stage. Eighty little voices rang out above the music, proclaiming their excitement and love for their Savior's birthday. Jonah and Emma were positioned on opposite ends of the stage. Too bad; I had wanted a picture of them together. Uncle Jeb panned the camcorder back and forth from one to the other. Aunt Wanda didn't even try to keep the tears from streaming down her cheeks. Uncle Jeb's eyes were glistening. I couldn't see Uncle DeWitt seated on the other side of Uncle Jeb, but I liked to think he was as moved by the procession as the rest of us.

Forty-five minutes later the curtain arose for the last time and once again the children held the bells in their hands. The music started again, an upbeat tune that had all of us tapping our feet.

Jonah was in the front row, near center stage, singing his heart out. I blinked away tears when I overheard two women behind us discussing the little darling in the blue vest. It took some looking to find Emma in the back with the older children, but when I finally found her, I was happy to see her ringing her bell, singing and smiling with her friends, her little hips swaying to the music.

The children sang the song through twice before leaving the stage in the same way they'd come in, still ringing their bells as they headed toward the fellowship hall. This time every bell was ringing enthusiastically; all signs of timidity had disappeared.

On the back of the programs was an invitation for the audience to partake in refreshments after the program in the fellowship hall. We all stood and waited our turn until we could leave our seats and go to claim our children. The bad part about having a good seat close to the front for the program also meant we would be among the last to leave the sanctuary.

"I hope they have some cake left by the time we get back there," Uncle Jeb complained jokingly.

"I hope the kids don't worry that we forgot about them," I fretted, refreshments the farthest thing from my mind.

"Oh, don't worry about that, Peanut," he said. "Didn't ya see the looks on their faces? They're havin' a blast."

Aunt Wanda turned in the aisle and squeezed my hand. "Wasn't it beautiful, Michelle? They did so good. All the kids were darling."

I nodded. "It was wonderful. I'm so proud of Emma. She's been just short of terrified all week."

"Don't forget Jonah," Uncle Jeb said. "Did ya see him up there beltin' out those songs? That boy's got real talent."

"Uncle Jeb, he's only three."

"Don't argue with me, Peanut. I know talent when I see it. That boy's got it; must take after my side of the family."

"Jeb, he doesn't have any Rowe blood in him," Aunt Wanda reminded him.

"Then he must have got it by proxy."

"What did you think, Uncle DeWitt?" I asked the tall, somber man at the end of the aisle, waiting patiently for our row to be dismissed. "The kids will be so happy you made it."

Uncle DeWitt kept his gnarled hands clasped in front of him. He gave me a slow nod and pursed his lips. He never spoke or reacted quickly to anything. We had learned over the years to let him speak his piece in his own time without rushing him. If you rushed him, he'd clam up and not speak at all. He was truly a man of few words. "Yup, fine job," he said finally.

We all waited politely to see if he had anything to add. He didn't.

I turned when I felt a hand rest on my shoulder. Kyle stood behind me in the next pew, his face aglow. "Michelle, Emma and Jonah did great tonight. They're like two different kids."

"Aren't they, Pastor?" interjected Aunt Wanda. "We're so proud of them—and of Michelle here too. She's just what they needed."

All eyes shifted to me. "I don't know about that," I said, suddenly uncomfortable. "I'm not the only one with input in their lives."

Aunt Wanda put her hand on my arm. "But you're doing the brunt of it, dearie." She dropped her hand and directed her next words to Kyle. "You should see her with them. You've never seen such sacrifice. She's practically refurnished her entire house. It isn't cheap raising two kids in this day and age, but you'd never hear her complain. Those two don't want for nothing, do they, Jeb?"

"Well, I—"

"She's given up all her free time, too, hasn't she, Jeb? They couldn't've asked for a better aunt. Nicole's lucky to have a sister who is willing to do what Michelle's done."

I was beginning to feel like a lame racehorse Aunt Wanda was trying to pawn off. Kyle was listening with a bemused expression on his face. I wanted to crawl under a pew.

"The teachers sure did a great job with the kids tonight," I said as soon as Aunt Wanda paused to inhale. "I can't imagine the hours that went into putting something like this together."

Kyle nodded. "Billie outdoes herself every year. I'm glad all I have to do is get up there and make whatever announcements she tells me to."

It was finally our turn to leave our pew. Kyle circled around the pew he was in and fell into step behind me. "Are you staying for refreshments?"

I couldn't explain how his question thrilled me when I was sure he was just being polite. "Yes. The kids'll be too wound up to leave right away."

"They did a great job. I know it thrilled you to see them up on stage."

"Yes, it did." If he only knew how much. "It's a shame their mother wasn't here to see them," I added.

He put his hand on my elbow and slowed down, forcing me to slow down along with him. Aunt Wanda, Uncle Jeb, and Uncle DeWitt moved on with the crowd unaware we were no longer right behind them. "Have you heard anything from Nicole?" Kyle asked, with his voice lowered.

I shook my head and whispered back, "Not a word."

He sadly shook his head in time with mine. "They're wonderful kids. How are you all getting along?"

"Really well, I almost can't imagine life without them." I felt the color rise in my face. Where had that thought come from? Life without them had been, and would be again any time now, much simpler.

Kyle squeezed my elbow before breaking contact. "I hoped that would happen. You're really good for those kids. Just what they needed, like your aunt said. I only see them now and then at preschool and even I notice the change in them, especially little Emma. She is absolutely precious."

I beamed with maternal pride. "Yes, she is, Jonah, too. He's so smart and curious. He wants to know the how and why about everything. Sometimes he drives poor Uncle Jeb to distraction, although I think Uncle Jeb secretly loves it." I clamped my mouth shut. Now I sounded like Aunt Wanda, promoting all Jonah's good qualities like I had to sell Kyle on him.

Kyle chuckled. "I'm sure he does. My dad's the same way. Sometimes he gets aggravated when the grandkids bug him about stuff, but I know he loves it." By now we had reached the fellowship hall, which was about to explode with preschooler energy. "Oh, my," Kyle said in mock horror. "They're actually feeding those kids refined sugar this late at night, as if they're not hyper enough."

"If there's one thing I've learned about kids," I said, "it's that they've got energy to burn whether you feed them sugar or not."

"I guess you're right."

I enjoyed Kyle's company, but it couldn't last. He was young, handsome and well respected, and everyone wanted a piece of his time. He left me to mingle with the crowd. I spoke with several of the parents I had gotten to know in the past four months. We talked about kids and kindergarten and babies; all the topics of conversation parents can't discuss too much. I spoke with each of the teachers and told them how pleased I was with the progress Emma and Jonah had made since coming to Noah's Ark. Each teacher, even if she didn't have one of them in class was responsible for them at least part of the day, and I was happy all nine women who worked there seemed to dearly love kids, especially my two. All the while I kept an eye open for Kyle. Our eyes met occasionally and we'd wave or smile across the fellowship hall. Was he watching me too? Did that explain the glances and ready smiles, or was it purely coincidental? I was relieved to see Barry in the company of his ex-wife. That meant he wouldn't come over to socialize. I had to admit I didn't want Kyle to see me talking to him and get the wrong impression. What impression that was, I wasn't sure. I wasn't involved with either man; I wasn't sure I wanted to be. Kyle was a church pastor, the worst kind of man to get involved with. Barry was just—well, he didn't set my heart to racing.

Emma zeroed in on Caitlyn, making it necessary that I go over and say hello to her parents.

"Hi, Barry," I said when I got within voice range. I turned to the pretty woman at his elbow and extended my hand. "Hi, I'm Michelle, Emma's aunt. She and Caitlyn are as thick as thieves." I wondered if that was an appropriate reference in church.

Neither Barry nor his ex seemed to take offence. She smiled, and a dimple appeared in her left cheek, reminding me of Caitlyn. "I'm Sue. I hear about Emma all the time. I would love to have her spend the night with Caitlyn and me sometime so I can get to know her."

A sleepover! First Jonah had asked at the birthday party and now Emma. I didn't like the idea of them sleeping anywhere but across the hall from me. What if something happened? What if one of them got hurt? What if they cried to come home? They were too young. "That would be fun," I said through clenched teeth, "but I don't know. Emma's very shy. I don't think she's ready to spend the night away from home."

"Oh." Her pretty face looked confused. She glanced at Barry. "I thought Emma was just staying with you until her mom came back. I assumed it wouldn't bother her at all to spend the night somewhere else."

It was my turn to glance at Barry. What had he told this woman? I didn't like people thinking Emma had no structure in her life or that she was just a wayward street urchin who flitted from pillar to post because no one cared for her. Maybe Nicole sent her to the neighbors to crash whenever she wanted a free night, but not me. I took care of her and Jonah. She wasn't left to her own devices. Was that what Barry thought? Was that the impression my words and attitude gave people?

"No, Emma likes routine," I assured them both. "She would be very upset sleeping anywhere but her own bed." I hoped Emma didn't stop playing with Caitlyn right this moment and contradict me.

"All right, it was just a suggestion," Sue said.

I was being too touchy. After all, it was just a sleepover. Kids did that stuff younger and younger all the time.

"Maybe at the end of the school year, we can plan something," she went on. "It can be like a celebration for both of them."

I smiled, determined to relax. I'm sure she wasn't planning to kidnap Emma or let her watch R rated movies. "Okay, that would be fun. We can talk more about it in a few months. I'm sure Emma would enjoy it. I just don't want to push her in anyway."

Sue smiled. "Oh, I understand that completely. People don't care anymore at all how their actions affect children, hustling them from one relative to the other. Kids can't adapt as easily to change as adults. It's too hard on them."

I looked again to Barry. He looked uncomfortable. Obviously he had been talking quite a bit to Sue about Emma and Jonah's situation. I didn't appreciate it, especially when he didn't know enough about it to be forming opinions. Besides, he and Sue were separated. How much did they care about how their actions were affecting Caitlyn? Everyone knew children of divorce were all screwed up.

Thankfully, I caught sight of Uncle DeWitt standing near the door, putting on his coat. "Oh, I think everyone's getting ready to go. It was nice meeting you, Sue."

"You, too, Michelle; if you ever need anything, let me know," she added sympathetically.

"Come on, Emma," I called to where she and Caitlyn were trying to pop some balloons that were tied to the back of a chair. "Uncle Dewitt's leaving. Let's go say goodbye." As I hurried away from Sue and Barry, I saw Kyle watching me from the kitchen doorway. When he caught my eye, he spun on his heel and started talking to a group of teens. I was too stirred up about Barry's big mouth to figure out what that meant. Barry had a right to explain Emma's situation to his ex, I supposed, since she was Caitlyn's best friend, but I didn't like it when people I didn't even know discussed my business.

Chapter Twenty

The preschool was closed from December twenty-third to January second. Miss Billie explained in a letter to the parents that it gave the staff the opportunity to spend the holidays, uninterrupted, with their families. I had a few days off myself at the end of the year, but called Angie to see if she could watch the kids on the days I worked.

Aunt Wanda offered to watch them, but I declined. Cousin Violet and her husband Cliff, had arrived on Christmas Day to spend a few days, and I didn't want to impose. They all assured me that Emma and Jonah were no imposition, but I figured they were just being nice. Violet and Cliff weren't used to kids, and Uncle Jeb and Aunt Wanda deserved some free time with their only daughter.

The day after Christmas, I stopped at Angie's house after my shift in the I.C.U to pick up the kids. Several extra cars were parked in the driveway. Her husband, whom I had yet to meet, was probably enjoying a few days of vacation with holiday visitors. I hoped Emma and Jonah's presence hadn't spoiled any family plans they might have had after I was so careful about not imposing on my own family. Surely Angie would have told me if it was inconvenient for her to keep the kids.

I rapped the door with my knuckles and pushed it open. Around here we didn't wait for Angie to answer the door. Sometimes it was inconvenient for her to stop what she was doing to answer the door, especially if she was in the middle of a feeding or a diaper change.

And we parents had been warned with bodily harm about making unnecessary noise during naptime.

I heard raised voices from the back of the house. It was nowhere near naptime so I called out. Most of the noise today couldn't be attributed to the daycare. Adult voices drowned out the usual childish ones. "Hello," I called out again. "Where is everybody?" An unnecessary question, but I asked anyway.

A voice that wasn't Angie's called out, "Back here."

I headed toward the daycare room that had once been the old family room. The open floor plan made games, playing with large motor skill toys, and naps possible. A bathroom was conveniently located off the room to the left. The open kitchen was separated by a long bar. Angie could prepare meals and get some of her own work done, while never taking her eyes off the children.

An older woman, who bore a striking resemblance to Angie, stepped into the doorway. "Everybody's in here," she said. Adult laughter erupted behind her. She looked over her shoulder at the cause of the noise and then back to me. "Hope you don't mind that nobody got naps today, although I'm about ready for one. I'm afraid the big children kept the little ones awake."

Angie appeared behind her. "Hi, Michelle, welcome to the nut house, at least for today. Have you met my mom? Mom, this is Michelle Hurley, Emma and Jonah's aunt. This is my mom, Janice."

Janice held out her hand and I shook it, "Nice to meet you. Your kids are wonderful, such little darlings. Not like those granddaughters of mine."

Angie smacked her playfully on the shoulder. "Now, Mom, if the girls are spoiled, it's because of you and Dad."

Janice grinned and crinkled her nose at me, admitting her guilt.

"Are you in a hurry, Michelle?" Angie asked. "We're having a little impromptu party. Mom and Dad came in the night before last for Christmas, and as soon as word got out, this place has been a mad house."

Before I could digest the invitation, Janice added, "We're visiting from Arizona. We retired out there a couple years ago. It was the only way we could get out of babysitting grandkids every weekend."

"Mom!" Angie cried, scandalized. "Michelle's going to think you're awful."

Janice gave me another smile. "You don't think I'm awful, do you, Michelle? I only speak the truth. Ask any grandparent. You can't refuse your grandchildren whatever they ask, so it's easier to move to a different time zone."

She looped her arm through mine and pulled me through the doorway between the kitchen and daycare room. The daycare area was full of playing, scrambling kids. The sofa cushions had been pulled halfway off the couch and throw pillows littered the floor. The TV was tuned to Nickelodeon, but no one was paying attention to it. Pieces from what looked like a hundred different puzzles were scattered over a Tiny Tikes tabletop. Coloring books, crayons, and Lego's lay all over the floor. Angie's standards had apparently gone out the window today. The other half of the room was filled with adults who were causing more of a disturbance than the children. They leaned against counter tops, perched on the barstools, and sat around the table. Soda bottles of every size and variety littered every surface, along with cellophane-wrapped containers of leftovers, presumably from Christmas dinner.

"Are you hungry, Michelle?" Angie asked.

"Here, have a buckeye." Janice said, thrusting a plastic plate of the peanut butter and chocolate confections toward me. I never met a buckeye I didn't like, but had never learned to make them myself. There was no need to. Every Christmas at least three different women on staff brought them to the hospital and left them in the break room.

"Yo, is that Michelle Hurley?" a voice called out. "Well, I don't believe it." I looked up and saw Angie's older brother at the far side of the kitchen table, with his hand extended in the air. Even with the middle-aged paunch and thinning hair, I'd've recognized him anywhere. Dave was a year ahead of me in school, while Angie had been a few years behind me. There were a few other brothers and sisters, but Dave was the only one I really remembered from the old days.

"Hello, Dave," I called out and waved back. I moved into the room and away from the buckeye plate. I'd eaten enough junk in the past three days. "Where've you been keeping yourself?"

"Oh, I've been around."

I smiled greetings to the other guests as I went over to where Dave sat. I recognized a few faces of Angie's other clients and family members, but couldn't put a name to all of them.

Dave put his arm around the smiling, buxom brunette to his left. "This is my wife, Penny. In case you don't know everybody else…" He went around the room making introductions and stopped at the last person, who had his head and shoulders buried in the refrigerator. "I guess you remember this ornery old bird," Dave added with a gleam in his eye.

The man backed out of the refrigerator and turned to face me. I felt the heat rise in my cheeks in spite of myself. It was Kyle. Of course Dave remembered that Kyle and I had been something of an item in high school. I hoped he wouldn't find it necessary to inform everyone else. "Yes, I remember," I said. "What brings you out today, Kyle?"

He patted his stomach. "Food. Hey, Angie, I thought you said there were deviled eggs in there."

Angie moved forward. "Oh, get out of my way. I'll find them."

"No, you won't," someone said with a laugh. "John ate the last of them."

Angie turned and glared playfully at the man Dave had introduced as Jenny's husband. I could no longer remember which one was Jenny. "John! How could you?"

John raised his hands in front of him. "I'm innocent. I didn't even know we had deviled eggs."

Angie reached around Kyle and pushed the refrigerator door shut. "Sorry, Kyle, my gluttonous family has eaten all the deviled eggs so I guess you'll have to do without them."

Kyle put a hand on her shoulder. "Don't fret, Sister. It doesn't look like I'll go hungry."

"Aunt Shell!" I had been spotted. Jonah jumped over a pile of toys and circled around furniture and legs to get to me. He hugged my legs and gazed up at me. "We don't gotta leave yet, do we? We wanna stay."

"I don't know if we'll have time. I've got to return some things to the store. Remember those pants Aunt Wanda got you that were too short?"

John clapped a large hand on my shoulder, "No need to be in any hurry. You ain't got nothin' to return that can't wait till tomorrow." He shoved a plate at me with his free hand. "If you go home now you'll just have to fix supper; might as well get yourself something to eat here. We've got plenty."

Angie took my arm and turned me toward the countertop lined with food. "There's no use arguing with him, Michelle. Get something to eat and make yourself at home." Jonah disappeared back into the daycare room glad someone had convinced me.

It looked as if everyone else had been eating most of the afternoon. I put a slice of cold ham and a scoop of potato salad on my Styrofoam plate and took a plastic fork out of a bag. A brother-in-law slid off one of the barstools to make room for me to sit down. Everyone was talking and laughing again, my arrival forgotten. Kyle sidled up beside me with a soda in his hand. "You still drink nothing but Pepsi?"

I arched my eyebrows in surprise. "After all these years, I can't believe you remembered that." I popped the top on the can and looked around for something to pour it into. "How long have you been here?"

"Too long," he said grinning. He found a depleted stack of plastic cups and removed one. "No, I'm kidding. I hung out with Dave a lot when we were growing up so I know their parents really well." As he talked he went to the refrigerator and filled the cup to the top with ice. I wasn't sure it was for me until he set it down next to my plate. Not only did he remember I drank Pepsi, but also that I liked a lot of ice. Amazing. "Angie called me the night before last," he continued, "and said I needed to come over and see them. None of us had to work today, so we all kind of gravitated here, kids and all."

"I hope Emma and Jonah didn't get in anyone's way."

"Are you kidding? The kids have been having a blast."

I looked over my shoulder into the family room. "Yeah, I can tell."

Kyle laughed. "I guarantee as soon as everyone leaves, Angie and Janice will have Chris and Pete in there, cleaning and restoring order."

I smiled and cut off a piece of ham with my plastic fork. It was one of those spiral sliced, honey-baked specialties they sell in the grocery store for the holidays, the kind that melts in your mouth. Kyle folded his arms across his chest and leaned against the countertop. We lapsed into a comfortable silence as we watched Angie's family enjoy one another's company.

"Did you have a nice Christmas?" I asked after a few minutes, then wished I hadn't. Kyle was a single man with little family left in the area; his parents had moved away while he was in the Air Force and his sister was much older. I imagined him sitting in his living room Christmas morning staring at a three-foot Christmas tree with no presents to unwrap and no one to talk to. I should have thought to invite him to Christmas dinner or something. Aunt Wanda would've been thrilled with an extra mouth to feed.

"It was nice," he was saying. "I drove to Texarkana in the morning to watch my sister's kids open their gifts; something I do every year. Then I came back here and had dinner with the Powell's." At my blank look, he explained; "He's one of the elders of the church and she runs the ladies' ministry. If you came to church more often, you'd know that."

I wrinkled my nose. "I suppose so."

"How was your holiday?"

I beamed, remembering the looks on Emma and Jonah's faces when they came downstairs yesterday morning. Aunt Wanda and Uncle Jeb got up at six A.M. to make sure they got to the house before the kids woke up. They wanted to see the kids open their gifts before they rushed home to put the finishing touches on Christmas dinner for Violet and Cliff's arrival from Fayetteville. Aunt Wanda made her special Christmas morning coffee cake and Uncle Jeb insisted we eat while he read the Christmas story out of the book of Luke before we were allowed to open presents. I remembered him doing the same thing with Nicole, Violet, and me when we were kids. I hated it back then, but now I appreciated the tradition.

"Emma and Jonah had a blast," I told Kyle. "I don't think their Christmases have been much of a big deal up until now. I probably could have bought them one gift apiece and used this opportunity as a lesson on the perils of materialism, and they would have been ecstatic. They'd already had a ball just putting up the tree and lights, and taking pictures of Gypsy in her reindeer antlers I'd bought at Hallmark. I admit I went a little overboard in the gift department. Aunt Wanda and Uncle Jeb did almost as much damage. Between the three of us, those kids made out like bandits."

Kyle smiled. "There's nothing wrong with that."

"I kind of wanted to make it up to them since this has been such a hard year and we haven't seen hide-nor-hair of their Mom since August."

"Don't put all the blame on Nicole," Kyle cautioned. "You bought most of those gifts for yourself."

I shrugged and popped another piece of ham in my mouth. After I swallowed, I said, "It was an awful lot of fun watching them tear into those packages. It's going to cost me a small fortune just getting all the pictures I took developed."

He laughed. "I'm glad you enjoyed yourself."

"Me, too," I pushed the plate toward him. "Here, help me eat this ham."

He shook his head and held up his hand. "Can't. Angie and her mom've been plying me with food for the last hour. For some unexplained reason, women always think unmarried pastors are starving. I don't know if they feel that way about all unmarried men or just us pastors. Either way, they're trying to fatten me up like a Christmas goose."

I arched my eyebrows. "Now that you mention it, you could use a little fattening up."

"Not you too." We smiled at each other and fell into another companionable silence. After a while, he asked, "Are you working through the new year?"

I shook my head in response, my mouth once again filled with ham. "Just till the weekend. Then I'm off New Year's Eve and New Year's Day."

"How about coming to the New Year's Eve church service? It starts at ten P.M. We worship for about an hour. I preach a little while and then we go into the fellowship hall for the traditional cabbage rolls and mashed potatoes."

"You don't pass up any opportunity to preach, do you?"

He smiled. "Not if I can help it. Our church has been doing the New Year's Eve service for a number of years now. It's very successful. It gives people an alternative to the partying scene, and you tell me, what better way to usher in a new year than by honoring the One who's given us so much?"

That's why I couldn't spend a whole lot of time around Kyle. He always reverted to that religion stuff; an occupational hazard I supposed. I suddenly remembered the two little excuses I had to get me out of jams like this. "I would if I could, but I have the kids. There's no way I can keep them up past ten o'clock. If I tried, they'd be grouchy as bears."

"Whew, dodged a bullet there!" So why was he smiling?

"No problem. All the kids love it. It is such a novelty for them to be up so late, they don't realize how tired they are. The whole thing is very informal. We never have a huge crowd. Some parents even bring the little ones in their pajamas. They get into the singing and worship time then once I start preaching, they all end up going to sleep in the pews."

"That must be a real boost to your confidence as a preacher."

"Oh, I don't mind as long as the adults don't start dropping off. After the service, a lot of the older kids wake up to go into the fellowship hall to eat, but many of them just stay crashed on the pews. I guarantee Emma and Jonah will have fun. They won't give you any trouble."

I winced inwardly. I guess now I was stuck. I said I would come if it weren't for the kids, now that excuse was shot. I gave him a half smile and lifted a shoulder in defeat. "Okay, pastor. I guess you got me. We'll be there around ten, pajamas, fuzzy slippers, and all."

Chapter Twenty-one

I hadn't seen Emma and Jonah so excited about anything as they climbed out of the bathtub, into their pajamas, and into the car. They wouldn't have minded going to the dentist if they could do it in their pajamas, in what they thought was the middle of the night. Kyle was right about the crowd. There were only about a third of the people that usually showed up for a Sunday service. The dress was more casual, very few suits and ties and many of the women in slacks.

We instinctively moved to the front of the near empty sanctuary and shook hands and greeted all those other brave souls who could've been home watching the ball drop in Times Square. I forgot my apprehension about being in church again, and caught the spirit of the occasion. The Youth Choir got the ball rolling with a toe-tapping ensemble of songs. Soon, everyone was up on their feet, clapping, singing, and smiling at anyone within range. Like Kyle predicted, Emma and Jonah had a blast. They stood on the pews, put their hands on the pew in front of them, and bounced along in time with the music. Ordinarily, I would have made them get down, but everyone was having fun, so I let them do their own thing. During a slower song, Jonah closed his eyes and raised his hands above his head like some of the adults around us. In their own innocent way, they were worshiping the Lord too, so how could I stop them?

Nearly an hour later the music stopped, Kyle took his place behind the pulpit. Emma and Jonah dropped off to sleep almost instantly, Jonah stretched out on the floor at my feet, and Emma with her head in my lap. I ran my fingers through her silken hair and struggled to keep my mind on the brief sermon and not the man delivering it.

Kyle assured the congregation his sermon would be brief and directed us to turn to the tenth chapter of John. Carefully, so not to disturb Emma, I reached for the Bible in the back of the pew; I hadn't brought my own, I seldom did, but I thought I should at least follow along. Kyle was halfway done with his reading by the time I found the passage. I tuned into the words coming out of his mouth in time to hear him reading from the fourteenth verse; "I am the good shepherd, and know my sheep, and am known of mine. As the Father knoweth me, even so know I the Father: And I lay down my life for the sheep. My sheep hear my voice, and I know them, and they follow me: And I give unto them eternal life; and they shall never perish, neither shall any man pluck them out of my hand."

By the time Kyle got to the end of the reading and looked up from his open Bible to survey the small assembly, tears pricked the backs of my eyelids. I absently fumbled in my purse for a tissue and dabbed the end of my nose. I had heard Jesus' words before; I'd spent more than my share of Sundays seated next to Grandma Catherine as the pastor droned on and on about Jesus, the Good Shepherd. But something about the words tonight pricked my heart.

No longer focused on Kyle and what he was saying, I reread the passage myself, and then I went back to the first of the chapter and read the whole thing. It seemed to come alive under my perusal. I could almost feel Jesus himself, reaching out to me. But that couldn't be, my logical brain told my heart. Christianity was a bunch of hogwash. Just a bunch of do-gooders who lived the way they did only to make themselves feel better in a rotten world. Hadn't I learned firsthand how good it felt to do something nice for someone less fortunate than myself over the past few months? I thought of Christmas morning as I watched Emma and Jonah open their gifts. Hadn't their expressions of delight and gratitude given me as much pleasure as the gifts had given them?

Kyle was right the other day at Angie's house when he said I bought the presents more for myself than for the kids. It was fun to give, a joy. I loved it. I loved the feeling. I was already planning Emma's February fourteenth birthday in my head. I wanted to see that expression again. I was selfish. I wasn't too good to admit it. I liked being the hero, the cool aunt who bought cool gifts and took them to cool places. Not like Grandma, who put herself on a pedestal for all the sacrifices she'd made on my and Nicole's behalf in the name of Christian charity. I took care of Emma and Jonah because I enjoyed it, not because some God in heaven was forcing me to. It wasn't out of obligation like Uncle Jeb said. It was pleasure on my part.

So, why did I feel Jesus reaching out to me right now? Years ago, I had convinced myself that if Jesus had existed in human form, He was no more than a really nice guy with a knack for teaching and reaching people on their level; nothing more. But if He wasn't real, if He was just a great teacher and humanitarian, why did I feel His presence so strongly beside me in the pew? Where was it coming from, emotionalism? That wasn't it. My emotions were screaming for me to be reasonable. This didn't make sense. Jesus died two thousand years ago. How could He be reaching out to me now?

I forced my mind back to what Kyle was saying. I concentrated on watching his lips move and not on the stirring in my heart.

"Like a shepherd is willing to lay down his life for the flock," Kyle was saying, his eyes aglow with passion, "Jesus was willing to do the same thing for us. He came to earth as a ransom to call people back to God the Father."

"Willing to lay down his life for the flock," Kyle's words reverberated around in my head. I looked down at the Bible page and tried to focus on the words, but they blurred before my eyes.

No, it couldn't be that simple. Christians were selfish. If they truly followed this man Jesus, they wouldn't make their own grandchildren feel like burdens. They would freely open their homes and their hearts to these lost children, instead of reminding them every day what an inconvenience they were, and what a louse their father was. They didn't act out of love and compassion the way Jesus taught, but out of obligation, every action laced with bitterness.

I heaved a shuddering sigh to bring myself under control. I closed the Bible and smoothed Emma's hair away from her face. The remaining fifteen minutes or so of the service, I focused on the poinsettia display around the piano, and the hairstyles of the women in the pews in front of me.

I'd just got caught up in the moment of the holiday and the notion of a Good Shepherd who knew his sheep and called them by name. That wasn't for me. I didn't need it. If it made these people feel good and helped them face another pointless year of work, heartache, and bills then good for them. I was fine; I could handle life on my own strength as I had for the last thirty-three years.

Chapter Twenty-two

The preschool's Christmas break ended January second. I only had to work an eight-hour shift so I picked the kids up from the preschool at three-thirty that afternoon. They seemed more wound up than usual after not seeing their friends for more than a week. It warmed my heart each time I entered the school and saw them playing and interacting with other kids. Emma had made other friends in the five months since coming here, though Caitlyn was still her best friend. She was always in the middle of a bunch of girls when I came in, playing baby dolls, working puzzles, or tripping around the play area in high heels.

Jonah had turned out to be a leader in his group. He liked to initiate games with the other boys, build things out of blocks, or careen around on the carpeted floors pushing oversized plastic trucks. I sometimes forgot the two little waifs I'd brought in here last August. The kids were so different now. I wondered if Nicole ever thought about them. I wondered if she planned to come back—where was she? What was she doing? Did she miss them? Was she spending this time to get her life in order and preparing for her return? What would I do when she did?

As always, when those thoughts crossed my mind, I pushed them aside. I didn't believe in crossing bridges until I came to them.

They ran into my arms when they saw me standing near the play area, determined to be the first to tell me about their first day back to preschool. You'd of thought they'd been gone for two months instead of ten days. They shoved their papers under my nose for perusal and I made the appropriate impressed observances.

My heart swelled with love and I forgot about the stressful day I'd had at the hospital. I didn't think about my sore feet or the negative run-in with Joan in administration. What did I plan to do when Nicole came back?

The kids were talking a mile a minute by the time we hit the parking lot. I could barely tell when one question or comment ended and another began. I herded them in the general direction of the car, nodding and trying to keep up with the flow of the conversation. I was pleased they'd had such fun and wanted to include me in it.

"Hey, Michelle, wait up," a masculine voice called out as I opened the car door.

Emma and Jonah threw papers and book bags into the back seat and then clambered in over them. The rugs on the back floorboards weren't doing much good keeping the January muck from getting tracked inside the car; a car I once kept immaculately clean. I reached down with one hand to straighten the rugs, while barely avoiding Jonah stepping on my hand, and looked over my shoulder at the same time. By the time I got the rug and I straightened up, Kyle was right behind me.

"How's it going?" he said. He put his hand on the car door to hold it open for me and leaned forward at the waist to peer into the back seat. "How was school today, guys?"

"Fine," Emma responded.

"Great, see what I made." Jonah said as he held his wrinkled paper into the air of some unknown object he'd drawn. A muddy shoe print made it even harder to recognize.

"Oh, that's wonderful."

Emma held hers into the air as high as she could from the confines of her booster car seat, the car seats they were balking at more and more every day. I didn't care how much they complained. They weren't getting out of those seats until they could no longer physically fit into them. I saw too many children in the emergency room with injuries that could have been prevented if they'd been properly buckled into a car seat.

Kyle made the proper noises of approval over the papers just as I had before turning his attention to me. "Where are you headed?"

"Uh—home."

He smiled. If it were possible, I think he would have blushed. "Yeah, I guess that was a dumb question. Actually, I've been wanting to talk to you. I was wondering what you thought of church the other night. I never got much chance to talk to you after the service. You didn't hang around long afterwards."

I fumbled in my purse for my car keys, remembering the service and how the words had moved me. I hadn't stuck around because I didn't want anyone asking me what I thought about anything. I wanted to go home and forget all about the gentle nudging I experienced during the service. I wasn't ready to admit that maybe I did need someone in my life, a Supreme Being to care for me. I was too logical for that. I'd seen Grandma Catherine serve her God, yet never the evidence that she was any better off for it.

"The kids were pretty wiped out," I said truthfully. That night I had taken them straight home after the service. I could've left them sleeping on the pew while I got something to eat in the fellowship hall, but I wanted an excuse to get out of there. "I got them home and we all just crashed."

Kyle still held onto the open car door. I hoped he didn't pursue the questioning. I wasn't ready to hear what he would have to say. He looked out over the top of the car at the parking lot with something on his mind. "If you're not in a hurry to get home," he began, slowly bringing his blue eyes down to meet mine, "how about going somewhere to get a quick bite? We haven't had a chance to really talk since we found out we're both living in the same county again. I'd like to catch up on old times."

"I don't know," I said, searching my mind for a plausible excuse, and wondering why I didn't want to give him one.

"It'd be fun," he said, "Just someplace for a burger or something. It doesn't have to be a big deal."

I don't know what he thought I was thinking. Was he worried I would make too big a deal out of it? Maybe I would. Maybe I wanted it to turn into something more than a burger and a chance to catch up.

"Okay," I finally acquiesced. "We just won't be able to stay long. I've had a long day and I'm beat."

"I wanna go to Burger King," Jonah said from the back seat.

"Yeah, Burger King," Emma repeated.

I looked apologetically at Kyle. His smile widened. "I was hoping you'd say that. Do you want to follow me?"

"Yeah, that would be fine." I waited until he backed out of his parking space and fell in behind him. The kids bounced up and down in their seats, excited about the turn of events. We didn't eat fast food as much as we had when they first came. It was reserved only for a treat these days, instead of a quick dinner when I wasn't in the mood to cook.

I ordered the usual and allowed Kyle to elbow his way in to pay. It took several minutes to stick straws into drinks and open ketchup packets and listen to the typical banter about who got the most fries. Kyle stood next to me, being as helpful and understanding as I could hope for a man without children to be. Finally the four of us were seated around a too-small square table. The kids clasped hands and bowed their heads automatically over their food. I was glad they were used to saying grace before each meal, a habit they'd picked up at preschool and brought home to me. At least Kyle wouldn't think I was a total heathen.

We exchanged charmed glances over the tops of their heads as they recited a favorite prayer.

"Thank you for the world so sweet. Thank you for the food we eat. Thank you for the birds that sing. Thank you, God, for Burger King. Amen."

My eyes flew open and I jerked my head up, mortified. Right in front of a preacher! What must Kyle be thinking? Should I correct them right now? Should we discuss it later so they could understand that making a joke out of prayer was inappropriate? Emma and Jonah squealed with laughter and proceeded to dig into their kids' meals. I darted a scandalized look in Kyle's direction.

"I have often found myself thankful for Burger King too," he said, a grin splitting his handsome face. "I just didn't know how to articulate it."

I smiled in return and relaxed. I guess if they meant what they said when they brought their petitions before the Lord, no prayer was inappropriate.

There wasn't much chance to catch up on lost time sitting at a table with two preschoolers, but I couldn't remember a better time I'd had at Burger King. Kyle was funny and so obviously not trying to impress me. We talked and laughed, almost exclusively about or with the kids. They had a way of taking the pressure off a potentially embarrassing situation for me. I still had feelings for Kyle, but didn't know what, if anything, I wanted to do about them. Kyle was handsome, sweet, and charming without effort, just as I remembered, only better with the passage of time.

But when I told Barry I wasn't ready for a relationship, I wasn't just talking out of the side of my mouth. Relationships were too much work. I had dated a few times in my younger days, but someone always expected something from me I wasn't willing to give. I didn't have female friends for the same reason. I was too busy, lazy, and selfish to invest the time necessary to build a lasting bond. But with Kyle, I didn't know.

I told myself I was worrying for nothing. Kyle had given no indication he was here for anything other than a quick bite at Burger King to catch up on old times like he said. He could be just as busy, lazy, and selfish as me, and just as unwilling to invest time into a relationship. He probably thought God would send him a woman when he was ready for one. I sure didn't need that kind of pressure.

The afternoon flew by. Before I knew it the kids had finished their meal and were eyeing the indoor playground. I usually didn't let them go in, cautious about freak accidents that had been to known to occur in places like this, but it was presently deserted, and I wanted to prolong my time with Kyle. We could supervise while still enjoying each other's company. At least, I enjoyed his company. I always had, from the first time I laid eyes on him.

What made him choose me out of all those girls in high school; girls much prettier, taller, richer, classier than me. Just like now, I was gangly and clumsy, always tripping over my own feet, or worse, my tongue. I would say something that sounded witty in my head, but as soon as it went from my mouth out into the world, it sounded stupid, even to my own ears. I learned to keep my mouth shut as much possible and not draw attention to myself.

I was such a loser. I couldn't do anything right; not at home, not at school. But somehow, I got Kyle Swann's attention. He thought I was funny and unusual. He didn't seem to notice I wasn't pretty or dignified. In his presence, I developed a confidence I never had anywhere else. I opened up and said whatever was on my mind, whether it sounded stupid or not. Talking to him was easy, natural. During our last two years at Winona High School we developed a close friendship that slowly evolved into something more without either of us realizing it.

High school couldn't last forever. Kyle's parents couldn't afford college, yet they made too much money to qualify for financial aid. But Kyle had his sights set on getting an education and maybe flying airplanes one day. When he told me the summer before our senior year that he was going to join the Air Force, I smiled and told him what a practical idea that was. Deep down I knew he was making the right choice; the Air Force would solve all his problems. On a more transparent level, I was angry that he was leaving me, knowing full well that I wasn't free to go anywhere. I had to stay in Winona. Someone had to be here for Nicole. Dad had already deserted her. Mom was off and gone to who knew where, calling to check in every year or two. I was all she had left. I wasn't going anywhere.

As angry as I was at Kyle for wanting to leave and make a life for himself, I didn't let it show. Our senior year we grew closer and closer, even though in my head I knew I needed to distance myself from him. How could I let him go to San Antonio if I fell anymore completely, madly, in love with him than I already was?

All my emotions had come pouring forth the night of our high school graduation. Everyone was standing around outside the gymnasium after the ceremony, hugging, taking pictures, exchanging small gifts, tears flowing, knowing full well many of us would never lay eyes on each other again. Not me, of course. I would be right here in Winona where anyone could find me if they took a notion to look.

Kyle laid a possessive arm across my shoulders and hammed it up for the camera. His arm grew heavier and heavier on my shoulders. I was too aware that in eight days he was going to San Antonio. I didn't know if I'd ever see him again. Why would he come back to this little nothing place after his stint was over? Whatever he learned there, he couldn't make an occupation out of in Winona. There was nothing here for him to come back to, certainly not me. If I were so important to him, he wouldn't be leaving in the first place. I was stuck and he was free, pure and simple.

The fight we had was a veritable free-for-all. It was easier to let him go after getting every hateful, inconsiderate, jealous thing off my chest. He said if I cared for him, I'd support his decision. I told him if he cared for me, knowing we would never see each other again, his leaving would rip his heart out like it was doing to mine. He called me spiteful and petty. I called him selfish and hateful. He left me standing in Grandma Catherine's driveway that night, tears streaming down my cheeks, as he drove away. We didn't speak again. He left for Texas without a good-bye phone call, and I hated him all the more.

I didn't fully understand how he could sit across the table from me now, after everything I'd said that night, and I told him as much.

He waved his hand dismissively. "That was a long time ago. Even at the time, I understood why you felt the way you did. It wasn't easy for me either, you know. I wasn't sure what I was doing. I'd never been out of Arkansas. It seems like everything's worked out like it should though," he said. He watched Emma climb over a net bridge. She was laughing and hurrying to keep up with Jonah.

I nodded. "I suppose. I wasn't really mad at you. You know that, don't you? I was angry that I had to stay here when it seemed like everyone else in the county had a future to look forward to. As far as I was concerned, nothing was going to change; just more school, looking after Nicole, and listening to Grandma's complaints every night."

His face filled with sympathy. "I hope it wasn't too terrible."

Was he trying to appease his conscious for leaving me here? "No," I said diplomatically, "I'd gotten used to the way things were long before graduation."

He nodded thoughtfully. The two of us watched the kids a few moments in silence.

"What about you?" I asked to shift the conversation away from myself. "You never did get to fly those jets."

He shook his head, "Wasn't up to the rigors of training. It wasn't as hard to accept as I thought it'd be. I realized before I was too far into the program it wasn't for me. I ended up training soldiers who would be in the air instead. I enjoyed it though. Four years, but by the time it came to re-up, the Lord had already made his plans known."

"How do you know?" I asked icily, suddenly uncomfortable. "What if you misinterpreted?"

I didn't," he said with a confidence I'd never felt about anything. "I listened for a long time. Make your call and election sure, the Bible says. I was sure. The Lord called me to preach and I never looked back."

"Haven't you ever wanted more?" I asked. "Like a family?"

"Who says I can't have both? I'm not a monk or a priest. I can have a wife. I'm looking forward to it someday, if it's God's will, of course."

"Of course."

He tipped his cup up to drink the last of his milkshake. He smiled at me over the rim of the paper cup. My insides turned to mush. "You don't sound like you believe in that sort of thing."

I picked at a French fry Emma left on her napkin, anything to keep my eyes off his. "Didn't God create us with a will so we could make our own choices?"

Kyle brightened, eager to talk about his passion, "Oh, yes, and I chose to follow His will. He did create me, so I figure I can trust Him to lead me down the best path for my life. After all, He holds me in the palm of his hand. He knows my tomorrow, so I don't need to worry."

"I guess you think I should trust God with my future, stop worrying about Nicole and her kids, and let God take care of the details."

"That would be ideal. Your worrying isn't going to change the outcome one bit anyway, so why bother? Trust God. Let Him work it out."

"Isn't that a pretty irresponsible attitude? I've got two little kids depending on me. Their mother obviously isn't concerned with whether they have a hot meal or a place to lay their heads. Somebody's got to see to all the boring details of taking care of them."

"And aren't they blessed to have you?"

"Humph. I guess some people would say that. Sometimes I wonder."

"Don't be so hard on yourself, Michelle." He looked pointedly at the top of the jungle gym. I followed his gaze and saw Emma and

Jonah laughing and playing together. "I can't imagine a better place for those kids to be at this point in time." He covered my hand with his.

I pulled my hand away and put it in my lap. The warmth stayed with me. Why was he being so understanding? Didn't he know how I mocked his profession and his faith in a God who couldn't make a mother care for her own children? He was only making things more difficult. He was too good for me. I didn't deserve someone like him. I wouldn't give him any reason to think there could ever be anything between us.

Chapter Twenty-three

I don't want to go to school," Emma wailed at the top of her voice. "I want to stay here with you."

I sat back on my haunches and looked up at the little girl on the sofa in front of me. For five minutes I'd been trying to squeeze her feet into her shoes. She continued to pull away and curl her toes in resistance. I was two seconds from losing my temper big time. "That's enough, Emma," I said sternly. "You have to go to school, you know that. If you don't get a move on, you're gonna make me late for work. Do you want me to get in trouble? Do you want my boss to yell at me?"

She sniffed hard and shook her head.

"Then put your foot in this shoe."

She jumped back on the couch and tucked both feet underneath her bottom. "I wanna stay with you."

I stood up and put my hands on my hips. "All right, that's it. I've had it." If I could force a sixty-year-old man to walk down a hallway when he looked like he had just come back from the dead, I could certainly put a shoe on one small child. I grabbed one ankle and pulled her foot out from under her. "I guess we'll have to do this the hard way." I held the shoe in one hand and jammed her foot into it with the other. She cried and wailed and struggled to pull away from me the entire time.

I couldn't imagine what had gotten into her this morning, and I didn't particularly care enough to pick her brain to find out. I was not a big fan of obstinacy. Open rebellion, I liked even less. When I wanted something done, I wanted it done two minutes ago. I'd lived by my own terms too long to change now simply because I was dealing with children. I had to be at work in forty minutes. I had barely enough time to drop her and Jonah off at the preschool and get to the hospital. I didn't have time to deal with a brat, and I wasn't about to. Let them get away with it once, and you had big problems on your hands down the road. That was my way of thinking.

After both shoes were secured, I scooped her into my arms and carried her to the front door. "Hurry up, Jonah," I yelled over my shoulder, out of breath and more than mildly irritated. "We're going to be late, thanks to your sister."

Emma was no longer crying. She rested her head against my shoulder in weary resignation. Pity welled up inside me. She wasn't a brat; something was bothering her, but why did she have to let it out right before I had to be at work? I set her down by the front door and kissed her tearstained cheek. I worked her limp arms into her jacket while Jonah bundled himself up beside us. He wasn't speaking. Whatever mood she was in had rubbed off on him. He stared at Emma's face, concern written all over his. My guilt and concern mounted.

"I'm sorry I lost my temper, Emma," I said softly as I zipped her up. "But I don't like being late for work. There's no time for tears or temper tantrums in the mornings."

"I'm sorry," she murmured. "I don't want you to get in trouble."

Now she'd worry about it all day. "I won't get in trouble," I assured her in a soothing voice. "But we have to leave now. Okay?"

She stared at her feet and nodded.

I turned to Jonah. "Okay?" I pulled his toboggan down over his eyes.

He tilted his head back and peered up at me from under the brim. Emma giggled. I sighed and opened the door to let them go out in front of me. Jonah went out but Emma remained where she was. I sighed again and squatted down to pick her up. Regardless of what was bothering her, I'd get to work quicker by giving in and carrying her to the car.

Fifteen minutes later, standing next to the pegs for the children's coats, the scenario repeated itself. "I wanna go with you," Emma wailed at the top of her voice. I had carried her inside the building, figuring a little extra attention was all she needed after everything she'd been through. As I leaned forward to set her on the floor, she tightened her arms around my neck and let the tears fall.

The last of my patience snapped. "Emma, I've had just about enough. Stop it this minute or I'm going to whip you right here in front of all your friends. Is that what you want?" I had never laid a hand on her or Jonah and I wasn't sure if I could go through with it, but if she kept this up, it wouldn't be hardest thing I'd ever done.

Miss Gail bustled out of the play area, "Emma, Emma, Emma, what's the matter, sweetie?" She knelt down beside us and smoothed Emma's hair behind one ear. Emma tightened her grip on my neck as if she'd been scalded. I suddenly couldn't draw a breath. I reached behind my head and took hold of both her hands and pried them loose from my neck; not an easy feat since I was bundled against the winter wind.

"Come into the play area with me," Miss Gail coaxed. "I need someone to help me with the puzzles. You're always so good at that. Don't you want to help me today?"

Emma shook her head and leaned against me. I put my arms around her but kept enough distance between us so she couldn't latch on again. "Okay, Emma, it's time to stop crying. I'll be here at three-thirty to get you." I was glad this wasn't one of the days Angie picked them up and kept them until I got off at seven. "Now you go into the play area with Jonah and Miss Gail and have fun."

Her tears had abated, but her cheeks were flushed and sweaty. Her hair was damp and clinging to her forehead. She shook her head, while not making eye contact. I straightened up and put her hand in Miss Gail's. "Go on now. Be a good girl. I'll see you at the end of the day."

I reached over and pulled Jonah's cap off his head. My heart sank when I saw the tears in his eyes. I pretended not to notice while I unzipped his jacket and helped him out of it. His eyes went from me to Emma. He sucked furiously on his bottom lip and tried not to cry. I kissed him on top of the head, and then Emma. "Bye, guys," I said cheerfully, beating a retreat to the door. "Be good. See you tonight."

Miss Gail was already turning them toward the play area, talking a mile a minute about all the fun things they would do that day. Instead of listening, they were watching me over their shoulders. I gave them another cheerful wave and exited the building. I cried all the way to work.

❦

I didn't cry when Mom left. For the longest time, I saw no reason to. She'd come back. She knew what it did to us when Dad left. She experienced Grandma's resentment firsthand. She bore the brunt of it in our stead. I knew she was weak and not designed to stand up to Grandma, but she also knew how Nicole and I suffered miserably. Surely she wouldn't do the same thing.

Now this thing, this curse or whatever it is was happening all over again with Nicole in Mom and Dad's place. I wouldn't have imagined it in a million years. Nicole wasn't Mom, not even close. She wasn't weak. Lazy? Yes. Self-centered? In a big way! But she was funny, clever, and had a warm heart. Why had she done it? How could she put her kids into the very situation that had devastated her?

By the time I realized Mom wasn't coming back, I no longer missed her. I resigned myself to the way things were and adjusted accordingly. Couldn't Emma do the same? She had to have known her mother couldn't be relied upon to do the right thing. Of course I was fourteen at the time, ten years older than Emma was now. In fact she was exactly Nicole's age when Mom left us. Was there any significance in that? Were the women in my family only capable of loving and caring for their children until they reached the magical age of four? Mom only lasted longer with me because she had Dad for ten of those fourteen years.

Mom had made it home. The first time was the summer after I graduated from high school. She'd just divorced a man none of us had ever met, and she showed up in a sporty Cadillac Cimarron she said she won in the divorce settlement. None of us really believed her. We figured the ex was looking harder for the car than he was for Mom. She hadn't put on an ounce of weight in the twelve years since she left us. She talked a lot and laughed too loud and tried to convince us her life was exactly what she wanted it to be. She was up to three packs of cigarettes a day and underneath the youthful makeup, her age showed terribly.

I was polite, Nicole, thrilled beyond belief. Grandma told her she looked like death warmed over. The visit lasted three weeks. She got several phone calls late at night that she wouldn't explain. One morning she was up earlier than usual, and when I got home that evening from my summer job at the Sack and Save, she was gone. I always assumed the ex, if he was an ex, had tracked her down. Mom was never any good at being without someone to take care of her.

I was in Mr. Cho's room, checking vitals and making notes on his chart, when a call came from Aunt Wanda. I never got calls at work. Everyone knew I didn't appreciate interruptions while I was working, even for what many people considered emergencies. Something must be terribly wrong. My first thought was Uncle DeWitt. He was getting on in years. He lived in that little house all by himself. I prayed he hadn't fallen and lain for days before someone found him. Then I remembered I wasn't a praying person.

"Aunt Wanda? What's the matter?"

"It's Emma," she said.

Immediately my concern for Uncle DeWitt changed to fear for the crying child I left at the preschool two hours earlier. "What happened?"

"Nothing," she said in that soothing, condescending tone of hers she used in the old days when explaining why Grandma had said or done something particularly hurtful. "She's just upset, that's all. The preschool called. They didn't want to bother you at work. She's been weepy and pouty all morning. Every time anyone looks at her crossways, she starts bawling. They wanted to know if there was anything they could do to calm her down."

I put a hand to my forehead. "I don't see why they had to call you."

"I told you, they didn't want to bother you at work if it turned out to be nothing. I told them I'd call and see if you cared if I went in and brought her and Jonah home."

Would wonders ever cease? Aunt Wanda, calling to ask my permission about something! I felt oddly touched and flattered. At the same time, this problem was out of my area of expertise. "What do you think? I don't want her thinking all she has to do is cry and we'll cave and she'll get what she wants. That's how kids end up spoiled."

"Oh, please. If you buying those two kids every toy known to man hasn't done it yet, a little coddling surely won't do any harm."

"You think that's all it is? She needs a little coddling."

"Sure it is," she said with all the confidence of someone who'd been doing this motherhood thing a lot longer than me. "The poor little thing's only four. Look at everything she's been through. Besides, Jeb and me love having them at the house, which doesn't happen near as often these days as I'd like. I'll go pick them up at the preschool and you can get them tonight at our house; plan on staying for dinner. I'll fix a batch of homemade beef and noodles. It's Emma's favorite."

I heaved a sigh of relief and appreciation for my family, who had suddenly developed charitable tendencies. "Thanks, Aunt Wanda. I hope she won't be any trouble."

"No trouble at all. I'll see you tonight, and Michelle, don't worry."

I hung up and returned to work feeling much better, knowing Emma would be happy spending the remainder of the morning helping Aunt Wanda roll out noodles. I didn't dwell on what could be the cause of the problem. I liked to believe Aunt Wanda knew what she was talking about and a little coddling would have everything back to normal in no time.

Chapter Twenty-four

The next morning was the same as the one before, and the next and the next. I couldn't let Aunt Wanda pick the kids up from preschool every time Emma decided she wasn't happy, and I let her know it. Our life was too busy for phone calls at work or tears in the middle of the night or temper tantrums when I had somewhere to be. Emma would have to realize she had to go to preschool and Angie's just like always.

But nothing I said seemed to matter. She didn't want me out of her sight. She took to standing outside the bathroom door when I was in the shower. While fixing dinner, she insisted on sitting at the kitchen table and keeping me company. As long as I was within sight, she chattered and laughed and talked about school as if she hadn't spent the whole day crying, inconsolable. But as soon as I headed toward the pantry or the back porch, she hopped off her chair and followed. She refused to watch TV with Jonah unless I was in the room too. Something was up; I just didn't know what. She and Jonah had been here five months. Had it taken all this time for her to develop a fear of being abandoned again?

Whatever it was, she wasn't talking.

I considered calling my caseworker and discussing the matter with her. But I dreaded involving the authorities. The woman might think I was behind the sudden developmental lapse; that I was abusing her or neglecting her somehow. No, this was something I needed to take care of myself.

Every day when I got to the preschool to pick her up, the teachers looked at me with their sympathetic, understanding glances. Maybe they understood, but I didn't. Why was she behaving this way all of the sudden? If it had suddenly occurred to her that Nicole was gone and possibly never coming back, why was she latched onto me and refusing to let go?

I stopped and picked up a pizza on our way home Thursday. I turned down the weekend work at the county hospital so I'd have three days to concentrate on Emma's problem. I hoped pizza would break the ice. There was a gallon of vanilla ice cream in the freezer at home. If it didn't placate Emma, I was sure it would at least do something for me.

I kept my questions and lectures to myself until after the pizza was gone and we were seated in front of the TV a couple of hours later. Jonah picked the movie for the evening, and I chose the twenty minutes of upcoming releases as an opportunity to broach the subject.

"Emma, you need to tell me why you've been crying this week every time we go to preschool."

She didn't answer. She kept her eyes glued to the TV screen, but I knew I had her attention. "You like going to preschool, don't you?" I pressed.

Still nothing.

"Come on, Emma, you have to tell me. I have to go back to work Monday. That means you and Jonah will go back to preschool. I know you like it there with all your friends. So I don't want anymore of that crying. It doesn't do any good, and it just gets everybody upset for nothing."

There, that should take care of it. Who could argue with logic like that?

Emma laughed nervously at something on the TV. She glanced at me out of the corner of her eye. I knew what she was thinking. She was hoping I'd stop talking about this uncomfortable subject and pay attention to the movie. I put my arm across the back of the couch and leaned forward so I could look into her face. She leaned to the right so she could see around me.

"Emma," I warned.

Reluctantly, she brought her face around to look at me.

"You're not going to cry again when I take you back to the preschool or to Angie's, are you?" I asked with no room for argument. "You're a big girl now. Next month you'll be five. That's too old to be crying like a baby when you don't get your way." I knew I was coming on too strong and I shouldn't resort to name calling, but I couldn't think of any other way. I needed to drive the point home, even if it took a little tough love and manipulation.

"I won't cry no more," she said in a tiny, defeated voice.

I put my arm around her and squeezed her against me. "Now, that's my big girl. How about after the movie, we pop some popcorn and play Old Maid?"

"Yea!" Jonah shouted.

Emma sniffed. "Okay."

Victory didn't taste as sweet as I'd imagined. I knew I had simply taken care of a symptom and not the disease, but I didn't want to ruin her weekend or mine. Enough talk for one night. She was a good little girl; she'd do whatever she could to please me, even if it meant breaking her heart in the process.

�֍

At the hospital, Louise Bell was taking her re-certification classes. I was covering her shift so, for the next two weeks, I had to be at work two hours early. Every night after dinner and bath time, I took the kids to Aunt Wanda's and tucked them into bed in Violet's old room. She got them up around eight and took them to preschool where I picked them up at my usual time. Emma's tears seemed to have disappeared. She was still clingy at home. She continued to follow me around in the afternoons, telling me about her day or something silly Uncle Jeb had done that morning at breakfast. But I didn't mind. At least I wasn't getting any phone calls at work telling me she was bawling her eyes out.

She pouted some when I dropped the two of them off with Aunt Wanda every night. She clung to my neck until I reassured her a dozen times I'd see her the next afternoon at the preschool. Uncle Jeb was there to read her and Jonah a story and supervise teeth brushing. My departure wasn't overly traumatic.

It wasn't until the beginning of February that Louise finished her re-certification classes and I was the one to drop the kids off at the preschool again. The trees along the driveway were beginning to bud. The tulips and crocuses had bloomed and died in the flowerbeds almost without my notice. Going to work so early meant I hadn't seen my house in the daylight hours for a couple of weeks. Spring was my favorite season and I hated to be missing this one. There was a scent of lilac and forsythia in the air, hinting of the beauty and glory to come.

I pulled lightweight pants out of the drawer to dress Emma and Jonah my first day back on my regular schedule. Emma stood in the middle of her bedroom floor, an obstinate set to her jaw. She looked just like her mother. "I don't wanna go to school. I wanna go with you."

Not again. This had to end right here and now. I glared down at her, my expression leaving no room for debate. "Emma, get dressed right now. We're not going through this again. You're going to preschool with your brother and I'm going to work. Now, hurry up."

She crossed her arms over her chest. "No."

I gaped. Open rebellion, from Emma, no less. I recovered quickly. "I said get dressed, Emma. I'm not standing for any nonsense this morning. We're not going to be late."

Rather than caving in to my demands like usual, her jaw tightened. She clenched her fists, opened her mouth, reared her head back, and bellowed, "Nooo! I ain't goin'."

By now I was as angry as she was, and only a little more under control. I advanced the rest of the way into the room. "Oh, yes you are." I took her by the arm, led her to the bed, and sat her on it. "You get dressed right this minute, little missy, or I'll do it for you."

She scowled up at me with no sign of acquiescence showing in her face.

"Which is it going to be?" I demanded.

The metamorphosis took over her face gradually. The scowl transformed from a pucker into a pout until silent tears slid down her cheeks. She never took her eyes off me as she blinked rapidly in a valiant, but failing attempt to keep from crying. I weakened. I tried to keep my serious look in place; the one that said someone who barely reached my belt buckle wouldn't boss me around. But looking into that sweet,

crestfallen face threatened to snap even my iron will. Before I could
say anything, Jonah appeared beside me and climbed onto the bed
beside his sister.

"Don't cry, Emma," he said. "She'll come back. She always does."

I ground my teeth in frustration and turned away so they couldn't
see the anger on my face. Nicole. Would she never stop causing me
grief? Wasn't it enough that I had given her children a safe home
while she was enjoying her respite from motherhood? Must I now argue with her daughter every time I wanted to walk out the front door?
It occurred to me to call Aunt Wanda and ask her to come over until
Emma calmed down. If possible, she could drive them to preschool
later in the morning. No, this was my problem. I couldn't keep letting
other people handle things.

Emma shook her head from side to side. The tears spilled faster.

After a covert glance at my watch, I lowered myself to the bed between them. I put an arm around each of them. "Sweetie," I said to
Emma, "you mustn't cry. I know you get scared sometimes, and that's
okay. I get scared too, but everything will be all right. I promise."

Jonah pulled away from me so he could look up into my face. "You
can't get scared, Aunt Shell. You're a grown up."

I smiled and squeezed him against me. "Grown ups get scared all
the time, Jonah. We worry that our kids will get picked on at school.
We worry about having money to buy you all the toys you want. We
get scared when you get sick, and it's okay. We just have to believe
that everything will work out all right. We have to trust..." I didn't
know how to finish the sentence. Trust, how could I explain such a
concept to preschoolers without a bunch of empty platitudes I didn't
believe myself?

"God?"

I turned to Emma in surprise. Wouldn't that be the easy way out?
Turn all my cares over to a Supreme Being who supposedly loved me
and wanted the best for me, if only I'd allow it. *"Cast your burdens on
Jesus, for He cares for you."* The line of a song from somewhere in my
past rushed unbidden to my mind. I gave up trusting Jesus years ago.
I had trusted, or wanted to trust, and it got me nowhere. Of course, I
couldn't tell the kids that.

I remembered the gentle urging I'd had during the New Year's Eve service at Kyle's church. What if He was up there, waiting to take my burdens, because He truly did care for me?

"Yes, we can trust God, Emma," I said with more confidence than I felt. "He'll help you when you're scared and worried about...things."

"How?" she asked. She looked around the room. "I don't see Him."

Good question. I wondered the same thing myself more than once. "Well, um..."

"He lives in your heart, silly," Jonah stated. "That's why you can't see Him."

"Yeah, right," I agreed. I tapped her chest with my finger. "He lives right here inside each of us. We just have to believe."

"I believe, Aunt Shell," Jonah said.

I gave him another squeeze. "Oh, I'm so happy, Jonah. Maybe you can help Emma be brave when you see she's scared or worried about something."

He nodded gravely. "I'll try."

Emma worked her bottom lip up and down and finally said, "I'll be brave."

"Oh, Emma, we know you will. You're such a brave girl already. You make me proud of you everyday. You know that, don't you?"

She looked doubtful.

I lifted her onto my lap. "You do, and Jonah, too. I'm so proud of both of you. Me, Gypsy, Uncle Jeb, and Aunt Wanda are so glad you came to live with us." I was shocked to feel tears sting my eyes. I *was* glad, but it took me actually speaking the words to realize it.

I kissed them both goodbye at the preschool, making as small a production of my departure as possible. Miss Gail stood at the ready, in case Emma planned to bolt or kick and scream like she had the last time I dropped her off. Miss Gail started chattering about needing a helper and she was wondering if Emma could do her such a favor. Emma lowered her head and alternately studied the floor and me. Her lip quivered dangerously. A fat tear glistened in the corner of her eye. My own lip started to quiver and I seriously considered for the first time in my life calling in sick.

I couldn't. I had to be strong. The girl had to learn those big tears wouldn't cause her to get her way every time. With fierce resolve, I reached for the door handle. I was needed at work, and I needed my job. I didn't have the luxury of a husband who brought in another paycheck.

I glanced back one last time and saw Jonah take her hand. "Don't cry, Emma," he said. "She'll come back. She always does."

Chapter Twenty-five

I hadn't been late for work in three weeks. Nor was I receiving distressing phone calls in the middle of a shift. I knew the problem wasn't over, just temporarily on hold. But I was relieved for the respite, however brief. Emma still dragged her feet and looked close to tears every morning when I dropped her off at the preschool, but at least she was going. That was something. On Mondays and Wednesdays, when I worked until seven and picked the kids up at Angie's, she reported Emma was withdrawn and clingy, but no tears. What nearly broke Angie's heart, she told me, was how Emma stared at the door and kept one ear cocked, regardless of what was going on, listening for the sound of my car in the driveway. Once I arrived, everything was right as rain; a happy, bubbling Emma vying for my attention, wanting to tell me everything she'd done that day all in one breath.

By Thursday I was ready for my weekend. Since I had come in early those two weeks for Louise while she took her re-certification training, she finagled her work load around to cover for me a couple of hours so I could leave early. The unexpected short workday and the three-day weekend staring me in the face put me in a better mood than I once thought possible. I used to be lost when I wasn't at work. Suddenly I was turning into one of those people who couldn't wait for the workday to end.

I hadn't worked contingency at the county hospital for nearly a month, and I was getting used to the three-day weekends, something I'd never taken advantage of in my entire adult life. I had the next few days at home with no worries about babysitters or leaving Emma while she suffered through whatever separation anxiety she was going through. Sooner or later she'd realize no amount of crying or feeling sorry for herself would make Nicole come back any faster. Instead of wishing she had a better mother, she'd see she was the one who had to adjust. I just hoped it would be sooner.

I wasn't even thinking about the time as I pulled into the church parking lot a little before two that afternoon. I saw the heavy curtains strung across the front doors. It was naptime, and would be until three o'clock. I hated to go in and wake Emma and Jonah. They got up so early in the morning that they were complete bears by evening if they didn't get their daily two-hour naps at preschool. Another thing I had to consider was waking up another child, a sure way of making enemies with the staff.

I was sitting there considering if I should wait or if I had time to run a few errands, when I saw the other set of doors farther down the building open and Kyle step outside. I watched as he went to the mailbox and gathered the mail. *"You would think a church this size could hire a secretary for jobs like that."* I thought.

I scrunched down in my seat and hoped he wouldn't see me. I hadn't seen him since our trip to Burger King. I didn't want to see him now. Watching him move around the parking lot in his rumpled khakis and untucked shirt was making my heart do uncomfortable things. It wasn't fair that a human being look so great without even trying. The lack of attention to his appearance apparently meant he wasn't planning to be in his office long. I hated that seeing him after all these years and striking up an old friendship bothered me so much. It shouldn't. Just like Emma needed to realize her mother would come back only when she was good and ready, I needed to get it through to my heart that there could never be anything between Kyle and me. I needed to forget he even existed, much as I had for the last fifteen years.

He spotted my car, squinted to make sure I was inside, and waved. I pulled myself up to my full height and waved back.

I groaned when he headed my way. I combed my fingers through my hair and ran my tongue over my teeth. I'd been up since five-thirty and would've done anything for a toothbrush. I didn't bother checking myself out in the rearview mirror. The less I knew the better. I turned the key in the ignition so I could lower the window.

"Hey, what are you doing out here?" he asked, approaching the car, his left hand clenched around the church's mail.

"Naptime," I said indicating the door with a nod of my head.

He followed my gaze and nodded. "Oh, yeah," He put his finger to his lips. "Gotta be very quiet," he said in a stage whisper, "or every teacher in there will have your hide."

I laughed. "Yeah, I found out the hard way. Back when the kids first started, I went stomping in during naptime, didn't even notice the curtains on the door till I was inside. It was pitch black and I couldn't see where I was going. I walked right into the cubby boxes before Miss Mary caught up with me and saved me from injuring myself."

By now we were laughing out loud. "That's always a possibility," he said. "I tripped over a kid once. I was on my way to Billie's office for some insurance paperwork and was concentrating on the ray of light coming from underneath her door, when I banged my shin on this little guy's cot. Fortunately, I caught myself before I fell on top of him."

I laughed even harder, picturing tall, athletic Kyle hobbling around in a circle trying to regain his balance without falling on, and crushing, a sleeping child.

"It's not that dark once your eyes get accustomed to it," he said, after he finished laughing at himself. "It's just the getting used to it that can hurt. I had a knot on my shin for two weeks." He glanced at his watch. "Why don't you come inside my office to wait? The kids' won't be getting up for another forty-five minutes or so. I promise the lights are on in my end of the building so you won't trip over anything. Besides, I'm freezing out here."

I hadn't realized he didn't have his coat on. It was February and still much too cold to be outside without something on. I glanced at the clock on the dash and then the front door. Spending the next forty-five minutes with Kyle sure sounded more appealing than a quick trip to the supermarket or waiting in line at the bank. Actually it sounded more appealing than most anything I could think of. I enjoyed his company even if I did find myself stumbling over words and worrying about my appearance way too much. He made me feel like a silly nervous teenager again. I needed to remember we were adults. What we had in high school was long gone. Whether or not we had ever been in love, I wasn't sure anymore, and it no longer mattered. All that mattered was the here and now. Kyle was a pastor; if he was looking for a relationship it surely wouldn't be with someone as hopelessly lost as me.

I got out of the car and followed him to the main entrance of the church, and down a short hallway to his office. "Care for anything to drink?" he asked as I settled into an oversized, leather chair. He went to a small refrigerator and opened the door.

"Bottled water would be great if you have it."

He removed two from inside the refrigerator and handed me one. He sat down in the chair next to mine. The chairs were angled to half face the desk and half face each other. Conducive to open communication, I supposed. Studies had probably been done to see which furniture arrangement got couples talking and problems solved in the most time efficient manner. Our knees nearly touched. Kyle discreetly slid his chair back a few inches to allow more space between us. He had also left the door open. No room for impropriety here.

"How's everything going with the kids?" he asked.

Always a first question now that I was playing Mommy.

"Great. Emma can recognize all her letters and numbers, and she can write most of them. Jonah has practically a photographic memory when it comes to new songs and scripture verses. He comes home quoting something new nearly every day."

Kyle rested his elbows on the arms of the chair and leaned toward me. "They're really bright kids," he said. "I knew once they got over their awkwardness, they'd settle in."

"Oh, I wouldn't say that exactly, Emma's going through a rough stretch right now. She'll hardly let me out of her sight. When we're staying around the house, it's not so bad. But it's murder every morning when I have to go to work. Sometimes I have to get a little rough with her, and then I feel like a heel all day."

"She's afraid you're going to leave one day and never come back, just like her mother did," he said matter-of-factly.

I shook my head. "No, it's not that. She misses Nicole, that's all, and she's displaced her frustration on me. I mean, we aren't that close. Well, we are, but not like mother and daughter or anything."

"Michelle, her behavior is classic. She hasn't seen her Mom in what…six months?"

"Five and a half," I corrected.

"You said yourself neither she nor Jonah has outwardly expressed too much concern over Nicole. It's you Emma is worried about. Her Mom disappears without a word. She survives. She and Jonah find out they are getting along pretty well without her; they're safe, happy, mentally stimulated for probably the first time. It's only natural that Emma start to feel insecure within her new world. What happens if you suddenly disappear just like Mommy did? Then what? Where will they go the next time? What if the new place isn't as nice as the one they're in now?"

I considered his words. "When I dropped them off at preschool the other morning, Jonah said, 'don't worry, she always comes back.' He said the same thing at home, but I thought he was talking about Nicole. I guess that makes sense. But I've never given them any reason to think I'm leaving. Nothing's changed. We do the exact same thing every day. They go to preschool, I go to work, and we come home, go to bed, and do it all over the next day. They say kids need routine, structure; well, they're not getting anything else but that at my house."

"Then keep it up. Eventually she'll realize she can trust you, that you're not going to disappear in the middle of the night."

I shuddered in spite of myself. "I guess that is an unimaginable thing for a four-year-old to ponder."

"It's unimaginable for anyone. I would suggest you talk to her. Tell her you know what she's afraid of and that you understand it. Don't tell her she has no reason to worry, because in her mind, she does. Just be understanding and patient. She'll start to feel secure again if she knows you care about what she's going through."

"You're actually pretty good at this," I said with a smile.

"It comes with the territory."

"Yeah, I guess I keep forgetting what your job is."

He smiled. "It comes naturally. Even before God called me, He made me a good listener."

"That's true. You were the one everybody came to for advice, even in high school."

"Everybody but you," he reminded me. "You were the together one, so aloof. You didn't need anybody."

"It was all an act, Kyle." There's no harm in admitting it now. Everything about everybody was an act in high school.

Kyle nodded. "I know. I must admit I started hanging around you because you were cool and mysterious. But it didn't take long to realize you weren't as together as you let everybody believe."

I took a sip of my water. "What was the giveaway?"

He shrugged, "Lots of things. For one, I learned a little bit about your home life, just what you told me, of course. It was a long time before you actually invited me to your house. I couldn't believe a teenager was almost wholly responsible for taking care of her little sister, even with all the other stuff you were doing. And then there was your Grandma." He grinned. "She was a piece of work. And the way you two looked at each other; like adversaries, on guard all the time."

"You do pay attention to what goes on around you."

"Only what interests me."

"Does that mean I interested you?"

"You already know the answer to that one." He sobered and gave me a piercing look. "Maybe you still do."

"Still what, interest you?"

His expression didn't change.

"In what way," I demanded caustically, suddenly irritated, "As a hopeless reprobate, in need of saving?"

He ignored my cynicism. "No, not in the least; maybe it'd be easier if that's the only way I thought about you."

I took another sip of my water and screwed on the lid, my knuckles white against the cap. I wished he wouldn't talk like this. He needed a godly woman, the perfect pastor's wife, not a heathen like me with no desire to change her life. It was bad enough that I couldn't stop thinking about him; he shouldn't waste his time on me. "I'm not the person I used to be, Kyle. You don't know anything about me, except that I'm not a Christian."

He sat back in his chair, deflated. "That I do know."

"Then why am I sitting here?" I didn't know why I was so angry with him. Did I think he was toying with my emotions, knowing full well there would never be anything between us? He belonged to the Club; the Righteous Club, the one you couldn't get into unless you were willing to play by the rules. He was even a charter member, and I was one of those they looked down on; a former member no longer good enough to belong.

I set the water bottle on his desk and tensed to stand. "Naptime will be over in a little bit. I think I'll wait in the hallway."

He leaned forward and held up his hand. "Michelle, wait, I'm sorry. I didn't mean to say anything to upset you."

I made an effort to relax the tension in my shoulders. I didn't want him thinking I was flustered because he said he was interested in me. Now I was embarrassed for getting bent out of shape in the first place. I had fun with Kyle. I didn't need to go making a federal case over everything that came out of his mouth.

"You didn't upset me, really."

He thought he was a good listener? That it came with the territory? I'd give him something to listen to, something to make him think twice about entertaining an interest in me. Besides, I'd earned the right to vent after the past five and a half months I'd had.

"My whole life I've tried to make the people I love, love me back. First it was Dad. He was the coolest person in the world as far as I was concerned. I thought he hung the moon. I was definitely Daddy's little girl. Then all of a sudden, he was gone. I was lost without him. Mom, of course, was devastated so I tried to be everything for her. Our relationship had never been as close as Dad's and mine, but she needed me and I needed to be needed. I was really into that back then, needing someone to need me."

I wasn't sure why it was so important to me for Kyle to understand. He remained silent.

"Mom moved us here and I tried to comfort her as best I could. Grandma seemed to relish tearing her down a peg or two everyday, so I became her buffer. I thought she appreciated it. For about four years, we muddled through—Mom, Nicole, and me against Grandma and Aunt Wanda, with their side always winning. But Mom needed me. I tried to be extra good so Grandma wouldn't be such a pill to live with. It was already hard to keep the house quiet and un-chaotic with a little kid like Nicole plowing through it, but I did what I could to settle things down. I didn't want Mom getting into more trouble than she already was. I thought I was doing a good job of holding things together.

"You should have seen the look on her face when she'd come home from an especially hard day at work and I'd have dinner cooking on the stove or the laundry done or Nicole already bathed and dressed and smelling sweet in her pajamas. That look of appreciation from Mom was worth giving up my childhood. I wanted her to love me, to need me, to realize that without me, life would be so difficult, so empty. I thought it was working. Then one Friday afternoon, me and my cousin, Violet, got off the school bus and found Grandma and Aunt Wanda sitting at the kitchen table with these grave looks on their faces. Aunt Wanda looked like she'd been crying. Grandma just looked mad, madder than I'd ever seen her."

I paused, remembering that awful day with absolute clarity. It was a day I seldom allowed myself to relive. It took about ten years to get those looks out of my thoughts during the day and out of my dreams at night.

Kyle listened with a look of compassion on his face, but no pity. I appreciated that. The time for pity was about twenty years too late. I took a deep breath and continued.

"Grandma told me and Violet what happened. I think she actually enjoyed the moment. She had this look of triumph in her eyes behind the aggravation, like she always knew her daughter would never amount to anything, and she'd just gone and proved it. "Your Mom's took off," she said. Just like that. Catherine Barker didn't believe in sugar coating anything. "She up and sneaked out this morning after you got on the school bus." My first thought was Nicole. Nicole was Mom's darling, and I was sure that meant she took Nicole with her and I was left alone. Grandma must have read my mind because she added real quick, "She left Nicole. Just up and left, leaving her own baby behind like an old dog you'd leave by the side of the road."

"I wanted to run upstairs and bawl my eyes out, but their eyes had me rooted to the spot. It was like they were blaming me. My mother was weak and spineless and because of my failure as a daughter, she couldn't take anymore. So I stood there and listened to the play by play of what they thought drove Mom out. Neither of them said it had anything to do with me, but they didn't have to. It was right below the surface. I knew what they were thinking. They were furious at Mom and Dad for leaving Grandma saddled with two kids she didn't particularly care for. I was old enough to know I would be the one to pay for it.

"I was pretty well finished with caring for anybody after that, except for Nicole. She was crazy about me, and I was pretty sure she wasn't going anywhere. But everyone else, forget it. They never cared for me the way I cared for them, and they ended up taking off on me anyway. I was through. No more getting burned. For about a year, I was pretty sullen. I tried not to let it show because I knew it gave Grandma some kind of warped satisfaction. So I put on a brave face, but anybody with half a brain could see through that façade.

"It was too hard to maintain for any length of time though. For one thing, I was only fourteen or fifteen. And then there was Nicole. She needed somebody to look after her, to be the buffer between her and Grandma, like I had been between Grandma and Mom. So good ole Michelle stepped up to the plate again. Now when I was fixing dinner and doing laundry and keeping Nicole out from underfoot, it was for Grandma. She so openly disliked my presence in her home; I was determined to make her see what an asset I was to have around. I don't know why I even bothered. It hadn't done a lick of good making Mom stick around."

I reached out a shaky hand and twisted the lid off my water. I took a long swallow. I didn't want to cry sitting so close to Kyle. I should stop talking, go get the kids, and go home. Reliving my past wasn't going to do either of us any good. But I couldn't stop now, even if I tried.

I set the water bottle back on the desk and continued, my eyes on the window over the desk instead of on him. "I lived at home while I went to nursing school so I could keep up with the housework and keep costs down. I started paying the taxes on the farm as soon as I could afford it. I brought food into the house every payday." My voice cracked, but I kept going. "Grandma never gave me as much as a thank you. After awhile she even started handing me lists on my way out the door on Fridays. I thought for sure all the help around the house and the money would make her love me, or if nothing else, at least respect me. But it didn't.

"Well, I don't know, maybe she did a little in spite of herself. I mean, she did leave me the farm. Some of the cousins actually had the nerve to be mad about that, even though I was the one here taking care of her in her old age and the one who took care of her affairs after she died. They never stopped their own busy, important lives for a minute or two to help me out, not that I blame them much. Grandma wasn't exactly someone whose company you'd seek out on purpose. But they sure balked when the will was read. She didn't have much, basically just the farm. Now it's mine, for as long as I live anyway. I can never sell it unless I offer it to Uncle DeWitt or the other brothers and sisters first. When I die, it goes to Uncle DeWitt first, and if he's gone, to Aunt Wanda or her descendants. I guess Grandma never considered the fact that I might have descendants of my own someday."

I chuckled humorlessly, "Neither did I. Like Grandma, I figure I'll live there till I die, and then let the family step in and do whatever they want with the place."

I shrugged. "I've spent my life trying to make people love me. I've done everything I could think of to earn their love, but nothing's worked. No one has ever loved me back so after a lifetime of beating that dead horse, I finally gave up. Obviously I'm not lovable. My own mother and father didn't love me enough to stay, or to even stay in touch after they took off. Grandma didn't love me, period. Even Nicole, who thought so much of me, didn't love me enough to listen to a word I said when it was for her own good. And as far as God's concerned, obviously I'm not worth his time either. I prayed to him the whole time I sat next to Grandma in that stuffy church of hers, listening to the pastor talk about God's grace and mercy. I asked him to bring my parents back. Then I asked him to make Grandma love me or at least treat me like a person. Finally I just prayed that He love me since no one else did. Even that didn't happen. I couldn't even be good enough to make God love me."

I threw up my hands in an exaggerated manner and smiled flippantly. "So, what's the point, Pastor? I'm too old to change now. Too much water has passed under the bridge. For the first time in my life, I have two people who love me unconditionally. And I love them back, unconditionally. Yes, they're just kids and they probably love me for the same reasons as I loved at that age—because I pulled them out from under the lilac bushes and took them to Wal-Mart and bought them pretty clothes and took them to birthday parties. I'm a good aunt. That makes them love me. If the good times ended tomorrow, they'd stop loving me too. That's just the way things are. I'll keep loving them, buying them stuff and taking care of them. Then someday they'll grow up and realize I'm not the asset they thought I was. They'll see they can do just as well without me, and stop loving me like everyone else has. So, I'm going to enjoy the feeling while it lasts. Afterwards, I guess I'll be on my own again. It's not like I can't take care of myself."

"But, God—no way. He may be up there in heaven showering His favored few with blessings. I'm just not one of them. Whatever it takes to earn His favor, I haven't done it, and I'm too stubborn to try. I guess I'm too old for games."

I sat back in my chair, too tired to bother with the phony smile. It hadn't been as easy as I thought to be flippant about all the pain of my past. It still hurt that my parents disappeared when I really needed them. It hurt that my grandmother had never seen me as anything more than a burden. It especially hurt that God chose to bless some, while people like me, He ignored. I could play the role of the agnostic all I wanted, but disregard from a God whose existence I couldn't deny no matter how badly I wanted to, was hard to laugh off.

Kyle's hand slid across the table and covered mine. I pulled it away and nibbled at a cuticle. Neither of us said anything for a long time. Kyle rested his elbows on the chair arms and made a teepee with his fingers. He stared at his hands while I continued to attack the cuticle, making mincemeat of my nails.

Finally he let his hands fall down in front of him. "That's the thing about God." His voice was soft and soothing. "You don't have to do one thing to earn his love or his favor. It is a free gift, waiting for you to reach out and take it."

Hadn't he heard a word I said?

"You've been trying to capture the wind in your hands, Michelle," he continued.

I brought my eyes up to meet his, confusion and anger written all over my face.

"The reason you haven't found God is not that He's been hiding from you. It's because you tried to earn His favor like you've tried with everyone else in your life. You can't earn His love, just like you can't push it away. God isn't a person who can fail you. He's your loving heavenly father. He's right there, waiting. The Holy Spirit has been working in your heart for years, Michelle. That's why you're the way you are. You are a gentle and tender spirit, always trying to please everyone but yourself."

"No, Kyle, I'm not. I'm selfish. I'm sitting here feeling sorry for myself, aren't I? I never wanted to be bothered with Nicole's kids. Why do you think I never stepped in before, even though I knew she was barely holding it together in the city? Why didn't I just go down there and take the kids? She would have handed them over and been glad to do it. Instead I convinced myself everything was fine. No, I'm not gentle and compassionate. I'm selfish. I want my life back. I truly resented those kids messing up my perfectly uncomplicated life, just like Grandma Catherine resented me."

At the sound of Grandma's name, my voice cracked again. I put my head in my hands and cried. "Just like Grandma," I sputtered between heaves.

The touch of Kyle's hand on the back of my head made the tears come even harder. I wasn't good with sympathy, but I didn't pull away this time. I didn't want the contact to end.

He pushed a Kleenex into my hand and smoothed my hair away from my face. "Shh, it's all right." His chair grated over the low pile carpet as he moved closer. The leather creaked from his weight and I sensed him standing over me. Still crying, I raised my head and wiped my face with the Kleenex, and then moved into his open arms.

"Shh, shh," he soothed over and over. One hand continued to smooth my hair away from my face. The other cradled my back. His arms tightened around me. I lifted my face upward at the same time that he looked down. He put his hand on my chin so I wouldn't turn away, not that I was considering it. He lowered his face to mine and our lips met. I leaned into him, grateful for his strong arms around me.

Abruptly, the kiss ended. He pulled back, his face stricken. "Michelle, I…"

A tiny noise of surprise escaped my throat. Words wouldn't form.

He dropped his arms to his side as if the touch of my skin burned him. He took a step back and his legs bumped against the chair he had been sitting in. "I—I'm sorry." Hastily he moved around the desk and straightened some papers with trembling hands.

My hands were shaking, too. Every part of me was shaking. I felt cold, disoriented. "Oh, I—no, Kyle, I'm sorry…" I reached for my purse that had slipped onto the floor. "I, uh, I'm sure naptime's over now. I'll—I'd better go get the kids."

He nodded while continuing to straighten the papers that didn't need straightening. Finally he forced his hands to stop, took a deep breath, and looked at me. "Michelle, you know I care for you. I don't want you to think…"

I put up my hand to stop him. I couldn't bear to hear another word. The last thing I wanted was to hear his apology for kissing me. "No, Kyle, I understand completely." I turned and hurried to the door.

"I don't think you do," he said from the safety of the other side of the desk.

Chapter Twenty-six

The kids were ecstatic to see me come through the swinging doors that separated the main part of the church from the fellowship hall. Emma reached me first. I leaned forward and she jumped into my arms, something I usually didn't allow for the sake of my back. I kept myself together. It wasn't that difficult; I'd been doing it all my life when yet another person found me unlovable.

"Guys, we've gotta talk," I said that evening over a dinner of corn dogs, baked beans, and coleslaw.

Emma licked a dollop of mustard off the side of her corn dog, her eyes on mine. My serious tone did nothing to dull the merriment in her eyes. All was comfortable and secure in her world at the moment. She sensed no cause for alarm.

I turned my head from her to Jonah to make sure he was listening too. His attitude was much the same as hers, concentration on food was more important at the moment than anything I had to say.

Maybe this wasn't the best time to broach the subject. Maybe I should wait till Sunday evening when they knew I'd be going back to work and our minds were all on the same page. Why bring up something that would only upset all of us? Too late; they were listening. I may as well get it over with.

"Emma, Jonah, do you worry sometimes when I leave for work or go to the store or something, that I may not come back?"

Jonah looked across the table at Emma. Emma put her corndog on her plate and stared at it.

I reached out and put a hand over each of theirs. Jonah turned to look at me. Emma continued to study her dinner. "I'm not going anywhere. When I go to work, it's because I have to. There are sick people at the hospital who need me to help them feel better. If I weren't there, who would give them their medicine? Who would help them get up and do their exercises so they can go home and be with their families? Who would help the doctors do their work? I have to go to work. I love doing my job; I'm good at it. But I also love coming home."

Jonah climbed up on his knees in his chair. "See, Emma. I told you she always comes back."

Emma turned on him; her cheeks flushed scarlet. "Not always," she snapped. "Mommy didn't come back."

"You will too come back, won't ya?" Jonah asked, looking up at me, his moist eyes large and pleading. "Tell her you'll come back."

I squeezed Emma's hand. "Of course, I'm coming back. Don't I come back every night when I tell you I will? This is my home, it's where I belong, here with you and Jonah."

Emma directed her next words at Jonah, as if I wasn't in the room. "But what if she's lying? Mommy lied. She said she'd always take care of us, but she didn't. She let Dean put us in the car, and she didn't even try to stop him." She jerked her hand away from mine, pulled her knees up into the chair, curled herself into a ball, and cried into her hands.

I jumped out of my chair and hurried around the table to her, Jonah right behind me. "Emma, Emma? Honey, please, look at me."

She thrust her face deeper into her hands and shrugged me away. I scooted her chair around so it was facing me and not the table. Jonah climbed down off his chair and came over to stand beside me. I knelt in front of Emma and pulled her long hair away from her face.

"Emma, honey, is this why you started crying over my leaving? Are you afraid I won't come home from work?"

She mumbled something into her hands.

"I can't understand you, Emma. If you want me to make it better, you have to tell me whatever is bothering you."

She turned her face just enough for me to make out her next words. "I don't want you to go."

I picked her up, sat down in her chair, and set her on my lap. She still wouldn't look at me. "Emma, I have to go to work. And sometimes I have to go to the grocery store, or the bank, or take Gypsy to the vet, but I always come back. You have to trust me and believe me when I tell you something. I'm not lying to you."

She wiped her wet face on her shirtsleeve. "Mommy always said the same thing when I cried."

Jonah nodded in solemn agreement. How could I dispute that? Why should either of them believe me when they couldn't trust their own mother? I pulled Emma close. I wrapped my other arm around Jonah and pulled him against me.

"Your Mommy loves both of you," I began. "I know she does. You know how I know? Because she's my sister and I took care of her when she was your age. She has a big heart and I know that's where she's holding both of you right now." I tapped Emma on the chest as I continued, "In her heart. But I don't think she can come back yet. She loves you and she'll come back as soon as she's able."

"Dean won't let her," Jonah piped up.

I hated to make Dean, whom I'd never met, the bad guy, but it would make my life a lot easier.

"Whatever the reason, Mommy decided you needed to stay here with me for awhile. I think we've been getting along just fine, don't you?"

Jonah nodded. I nudged Emma's shoulder and she nodded too. "We've been having a lot of fun. You like preschool, and everybody says you're doing great there. Uncle Jeb has somebody to go fishing with him. Aunt Wanda's teaching you how to cook."

"We've never had a dog before," Emma said with a sniff.

"Hey, that's right. Now you've got a dog and your own rooms like big kids." I hugged them both and kissed the tops of their heads.

"Aunt Shell?"

I turned to look at Jonah.

"When Mommy comes back are you gonna tell her we want to keep living here?"

I swallowed hard. They'd asked this question before and I promised I'd make everything all right with Nicole. I had hoped they'd forgotten. I hoped by this time they would want to go back with their mother…in the event she still wanted them, no matter what it did to me.

"Well, Jonah, are you sure that's what you want?"

He and Emma exchanged solemn looks. Then they both turned to me and nodded.

I tightened my arms around them. "All right, then. I'll talk to her."

"You promise?" Emma asked.

"She might be pretty mad," Jonah pointed out.

"That's okay," I said confidently. "I'm the big sister. She has to do what I say."

That satisfied them, even though I wasn't so sure.

So Kyle was right. I was the one Emma worried about leaving and not coming back, not Nicole. I wondered why it took her all this time to start worrying about it, but I figured it didn't really matter. Maybe it took her all this time to really feel like a part of a family again; a family that included me.

I smiled to myself as I poured myself the last of the coffee and switched off the pot. I was part of this family, her and Jonah's family. They needed me. They hurt when I was absent. If that didn't beat all! When I found them in the front yard under the lilac bushes six months ago, I never thought it would come to this. It felt kind of nice. First I told them I was happy they'd come to live here, and now I was calling us a family; a family I was adamantly opposed to six months ago. What was happening to me? What about the independence I prized so highly? What about my determination to keep them at arms length in preparation for the inevitable day when Nicole would come for them?

I banished that thought from my head. I didn't want to think about Nicole coming back. Especially after the promise I'd made, twice. Maybe it's what the kids needed; I knew firsthand what it was like to know my own parents had no interest in me. Even if she couldn't take care of them properly, they'd know she cared. But for my sake, I hoped she didn't come back for a good long time.

Chapter Twenty-seven

Kyle was right about me wasting my time trying to catch the wind with my hands. I couldn't change people into who I wanted them to be. I couldn't make someone love me or need me, simply because it was imperative to me that I be loved and needed. It wasn't a given that husbands love their wives and parents love their children. It was a cold hard fact I'd learned during my thirty-three years on the planet, and something I had to accept.

Another fact I had to accept was that Kyle could never love me. Regardless of whether he was interested or not, there would never be anything between us. Our kiss had been a mistake; we both saw it. But there was someone who did seem to care for me—and maybe a lot. He sure took a lot of abuse and neglect with no reward, and kept coming back for more. I wondered how he'd react if I called.

"Hi, Barry, how are you? Long time no see."

His end was silent for a moment. He was either trying to identify my voice or come up with a way to let me down gently. "Michelle?" His voice croaked in disbelief. "I'm good, how are you?"

"Fine," I couldn't remember now what I planned to accomplish with this call, but it was going well. At least he hadn't hung up on me. "Hey, I was wondering, would you be interested in dinner or something maybe, um, tomorrow night? I'm off this weekend and thought we might get together."

"Just the two of us?"

Make him think it was his idea. "Sure, if you like. You mentioned that Italian restaurant in Geneva a while back."

"Angelino's?"

"Yes, Angelino's; I still haven't been there."

"Me either."

"Well, how about we try it out together, around seven?"

"Okay, that works for me."

"Great. Do you want to pick me up here at the house?"

"Perfect, I'll see you about seven then."

"Okay, great. See you then. Bye."

"Bye."

I hung up the phone and stared at my reflection in the thin sliver of mirror attached to the coat rack by the front door. Dinner with Barry, I could think of less attractive ways to spend a Friday night. It was better than what I usually ended up doing. Why exactly was I doing this? Sure Barry didn't exactly send my heart into overdrive, but he did seem interested in me. Was I that hard up for company? No, this wasn't about me. It was about the kids, and Barry, and Caitlyn, and my future. I couldn't keep living like this. I might want a child of my own someday, a real relationship, something.

Barry was a nice person, a good provider, and a great father who wasn't afraid to get down in the trenches. Good husband material. And he liked me. What was I saving myself for? Fireworks didn't always happen. That didn't mean two intelligent adults couldn't make something develop if they tried hard enough. A union between us would make three little kids very happy. Who knew? It might also be what I was looking for.

❧

I fed the kids around five Friday evening and walked them across the field. I gave Aunt Wanda few details about my plans for the evening other than a reminder that she could reach me at any time on my cell phone. The kids knew I was having dinner with Caitlyn's dad, and it wouldn't take much prying before one of them told her; *"Aunt Shell's on a date. She's gonna find us a daddy."*

Good grief, was that what I doing? I wanted to go upstairs to my room and hide under the covers for a week or two.

I tried to shake the discomfort of everyone knowing my business and set about making myself beautiful. It didn't take much sitting in front of the mirror to realize Barry was going to have to accept me basically the way I was. With the help of eyeliner, foundation, mascara, and a little blush on my cheekbones, which I wasn't exactly sure how to apply, I was about as beautiful as I was going to get. But he'd seen me at my worst during those long, sweaty field trips last summer, and still came around. He basically knew what he was getting.

The restaurant was fashionably lit. Hopefully no one would notice my lack of cosmetic expertise. The maitre d' led us to a secluded table, offered the wine list, which we declined, and made his retreat.

I fingered the crisp stitching on the linen napkin and fiddled with my water glass. Barry clasped his hands in front of him. "I'm so glad we're finally doing this, Michelle. You look lovely tonight."

I smiled demurely. I never knew how to take a compliment, not that I'd received that many. "Thank you. You're not so bad yourself," I quipped.

He grinned. "Why are we so much more comfortable together with three preschoolers vying for our attention?"

I exhaled, relieved. "Oh, good, I thought it was just me."

After that, the evening went much smoother. We found plenty to talk about, most often the kids, sometimes work, with no uncomfortable lulls in the conversation. After dinner we drove downtown to the renovated historic district. Quaint shops, which couldn't make much money in a town the size of Geneva, lined the sidewalks. We strolled along in companionable silence, and window-shopped. Halfway down one street, Barry took my hand to point out a particular window display, and didn't let go. I knew he had done it on purpose. I didn't mind, although it didn't feel quite natural. I ignored my discomfort and reminded myself this would take some getting used to. We weren't an old married couple who'd been holding hands for years, and we certainly weren't teenagers. This was how dating worked when you were in your thirties.

All the way home, I agonized over the goodnight kiss. Should I or shouldn't I? Would he expect it? What was the big deal? I was a grown woman. Why should I agonize over something as simple as a goodnight kiss? They didn't even mean anything these days. People who were practically strangers did it every day.

It wasn't that I didn't like Barry most of the time. Some of the things he did and said didn't always sit well with me, but he was a nice person. He was funny and caring and a great father to Caitlyn. I could see us becoming friends someday, soccer parents, but kissing… the thought didn't appeal to me at all.

Yesterday I thought for sure I wanted someone to care for me like everyone else. I wanted a future, possibly even a child of my own. Well, that would be pretty hard to achieve if I wasn't willing to kiss a man. Feeling like a rotten crumb, I realized it was kissing Barry that I had a problem with. I didn't have anything against kissing a particular man who came to mind. In fact, I would love the opportunity to repeat what had happened the other day in Kyle's office. But Kyle wasn't here. He hadn't called. He hadn't dressed up and paid too much money for dinner at the nicest restaurant in the county, per my request. He made no move whatsoever to spend time with me. He was a counselor, a searcher of lost souls. To him, I was another part of his job.

Barry pulled his car into the driveway behind mine. The house was dark except for the porch light. I wished I'd left a light on. The house looked lonely without the children inside. We both looked toward the house. My hand was already on the door handle. "I'm glad you called me yesterday, Michelle," he said.

"So am I. I had a good time."

"We'll have to go back sometime. The food was really good."

"Yes, I thought so too." Was I supposed to invite him in for drinks or something? Didn't a man always think invitations like that meant more than the woman intended? I tightened my grip on the door handle. "Well, thanks a lot, Barry. I had fun."

He picked up on the signal and put his right hand on the key in the ignition. "So did I. I'll call you later then."

I nodded brightly. "Okay. Drive carefully." I hopped out of the car, ignoring the disappointed look on his face. I darted up the walk as if a rabid dog was on my heels. I listened to his car drive away as I rummaged in my purse for my house keys. What a jerk I was! I initiated this thing and I couldn't even pretend I enjoyed myself.

I let myself in and leaned against the door, more depressed than before my heart-to-heart with Kyle. What was wrong with me? Barry was great. If I'd punched his qualities and my needs into a computer, it would say we were meant for each other. Two lonely people with preschoolers, hard working, generous; we should be a perfect match.

Kyle and I, on the other hand, had nothing in common, unless you counted a minor relationship fifteen years earlier before either of us knew who we were. Kyle was a man after God's own heart. I was a cynical ex-church goer who doubted God's existence. Anybody would know a pair like that had absolutely no future together. Then why couldn't I get him out of my head?

Why had I let Barry drive off tonight without as much as a simple kiss? I went through the house to the kitchen and dropped my purse on the table. I opened the back door to let Gypsy out and then headed up the back staircase. It was barely ten o'clock, but I was ready for bed.

Chapter Twenty-eight

A smile stretched across Jonah's face from one ear to the other. "Miss Billie let me sing into the microphone today."

I was only half paying attention. I gave him a quick glance before returning my gaze to the checkbook in front of me. "She did?"

"Yeah, she let me sing the whole song. All the other kids had to sit on the pews and watch me. It was awesome."

He finally had my full attention. "You sang onstage, all by yourself?"

He nodded eagerly, "Yeah, all by myself."

"Hmm," I guess Billie knew what she was doing, letting a kid handle such expensive equipment. She was always telling me Jonah was quite the performer. Maybe he'd hit the big time someday. An image of Bones, Nicole's old guitar-mutilating boyfriend flashed through my mind. I grimaced. I was sure Nicole was already carrying Jonah by the time she moved away from the farm the last time. She didn't meet Bones until after that, at least that's how I always thought it happened.

I studied Jonah out of the corner of my eye. He didn't look anything like the Bones I remembered, although I'd only had the pleasure of meeting the guy once. I remembered straggly brown hair, a long wiry body without an ounce of muscle, a big nose and glazed over eyes. Jonah couldn't be his. Oh, I prayed he wasn't. Jonah's hair was dark blonde, the color that would eventually turn to brown like everyone else's in the family had done. I had read somewhere that something like seventy percent of the human population had brown hair so that wouldn't implicate Bones. He had pouty lips and an upturned nose like Emma's, alarmingly long eyelashes and chubby baby cheeks. Nope. No Bones in his DNA. His musical ability couldn't have come from there either since I didn't recall Bones having any.

"Why were you singing by yourself?" I asked.

Jonah shrugged.

"'Cause he sings the best," Emma piped up from her end of the table, her blonde head bent over a coloring book.

"He does?"

She nodded and chewed on her bottom lip as she searched the box of crayons for the perfect shade of purple, her favorite color. "He's a good singer. Miss Mary says he's gonna sing by himself in church."

"In church, you mean during a service? Surely she didn't say that. He's only three."

"I'm four," Jonah countered. We'd had a birthday at McDonald's on the last day of March with six little boys from preschool and Caitlyn in attendance for Emma. Barry had been a no-show. I hadn't seen him since our ill-fated dinner date in February. Sue, Caitlyn's mother, had dropped her off and picked her up an hour and a half later.

"Oh, that's right, I forgot, four. But still, singing on stage by yourself at church."

"That's what she said," Emma repeated gravely.

Jonah nodded and went back to his coloring book.

A week later I ran into Billie at the preschool. "Michelle," she said, hurrying over to where I was signing Emma and Jonah in for the day. "I've been meaning to talk to you about our Easter program. I'm sure you got the announcement by now."

"Yes, I got it." On Good Friday, the preschoolers would be performing in a program put together by the youth in the church. They would open the program with a few songs, a finger play, and a memory verse they'd learned over the last month.

"I want to make sure you'll be there," Billie was saying. "We're planning to have Jonah sing a solo, well, part of a song anyway. The other preschoolers will be on stage with him and after he sings his part, they'll join in for the chorus."

I was flabbergasted. "He and Emma said you let him sing on stage a week or so ago. They mentioned a solo but I thought they were mistaken. I can't imagine him singing in front of the whole church. Not by himself."

Billie's perennial smile widened, "I wanted to see how he'd react with the other kids watching him. Oh, my goodness, Michelle, his little voice just gave me chills. He definitely has a gift, I'm telling you. We've never had a child Jonah's age show such promise."

I couldn't believe she was talking about *my* Jonah. What if he couldn't do it? What if he made a mistake and the other children laughed? "Are you sure he's up to this? He's so little," I pointed out. "What if he gets up there and freezes and can't remember a word he's supposed to sing?"

"Then we'll all just sit in our seats and watch him standing up there all handsome in his Sunday clothes."

I stared at her. Surely she wasn't serious.

"That's the thing about preschoolers, no matter how well or how poorly they perform, it doesn't matter. If they just stand there, parents are absolutely thrilled to see them onstage. Even the criers are irresistible. But I have every confidence in Jonah." She laid a reassuring hand on my arm. "I know he'll do his best. All we can do is make sure he knows when to start singing and when to stop, and pray, of course."

I grinned at her like she possessed all the wisdom of the ages, and nodded. "Yes, that's all we can do."

Miss Billie had certainly lost her mind. Jonah singing a solo in front of the whole church, Kyle included. I didn't know what good prayer would do. Only Jonah could control his reaction when he looked out over the sanctuary and saw three hundred strangers staring back at him. I was sure God had more important things to worry about than if Jonah got up on stage and wet himself out of sheer terror.

Chapter Twenty-nine

I bought Jonah a new shirt in a robin's egg blue to go with his black trousers. He was set for the Easter program as far as I was concerned. Apparently Aunt Wanda thought differently. She came by the house Saturday morning to take the kids to the mall in the next county where I worked. Not long after lunch, the three of them burst through the back door bearing packages.

"Aunt Shell, look what I got," Jonah exclaimed. He tore through the packages looking for what belonged to him.

"Careful," Emma cried. "You'll tear up my dress." She snatched the largest bag out of his reach.

"Hey, I need that one. I want to show Aunt Shell what I got."

"So do I."

"Okay, you two." Aunt Wanda positioned her body between them and extracted the bag from Emma's clutching fingers. "We'll show Aunt Michelle our stuff together." She opened the largest bag and pulled out the frilliest concoction I'd ever seen.

Oh, my stars! Had Aunt Wanda lost her mind? A white dress trimmed in the subtlest blue piping—I'd never keep that thing clean.

"That's mine," Emma exclaimed proudly, as if there were any doubt. A white straw hat with coordinating ribbons streaming down the back followed the dress. Jonah made an impatient grab for the bag but Aunt Wanda held it out of his reach.

"Hold your horses, big guy." She winked at me, paused dramatically, and then handed the bag to him.

He reached inside and pulled out a vest and tie to match the blue shirt I'd bought. I saw the receipt at the bottom of the bag, but didn't bother to look at the total. It was probably more than Aunt Wanda and Uncle Jeb spent on groceries in a month. I had given up a long time ago telling her not to spend money on clothes the kids would probably only wear a few times. Every time I did, she'd puff out her bottom lip and lament that Violet and Clifford, that awful husband of hers, would probably never give her grandchildren, and must I deny her this one pleasure in her life?

The Easter outfits came complete with new black slip-ons for Jonah and white patent leather pumps with a daisy on top for Emma. They were from the finest shoe store in the mall, one of the few remaining whose clerks still measured your foot with those cold metal slides and offered complete individualized attention.

At the look on my face, she held her hands out in front of her. "I know—I know what you're going to say, but I noticed Jonah's church shoes had some scuffs the last time I saw him wearing them." She turned the box around so I could see the size while keeping her thumb over the price sticker. "I bought one size larger so he can grow into them."

"Thank you, Aunt Wanda," I said graciously. "The old ones were getting too small."

After some more admiring of the new clothes the kids lost interest and disappeared into the back yard with Gypsy.

I put my arms around Aunt Wanda. "I do appreciate everything you and Uncle Jeb do for the kids."

"I know you do, honey, but believe me, it's nothing we don't want to do. In fact, while me and the kids were shopping for clothes, your Uncle Jeb was out buying blank tapes and a back-up battery so he can video tape the Easter program with no chance of missing a second of it."

We both chuckled as she deposited her purchases on the kitchen table. I was amazed at the change in our relationship since the kids had arrived here last summer. Aunt Wanda and I never had much to say to each other before; there was too much baggage, but in the past eight months some sort of camaraderie had developed between us without our realizing it. Had she changed—or had I? Would we have realized on our own there had never been a real rift between us, without the kids arriving and changing everything?

"How about some tea?" I asked. "I just made a fresh pitcher."

"That'd be great." She pulled out a chair and dropped into it. "I have such a good time shopping for those kids. It reminds me of when Violet was little," she added wistfully, brushing her hand across the multi-layered ruffles of the dress's skirt.

I gave her a smile before heading to the refrigerator. For the first time, I could understand how difficult it was for Aunt Wanda to lose the close contact she'd enjoyed with her only daughter.

Violet moved away in 1997 when Cliff, her husband of eighteen months, was transferred by the forestry service to the western part of the state near Fayetteville. Aunt Wanda was an absolute nightmare to be around for the entire three months leading up to the transfer, and pretty much for a couple of years afterwards. Even Uncle Jeb couldn't make her see reason. Cliff, who up to this point had been a relatively decent son-in-law as sons-in-law go, instantly became the Devil, incarnate. I wouldn't have traded places with him for all the tea in China. It was difficult enough just being her niece, her butcher, her drycleaner or even the new bagger at the A&P who set a dozen eggs on top of a loaf of bread. The eggs, of course, slid off the bread on the way home and cracked, and the bread was too smashed to fit into the toaster. What a scathing call the store manager received over that one!

I, on the other hand, felt the relief of a sixteen-year-old burden lift from my shoulders when Violet moved two hundred and fifty miles away. At times Violet had been my only friend, at other times, my nemesis. Ours was a love/hate relationship, the love more likely when Grandma and Aunt Wanda weren't around. In the clear sight of adulthood, I could see that Aunt Wanda had been threatened by any friendship between Violet and me. She had built her life on that little girl, while I was the tainted daughter of her wayward sister's dalliance with a worthless rogue. The influence she feared from me came instead from Cliff, whose name she still spoke with a sneer.

"I never realized how much I missed this," she said, stroking the dress fabric. I wasn't sure if she was talking to me or thinking out loud. "You don't I guess, I mean you don't realize what you've got till it's gone." She looked from the dress to me, her eyes misty. "I remember how you girls played around here when you were little. You made so much noise. This place was so quiet when it was just Violet, before you and Nicole got here. Oh, how it got on my nerves. Mom's too. She had no patience with kids. How she'd react to this." She chuckled. I couldn't tell if she was talking about the amount of money she'd spent on Emma's dress, or her and Jonah being here at all. "She always said Nicole was trouble with a capital "T." I guess she was right."

Question answered. I opened the cabinet door and took out two tall glasses that had been in the kitchen for as long as I had.

"Jeb and I enjoy those young 'uns so much," she continued. "They can be a handful sometimes, especially on those mornings we get 'em ready for preschool. But I do love it, Jeb, too. He always had a way with kids. You remember that, don't you, Michelle?"

I nodded as I poured the tea over ice.

"That's why I don't let myself get uptight the way I used to," she went on. "One of these days, we're going to wake up and they'll be gone, and I don't want to have the same regrets."

I wasn't sure if she was talking about Emma and Jonah growing up and moving away like Violet had done, or if she was referring to the inevitable day when Nicole would return. I didn't want to think about it either way.

"Have you given any thought about what you'll do?" she asked. "I mean I know you've gotten attached to the little buggers. A' body couldn't keep from it. If they could soften an old bird like me, nobody stands a chance."

I didn't want to talk about what I'd do when and if they left. The woman from Children's Services had called a couple weeks ago, "just to check on things" and she had alluded to the same thing. I didn't have an answer for her either.

"I never expected it to happen so completely, but I have gotten attached," I admitted to Aunt Wanda.

She studied me a moment and then asked, "So? What are you going to do about it?"

I knew exactly what she was asking, but I didn't have an answer. I really didn't want to think about what would happen when Nicole came back. Every time that little nagging voice started in the back of my head, I pushed it aside. I didn't like to stew over problems that hadn't materialized yet, especially when my fretting wouldn't do one bit of good.

I focused on my glass of tea and absently slid my fingers up and down the sides, leaving little tracks in the condensation. I shrugged. "I guess we'll cross that bridge when we come to it."

She shook her head sadly, "If it were only that simple. You've got to think about those kids, Michelle. How long's it been now, six months? Isn't that enough time to charge Nicole with abandonment? She's not coming back, and if she is, she's already proven to any court in this county that she's not fit to be those kids' mother. You need to talk to that welfare lady about doing something legal. If you don't, Nicole can waltz in here any time she wants and take them away. What happens the next time she decides she's tired of playing Mommy? Where will they be then? She might be ticked off at you for any number of reasons so maybe she'll turn them over to foster care, a drunken neighbor, or leave them on the doorstep of a church. We can't trust her to consider what's best for Emma and Jonah. She's incapable of doing that. You've got to do something, Michelle. You can't let her take them to God only knows where, where we might never see them again."

I suddenly had a pounding headache. And to think, this day had started out so well. "I know, I know, but this is really tricky. If I act in haste or do the wrong thing, I can do irreparable damage to the family."

"What a bunch of baloney. It sounds like a fancy way of saying you aren't going to do anything except dodge your responsibility. Nicole is not your concern anymore, Michelle. You need to think about Emma and Jonah. You're obligated to them. You do for family, that's all there is to it."

"Nicole *is* family," I reminded her.

She sniffed and took a sip of her tea and made a face. I'd put in too much sugar for her taste. "Nicole is a big girl. She can take care of herself. Emma and Jonah need you right now. It's the right thing to do, Michelle, and you know it; Christian charity. You don't have a choice."

"There's no sense worrying about it now, Aunt Wanda. Nicole isn't here yet. I haven't heard a word from her. It could be another year before she shows up. I'm not going to borrow trouble."

She sniffed again. "Well, somebody better because that girl will come back, and when she does, it's going to tear those two little kids apart. They need to know that things are taken care of, that they're not going to get ripped out of the only home they know."

"Technically, this isn't their home. Nicole has more leverage, as far as the courts are concerned, than I do. There's nothing I can do to keep her from her kids is she wants them back."

"If you believe that, you're either terribly naïve or just looking for an excuse not to keep them. Any judge in this county will find her unfit, especially after I take the stand. But if you don't want the responsibility, well, Jeb and me haven't changed our minds. We've discussed it quite a bit in the past six months, seein' how we don't know what your plans are. If you aren't going to fight for those kids, we will. I don't care how long or how much money it takes. They don't need to go back with Nicole. God in heaven knows she has no business taking care of a dog."

The glasses of tea sat forgotten before us. "I didn't say I didn't want the responsibility, Aunt Wanda. I just said I didn't see any point in worrying about it when Nicole isn't even here. I don't want the kids to leave. As far as I'm concerned, this is their home. But Nicole is still their mother. I know for a fact that the courts and social services do whatever they can to keep children with their biological parents."

"Well, not in this case. Nicole is unfit. You have turned your whole life upside down to accommodate those two kids; everybody sees that. It would give me peace of mind if you'd just talk to that woman from the welfare and find out what to expect when Nicole does show her face."

I puffed out my cheeks and released a defeated sigh. There was no arguing with Aunt Wanda once she got something into her head. I even agreed with her to a degree. But if I went to a lawyer that would mean I was thinking about it, and thinking about losing Emma and Jonah was something I didn't want to do.

Chapter Thirty

I f Aunt Wanda had intended to get me all upset over Nicole's inevitable return and how it would once again turn my well ordered life upside down, but in the opposite way that it had the first time, she succeeded. After she left that afternoon, I kept busy in the kitchen. Then I went outside for a few chores I'd avoided all winter; picking up sticks and carrying them to the burn pile, sweeping off the back porch, oiling the barn door. Emma and Jonah tore around the yard after Gypsy, who kept taking the sticks I threw onto the burn pile and running off with them. It was a game of hers. She only wanted to be chased. If I ignored her long enough and let her steal a few sticks, she'd eventually lose interest in the game and stop and leave me to finish my work in peace. But the kids fell right into her trap and gave chase until all three dropped from exhaustion.

By the time the yard was cleaned up, it was time to think about dinner. I set Emma and Jonah at the table with hot chocolate and marshmallows, sure to spoil their appetite, while I fixed macaroni and cheese and hotdogs. I opened a can of peas, knowing full well the kids would barely touch them, but at least something green had been provided in case anyone asked—like a judge who wanted to return them to their mother.

A judge; what was I thinking? I had no reason to impress a judge. Didn't I want Nicole to come back and get her kids? They belonged with their mother. I was the one who didn't like kids and had never wanted any. They were too much trouble. Didn't I remember all the aggravations everyone at work went through planning holidays, missing work for doctor appointments, or swinging extra money for braces? I didn't need all that in my life. I had Gypsy. It had been wonderful all those years coming home after a long day at work, falling into my chair, fixing what I wanted for dinner, no demands for my attention, no bickering, no struggling to get a preschooler into the bathtub.

If preschoolers were difficult, what did I think the next few years were going to be like? Starting school was when kids really began to cost money. New clothes, those outrageously overpriced name brand shoes, school supplies, field trips, extra curricular activities; the list went on and on—and money wasn't even the main issue.

What would I do when Jonah got into a fight at school, Emma came home crying because someone teased her or, God forbid, she got a boyfriend?

I wasn't up to this. I didn't need it. They weren't even my kids.

When had my life gotten so complicated?

Aunt Wanda was right; I had grown attached to them. I was used to having them around. I couldn't imagine the day they would leave, whether with their mother or when they joined the Navy; if they stayed that long. I was beyond simple attachment. I was in love. I didn't want them to go away. I wanted them to stay with me forever. They were mine now—yet, they weren't. They really didn't belong to me. No amount of wishing, praying, or providing them with a good home now would matter one way or the other when Nicole came back. Regardless of what Aunt Wanda thought she might say on the stand to sway a judge, they belonged to Nicole. If she could prove she was repentant for leaving them with me in the first place and that she'd turned her life around, she would probably win in court. Even if she didn't, was I up to a bloody fight with my own sister?

In bed that night I tossed and turned, and then slept fitfully, wishing the alarm would hurry up and ring already so this night would end. I stared at the ceiling and thought of all the changes that had occurred in the past few months. Not only did I have two little people depending on me for food, shelter, and everything else that came with parenthood, I attended a church semi-regularly for the first time in six years, Kyle was back in my thoughts, if not my life, and I had met many wonderful people. I tried to form a prayer in my head, but was so out of practice, I couldn't think of how to begin. If God was up there and knew everything about the situation like Kyle and the teachers at the preschool claimed, wasn't I wasting His time and mine anyway? He knew what was best for Emma and Jonah without me keeping him apprised of the situation. He knew I never wanted kids, yet my insides were all torn up over the thought of losing them.

"Go so sleep. Stop thinking about it," I told myself. *"Nicole hasn't even called. You can obsess over it after she comes back…if she ever does."*

But I kept thinking; borrowing trouble.

I managed to put it out of my mind enough to get through the next two days. It wasn't that difficult with Emma and Jonah talking about nothing but the Easter program. Jonah didn't seem the least bit concerned about singing in front of an audience, while Emma looked petrified every time he brought it up.

Aunt Wanda and Uncle Jeb picked us up in their minivan the night of the program, and drove us to the church. Uncle Jeb headed immediately to the sanctuary to stake out the perfect spot to set up the camcorder, while Aunt Wanda and I herded Emma and Jonah down the hall to the classrooms, where the teachers were getting everyone organized.

A father was videotaping as his wife struggled with a lopsided barrette in their daughter's hair. The little girl's eyes glistened with unshed tears. "Tonight's the big night, Jessica," Daddy said in a high-pitched voice designed to build excitement, "Our little girl's stage debut. Smile for the camera, baby—a big smile for Daddy now. Let me hear your memory verse again."

The little girl shook her chestnut head, barely holding the tears in check. The barrette slipped farther out of place. Mommy shot Daddy an evil look. "Troy, do you mind?"

"Smile into the camera, Jessica," Daddy said, ignoring Mommy's irritation. "Right here, Dumpling. Give Daddy a big smile and say 'Happy Easter'."

Jessica shook her head more adamantly this time and turned into her mother's arms, dislodging another barrette. "Troy, please, leave her alone. She'll calm down if you get that camera out of her face."

Troy clicked the off button and lowered the camera. "Well, excuse me for wanting to capture this moment in our daughter's life."

"You can capture it, darling, just not in this room." The mother looked up and saw me and Aunt Wanda standing within arms reach of her. She grabbed the little girl's arm and ushered her to a chair, away from us and far away from Daddy, to finish her job on Jessica's beautiful long hair. I was under the impression life with children would be easier with a responsible father figure in the picture. Apparently it didn't always work that way.

Aunt Wanda and I joined Uncle Jeb in the sanctuary, who had procured for himself an aisle seat on the very front row. The sanctuary steadily filled up around us. I spotted Barry entering the room with his ex-wife and an older man and woman I had never seen before, Caitlyn's grandparents I assumed. On which side of the family, I couldn't be certain. The man was tall and broad like Barry, but lacking the necessary red hair. I didn't want to let him know I was watching by looking too closely. I was almost embarrassed to see him. I had kind of strung him along: not returning his calls, and then asking him to dinner out of the blue, only to pretend later that he no longer existed. When had I become such a fickle person? When did I decide I would do anything to have a man in my life, including a man who didn't particularly appeal to me? He spotted me just as I turned away, and lifted a hand in a lackluster greeting. I waved back, feeling like a crumb. I kind of hoped he and Sue would get back together. She seemed to be on his arm at every preschool function lately. I took that as a good sign that they didn't hate the sight of each other. Maybe there was a chance for them. Good for him. Good for Caitlyn. Kids needed both their parents in the picture, ideally together and not biting one another's heads off.

Eventually the music started and the children filed in two-by-two up the center aisle. There were no bells this time. I leaned forward in my seat to see around Aunt Wanda. The instant I caught sight of the procession, my vision blurred with tears. An idiot grin spread across my face. After some confusion getting everyone situated on the stage risers, Miss Billie stepped to the mike and made her usual welcoming speech. I settled back into the padded pew to watch.

One preschooler is a hard thing to tame, a whole pack of them in one place, impossible! Their portion of the program was markedly brief: a prayer from one of the teachers, a few words from an older gentleman I'd seen at church a few times, telling us what a marvelous group of teachers we had caring for our children, a couple of memory verses, followed by three songs. Jonah's solo was first.

Aunt Wanda tensed, and my eyes misted over anew as he made his way to the center of the stage, looking dashing in his new blue suit. Miss Gail handed him a microphone, offered a smile of encouragement, and backed away where she would be out of the way, but available for moral support if he needed it. He didn't.

He kept his eyes on Miss Gail. Although he knew the piece by heart, he watched for her cue on the correct note of music. Then he opened his mouth and started to sing. My heart soared as his tiny voice resounded through the sanctuary. By the time he got to the second or third word, all signs of timidity and uncertainty had vanished. *"Your powerful love is shaping me, molding me, changing me into someone brand new. Your powerful love is shaping me, molding me. I'm brand new by Your powerful love."*

I didn't even notice the tears streaming down my cheeks until he repeated the opening.

That was it exactly. The power of his love, and Emma's, had changed me over the past eight months without me even realizing it. I was no longer the detached business professional married to her job, who found them under the lilac bushes. I was a mother who felt pride in their accomplishments and grief over their pain. Little things that had gone past without my notice suddenly had meaning because I shared them with someone other than Gypsy. I wasn't the aloof girl Kyle dated in high school. The people at work no longer asked me to work their weekends because they knew without asking what the answer would be. I wasn't alone in the world anymore. Someone needed me and I needed them right back. Nothing in my life was the same and I hadn't even seen it happening.

I wasn't the only one who'd changed. Emma and Jonah were different, too. They knew they were loved. They could sleep at night without fear of the unknown upon awakening. Emma was no longer afraid of her own shadow. She talked and smiled all the time. She didn't suck on her fingers. The confident, intelligent little man inside Jonah had blossomed.

Jonah sang the stanza again and then a little girl stepped up to the microphone beside him and started to sing. He looked out over the crowd while he waited and spotted us in the front row. He raised his tiny hand and wiggled his fingers, grinning. I grinned back and mouthed, "Good job." His grin broadened. Aunt Wanda nudged me in the ribs, beaming with pride.

I scanned the risers for Emma and gave her a big smile. While she didn't look as comfortable as her brother, she did manage a tremulous smile in return. My heart swelled with love. When had the scales tipped in their favor? When had I stopped seeing them as a curse and realize what a blessing they were to me? I didn't deserve their love. I was afraid of it, afraid of being hurt again. I didn't know how to love anyone. I held the world at a distance. Yet somehow my life had turned around when these two wonderful children entered it.

"*Why?*"

"*Why, God?*"

Tears of joy streamed down my cheeks. It took me a moment to realize I was praying.

The music built in crescendo and the rest of the children joined in the song. The crowd went wild. They were no longer proud parents, but the Body of Christ touched by the Lord's presence. Amen's rang out all around me. Hands lifted toward heaven, tears flowed freely. The children continued to sing.

My heart swelled with a praise I had never experienced before. It wasn't the children's love that had changed me, or even my love for them. How could I have been so blind? It was the power of God's love that had changed me from the woman I had been my entire adult life. For the first time, I felt free of judgment and condemnation. My Creator loved me, certainly not because I deserved it; I would never deserve it, but because He was a merciful God.

"*Forgive me, Lord,*" my spirit cried out, "*for ignoring you all these years. I know I'll never be good enough on my own, worthy enough for Your love. You blessed me when I didn't deserve it. It's the power of Your love that's changed me. You brought these two wonderful children into the life of a lonely miserable old aunt when she needed it most. They're here for a reason, to teach me of Your blessings. I want to serve You, Jesus, to live for You. Come into my heart and begin a new work in me. Start me over again, fresh and new."*

Without even realizing it, my hands lifted in praise along with half the congregation. The music faded and the crowd rose to their feet in applause. I joined in. As proud as I was of Jonah, it was the Lord I praised. He did love me. He accepted me, just the way I was. Nothing I could do would win His favor. He loved me just because He did.

Chapter Thirty-one

Aunt Wanda could tell something had happened to me—something far beyond the usual pride over the kids' performance. She pulled me against her. Tears streamed down her cheeks. I sank into her softness. A love I never knew I possessed for this woman came pouring out of me. At this moment I wanted to show everyone I knew how much I loved them. I almost wished Grandma were here so I could tell her how much I appreciated the sacrifices she made for Nicole and me. What would have become of us if Grandma hadn't taken us in? I had never even considered it before.

Aunt Wanda pressed a tissue into my hand as the last notes of the song died away. She reached up and brushed a tear from my cheek, we took our seats.

The program continued, and I listened with a new intensity. The preschoolers left the stage and were replaced by the Youth Choir. Each song seemed to have been chosen specifically for someone like me who wanted to praise the Lord but didn't have the words or means with which to articulate. Several more tissues were passed my way and I used every one. Uncle Jeb reached around Aunt Wanda and patted my knee. I squeezed his hand as fresh tears flowed down my cheeks. I felt like I wanted to wrap my arms around the whole world and hug it. Then I felt like a jerk for being so ridiculously sentimental.

After the choirs exited the stage, Kyle stepped behind the pulpit to thank everyone for coming.

"We often forget at this time of year, just how important our Savior's death on the cross was. It reconciles us to God; something that wouldn't have been possible had Jesus not been willing to sacrifice Himself for our sins. When I was a kid I didn't understand the significance of His sacrifice. I thought, "Well, wasn't that what He was supposed to do; the whole reason He was born?" I didn't understand that He was flesh just like us, yet He was willing to pay the ultimate price that we might live.

I listened earnestly. Why had I been fighting this so long? God did love me. He wasn't responsible for all my misinterpretations of faith. He wasn't responsible for Dad taking off, Mom leaving, and Grandma not loving me. The Christian charity I'd grown up with had nothing to do with true Christianity. Jesus never made anyone feel indebted to Him. True Christians who wanted to follow His example wouldn't either. They lived and behaved in a way that pleased Him; not to fulfill some distorted sense of Christian duty.

After their part in the program, the preschoolers had been taken to one of the classrooms to wait. Kyle dismissed the assembly with prayer and Emma and Jonah ran up to us waving treats. They were so full of energy and excitement over the program, they barely acknowledged our compliments on their performance. I took my camera from my bag and took some pictures and then posed for a few. I kept an eye out for Kyle. As excited as I was over the kids' performance, I couldn't wait to tell him I had accepted Christ. For the first time since seeing him again after all these years, I didn't think of him in a romantic sense; I just wanted him to know I finally understood what he'd been talking about a few months ago when I spent the afternoon in his office, the day of our kiss. It didn't matter how handsome he was, how I wished things could have worked out differently between us, or that I regretted all those wasted years. I just wanted him to know I understood. I had finally accepted into my cold stone heart that God loved me, and always had.

We headed to the fellowship hall for refreshments like always after a church function. I'd never seen a group of people who would use any excuse to eat cake. I could barely contain my excitement. I knew I was glowing. Everyone around me probably attributed it to maternal pride. Of course I was proud. Even people I didn't know stopped us along the way, bending at the waist to congratulate Jonah and Emma. Emma shrank against me, unnerved by the attention. Jonah wanted to hurry up and break away from our group so he could play with his friends.

I offered to stand in the cake line for Aunt Wanda and Uncle Jeb while they claimed some chairs at the tables set up for us. Personally, I was too excited to think about cake. I smiled greetings to parents and spoke to a few as I made my way though the crowd to the front of the room.

Just as I got into line, someone grabbed my elbow and spun me around. It was Angie. She pulled me into an embrace. "Michelle, you must be so proud," she said after releasing me. "Jonah did wonderful." She put her hand to her chest. "Oh, his little voice just touched me so much. I was bawling my eyes out."

"Me too," I managed before she went on.

"Chris got a bunch of pictures, so I'll make sure you get copies. Emma did wonderful too. She looked like such a doll baby. She has really come a long way, you know. I know you are so proud of them both."

Finally she stopped talking long enough for me to do more than smile. "I am proud of them, but I have something else to tell you."

Angie's eyes widened in anticipation and suddenly I felt a little embarrassed. What if no one else thought it was a big deal? Or worse, what if I did it wrong and God hadn't accepted me like I thought or I hadn't gone through the proper channels? What if there was more I needed to do before I was worthy enough to go before the Lord? What if I had fallen too far; spent too many years scoffing at Christianity? *"No, none of that matters,"* I chided myself. I knew in my heart what happened to me and no one could take it from me!

I took Angie's hand. "I accepted Jesus as my Savior tonight." I blinked away tears. "He saved me, Angie!"

She gasped and tears sprang to her eyes, "Oh, praise God," she nearly shouted. I looked around, afraid someone had heard her. Angie apparently didn't care who did. She threw her arms around me and squeezed me to her just like Aunt Wanda had done. "Oh, sweetheart, how wonderful. I'm so happy for you."

"Thank you. So am I."

She hugged me again and then let go. "Michelle, this is what the whole resurrection story is about; death to the old fleshy ways isn't an end, it's a beautiful beginning. After we die to the flesh and are born again spiritually, we have the promise of reigning forever with our Father in heaven."

I nodded. I understood the semantics. It was the getting it through to my heart that had taken so long—too long.

"Oh, my goodness, there's Kyle." Angie grabbed my elbow and spun me around again. Aunt Wanda and Uncle Jeb were never going to get their cake and punch. I stiffened, no longer sure I wanted to tell Kyle right now, especially in front of Angie, but she was hard to deter.

"Pastor, Pastor," Angie called out, dragging me along behind her. Kyle turned and we came to a stop in front of him. "Praise the Lord, Pastor, our sister accepted the Lord tonight during the service. Isn't that wonderful!"

Kyle turned his gaze to me. I blushed under his smile. "Well, glory to God." He grabbed my shoulders and pulled me into a rough hug. "That's so exciting. I'm so happy for you, Michelle."

I didn't know exactly how to respond. This church was nothing like the one I'd attended with Grandma Catherine. I hoped he wasn't going to make me testify or something in front of all these people enjoying their cake. "Um, thanks."

"Praise the Lord!" He turned to whoever was within earshot and relayed the news. I was instantly surrounded by smiling, crying brothers and sisters in Christ who wanted to hug me and welcome me into the fold. I found myself crying all over again. No one asked for my testimony.

After the others cleared out, only Kyle and I remained. Even Angie had conveniently drifted away. "How exactly did it happen?"

My eyes misted over. "It was during Jonah's solo when he sang about God's love shaping him and molding him. My brain kept telling me it was Jonah and Emma's love that had changed me. It's true, I'm not the same person I was when they first came, but suddenly it hit me, it wasn't them. It was God. His love had changed me. Maybe He used Emma and Jonah coming into my life to get my attention, but He's the one changing me every day."

Kyle grinned. "I am happy for you, Michelle," he said sincerely. "I could see the Lord working in your life from that first day you came to the preschool."

"Looking back, I guess I can too. I'm glad He was patient with me."

"He's patient with all of us, and it's a good thing. I don't want to overwhelm you right off the bat, but I'd really like to see you start in our New Converts Class. You may be interested in spending some time with the Ladies' Ministry, too. You will find some wonderful godly mentors there, women like Angie, who've been where you are now."

I nodded, still smiling. I imagined I'd be smiling for a long time. "That would be great. I'd appreciate it."

"This Sunday's Easter, so we have our early morning service. Maybe Sunday afternoon I could squeeze in a brief counseling session for you. You're welcome to bring the children along."

"That'd be great, but if you're too busy with the extra services and everything I'm sure I could talk to Angie."

"Whatever makes you comfortable." He pulled me into his arms for a final brotherly, pastoral hug. "This is wonderful news, Sister Hurley."

My smile widened. *"Sister Hurley, my new identity."*

Chapter Thirty-two

The kids and I colored eggs Saturday evening, loaded them into two empty ice cream buckets, and carried them across the field to show Aunt Wanda and Uncle Jeb. Earlier in the week I'd bought baskets and filled them with every chocolate, candy-coated, marshmallow confection they carried at the Geneva Wal-Mart. I wrapped the final products in clear plastic gift-wrap and hid them in the mudroom. I'd bring them out after church so Emma and Jonah's minds would be on Sunday School and not the Easter bunny.

There was an Easter egg hunt on the grounds outside the church after service. Even Uncle Dewitt, dressed in his circa 1970's coat and tie, joined Aunt Wanda, Uncle Jeb and us at the church. Neither Aunt Wanda nor Uncle Jeb had said anything, but I think they were seriously considering changing churches. They'd been attending the same church since the day they married, but now it seemed only right that the whole family attend church together. Years ago I would have done anything to remove myself from family and tradition, but my way of thinking had changed drastically in the last eight months.

Another wonderful thing I hadn't noticed in church services past was the Easter message. It didn't even matter that Kyle looked beyond handsome in his immaculate blue suit. I leaned forward and listened intently to the message. His face was intent, his voice resonating through the packed sanctuary. As he delivered the sermon, I fumbled through the Bible in search of passages I hadn't read in years. My heart swelled with peace and gratitude toward God for allowing me to be here as His servant brought forth the Word. What a merciful God I served that He had given me another chance to hear and accept His Son. My only regret was that it had taken so long to hear and understand what Jesus had said and what He had died for.

Dinner was at Aunt Wanda's following church. Like every year, she went overboard on the ham and fixings. Instead of her usual desserts, she bought one of those grocery store cakes shaped like a rabbit covered with white frosting and coconut. We ate until we could barely move and then went outside to hide eggs in the tall grass.

Uncle DeWitt, always a man of few words, sat on the porch and watched the proceedings. Jonah went to him to show off his full basket. I wasn't close enough to hear the exchange, but Jonah was explaining something with great intensity and Uncle DeWitt actually seemed to be paying attention. Then much to my amazement, Jonah climbed into his lap to continue the conversation. Uncle DeWitt draped an arm over the little boy's shoulders and kept nodding and smiling. He must have sensed me watching because he looked up and winked. I smiled back and turned away, a strange knot in my stomach.

The words from the song Jonah sang the other night at the program filled my head. *"Your powerful love has changed me into someone brand new."*

Love had changed me all right. I was a totally different person than before God sent those two kids into my life. My life suddenly had meaning. It was still important to me to be needed, and suddenly I was. I was in love with two wonderful little people and I was a child of the King.

How could things get any better?

"Whose car is that?"

Just as the question was out of Jonah's mouth, Gypsy noticed the strange vehicle parked in the driveway between the house and the fencerow we were approaching. She lunged forward, her deep-throated, don't-mess-with-me barks shattering the afternoon stillness. Emma reached out and took my hand. Jonah ran on ahead after Gypsy, the basket of eggs he'd gathered at Aunt Wanda's swinging precariously in his left hand.

"Gypsy, no!" I shouted. She was full of bravado. I didn't think she'd ever bite anyone, but I wished she didn't have to act so fierce every time she saw someone she didn't immediately recognize. "Jonah, wait up." I tried to get a better view of the car on the other side of the fence, but could only make out a blue, older model vehicle. Who would be visiting on Easter Sunday? The only family I had living locally was back at Aunt Wanda's. It was probably someone from church. I envisioned Gypsy jumping up on a dear sweet sister who had come all this way to invite me to a Ladies' Meeting, only to have her new Easter dress ruined with dirty paw prints.

I picked up my pace, wordlessly urging Emma forward. "Gypsy, stop. You come here right now. One of these days I'm going to wring that dog's neck," I added, smiling down at Emma. Jonah had already reached the gate that separated the field from the yard and was climbing over; always climbing over something. It was a miracle he'd never fallen on his head and broken something important.

Gypsy slithered through the slats in the gate and disappeared. Jonah balanced at the top. He held on with one hand and clutched his Easter basket in the other. I could see he was making a decision. The Easter basket was slowing him down. He swung one leg up and over the gate, but couldn't quite get the other leg over without holding on with both hands.

My heart leaped into my throat. "Jonah, stop!" I shouted. "Wait for us. I'll open the gate."

It was then he decided he wanted over the gate more than the Easter basket full of eggs and candy. He let go of the basket, watched it fall to the ground, swung his other leg over the gate, and climbed down far enough to jump the rest of the way to the ground. He picked himself up, brushed his hands on his pants, gathered a few things back into the partially spilled basket, and took off toward the house.

I shook my head at the futility of trying to keep the boy in one piece. When Emma and I reached the gate, I lifted the latch to open it wide enough for us to squeeze through. I went first and turned to wait for Emma, who didn't want to get rust from the gate on her clothes, when Jonah's voice rang out.

"Mommy!"

Emma and I froze. She turned her little face up to me and I stared down at her for a fraction of a second. Then her face lit up and she tore around me and disappeared after her brother. She no longer cared about what the rusty gate might do to her clothes. My heart plummeted to my feet. Not Nicole. Not today. I wasn't ready. *"Please, God, don't let it be Nicole,"* but I knew it was her. Jonah wouldn't have made that mistake, even after all this time.

This doesn't have to be a bad thing, I told myself. Wasn't this what I wanted—my family together again, my sister finally accepting her responsibilities like a mature adult, my life back?

I carefully replaced the latch to keep the gate from swinging open where it would inevitably catch on a rut in the ground, making it impossible to swing shut again without the help of three men and a mule. I took a deep steadying breath. I adjusted my blouse on my shoulders, smoothed my hands through my hair, and turned toward the house. After a few steps forward I could see what Jonah saw. Gypsy was running around the car, still barking, but no longer threatening. She loved everyone, even ratty sisters and their loser boyfriends. Nicole was squatted on the ground next to the car, Emma and Jonah locked in her arms. There was no mistaking the rapture on all three of their faces. A rough looking character about my age, wearing faded jeans and an old tee shirt, stood next to the driver's side door. His arms rested on the roof of the car while he watched the reunion. His face was a study in complete disinterest. Was this the infamous Dean I'd heard so much about? So far, neither the kids nor Nicole had acknowledged him.

Nicole saw my approach and disentangled herself from the kids. She straightened up to her full height. She was still several inches shorter than me. "Michelle."

"Hey," I said, trying to sound as detached as the man watching us, "Long time no see."

Nicole ducked her head in polite embarrassment and rested each hand on top of the kids' heads. "Yeah, I guess it has been." To avoid offering anything that resembled an explanation or apology, she squatted before Emma and Jonah again and put her arms around them. "I've missed you guys so much. Look how big you are. I can't believe you grew up so much on me."

They beamed under her praise. I resisted the urge to remind her that kids do tend to grow in eight months time. Gypsy stopped circling the car and sniffed at the man's feet. He looked down at her but didn't move. I always heard dogs were excellent judges of character. I wondered if he had heard that too, and expected her to attack at any minute.

I took my eyes off the man I supposed was Dean to look at my sister. She looked like she'd lost weight, but I couldn't be sure from the way she was holding Emma and Jonah against her. She had always been willow thin. Now I noticed the bags under her eyes. Her long brown hair hung loose and unkempt around her shoulders. Her high cheekbones and narrow chin were pronounced, but she was still pretty. It had been so long since I'd seen her I was amazed at how I could see both of the kids in her face. For some reason, it made me envious. I wanted her to get back in her car and go away. These two little kids who looked nothing like me belonged here.

She took Emma and Jonah's hands in hers and stood up.

Jonah gazed adoringly up at her. "I sang in church the other night, Mommy, all by myself."

Nicole gasped. "You did? Oh, Jonah, how exciting. I'm so proud of you."

Jonah grinned proudly. *"Don't tell her, Jonah,"* I silently begged, possessiveness getting the better of me. I wanted to snatch his hand away and lead him into the house. *"She doesn't deserve to know one thing about you and Emma. Don't tell her about the Easter program. If she wanted to be involved in your lives so badly, she wouldn't have left you here in the first place. You're too good for her."*

"I had my birthday party at Chuck E. Cheese's," Emma piped up.

"You did? How fun!"

What I wouldn't give to smack her. She'd had plenty of birthdays for which to throw cool parties, but she never did. It was all me. Me! I glared at her hands on my children, and resisted the urge to slap them away. Why was she here? What did she want? Aunt Wanda's words had proven prophetic. Just when I got them straightened up, Nicole waltzes in and messes everything up.

No, this was how things were supposed to work. Children belonged with their mother. I was here when they needed me, and now my job was done. I could go back to my life and they could go back to theirs. I should be relieved. I could smell my own freedom.

"Let's all go in the house," I said cheerfully, my tone amazing me. "I've got some lemonade and ice tea," I added, looking at the man leaning on the car.

The corners of his mouth twitched as though trying to smile for the first time in his life. It was plain to see he didn't want to be here. He heaved a sigh, removed his arms from atop the car's roof, and trudged after us to the house. The kids led Nicole ahead of us, chattering like magpies. Had they forgiven her already? They hadn't even asked where she'd been. Of course they probably knew how this game was played. They didn't ask and she didn't offer information. It's easier on everybody that way. They still hadn't acknowledged Dean, if that's who he was. I was sure they hadn't purposely excluded him. They were too young for such behavior; they were just too excited over Nicole's appearance to notice anyone else, even me.

I had turned down Aunt Wanda's offer of leftovers after Easter dinner, so I didn't have much in the kitchen to offer our guests. "Are you hungry?" I asked nevertheless. I went to the freezer and pulled open the door. "I can pop a pizza in the oven, or if you want to wait, I can cook something."

Nicole shook her head and continued to gaze lovingly at the kids. "No, thanks, we're fine. We ate on the way, right, Dean?"

He gave a stiff nod and sank uninvited into a kitchen chair. I wanted to hate him after everything he'd done. I didn't believe my sister would walk out on her kids for eight months without someone like him influencing her, but that was the old me. The new me would show him charitable kindness even though he didn't deserve it. I walked over and stuck out my hand. "I've heard a lot about you, Dean. I'm Michelle."

He took my offered hand only because he had no other choice and gave it a half-hearted shake. "Hmm," he mumbled.

"Oh, my, where are my manners?" Nicole tittered. "I always forget introductions."

"Don't worry about it," I said, amazed at my diplomacy. "Well then, if you're not hungry, I'll pop a casserole in the oven in a few hours. The kids and I had dinner at Aunt Wanda's so we won't be hungry for awhile."

Nicole pulled her face into mock surprise. "You? Pop something in the oven? Michelle, what's happened to you? You don't cook."

"Oh, I don't know." I looked pointedly at Jonah and Emma. "A lot of things have changed around here, I guess."

My sarcasm was lost on Nicole. She looked at Dean and laughed. "My sister could never boil water," she explained. "Grandma Catherine went to her grave lamenting Michelle's inadequacies in the kitchen."

"It wasn't that I couldn't cook. I just never wanted to. I was too busy getting an education and a job." I immediately bit my tongue. Why did I let her pull me in so easily? Hadn't I learned anything over the years?

Nicole rolled her eyes. "Well, that didn't take long." She directed her comment to Dean, whose focus was on Gypsy still sniffing at his feet. "I'm not in the door five minutes and she reminds me how she's the perfect one, always trying to improve herself, while I'm the slacker."

"You started it," I said and again regretted my words the instant they were out of my mouth. The last thing I wanted to do was let her draw me into a disagreement in front of Dean and the kids that made her look like the victim and me the cold, unfeeling tyrant. I'd been down that road before.

She continued her one-sided conversation with Dean as if I hadn't spoken. "My sister, Michelle has never made a mistake in her life. The rest of us can never measure up to her." She put her hand on her hip and glanced over her shoulder at me before looking back at him. "I was always the screw up in the family, just ask Michelle. She had everything together while I made one mistake after another."

I glanced anxiously at the children, who had grown quiet and pensive. I forced a smile and said; "Really, Nicole, Dean doesn't want to hear about our dysfunctional family. Emma, Jonah, where are the pictures you made in Sunday School this morning? I bet Mommy would love to see them."

Their faces lit up. "Okay." They took off through the living room door to the stairs. As soon as I heard their footsteps thundering up the stairs, I turned to Nicole and set my hands on my hips. "Why do you have to do that? Start something in front of the kids? Don't you think they've been through enough?"

Nicole rolled her eyes yet again. "Oh, yes, Michelle, you're right, as usual. You know what's best for *my* children. You know what's best for everyone."

Now was not the time to lose my temper. I didn't want this to turn into a shouting match I simply wanted her to see what was so obvious to anyone in possession of a few functioning brain cells. "I'm not trying to say that, Nicole. I just don't think it's a good idea for them to hear us bickering. It's the first time they've seen you in eight months. I'd like it to be a nice afternoon."

"So would I, Michelle. You just know how to push my buttons. Don't pretend you don't do it on purpose."

"I'm not pushing your buttons. The kids and I were having a wonderful afternoon until you showed up out of the blue and started in on me."

"Oh, of course it's my fault your afternoon is spoiled. But I wanted to see my kids, or don't I have the right to do that anymore?"

The muscles tightened in the back of my neck. I couldn't believe she was actually miffed about her parental rights after months with no contact whatsoever. There was so much I wanted to tell her, so much I wanted to ask: like, who did she think she was walking into my house after all this time and accusing me of trying to make her look bad? Where had she been all this time? What was she doing here? How long did she plan to stay? Was she taking the kids with her when she left?

Instead of answering I watched Gypsy tire of sniffing Dean's boots and flop down on the floor at his feet. She sighed and rested her chin on her paws. Had she decided he was not a threat and she could let down her guard or did she realize he wasn't going anywhere and she may as well accept it?

The kids charged back into the kitchen and went straight to Nicole. She dutifully took the Sunday School pictures offered her and squealed approvingly. When she turned Emma's over, the smile froze on her face. With a sinking heart I remembered what Emma had written on the back of her paper. She had just learned that by stringing letters together, she made words, and then sentences. She could write every letter of the alphabet now. Her new thing was asking whoever was around how to spell whatever message she wished to convey.

I could imagine her in Sunday School this morning, her lips pursed in concentration as she wrote each letter the teacher told her to complete her message. In oversized, lopsided script that ran to the edge of the page and down one side, were the words; *I love Aunt Michelle.* Nicole's knuckles whitened on the paper. She stood up abruptly and glared at me as if I intentionally insulted her. While Jonah and Emma were stung by her rebuff, they had no idea what caused the sudden shift in tension.

I couldn't take much more of this. I hated seeing the confusion and helplessness on Jonah and Emma's faces. It had taken months of living here to lose those looks, especially for Emma. I wanted to scream at Nicole to open her eyes, to look at what she was doing. She was upsetting everyone. We were all happy to see her, if she was here for the right reasons. If she had actually learned something in the last eight months, gotten her life straightened out and was ready to be a responsible parent to these two kids, then we were thrilled she was back. But if she was only here to upset the fine balance we'd struck, she could get on down the road this minute.

Of course I couldn't say any of that. I would have to surreptitiously figure out what was going on in her head; I couldn't come right out and ask. Even if I had the nerve, I was almost afraid to hear her answer.

I would be patient with Nicole, patient and compassionate—like I wanted people to be with me. My flesh wouldn't rule my actions. No matter what my mouth wanted to shout at her, I would behave like Christ. *"Lord, help me control my tongue. Let me put the needs of the kids first and also those of my sister. She needs You in her life, Lord. Give me the words to say to her; words that won't offend her."*

The quick prayer offered no comfort. I may as well have been praying to the ceiling. If only Kyle or Angie were here. They would know the right way to ask Nicole what we all wanted to know lovingly and without guile. They would understand her pain. They could explain in words that she understood that God loved her and wanted to reach out to her right where she was. All I wanted to do was wring her skinny neck for all the trouble she'd caused everyone.

Nicole still clutched the Sunday School paper in her hands. Her jaw worked back and forth in an attempt to control her anger. Maybe she was thinking up the perfect slur to throw at me about how I stole her child's affections or something ridiculous like that.

I had to diffuse the situation before she upset the children anymore than she already had. "Nicole, would you like to see the kids' rooms? Jonah has your old room and Emma is in mine. We painted and changed the linens. It looks totally different upstairs from what you remember. You are spending the night, aren't you? We can put Emma and Jonah in one room and you and Dean can have the other."

I was rambling, but couldn't make myself stop. I also realized putting two unmarried people in the same room was something Kyle or Angie would never do. However, I was desperate to make her happy and get those cold angry eyes off me.

Jonah grabbed her hand. "Yeah, come see, Mommy; we painted my room yellow and blue. Emma's is pink and green. Aunt Shell let us help. Uncle Jeb painted Violet's old toy box and let me have it. It's big enough to climb in if I take most of the toys out. Gypsy and me hide in there from Emma sometimes, but Gypsy's so big I can't close the lid, that's okay though, 'cause I'm kinda scared to close the lid all the way."

With Jonah prying at her hands and talking a mile a minute, Nicole had no choice but to look away from me. "All right, all right, Jonah," she said impatiently. "Would you let me think for a minute?" She made a visible attempt to quell her irritation. "What do you think, Dean? Would you mind staying here? I hate the thought of staying in a motel when my kids are here."

Dean shrugged and a glance passed between them. A glance that said they'd discussed it already in the car on the way over and had every intention of staying with us.

I clasped my hands in front of me. "Then it's settled. You two go on upstairs and enjoy your tour and I'll lay out something to thaw for dinner."

Nicole gave me another glance before allowing the kids to turn her around and lead her from the room. Dean wearily pulled his legs in and rose from the table to follow them. I headed for the mudroom and the deep freeze, and tried to squelch the dread rising up in me. Surely this was God's plan. Nicole needed her kids back. I was ready to resume my old life. How peaceful it would be to come straight home from work, without swinging by the preschool first to pick up the kids, and then planning dinner in my head while they chattered incessantly about their day. My weekends would be mine to do with as I pleased. I could start saving money again and working some overtime. Maybe not as much as the old days, just whenever it suited me. If I'd learned anything in the last few months, it was there was more to life than work.

I thought of Kyle; handsome, single, available, unless he considered himself married to God. Was there a chance of something developing between us? Now we'd have all the time in the world to pursue a relationship if that's where it was headed. Not that I had any idea of how his brain was working. He said he'd know if and when God sent him the right person. He was still a pastor, whether I was born again now or not. Marrying a pastor would have to be the second worst position to be in, the first being the pastor himself.

Marriage! Good grief. Where had that come from? I was staring down the barrel of getting my old life back for the first time in eight months and my mind was suggesting marriage—to Kyle. I definitely needed to get hold of myself!

Freedom, I opened the freezer and let a sigh escape my lips. What a beautiful word. Buried under the frozen pizzas, chicken nuggets, and fish sticks I found a pack of chicken breasts. Yes, if Nicole took the kids, she could take all this junk food with her. I wouldn't need it anymore. I lowered the lid and headed back into the kitchen, trying to ignore the heaviness that had settled into my chest.

ꙮChapter Thirty-three

"A unt Shell."

I was instantly awake. I hadn't heard that in the middle of the night from either of the kids in months. They had outgrown many of their childish mannerisms in the eight months they'd been here. Now I worried that Nicole's presence would bring all of them back. I opened my eyes and saw Emma's face just inches from mine. She'd given up her worn "blankie" months ago too, yet there she was, clutching it against one cheek. She rested her free hand on my bare arm. I propped myself up on one elbow and rubbed my face. "What's the matter?" I mumbled through my sleep-fogged brain.

"I can't sleep."

"Okay." I slid over to make room. She scrambled up beside me, immediately turning away and curling into the curve of my body. She hadn't got into bed with me in ages; it was a habit I tried to discourage. But I figured I knew what was keeping her awake. "Did you have a bad dream?" I asked the back of her head.

In the pale moonlight coming through the window, I saw her shake her blonde head no. "You just couldn't sleep, huh?"

She nodded. I put an arm around her middle and snuggled against her. I lowered my head back on the pillow and breathed in the scent of her freshly shampooed hair. The springs creaked down at the foot of the bed as Gypsy's weight settled against my feet. "Gypsy, is that you?" I asked gruffly.

Emma giggled. Within minutes, all three of us were asleep.

Hours later, it took a moment to remember why my bed was so crowded and I was in so much pain. During the night, Emma had worked herself down to the center of the bed and Gypsy had maneuvered her way up so that they met right in the spot where I usually slept. A bony knee jabbed my lower back and the blankets had been pulled off my lower legs. I disentangled myself from a web of twisted sheets, arms, and dog parts, and slid out of bed. I put my hand on the small of my back and twisted to work out the kinks. Gypsy raised her head off the bed to look at me, clearly annoyed that my bones and joints made so much noise popping back into place.

There was no point in trying to get back to sleep. It was nearly five, almost time for the alarm to go off anyway. "Dogs don't belong on the furniture," I hissed at her in Grandma Catherine's voice. She responded by stretching out on her side next to Emma. Emma reached out in her sleep and put her arm over Gypsy and snuggled against the dog's broad back. She looked like an angel lying there, a tangle of blonde hair across her face, her jaw relaxed and lips slightly parted.

I checked on Jonah on my way to the bathroom. He was sound asleep in what used to be my room, recently renovated per Emma's preferences, unaware he had slept on the double bed the last few hours without his sister. The two of them spent the night there last night while Nicole and Dean occupied Nicole's old room. After straightening the covers and kissing Jonah's downy cheek, I went to the bathroom for my morning ritual.

The night before had gone relatively well, considering. After a dinner of oven-fried chicken and rice pilaf, we spent the evening in front of the TV watching the kids' favorite videos. Nicole popped popcorn and had the kids laughing and carrying on about every little thing. Dean sat apart from the rest of us, still detached but warming up as the evening wore on. Jonah sat on his lap a few times and Emma showed him some of her books from the bookshelf. I spent the evening quietly in my chair, a part, but not obtrusive. Maybe that was the balance Dean was shooting for.

I finished in the bathroom and then went down the back stairs to the kitchen. I hit the button on the coffee pot and sat down on a kitchen chair. I opened the novel I had been reading for the past week and a half. It was due to go back to the library in a day or two, and I was only halfway through it. Though I loved to read, I never found the time, now more than ever. With Nicole and her sudden appearance on my mind, I couldn't even remember what struggle my heroine was facing.

"I thought I smelled coffee." Nicole stood uncertainly in the doorway. She was still dressed in the baggy tee shirt and cotton shorts she had slept in. Her hair had been hastily combed but not much else by way of making herself presentable. Regardless, she looked rested and pretty. Go figure. "Got enough for two?"

"More than enough," I replaced my bookmark and closed the book.

"What are you reading?" she asked, approaching the table.

I slid the book across the table to her. I knew she didn't really care. Nicole hadn't read a book of her own volition in her entire life. She was just trying to make conversation to keep me from asking questions she might not want to answer.

She glanced at the cover and nodded thoughtfully, as she'd been meaning to read it as soon as she got the chance. Then she lowered herself into a chair. "I checked on the kids on my way downstairs. Jonah was alone in the bed. It took me awhile to find Emma." Her voice took on an accusing tone.

She was hurt that Emma chose my bed instead of hers. "She came in and got in my bed during the night," I said.

She sniffed. "I never thought it was a good idea to let kids get in the habit of switching beds during the night."

She had to be kidding. "Yesterday was a stressful day," I pointed out. "She couldn't sleep."

"I don't understand why it would be stressful," she said, wounded. "I would have thought it was the best day of their lives; seeing me after all this time."

"Nicole, they're little kids. You scared them half to death. You disappear for eight months and then breeze back in here like nothing's out of the ordinary. They don't have any idea what's going on."

Nicole exhaled and looked away, like I was the most obtuse person she'd ever come across. "Michelle, I did them a favor by leaving them here for eight months. I couldn't take care of them properly at the time. I'm the adult and I made the tough decisions. I did what I had to do...for their sakes."

I resisted the urge to grab her by the throat and give her a good, hearty shake. "You could've explained it to them first. Even if they had hollered and begged you not to go, at least they would've known you were coming back."

"I handled it the best way I knew how."

By taking the path of least resistance, I thought.

The coffee maker was sputtering and hissing, its ancient mechanism going through the motion of making coffee. I got up and took two mugs from the cupboard. I filled the mugs and replaced the pot under the drip. I took the milk out of the refrigerator and added a splash to my cup. I set the jug on the table next to Nicole. I couldn't remember how she took her coffee.

I sat down and took a cautious sip of the hot brew. "We are glad to see you, to know that you're all right. I just can't help but wonder what you've got on your mind. I'm sure Emma does too. That's why she couldn't sleep."

Nicole added milk to her coffee and let out a belabored sigh. "I wish everyone didn't feel the need to analyze everything I do and second guess me all the time. Maybe I miss my kids. Did you or Emma ever think of that? Maybe I miss my sister. Maybe I just wanted to come home."

Her voice cracked appropriately on the word "home."

I bit my tongue and took a deep breath. Speaking my mind would only make Nicole resentful and accomplish nothing. "I'm sure you miss the kids," I said instead. They miss you too."

"Well, you sure couldn't prove it by me," she said, puffing out her lower lip. A tear glistened in the corner of her eye. "Emma didn't even come to me when she couldn't sleep. How do you think that makes me feel, Michelle? I'm her mother." Again, her voice cracked in all the right places.

With great effort, I kept the condemnation out of my voice. "You should be more concerned about how they feel, Nicole. You are practically a stranger to them. Eight months is an incredibly long time in the life of a five-year-old. They've both had birthdays since the last time they saw you. Emma's reading. Jonah's turned into a little performer. They've grown up a lot and you haven't been here."

Nicole slapped the table, rattling our cups. "See? I knew you were blaming me. I knew you couldn't understand. You're so perfect."

"I've been here, Nicole, raising your kids. Just look at how they've blossomed with me."

"Well, not all of us are as put together as you are, Michelle. Some of us are mere mortals who sometimes need a little time to get our lives worked out."

My patience was wearing thin, especially since I was somehow at fault for behaving like a responsible adult. "Come off it, Nicole. No one expects you to be perfect, but when you choose to bring two complete people into the world, you have to put your own needs aside for theirs. The world is no longer about you; it's about them. It's all about them. You need to stop worrying about all the crap going on in your own life and consider how your actions affect them."

"You know so much about what you're talking about," she retorted scathingly.

"I've never had children of my own, if that's what you're getting at," I snapped. "I've just had other people's children thrust upon me."

"Michelle, I needed you. I didn't think you'd hold it over my head for the rest of my life."

"I wasn't talking about you," I said.

I forced myself to stop shaking. I was losing control, something one shouldn't do when talking with Nicole. I took another sip of the coffee and sent a quick prayer heavenward before I spoke again. "I was talking about Mom and Dad."

"Oh, here we go again."

I ignored her sarcasm. "I was fourteen when I started raising you. Grandma made it plain she wasn't going to do it. I couldn't participate in anything after school or have a boyfriend because I had to come straight home to take care of you."

"You never had a boyfriend because you acted snotty and had no clue about how to have fun. Men don't like an ice princess, Sister. Yes, you came straight home from school every day—but you loved it. You loved playing the martyr. You could blame it all on me and your evil grandmother that you were cold, distant, and incapable of loving anyone even if you wanted to. We were your perfect alibi."

"Aunt Shell?"

Our heads snapped in the direction of the voice.

Jonah stood in the doorway, rubbing the sleep from his eyes. "Why's everybody yelling?"

Remorse washed over me. What kind of a witness was I creating for my lost sister? I could just imagine her snide comments about hypocrites who preached one thing and lived another when she found out I had become a Christian in her absence. "We're sorry, honey," I said. "We didn't mean to wake you up."

Nicole jumped up from the table and scooped him into her arms. "It's all right, darling, Mommy's here." She gave me a dark look over the top of his head. "Come on, I'll take you back to bed."

After they left the room, I put my elbows on the table and rested my chin in my hands. That went well. Why couldn't I learn to hold my tongue? What a mess everything was. Aunt Wanda was going to throw a fit when she found out Nicole was back. I never had gotten around to talking to a lawyer—too late for that now. I drained my coffee cup and set it in the sink. I'd have to hurry if I was going to get to work on time. I still had no idea what Nicole wanted by being here.

Chapter Thirty-four

I needed to let them know at the preschool that the kids wouldn't be coming in today. Then I had to call Angie and tell her not to pick them up there at four o'clock like she ordinarily did on my long workdays.

Last night I had suggested to Nicole that Emma and Jonah go to preschool as usual while I was at work. She wouldn't hear of it. "I'm here now," she'd said. "There's no point in having strangers baby-sit them when their own mother is sitting at home."

I didn't bother to tell her the teachers were neither strangers nor babysitters. But I didn't plan for a minute to leave her and Dean here alone with them while I worked a twelve-hour shift twenty miles away. After calling the preschool, my next call would be to Aunt Wanda. It wouldn't be a problem at all to have her and Uncle Jeb spend the day here at the house keeping an eye on Nicole. I knew they'd move heaven and earth to make sure she didn't high tail it out of here with the kids the second my back was turned.

I carried the cordless phone out on the front porch for privacy, but instead of dialing the preschool's number, I dialed the church. I planned to leave a message for Kyle to call me on my cell phone as soon as he got a chance today.

"Abundant Life Fellowship," he answered on the first ring.

I knew he stopped by his office early most Mondays before heading to the hospitals to visit those whose family had requested visits on Sunday, but this was early, even for him. It was a relief to hear his voice. "Kyle, it's Michelle," I said in a hushed voice. "I can't believe I caught you."

"Michelle," he said, surprise in his voice. I imagined the confusion on his face, wondering what had me calling him this early in the morning. "Hi. Shouldn't you be getting ready for work?"

I was suddenly dangerously close to tears. I cleared my throat. "I have a feeling I'm going to be late. Nicole showed up yesterday."

There was a short silence in which I imagined him feeling sorry for me, searching for words of comfort. "Is she staying with you?"

I glanced toward the door to make sure no one had discovered me. It was a shame I had to hide to use my own phone. "Yes," I replied in a hushed voice, "for the time being anyway."

"Has she given you any idea what her plans are? How long she's going to stay?"

"No. She hasn't said a word."

"I'm so sorry, Michelle. I know how hard this is for you."

My throat thickened at the sympathy in his voice. It was a moment before I could respond. "You know what they say; the Lord works in mysterious ways."

"I guess the kids are happy to see her," he answered.

I had hoped he would tell me this wasn't God's plan; that the kids belonged with me, not Nicole. My heart sank even farther. "Yes, well, I think so," I managed. "They've picked up on the tension between us even though I'm trying hard not to get into anything with her. Emma got in bed with me last night. She hasn't done that in ages."

"How's the rest of the family taking it?"

"No one else knows yet. I'm going to call Aunt Wanda and Uncle Jeb after I hang up from you. I can just imagine what their reaction will be."

"I am sorry, Michelle. Is there anything I can do?"

"Would you mind letting Miss Billie and the rest of the teachers know what's going on? Nicole wants to keep the kids home with her today when I go to work. I have to tell you I'm not real thrilled about that, but regardless of what her plans are, I can see a lot of adjustment problems down the road for the kids. I can't imagine what's going through their heads."

"It has to be strange for them. But no, I don't mind. We'll all pray for you."

"That's probably a good idea. I think I lost my religion when I saw Nicole standing in the driveway. Anyway, tell Billie I hope to have the kids back at the preschool tomorrow. Well, I'd better get back in the house before she comes looking for me. I'm hiding on the front porch.

"Michelle, hang in there, will you? Remember God is with you all the time. He'll see you through this. He already knows the outcome."

"I know. I just wish I had a little insight of my own."

I hung up the phone, braced myself, and dialed Aunt Wanda's number. I still needed to call Angie, but I wanted to get my other phone call over with first. Aunt Wanda was going to be fit to be tied.

Dean had barely spoken a word to any of us. He sat up late watching TV while Nicole and I gave the kids their bathes, and was still in bed when Nicole and I had our encounter in the kitchen. By the time I had finished my telephone calls, spent some time in prayer, and went back into the house, he was in the kitchen with Nicole. She was rummaging through the kitchen cabinets for something to cook for breakfast. Emma and Jonah were at the table, oblivious to the activity around them.

"Everything's where it's always been," I said when I realized what she was doing. "You know me, I never change anything."

"You've got that right," she said with a chuckle. "I think I found a box of raisins that's been here since before Grandma died."

"There's cereal in the pantry and plenty of eggs in the fridge," I said, taking no offence. "The kids love scrambled eggs doused in ketchup."

She glared at me. "I know that, Michelle."

"Sorry."

Her face softened and her shoulders relaxed. "I know. So am I."

Emma sat on her knees on one of the kitchen chairs, coloring in a coloring book. She was still wearing her pajamas. She looked up at me. "We're gonna be late for school."

Nicole and I exchanged glances. "You're going to stay home with

Mommy and Dean today while Aunt Michelle goes to work," Nicole announced with an exaggerated grin. "Won't that be fun? You can take me for a walk down to the creek and we can watch more of your movies."

"We're 'posed to go to school on Mondays," Jonah declared from the other side of the table. "That's when Miss Jennifer goes over the calendar and tells us what our letter for the week is."

It was immediately apparent that Nicole wasn't happy Jonah hadn't reacted the way she thought he should. "It doesn't matter if you miss one Monday, Jonah. She can tell you tomorrow what letter you're doing."

"Yeah, but all the other kids will already know. Their papers will already be hanging on the bulletin board and mine won't."

Nicole set a carton of eggs on the counter and slammed the refrigerator door shut with her foot. "Knock off the whining, Jonah. You know I can't stand that. She can hang your Tuesday paper on the bulletin board."

He hadn't been whining before, but he was now. "But it won't be the same paper as the other kids'. Mine will be different and I'll look stupid."

"You won't look stupid. Now stop acting like a baby. You're not going to school today, and if you don't shut up, you won't go tomorrow either."

Jonah slammed his fist onto the table. It was the closest I'd come to seeing easy-going Jonah throw an all out temper tantrum. "I hate Tuesday. I wanna go today. Aunt Shell, tell her we gotta go today." His bottom lip quivered. He was close to losing control and bawling in front of everyone, but his pride wouldn't allow it. He crossed his arms over his chest and glared at Nicole. Emma looked as close to crying as her brother.

I wanted to tell Nicole they weren't used to raised voices or their concerns being disregarded as if they were trivial. The teachers at the preschool treated them with respect while still maintaining authority. I tried to do the same. I kept my mouth shut. She was already mad enough. Any parenting advice from me would not be appreciated.

I went to Jonah instead and put my hand on his head. "Jonah, you don't have to go to school today. I've already called the preschool and told them you and Emma aren't coming so you may as well stay home and have fun with Mommy."

Jonah slumped forward on his elbows on the table. He didn't complain any further.

Nicole slammed the cabinet door and set a skillet on the stove with a bang. She spun around to face us. She set one hand on her hip and glared at me. I knew immediately what was wrong. She didn't like it that I had been the one Jonah listened to rather than her. *"Please, please, Nicole, don't make an issue of it,"* I silently begged. *"He hasn't done anything wrong."*

Apparently she had learned to read minds. A range of emotions flitted across her face as she made an effort to calm herself. She picked up the egg carton. "Who wants eggs?"

At precisely that moment, Aunt Wanda stuck her head in the back door. "Yoo-hoo, anybody home?"

I saw the irritation flash across Nicole's face and then disappear behind a wide smile. "Aunt Wanda!" she called out. She set the eggs on the counter and hurried across the kitchen to embrace the older woman. I had to hand it to Aunt Wanda; she had great timing.

Aunt Wanda managed to look duly surprised. "Nicole, child, is it really you? Where'd you come from?" She loosened her arms from around Nicole and pulled back. "Well, honey, you're melting away to nothing. You need some meat on your bones."

"All in good time." Nicole said playfully, "Seems to me you were a tiny little thing back when you were my age."

Aunt Wanda's cheeks turned pink. She dropped her arms from Nicole's waist and patted her own hips. "Well, I suppose I was. Been so long ago, I didn't even remember." She turned her attention to the rest of the room. In an instant her eyes registered the hard set of Jonah's jaw and Emma's tearfulness, Dean seated on the opposite side of the table where it butted up against the window, and my own cautious presence.

"What's the matter with everybody?" she demanded. "Jonah, you look like you've been sucking on a sour pickle. And, who might you be?" She approached Dean and stuck out her hand.

He actually managed sort of a smile and shook her hand. "I'm Dean," he said, before Nicole could do it for him.

"Well, nice to meet you, Dean. I'm Michelle and Nicole's Aunt Wanda, their mother's sister. I presume that's your car I saw in the driveway. You're the one who brought our Nicole home where she belongs."

Nicole's smile faltered. "Aunt Wanda," she cautioned.

"What? I was just asking the young man a question."

"Nicole was just getting ready to fix everybody some breakfast." I glanced at my watch. "I've got to be getting to work, but you're more than welcome to stay and eat."

"Lands, no, I ate with Jeb hours ago, but I wouldn't mind cooking for everybody else." She turned back to Nicole. "You're not just going to have eggs, are you?"

"Well, whatever everybody wants."

She headed to the refrigerator. "Surely you have some bacon or sausage in here. How about some homemade biscuits? Nicole, you haven't had my biscuits in ages. It'll only take a minute to whip up a batch. Michelle, you run along and I'll take care of breakfast. Are you kids hungry?"

"I can fix breakfast," Nicole said meekly, clearly pleased the job was out of her hands. She went to the coffee pot and poured herself another cup.

Aunt Wanda took the cup away from her and poured the coffee down the sink. "That's old. Let me make a fresh pot. Now, go sit down and relax."

Nicole didn't have to be told twice. She settled into the kitchen chair against the wall next to Dean so she was facing the kitchen. "You don't come over here and fix breakfast every morning, do you?" Her question was directed at Aunt Wanda, but she eyed me suspiciously.

Aunt Wanda was already poking through cabinets rounding up the ingredients for biscuits. "Lands sakes, no, girl, but I do pop in from time to time, especially when Jeb has a slow day on the farm and hangs around the house driving me crazy. That's what he's doing today, so when he turned his head for a minute, I made a beeline out the door. I'll call him after I get the biscuits in the oven and tell him you're here. He'll be so excited. Do you have any plans for today? We'd love to get caught up with you. We never get to visit since you moved off after little Emma here was born. Jeb and I are so happy about getting to know these two. It's been the most wonderful time for us. Jeb's just taken to these kids like a duck to water. It's not all him though, I'm having the time of my life. You know Violet. I don't think that girl's ever gonna give me grandbabies, so these two've just filled a void in Jeb's and my heart."

Emma had gone back to scribbling furiously in her coloring book. Jonah sat next to her with his shoulders hunched, looking resigned now rather than belligerent. Aunt Wanda beamed lovingly at the backs of their heads. She didn't say anything about the altercation she had obviously walked in on.

I eased out of the kitchen, relieved. Aunt Wanda had everything under control. In her mildly manipulative way, she had ingratiated herself and Uncle Jeb into Nicole's day. She'd make sure Nicole and Dean were not alone with the kids for a minute. She'd probably have Uncle Jeb keep Dean busy somewhere on the farm while she talked Nicole's ear off in the kitchen. Nicole would be too relieved that she didn't have to cook or entertain her own kids to get suspicious about why they were here in the first place. I could go to work in peace and not worry that I'd come home to an empty house.

Chapter Thirty-five

The first thing I noticed when I got home that evening was that Aunt Wanda's car was still parked in the same spot as it had been this morning. Dean's battered car was missing from the driveway. My heart in my throat, I scanned back to the old barn where I sometimes parked the Mazda on stormy nights. What if Aunt Wanda left today for a little while and when she got back, Nicole and Dean had packed the kids into the car and gone? Surely she would've called me at the hospital. I had made sure I was easily accessible if anyone needed to find me during my shift, just in case.

I pulled alongside her car so that my headlights shone all the way to the barn. Dean's car was definitely missing. The kitchen light was on along with a few lights throughout the house. He probably went to town for cigarettes or something. I could imagine he was going stir crazy trapped in this house all day with Nicole, Aunt Wanda, Uncle Jeb, and two kids. Just thinking about it almost made me want to take up smoking myself.

I grabbed my purse, exited the car, and hurried around the house to the back door. Aunt Wanda was at the sink finishing up the dinner dishes. Uncle Jeb sat at the kitchen table, leafing through the TV guide. "Evenin', Peanut."

Aunt Wanda turned halfway from the sink, her arms immersed to the elbows in sudsy water, and gave me a smile in greeting. My heart rate returned to normal. They wouldn't be so calm had Nicole taken off with Emma and Jonah.

"Where is everybody?" I asked, just to be sure.

Aunt Wanda nodded her head toward the living room. "Nicole's watching TV. The kids are upstairs. Nicole told them they could go to preschool tomorrow. I think she gave in so they'd quiet down and get out of her hair."

"Rough day?" I asked in a stage whisper.

She shrugged and Uncle Jeb chuckled from his place at the table. "No more'n any day when you've got two bored kids under your feet."

I went to him and patted his hand. "I appreciate you two sticking around today."

He stood up and kissed my cheek. "Why don't you go talk to your sister," he said gravely.

"Why? What's the matter?"

Aunt Wanda let the stopper out of the sink and dried her hands on a dishtowel. "Well, I'm ready to go home, Jeb. My feet are plumb wore out."

"Mine too, dear. Good thing the car's here."

"What's wrong with Nicole," I hissed again. They weren't leaving without giving me some kind of heads up.

Aunt Wanda rolled her eyes. Uncle Jeb leaned in close and whispered, "Trouble in paradise."

"You mean Dean? Where is he?"

Uncle Jeb shrugged. "Don't know, but Nicole's been upset all evenin'."

Aunt Wanda put her hand on my shoulder and kissed my cheek. "They spent a lot of time talking in private this afternoon, but by the sound of things, anybody could tell they were fighting. Finally he took off and she came stomping in here like a thundercloud. The kids knew to stay out of 'er way. She's spent most of the night staring at the television."

I didn't know if this was good news or bad. Dean definitely wasn't happy about being here. He could be the force that talked Nicole into going back to wherever they came from, leaving us in peace. On the other hand, Nicole could be so mad she'd do something just to spite the kids and me. But is that what I really wanted? Without Dean, Nicole would have a hard time making a living to support two kids and I'd be stuck supporting all of them. Nicole had already shown she was irresponsible when it came to earning a living. Did I want her and her kids living here and sponging off me indefinitely? My thoughts were in turmoil.

Nicole appeared at the kitchen door. Her eyes were red and puffy. She looked like she could use about sixteen hours of sleep. She crossed her arms over her chest. "You can leave now. Michelle's here to keep an eye on me."

Uncle Jeb grinned. "Good. It's past my bedtime."

"We weren't keeping an eye on you, honey," Aunt Wanda told her, in spite of the fact that an idiot could have figured out our little scheme. "I was happy to spend the day with you and the kids. Like I said, I haven't seen you in a coon's age."

"I'm serious, Michelle," Nicole said as soon as the door slammed shut behind Aunt Wanda and Uncle Jeb. "You don't need to send a baby-sitter over every time you leave the house."

"That's not what I was doing."

"Whatever. I'm just telling you it isn't necessary."

Her face softened and her arms relaxed at her sides. We smiled at each other. "You want me to fix you something?" I asked gently. "Are you hungry?"

She shook her head, "Always the big sister."

I held my hands up in front of me. "I can't help myself."

She smiled again. "You've been on your feet all day. I should be the one fixing you something."

"In that case, I'll have a steak, medium well, baked potato, and a huge chef salad with tons of fresh…"

"Easy now," she interrupted. "I just said I *should* fix you something; I didn't say I would."

We laughed easily. It felt good. There were times I loved being in my sister's company. She was a loving person, if not a little selfish, but she was still my sister and I loved her, faults and all.

I went to her and linked my arm in hers. "Let's go sit down. I am dog tired." We moved into the living room together. "Anything on TV?"

"No." I let go of her arm, and she reached out and clicked off the old set. "I've just been sitting in here to avoid Aunt Wanda. She has talked nonstop all day."

I laughed. "She means well."

"Maybe, but she's exhausting."

I sank into the easy chair and propped my feet on the ottoman. Nicole sat down across from me on the couch. I had to ask; it would look suspicious if I didn't. "Where's Dean?"

Nicole sank back into the couch cushions and sighed. I could see she was fighting tears, tears that she'd probably been shedding all night with just the television set for company. "He's gone. We had a big fight and he left."

"Oh, Nicole, I'm sorry," I said, although, I wasn't sure if I was or not. How would his leaving affect the kids and me?

She stiffened and crossed her arms over her chest. "Oh, I don't care. I'm sick to death of him anyway. It's his fault my life is in the mess it's in right now. I just hate him. Maybe he'll drive that old clunker of his off a cliff."

"Nicole!"

"Give me a break, Michelle, you don't like him either."

That was neither here nor there, but I wouldn't debate it with her. "What did you mean by it was his fault you're in the mess you are now?"

She swept her arms away from her in a large gesture, "This—leaving my kids here with you in the first place, no job, no home. I guess I'm better off without him. But we've been together so long, it doesn't seem right that he just took off. He knows how much my kids mean to me."

I resisted the impulse to roll my eyes. "You always have a home here, Nicole," I assured her, wishing there was something else I could have said besides that.

"You don't mean that, Michelle. If you did, you would've invited me to stay here a long time ago."

She had me there. "I didn't think I had to say it. You're always welcome."

She arched her eyebrows. "But not if I keep living the way I've been living."

"Well, um, I can't have drinking going on in the house, especially with the kids here."

"You mean my kids?"

"Nicole, it is my house. I don't drink and I don't want anyone else doing it here either. In fact, I'd prefer the cigarette smoking be done outside, too."

"See, that's what I mean. No one's welcome here unless they're willing to abide by your rigid rules and regulations. You have to control everyone and everything, Michelle. You've always been that way."

"I'm not saying that, but since I am the one who pays the bills, I guess that entitles me to make up the rules." There I went again, throwing my weight around because I had a good paying job and she probably never would. I took a deep breath, determined not to turn this into a money and power issue. Maybe she was right and I was some kind of control freak, but was it my fault everyone else was always wrong?

I began over again. "Nicole, you're my sister and I love you. You're always welcome here. But it isn't fair that you come into anyone's home, not just mine, and expect to have things the way you do in your own house. It's only common courtesy that you do things the way your hostess likes. You'd do it anywhere else, I know you would."

"You're right I guess, but you forget, this was my home once, too. I was raised in this house like a lot of other people. So it isn't just your home alone, it's mine too and Aunt Wanda's and Mom's and the whole rest of the family's."

"Then where are all of you when the taxes come due or how about pitching in on replacing these drafty, old windows?"

"Oh, Michelle, everything with you is either white or black, nothing in between. I'm not saying I'm a partial owner. I just think I should always feel welcome here, whether I'm willing to live by your rules or not."

"I'm sorry if I made you feel unwelcome," I said sincerely. "I just thought you were living the life you wanted to live. Every time I talked to you, you were in a relationship, telling me how happy you were and how excited you were about a new job. How was I to know you were miserable and wanted to come home if you didn't speak up and tell me?"

Nicole hung her head. "I didn't say I really wanted to come home. Oh, I don't know what I want. For the most part, I was happy, but sometimes I'd be with someone simply because I didn't think I had any other options."

I pulled my legs off the ottoman, leaned forward in my chair and rested my elbows on my knees. "That's no way to live, Nicole. You have a lot to offer. You don't have to settle for some man, simply because he's there. You need to decide what you want to do with your life and then do it. You're still young. You can go back to school. I'm sure you have interests, a vision of what you want your life to be like ten years from now."

She shook her head. "I'm not like you, Michelle. I never liked school. I was never happier than the day I walked out of Winona High School for the last time. I don't have some fancy career in mind. I want a man in my life. Not just for security. I couldn't stand living alone like you do. I'd go stir crazy. I have needs."

I definitely didn't want to discuss her needs. "I'm not suggesting you become a nun. I'm sure there's a man out there who would treat you decently. You shouldn't put up with some low life because you don't think you have any other options."

"You don't know how it is out there."

"I'm out there everyday," I reminded her.

"But you're not looking."

An image of Kyle flashed through my mind, but I pushed it aside. Just because I was a Christian now, didn't mean I would ever be good enough for someone like him.

"It's a jungle out there, Michelle, full of creeps and jerks and users. At least Dean treats me good most of the time. He works pretty steady and we have a good time together."

"But isn't he the same one who influenced you to give up your kids?"

"It's not like that. We were having problems. He had been out of work for a long time and we got evicted from our apartment. He was always saying things like how much easier it would be to find a place if it was just me and him with no kids. We'd have more money too. Everything he said was absolutely true."

"But they're your kids. They're not to blame for your money problems."

"I'm not saying they are. They're great kids and I love them more than anything in this world. But Dean was on me constantly. I'm weak and he knows it. He always could wear me down."

"And you put up with that?" I interjected, the blood rising in my cheeks.

Nicole raised her hand to silence me. "You don't know what it's like, Michelle." She snorted derisively. "How would you? A relationship takes work and compromise on both sides."

"That's not compromise," I interrupted again. "You're talking about giving up your own kids because some man knows you're weak and takes advantage of it."

She shook her head wearily. "Are you going to listen or are you going to keep insulting Dean?"

I sat back in the chair and gave her the go-ahead with a wave of my hand. While she was totally wrong and Dean was obviously pond scum, I did want to hear what she had to say.

"I know I shouldn't've given into Dean. That was wrong, but he kept hounding me. He wouldn't let up and he always waited until I had a headache or didn't feel well, then he really let me have it."

"You mean when you were hung over."

"Not all the time. Anyway," she gave me a warning look not to interrupt again, "finally, I couldn't take it anymore. He caught me at a weak moment and I gave in. It was just supposed to be for a few weeks until we could work things out. He had some job opportunities lined up…"

She paused when she saw me roll my eyes toward the ceiling in spite of my best intentions. "Sorry," I said. "Go ahead."

"He was trying to find work for me too. He said no one would give me a job if they knew I had two kids at home to worry about. Once we were both working regular, we'd look into daycare and come take the kids off your hands. I was really hesitant about bringing them here in the first place. Frankly, I didn't want a lecture from you or Aunt Wanda. You always make me feel like such a failure, even in the best of circumstances. When I explained that to Dean, he said, 'No problem, I'll take them for you'."

I was sorry I made her feel like a failure but I couldn't keep quiet. "Did you also discuss leaving them so close to the road where a car might run over them or under the lilac bushes where I've seen snakes before? Didn't you worry about their safety?"

Nicole straightened her spine. "I did not know about that for a couple of weeks. He told me he was going to go to the front door, face you, and tell you this was something we had to do so here they were. We both knew you wouldn't turn them away but I just couldn't make myself come. The whole thing had me very upset. I stayed at the motel on Highway 92 while he dropped them off. I couldn't bear the thought of giving up my babies. Besides that, I was a little hung over."

I clenched my teeth, determined not to say a word. It never did any good, and there was no going back to undo the damage she and Dean had done.

"Dean said he left them at the house, and I didn't really ask for details."

"At six o'clock in the morning with barely anything more than the clothes on their backs?"

"I told you, I didn't know about that. I was sound asleep."

"Frankly, I'm amazed you were able to sleep, dealing with all that grief the way you were."

"Not all of us can be as perfect as you, Michelle."

"This has nothing to do with perfection, Nicole. This is about being a responsible adult. Most people wouldn't leave a dog on the side of the road, let alone a child."

"You are so dramatic. Nothing happened, did it? They didn't wander into the road, not that any traffic goes past this dump anyway. They are well-behaved children. If Dean told them to stay put, then they would stay put. No snake slithered out of the bushes and swallowed them. They were fine. Dean said that dog of yours started barking as soon as he pulled up to the gate, so he knew you'd be down in a matter of minutes. It wasn't like they spent the night out there."

"Did you bother telling Emma and Jonah what was going on? That they were going to live with an aunt they didn't know until you and Dean got jobs?"

Nicole pursed her lips thoughtfully. "They probably overheard some of our plans. They're smart kids. I'm sure they figured some of it out."

"Nicole, Jonah was three. How much should he be expected to figure out?"

Nicole exhaled wearily and stood up. "Just forget it. I'm going to bed." She headed for the stairs, but then turned back. "You know, I am really sick of your holier-than-thou attitude. We all know the great Michelle would never make a mistake raising her kids. I'm sure they'd be as perfect as you are; but we'll never know that, will we, because you'll never have kids. You need a man for that, and you're incapable of giving a man what he wants."

I jumped to my feet and clenched my fists at my sides. How dare she talk about me that way! If I seemed cold and aloof, it was because I'd been programmed that way. I'd put up with plenty in my nearly thirty-four years of living that earned me the right. But I couldn't tell Nicole that. She only heard what she wanted to hear and understood what she wanted to understand.

"If it makes you feel better to turn this around to be something about me, then go ahead," I said through clenched teeth. "But don't make excuses to my face about why you left the kids here. You were about as serious about getting your life together as you were about becoming a brain surgeon. You left the kids with me for no other reason than you're lazy. You and Dean didn't want to be bothered with them for awhile. I don't want to hear one word about how it was for their good, and they understood. They didn't understand. Emma didn't speak for weeks and when she cried, it was for Carrie whoever that is. She didn't even ask me about you. She just wanted Carrie."

I said it to hurt her. I was mad over her calling me holier than thou. I wanted her to feel a little of the pain she put her kids through, but as soon as I saw the look on her face, I regretted mentioning the woman's name.

A real tear formed in the corner of her eye. The first genuine one I'd seen in years. "She wanted Carrie?"

I felt like a jerk. "Yes," I mumbled, looking away.

As suddenly as the contrition appeared, it was replaced by anger. "See what I mean? Those kids are ungrateful brats. Everything I do is for them, but all they see is how much fun they have at Carrie's." She threw up her hands and stalked a few feet away. "I am so sick of this. Nothing I do makes anybody happy. Dean's gone. Now that he's not getting his way, he throws me aside. My own kids don't even ask about me when I'm gone. All I heard today was how great Aunt Michelle is. 'Aunt Michelle does this.' 'Aunt Michelle buys us that'."

She turned to face me, her venom again directed at me. "Well, Michelle, I'm sorry I can't show my kids the good time you do. I don't have a good paying job and a farm left to me by a bitter old lady, but kids don't understand that. They just know who throws them cool birthday parties and drives them around in a flashy sports car."

I took a deep breath. I wanted to set her straight, but I no longer wanted to hurt her. "That isn't all I do for them. I worked hard to get the job I've got now. The only reason Grandma left me the farm was because she knew I'd never leave it or sell it to an outsider. None of that is the kids' fault. The only thing you have to do to make kids love you is love them first, be there for them, tuck them in at night, wash off their scrapes, and listen when they talk."

I honestly wasn't trying to be condescending, but Nicole sure took it that way.

"You're giving me parenting lessons?" she shrieked. "Well, isn't that priceless. Where did you pick up these little tidbits? Are you watching Dr. Phil now?"

"Nicole, please." I glanced toward the ceiling and purposefully lowered my voice. "There's no sense fighting about this. I'm not trying to give you parenting tips. I just wanted you to see what kids really want. They're not impressed by what kind of car you drive or how many toys you buy them."

"Oh, yeah, that's easy for you to say. Your life is perfect and mine is anything but. Well, believe me, I don't need advice from an old spinster who can't buy a date. So mind your own business."

My temper flared in spite of my determination to remain calm. "You've made this my business, Nicole. I never wanted those kids here, but you didn't give me a choice, did you? Your loser boyfriend dumps your mistakes in my front yard and once again, I'm here to clean up the mess."

"Aunt Shell?"

Nicole and I snapped our heads toward the stairwell. Emma stood halfway down, her hands gripping the banister. Her blonde hair was tousled and her eyes clouded with sleep. Gypsy sat on the step below her, reproving me with her eyes. My breath caught in my throat. What had I just said? I was so mad, I couldn't even remember, only that it wasn't good. Something about her and Jonah being mistakes that I had to clean up.

She buried her hand in Gypsy's red hair, searching for the collar, like she used to when she first came here and needed a lifeline to hold onto. She hadn't done it in months. She had come so far out of her shell. A few careless and angry words out of my mouth, and I pushed her right back in.

"Why are you yelling?" she asked me, her voice barely audible.

Nicole recovered quicker than I did. She rushed to the bottom of the stairs. "Oh, baby, did Aunt Michelle scare you?" She started up the stairs. "Everything's all right. Mommy will take you back to bed."

Emma acted like she didn't even hear Nicole. She kept her eyes on my face. Gypsy sensed the tension and stood up, blocking Nicole's path. Nicole stopped climbing and stared wide-eyed at Emma and the dog.

"I'm sorry, Emma," I said from my position on the floor. "I didn't mean to wake you up. Let Mommy take you up to bed so you can get some sleep. You've got school tomorrow."

"Gypsy and me woke up and went to your room, but you weren't there."

"I know. I didn't get off work till late but everything's okay. I'm home now. I'll be up in a little bit."

"Will you come in and kiss me goodnight?"

"Sure."

Emma nodded and turned to look at Nicole for the first time. Nicole pasted a bright smile on her face. "Come on, sweetie; time for bed." She stepped cautiously around Gypsy and scooped Emma into her arms. She grunted audibly. "Oh, my, when did you get to be such a big girl? Before long, you can carry Mommy." She gave me a quick look before heading up the stairs, a look of pure hatred.

I winced inwardly. I knew that look. Nicole would make me pay for taking her place in the eyes of her children.

Chapter Thirty-six

As mad as Nicole was last night, I didn't know if she'd stand behind her word and let the kids go to the preschool while I was at work. I tried to stay as quiet as possible while I got them ready to leave. Nicole hadn't made an appearance yet, and I was hoping she'd stay in bed until we were long gone. It was a little after six when we left, both kids strapped into their booster seats in the back, their heads bobbing from side to side as they dozed in the car. I dreaded facing my sister that afternoon; she'd probably accuse me of avoiding her on purpose, but I had neither the time nor the desire to wake her and get into another fight.

Only one car was in the parking lot when I arrived at the church. Miss Julie usually opened the preschool at six-thirty and the other teachers started arriving at seven depending on which shift they worked. I knew Kyle wouldn't be here this early, if he came to his office at all, but I looked toward his end of the building anyway and swallowed my disappointment. I needed to talk to someone. Nicole's animosity toward me, and not knowing what she was up to, had my stomach in knots.

I signed the kids in and got back in my car for the twenty-minute drive to the city. I drove on autopilot, unaware of the exits I took or the traffic around me. My day was quiet and routine. I spent most of my eight-hour shift monitoring Mr. Hooley who had come out of his six-way bypass surgery yesterday. Tomorrow I'd get him out of bed for the first time. But today, he was only capable of sitting up and holding a heart-shaped pillow against his chest while he coughed as I instructed, even though he whined and called me a sadist. Between visitors, we chatted about the construction company he owned and the trip to Hawaii we'd take if I promised to cease causing him pain.

I managed to push most of my concerns about Nicole to the back of my head until the drive home. As soon as I was on the highway, I called Angie on my cell phone to fill her in on what was going on. As far as I knew she'd be picking the kids up tomorrow from preschool while I worked my Wednesday twelve-hour shift.

"I'm glad you called," Angie said when I got hold of her. "I've been praying for you ever since you called yesterday. How's it going? Are the kids doing all right?"

"As well as can be expected. Nicole and I got into a shouting match last night and woke Emma up. She wanted me to tuck her back into bed. Needless to say, Nicole didn't appreciate it at all."

"Poor thing."

I couldn't tell if she was talking about Emma or me.

"Do you have any idea what her plans are?"

"No. Her boyfriend took off yesterday. I don't know if that's good or bad. Without him, she doesn't have any money to go anywhere else, so I don't have to worry about her taking the kids anywhere. But that also means I could be stuck with her indefinitely."

"Oh, Michelle, you don't think…hold on a minute." I heard some moving around and children's voices in the background. Then all was quiet. "Okay, I'm back," Angie said in a quiet tone. "I'm in the bathroom, in case any little ears are listening. Where was I…oh, yeah, you don't think Nicole's actually considering leaving with the kids, do you? She has to realize they're better off with you."

"I don't know, but maybe—maybe it'd be the best thing for them," I stammered, trying hard to believe it. "She is their mother. Aren't all kids better off with their mothers? Maybe this is all God's plan."

Angie didn't reply right away. "It's possible," she said finally. "If Nicole's turned her life around and has accepted her responsibilities, then yes, it is God's plan that she raise her kids; but if nothing's changed, and she's only here for convenience sake, then no, I don't think it's God's plan."

I was quiet while I considered her words. I wasn't sure how I felt about it. Didn't I want my freedom back? Wasn't this what I'd been wishing for all along?

"Michelle, are you okay?"

"Um, yeah, I'm fine. I've got to go. I'll call you if I don't need you to pick up the kids tomorrow night." I clicked the phone off and drove the rest of the way to the preschool deep in thought.

"I don't like staying here alone all day," Nicole announced as soon as the kids and I walked through the door a half an hour later. "I want the kids to stay home with me tomorrow."

Why did she have to bring this up in front of them? Emma and Jonah turned expectant faces toward me. They loved school, but they also missed their mother and wouldn't be totally against sleeping in and spending the next day doing whatever suited Nicole.

"There's only a little over a month before Emma graduates. Why don't we keep their regular schedule going till then?"

Nicole planted her feet and glared at me. "Because I'm bored. I want them here."

"Come on, Nicole, it's only four days a week. You can't come in here and upset their routine just so they can entertain you. Tomorrow's Wednesday; only two more days and they'll be home the rest of the week."

I could see she didn't appreciate my logic, no matter how… logical. "They're my kids, Michelle. That makes it my decision."

I gritted my teeth. She had a point, as much as I hated to admit it. All the logic in the world didn't change that, and I didn't want to be the one to keep Emma and Jonah from spending time with her. What could I do? "What if Aunt Wanda lets you borrow her car tomorrow. You can drive the kids to school by nine and then go pick them up after lunch. That way, they'll at least have their class time, and you can have the morning to yourself. It's a shame that Emma's come so far and then won't be able to get ready for the graduation ceremony with her friends. They're already practicing for it."

Emma and Jonah turned to Nicole. Nicole exhaled and looked from them to me. Her inner turmoil was obvious. She saw giving in as a small victory for me, but she did like the idea of mornings to herself. "All right," she conceded after a moment's thought, "but only if you get permission for me to use Aunt Wanda's car."

"Great, I'll take care of it after dinner." I hadn't smelled anything cooking when I came in so I figured I might as well get to that too. For someone who was so bored all day, Nicole sure didn't entertain herself with housework or food preparation.

❧

"What's Nicole up to, anyway," Aunt Wanda demanded after granting permission for the use of her car the following morning. I called while washing the dinner dishes. Nicole had gone upstairs to give the kids their baths. Her maternal moments usually didn't last long so I was taking advantage of the respite to make my phone call in private.

"I don't know," I replied honestly. "Dean's gone for the time being, but I don't have any idea what her plans are. I don't know if she's thinking of staying around here and getting a job, taking the kids back to the city, or what."

"That's why I tried to get you to take some kind of legal action so this sort of thing couldn't happen. She don't have any rights to those kids and you know it. Now, here she is, making demands, turning things upside down. She don't care one thing about those poor little babies. She just ain't got nowhere else to go right now, so she's messing up our lives."

"I know, Aunt Wanda, but she's family. You're the one always telling me we do for family. I can't very well turn her out. The kids are hers to do with whatever she wants." Before she could interrupt I hurried on. "Did you ever think this is exactly how God's got it planned? Maybe He's using the kids and Dean's exit to light a fire under Nicole. What if she's truly ready to get her life turned around and we do something to sabotage it? We've got to give her all the support and understanding we can."

"That's hogwash and you know it. She ain't never thought of nobody but herself, and that's exactly what she's doing now."

"God can change anyone's heart, Aunt Wanda."

"I think I know better than you what the Lord will and won't do. You've only been back in church a week, Missy. That hardly qualifies you to go preaching at me when I've lived my whole life according to Scripture. It sounds to me like you're just wanting rid of those kids so you can go back to doing things the way you've always done 'em."

"That's not it at all," I exclaimed, hurt that she could even think that.

"Oh, isn't it? Don't tell me you haven't thought about how nice it'll be when your duties as benevolent aunt are over. You've done your part, providing them with a good home this past year, but I think you're glad Nicole's back. She can take them off your hands and you'll be free to hole yourself up in this house again, hiding from the world. Well, let me tell you, Missy, I am sure disappointed in you. I thought you had a changed heart. I thought you fell in love with those kids. Now you're ready to give them up without a fight."

"No, I…"

"Well, Jeb and I aren't willing to give up. If you're not going to fight for them, we will. I'll lose everything I own to some high priced attorney before I let Nicole take off to God knows where with those kids. Talk about doing for family; Emma and Jonah's family, too. They're innocent in all this, and I for one, won't let them down. Yes, I feel sorry for Nicole, and I'll pray for her. I'll even help her out financially if she needs help getting an apartment or something, but I will not help her ruin those poor babies' lives."

I sighed and clutched the phone. How could I argue with her? I couldn't dispute one thing she said. Was I being lazy? Did I want my own life back so badly I was willing to sacrifice the kids' safety and well-being?

"I hadn't thought about it like that, Aunt Wanda. I don't want her taking the kids somewhere where we don't know if they're safe either. I suppose something should be done."

"You're darn right I'm right. You tell Nicole she can come over tomorrow morning and pick up the car. In the meantime, Jeb and I will be going through the phone book for lawyers who specialize in custody or family disputes or whatever this is."

"You don't have to do that," I said. "This is my problem and I'll take care of it, but I'm going to do everything else before I bring lawyers and courtrooms into it. This is how families get torn apart. If I can convince Nicole this is the best situation for everyone, then maybe we won't have to go to court. I think that would make more problems than it solved."

"Michelle, I think you're making a big mistake. You're not going to convince Nicole of anything unless she's already made up her mind in the first place. You know how hard-headed she can be. It would be wonderful if she agreed to stay here and get her life straightened out. Or if she left town to get a job, and let the kids stay here, but we all know that isn't going to happen. I don't want to take her to court either, but I don't see anyway around it."

I massaged a pain in my left temple. "There has to be, Aunt Wanda. I can't sue my own sister. I just can't. She already thinks I've taken her place in the kids' eyes. If I take her to court to get custody, she'll never forgive me. I have to do this with her best wishes."

"Well, you're wasting your time. This is Nicole we're talking about."

"I don't know, she might see reason, I know she misses Dean, and she never has been satisfied to live on this farm for more than a month or so. All I need is for her to realize that it won't only be the kids who benefit by them staying here. If she sees it's in her best interest too, then maybe she'll let me have permanent custody."

"Oh, Michelle, I think you're setting yourself up for a disappointment, but you go ahead and do what you think you have to do. Just don't take the rest of your life figuring it out. These kids need stability now."

"They also don't need their mom and their aunt tearing each other apart. I'll know when the time's right to approach Nicole."

"Just pray, dear, and let the Lord guide you."

I hung up the phone, under the assault of a massive headache. Aunt Wanda was right about the kids needing someone to take care of them. Freedom was an ideal lost to me as long as my niece and nephew were too young to take care of themselves. Like it or not, I needed to intervene on their behalf and do what was best for them. But what would happen to my sister if I took her to court to get custody of her kids? She wasn't the most stable person on the planet. Would this push her over the edge? What would happen to our relationship? We barely had one now. There had to be a way to reason with Nicole. Surely she wanted the best for her children the same as I did. Unfortunately her idea of the best differed greatly from mine.

How could I get her to agree with me? What if she never did?

Chapter Thirty-seven

I peeked in on Nicole before leaving for work the following Monday to make sure she had her alarm set early enough to get the kids to the preschool by nine. Emma and Jonah were both in bed with her. I guess it only bothered her when kids shared beds with adults if I was the one doing it.

I put it out of my head and went to work. This was a minor infraction. I could understand why Nicole wanted to spend time with them and spoil them a little. I was sure it was harmless. *"She won't be here long,"* I reassured myself. *"She'll get itchy feet. Maybe Dean will even come back, and then she'll be gone like the wind."* I hated to think she'd hurt the kids again like that, but for my sake and their own good, I wanted her out of here.

Things were already changing for the better. She didn't go to church with us yesterday morning as I had hoped she would, but there was a hot dinner waiting on the stove when we got home. She was smiling more and the color had returned to her cheeks. After dinner she played on the floor with the kids while I cleaned the kitchen. Maybe this situation would work out after all.

At church the day before, I saw Kyle for the first time since the Easter service. We didn't have time to do more than exchange a few pleasantries. He asked how Nicole was doing and if the kids needed anything. I told him we were fine and I had everything under control. I decided not to bother him with all the questions whirling around in my head like; why was Nicole back after I had finally started serving the Lord and everything was going so well? What did she want from me? What did God want? Was I supposed to eat my words about Grandma Catherine and her Christian charity?

Was God testing me? I just didn't know exactly what He required, or if I'd pass or fail.

"How was school?" I asked Jonah Monday evening when I got home from work.

He was sitting on the front porch, an army of tiny green plastic soldiers positioned around him, prepared for battle. He set one on the top of a stack of wooden blocks and aimed the soldier's rifle into the air. "We didn't go today."

"What? Why not?"

He shrugged and made shooting noises with his lips. "Mommy didn't get us up."

I headed into the house without another word. I didn't want to risk yelling at my innocent nephew when it was his mother I was angry at. I found Nicole in front of the television.

"There's frozen pizza on the stove if you're hungry," she informed me.

I positioned myself between her and the television. "Why didn't you take the kids to preschool today? Jonah said you didn't get them up."

She gave me a dirty look and leaned to the left to see around me. "I tried, but they wouldn't get out of bed. I got tired of begging them. When they finally did get up, they said they didn't want to go."

"They're kids. You don't ask them, you tell them."

She finally gave up watching her program. She sighed and looked up at me. "Michelle, you know I'm not a morning person. I can barely get myself out of bed without worrying about getting two whiny kids up. I don't see why you're getting so excited, it's just preschool."

"Preschool that I'm paying a fortune to send them to!"

She raised her hands in front of her. "Ooh, sorry. Just put it on my tab."

"It's not the money, Nicole. It's very important that they go. I don't know what I would've done if it hadn't been for the teachers at that school. It's a wonderful place for the kids to be. They've learned a lot and have really grown spiritually while they've been going there. I already told you Emma graduates next month. I don't want her to miss out on that."

"I'll send them tomorrow, now will you please get out of the way so I can finish watching my program."

"No. I won't get out of the way until I make you understand how important it is that the kids get up and go to preschool. They are building habits that will be with them the rest of their lives. If you can't make them get up now, what are you going to do next year when Emma is in kindergarten? If you don't make her go then, they'll put you in jail."

"All right, all right, I said I'll send them tomorrow. You're right, as usual. I'm a terrible mother and I don't deserve to live. I promise I won't waste anymore of your precious money. I'll have them up at five A.M. tomorrow and ready to go. Now, will you get out of the way?"

I wanted to kick in the TV screen, snatch Nicole up by the hair of the head, and make her listen to me. Instead I turned and went upstairs. She wasn't going to listen to a word I said. As usual, she saw me as an anal retentive bully and herself as the victim. She didn't think it was important that the kids keep going to preschool. Maybe I was making it more important than it really was. Millions of kids didn't go to preschool. Was I making too much of it? Maybe I should relax and let the kids sleep in if they wanted to. When it all boiled down, it wasn't even my decision to make. Before I got myself all worked up, I'd see how things went tomorrow.

Tuesday and Wednesday, the kids made it to school. On Tuesday, Nicole picked the kids up during lunch causing the cooks to bag what they hadn't eaten and send it with them. Wednesday, Nicole lost track of time and didn't go get them until after Aunt Wanda called inquiring about her car. It was nearly five o'clock before they left the preschool that day. I didn't like the irregularity of their new schedule, but I decided worse things could happen to a kid, such as living alone with Nicole in the city somewhere without me having any knowledge of their whereabouts. I needed to relax and not imagine that the fate of the world hung in the balance if they were late to school once in a while. I needed to learn a little flexibility; everything didn't have to work out the way I wanted it to every time.

I was just grateful Nicole hadn't said anything about leaving. I didn't want to get into it with her about custody. I knew exactly how she'd react if challenged; like a she-wolf protecting her cubs. It was best for the kids to remain here with me, but I don't know if I had the nerve to take a stand, especially if that meant threatening her with litigation.

I prayed every night that she'd realize she needed a job and stability here on the farm. Deep down, though, I braced myself for the storm just beyond the horizon.

❧

"No, I don't have to."

Jonah stared up at me, his eyes defiant.

"Pick up those toys right now," I repeated. "I'm trying to cook dinner and you're in my way. Those toys don't belong in here anyway."

"Mommy lets me play in here while she's cooking." He gave the army men scattered at his feet an angry kick. Several skittered across the floor. One slipped under the refrigerator and disappeared. Perfect, gone forever, since I never bothered to clean there.

"Jonah, I'm not telling you again. You can't play in here while I'm cooking. Someone could trip over a toy and get burned on the stove. Now, get these toys out of my way. I've got things to do."

"I don't have to listen to you. You're not my Mommy."

The attitude that had pervaded the house the past two weeks, since Nicole's arrival, had not been put into words, until now.

"I may not be your Mommy," I said, struggling not to give into the emotions warring inside me, "but this is my kitchen and you'll do as I say, when I say it."

"You're mean." The little boy sat down among his toys, crossed his arms over his chest, and glared up at me.

"So you're not going to pick up these toys?"

"Nope."

"Fine." I went to the mudroom and got the broom. Jonah bent his head over his toys, but I could see him watching me through the blonde fringe of hair that hung over his forehead. I brought the broom and dustpan into the kitchen and began to sweep. I started near the refrigerator where the farthest army men had landed and worked my way toward Jonah. I moved slowly and deliberately, carefully reaching under the table and along the counters. Finally I swept against Jonah's backside.

He whipped his head around to stare at me. "Hey. What are you doing?"

"I'm cleaning up the kitchen so I can get dinner started. Are you sure you don't want to help?"

Without answering, he spun around on the floor to face me and re-crossed his arms over his chest. He didn't say another word when I knelt down to sweep the army men, and an alarmingly significant amount of dirt, into the dustpan. I straightened up, went to the trashcan, and dumped the contents inside.

That brought a reaction. He was on his feet in an instant. He ran to where I stood next to the trashcan and peered inside. Tears formed on his lashes. "Hey! Those are my toys," he announced tearfully. "You can't throw them away."

I snapped the lid closed. "I can and I did. I gave you more than enough chances to pick up your toys. You wouldn't do it so you left me no choice."

"But you can't throw my stuff away. Now what am I supposed to play with?"

"You should've thought of that earlier."

"You're mean Aunt Shell," he reiterated. I didn't care. I was feeling quite proud of myself. "I hate you. I wish we didn't have to live here." He ran from the room, hollering for Nicole.

My satisfaction over finding a practical solution to the problem of a preschooler who wouldn't pick up his toys vanished with him. He hated me now, or at least he claimed to for the moment. In an hour he'd forget about the altercation and try to warm up to me so I'd buy him new toys, but for this moment, he hated me. For the past nine months, we'd been best friends. He'd made me cards and tacky presents at school; he curled up against me at night to watch television; the bond we'd formed had seemed indestructible. Now I was the hated, unreasonable aunt.

I returned the broom and dustpan to the mudroom and started dinner. Everything was falling apart. Nicole had only been here two weeks and she was wrecking the fine balance the kids and I had established. If only things could go back to the way they were before she came. Wistfully, I thought back to last summer before Emma and Jonah came. It seemed like a lifetime ago. Ah, how peaceful my life had been: dinner out of the microwave or paper sack, no toys on the floor, no arguments that always served to ruin my appetite, just Gypsy and me, happy as clams in our big empty house. But Gypsy wasn't even my dog these days. She belonged to the children. She was happy and fulfilled; she had no clue that the two of us were being used and mocked behind our backs.

I had become a guest in my own home. I had to do something. I had to regain control of my house and my life. If I didn't want toys littering the floor and a fresh-mouthed kid spouting hatred, I shouldn't have to put up with it. And, by cracky, I wasn't going to. This was my house. My name was on the mailbox. All the bills came addressed to me. Things were going to change, starting now. When Nicole came in to find out why I threw Jonah's toys away, she was going to get an earful. If she didn't like it, she could find the door. Maybe it wouldn't be the end of the world if she left and took those kids of hers with her.

Chapter Thirty-eight

Generally I wasn't much of a crier, I couldn't remember the last time I'd had a good throw-yourself-across-the-bed-and-wail session, but I sure felt like it now. The night had gone from bad to worse with Jonah whining and Nicole accusing me of overreacting. Even Emma ignored me and sat next to her mother on the couch, as I squirmed against their onslaught.

It was only eight-thirty when I went upstairs to my room where I could find some peace and quiet. I lay across the bed and took my Bible from the nightstand. I couldn't remember the last time I'd felt so alone, but I knew there was one who sticks closer than a brother. I flipped the Bible open to the Psalms and started to read. Unfortunately I had opened to the part where David cried out to God because his enemies besought him on every side. That made me more depressed. I flipped over another fifty pages and landed in Proverbs. Somewhere in here was the assurance that if you beat a child with a rod, he would not die. That's what I needed to hear, confirmation that I had done the right thing by throwing the army men in the trash.

I tuned out the noise drifting up through the old fashioned heating grates and read. When the phone next to my elbow rang, I nearly jumped out of my skin. I pounced on it, my heart hammering in my chest.

"Hello?"

"Michelle? Is that you, everything okay?"

I exhaled, more relieved than I had a right to be. "Hi, Kyle, yeah, I'm fine. I was reading, and the phone startled me."

"Well, I thought I'd call to check on you. I haven't had much of a chance to talk to you lately and I know you're going through a lot. I understand why you haven't had a chance to attend any of the New Converts Classes. How is everything?"

The tears from earlier threatened to spill now. But I would hold it together. He was a busy man with no time to waste on someone feeling sorry for herself. "Oh, we're getting along," I replied vaguely.

"Michelle, I want you to be honest with me. That's what I'm here for. I wouldn't be calling if not for the Lord putting you on my heart."

"He did?"

"Yes, I've been praying for you all evening. Is there anything you need to talk about?"

"I guess you could say that, but I wouldn't even know where to begin."

"I've got an idea. Why don't we get together somewhere for lunch tomorrow? You don't generally work on Fridays, do you?"

I was incredibly flattered that he remembered so much about my schedule. Then I remembered he only knew my schedule because the kids never went to preschool on Fridays. I tightened my grip on the phone as if I was holding onto him and smiled. "No, I'm free."

"Good. Why don't we meet around noon at Giovanni's in Winona for pizza? Then we can have the whole afternoon to talk, unless you'd rather discuss things now over the phone."

I don't know what happened to my desire to spill tears. "No, tomorrow will be fine. I'll see you around twelve."

We said our goodbyes and hung up. I lay back against the pillows and hugged the open Bible to my chest. *"So, Kyle's been praying for me all evening, huh, Lord? Does this mean something or am I just one of his flock?"* I was determined not to read more into it than what was really there but I couldn't still the butterflies suddenly flitting around in my stomach.

❧

"Kyle's not interested in dating you," I reminded myself all morning and as I drove the four miles into Winona for our lunch at the pizza

place. *"You're not exactly pastor's wife material. He's just offering a listening ear for an old friend."* One kiss wasn't enough to indicate that his feelings ran any deeper than friendship.

I was through pretending that Kyle didn't mean anything to me, even if he could never reciprocate. I couldn't deny the fluttering in my stomach every time I heard his voice or thought about running into him at the preschool. I'd had feelings for him since high school and I was too old to try and convince myself they didn't exist. I was destined to be an old maid, another thing I was too old to deny, just Gypsy and me living alone in that big old farmhouse. But I could have my memories of today.

While waiting for our food to arrive we exchanged pleasantries. He told me about a few of the people he'd visited at the hospital this morning. He definitely had a pastor's heart. It wasn't just the members of his own flock he visited at hospitals. While moving down the hall to the room of a patient he knew, he would stop in other rooms for a quick hello to its occupant. Before leaving the hospital, he would always go by the chapel to offer to pray with anyone who may be there. If the chapel was empty, which was often the case, he prayed alone. He cared for everyone, and it made me love him all the more.

It wasn't until we had nearly polished off every pepperoni and bread stick on the table that he asked me about Nicole.

"Has she given any indication about why she's here?"

I shook my head. "No. She and I barely talk. She spends her time with the kids, which is good, and I'm always at work. I don't know any more about her plans than I did when she first got here. I don't think she even has plans. She's always been that way, living each day as it comes."

"Sounds good in theory, I guess, but not very responsible."

"Well, that's our Nicole." I took a sip of soda and played with the straw. Kyle didn't speak, he just watched from his side of the table. "I am totally losing control," I admitted finally. "The kids are fighting with me about everything. They don't go to preschool half the time when they're supposed to. Nicole says I'm too controlling. I don't want to control anybody, but some things have to be done, don't they? Emma starts kindergarten next year and we don't even know where she's going to be living. Aunt Wanda wants me to get a lawyer and take Nicole to court. Maybe that's best for the kids, but what if Nicole's really changed this time? Shouldn't I give her a chance to prove herself before I hire a lawyer? Any influence I have on her will be lost then. I almost think she wants the kids to hate me too. You should've seen the look she gave me the first time Emma wanted me instead of her. I don't know what to do.

"All I do know, is I'm losing it, big time. I can't keep living like this. Everything I believe in is suddenly insignificant. I tell Nicole something and she gives me this look like, "Michelle thinks she's so perfect. Look at what a mess her life is." I hate this. Sometimes I think it would be so much easier if Nicole just left and took the kids with her. Isn't that awful? Aunt Wanda would hate me if she knew I was thinking this way, but I can't help myself."

I stopped talking. "Sorry, I didn't mean to get so carried away."

"No, it's fine; you need to talk."

"Do you think I'm terrible? I know the kids are better off living on the farm with me, but it's taking everything out of me to have them there."

"Them or Nicole?"

"Well, Nicole, of course, but they're a package deal."

He pushed his glass aside, leaned his elbows on the table, and gazed into my eyes. "I don't think you're terrible, Michelle. Nicole is using you. She knows you care too much about those kids to risk saying anything to her. I also think she knows exactly what she's doing."

"Which is…?"

"She's sponging off you until something better comes along. Do you think she'd hesitate for a minute to leave if that boyfriend of hers came back? For the time being she doesn't have any options so she has to put up with you but something will happen and you need to be prepared."

"That's what Aunt Wanda tells me."

"You have to decide what you want. Do you want to keep Nicole's kids? If you do, then you need to talk to her about it."

"I know I do, but right now she's staying put and the kids love having her around. I hate to rock the boat."

"And she's counting on that. She knows you won't kick her out as long as she has the kids for leverage. But you said yourself you can't keep living in limbo, not knowing what's going to happen tomorrow. You need to confront her."

"I can't do that. Emma's graduating from preschool next month. Jonah's been acting out ever since Nicole came home. I can't throw the kids into anymore turmoil than they already are."

"What about you? What about the turmoil your life has been thrown into?"

I blushed over my glass of Pepsi. "I didn't expect this, Kyle," I said smiling. "I figured you'd give me one of those turn the other cheek lectures and tell me how I need to be patient and understanding with her."

"You do, of course. But your top priority is those kids."

"I wish we could have one conversation that wasn't about my messy life."

"Oh, we will." He arched his eyebrows playfully.

I felt the heat rising in my cheeks. "What's that supposed to mean?"

He reached across the table and put his hand over mine. "Please, Michelle, just one problem at a time."

What was he doing? Did he have any idea what affect his physical contact had on me? I gazed into his deep blue eyes. No doubt about it. He knew.

"So after all this is over with Nicole, you're going to start giving me trouble?" I asked.

He smiled. "I might. But you can't handle it right now." He didn't give me time to process the meaning behind his words before he switched gears. "If anyone else came into your house and turned your routine upside down like Nicole has, you wouldn't stand for it. You would realize it was totally unacceptable behavior in a houseguest, and probably do something about it."

"She's not a houseguest, she's my sister."

"Still, she's a guest. You have certain rules and expectations for what can and cannot go on under your roof and as any decent human being, she has to respect that. It's time you stood up for yourself."

"I guess," I muttered, "but I've never been strong when it comes to my family. Every one of them has always bowled me over."

He squeezed my hand again. "You can do whatever you need to do, Michelle."

"I wish I had your faith in me."

"My faith is in the One who saved you from your sins. Trust Him, Michelle, He promised to never leave you or forsake you."

ᎶChapter Thirty-nine

I left the restaurant that afternoon with a new determination. I had to get over my fears of what Nicole planned to do. Like Kyle and Aunt Wanda said, Nicole was taking advantage of the hold she had over me. She knew I couldn't stand up to her for fear of what she'd do with the kids. I had to get my life back. I could no longer stand the way she and the kids were ruling my house. They were living under my roof, I was picking up the tab for every single thing from food to toilet paper; like it or not, Nicole was going to start doing things my way. She wasn't going to intimidate me anymore.

I parked in my usual spot next to the kitchen door, squared my shoulders, and marched into the house like I owned the place. All was quiet except for the muffled sound of the television set in the living room. I headed in that direction. The shades were drawn against the afternoon sun and the room was cloaked in shadows. It took a moment to make out the shapes of my niece and nephew asleep on the couch. Gypsy raised her head and looked at me from her position on the floor below them, and then lowered it back to her paws. I tiptoed to the TV and clicked it off. The kids didn't stir. Where was Nicole?

I tiptoed from the room, dropped my car keys on the sofa table in the foyer, and headed upstairs. She had probably set the kids down in front of the TV and then went upstairs to take a nap or a bath; typical, irresponsible, Nicole behavior.

Just as I figured, I could hear movement coming from her room when I reached the landing. I pecked on the door and stuck my head inside. She had just sat down on the bed when I looked in. She held something in her hands. It looked as if she'd been crying.

"Nicole, are you all right?"

She looked up startled. "Oh, it's you. I didn't hear you come in."

"I just got home." I went the rest of the way into the room and pushed the door shut behind me, "What's the matter?"

Her shoulders lifted slightly. She stared at the object in her hands. "Nothing."

By now, I could see what had held her attention. It was a ceramic ballerina that used to sit on the shelf in her room. Mom had sent it from where she was living in Texas at the time, a few weeks after Nicole's tenth or eleventh birthday. I remembered thinking at the time it was a little childish for a girl Nicole's age. But who could expect Mom to know enough about either of us to send an appropriate gift. The gift came with a card that didn't even apologize for being late. The inscription read something like, *Love, Mom. Wish I could be there.* Of course, there had been no explanation as to why she couldn't be here. No *"I miss you," "Call me"* or *"I'll be there as soon as I can get away."* Nicole had cherished that ballerina. Anytime she was feeling particularly low she'd take it off the shelf and stare at it and caress it, sometimes for hours.

I sat down beside her on the bed and took the ballerina out of her hands. I smoothed my fingers over the line-splayed porcelain. The blonde hair and pink tutu had faded over the years. The seam that held the thing together had grown wide enough to be felt with one's fingers. I turned it this way and that in my hands, and could easily make out the Made in Taiwan on the back of its neck; a cheap trinket that had brought a little girl such comfort over the years. I wondered if Mom even remembered she'd sent it. Not likely even though she only sent three or four packages during the years we were growing up without her.

"Do you remember when Mom sent that to me?" Nicole asked.

"I was just thinking about that."

She sighed wistfully. "I used to lay here on this bed and stare up at her on the shelf, and imagined her dancing in some big auditorium. Of course, I was the ballerina. I would pretend that Mom helped me get my hair styled that way and made the costume for me. Then I would go to my dance recital and Mom and Dad would be sitting in the front row watching me dance in Swan Lake. When the music ended, the audience would come alive with thunderous applause and everyone would stand to their feet. I would bow and people would throw roses onto the stage. I'd look out at the audience and Mom would be clapping hardest of everyone with tears streaming down her cheeks. She'd smile and nod and give me this little wave and keep right on clapping. Dad's face would be wet with tears. He'd reach over and kiss Mom's cheek, and the two of them would be so happy."

I sat quietly beside her for a few moments, letting her remember. "Then what happened," I asked.

She took the ballerina out of my hands and stood up. "Nothing." The wistfulness was gone from her voice. "That's where the daydream ended; Mom and Dad clapping and crying and being proud of me." She set the ballerina back on the shelf. "What could be better than that?"

I suddenly felt very depressed. I wondered what got her thinking about that, but it seemed cruel to ask.

She ran her fingers over the front of the doll one last time and then turned to face me. "Dean called while you were out."

I felt as if I'd been punched in the gut.

"We talked for over an hour. He said he'd made a big mistake by leaving. He can't stop thinking about me. He told me he's sorry and wants me back."

"What about the kids?"

"He's sorry about that, too. He says he was wrong to hassle me so much about them. He wants to come get me and move all of us back to the city."

My heart sank even farther. Here it was, the moment I'd been dreading, but knew would come nonetheless. I sent a silent prayer heavenward and said, "Don't take the kids, Nicole. Let them stay here with me, just until you and Dean get on your feet." Even as I said it, I knew it was a lie. I never wanted her to take them from me. I continued, "Or they could stay here indefinitely. I love having them here. It isn't like they're…"

"No, Michelle, they're mine, I can't live without them."

I thought, *"You did for eight months."* But I didn't say it out loud. "What about when Dean gets tired of them again and you two get in another fight?" I gently reminded her. "It would be so much better if they just stayed here."

"Better for you maybe; you've always been jealous of what I've had. You can't have children of your own to control, so you think you can steal mine. I see how you are with them, Michelle. Everything has to be your way. Throwing Jonah's toys away just because he wouldn't pick them up the instant you asked. That was plain cruel and childish. Do you always have to be right, Michelle, even when it breaks the hearts of everyone around you?"

I couldn't believe she was attacking me. "I told him several times to pick up the toys. He wouldn't and I had work to do," I stopped talking and took a deep breath. "Nicole, I don't want to defend my childrearing methods. I'm not an old pro at this. I'm learning as I go and I'm sure I'm making mistakes, but the kids are happy here. They're going to school, they're involved in church, this arrangement is good for them," I prayed again for strength, "and I think we should think about making it permanent."

Her mouth dropped open. "You've got to be kidding. You want my kids? No way," she said as she sliced at the air with her hand. "No way."

"Come on, Nicole, think about it. This is the kids' home now."

"No, it isn't. This is your home. You make that evident every minute of the day. I know you don't want us here and you resent getting stuck with the kids in the first place. There's no way I'd leave them here so I'd be indebted to my big sister the rest of my life for saving me."

"This isn't about you and me, Nicole. It's about the kids. I admit, I did resent them being here in the first place but not now. Now I can't imagine life without them. At least think about it. Think about what's best for them. It isn't fair to uproot them after they've finally got some stability in their lives."

She set her fists on her hips, "See, you always do that. You make everything to be my fault. If I don't take them, I'm a terrible mother. If I do take them, I'm robbing them of the only stability they've ever known. God knows I never gave them any stability, isn't that right?"

I stood up, vigorously shaking my head. "I'm not trying to make this anyone's fault. I just want you to see that they're settled here. They're doing great in preschool. Emma starts kindergarten in the fall. If you leave now, it's only going to upset them and make it that much harder for you to get settled with Dean in the city. Isn't that why you gave me custody in the first place?"

Nicole shook her head. She didn't like what she was hearing. "I gave you temporary custody to help me out of a tight spot. We've already discussed this, Michelle. Dean is coming to get me. Now, I know what I'm doing. I'm ready to be a mother to my kids."

"You just said he called. You never mentioned anything about agreeing to go with him."

"I didn't think you were interested in hearing a replay of the entire conversation. But, yes, we made up. We're going to be a family. We might even get married."

I slapped my own forehead, "Nicole, no. Think about what it will do to the kids. This isn't fair to them."

"And think about what it will do to them if we do it your way. They'll grow up thinking their mother deserted them just like you and I did. No thanks. I'm not doing that to my kids, Michelle. Look what it did to us. I can't keep a job or a man, and you've turned into a bitter old shrew just like Grandma."

"I'm nothing like Grandma."

She snorted derisively, "Yeah, right. Keep telling yourself that, Sis. Anyway, I don't want my kids to grow up with the same feelings of inadequacies that we had. Do you think if Mom or Dad had put one ounce of energy into making me think I was special or that they loved me, I'd be so bent on taking the word of the first worthless man who showed me any attention? Of course not. I know the guys I hang out with are no good. But I figure I don't deserve anything better." She stared into my eyes. "And you feel the exact same way but instead of choosing losers, you went the safe route and avoided men altogether."

I ground my teeth together in frustration. I had to hand it to her; she was right this time. I had realized years ago that I didn't feel worthy of anyone's love. But rather than think about it, I buried my head in my work until I didn't have time to think.

"If you're so sure Dean is worthless, then why are you leaving with him?" I asked. "Especially when you know he isn't exactly thrilled to play the Daddy role."

"Maybe he's not my knight in shining armor, but he's here. I think he cares for me like he says and I think we can make it work. I'm not stupid enough to think it'll be perfect, but I want to try. What else have I got?"

"You've got your kids, Nicole. You've got them, and you need to think about what's best for them."

"I am thinking about them. They need a daddy. Heaven knows living here they'll never have a male role model. I want my kids to have what we never did."

I wanted to tell her they'd be better off with no role model than with Dean, but I kept my personal opinions to myself. I had to make her see reason before this situation escalated into an all out battle that neither one of us could win.

I spoke as calmly as I could, sort of the way you do when facing a dangerous and potentially unstable animal. "We're not talking about you and me, Nicole. We're talking about Emma and Jonah. They know they're loved here. They've got me and Aunt Wanda and Uncle Jeb and their teachers at the preschool. We could explain that while you still love them, we've decided, as the adults in their lives, that it's better that they live here. It wouldn't be like Mom and Dad, where you just drop out of their lives altogether. You'd still come by to visit and when they got older if they wanted to spend a week or two with you over summer vacation, they could. They wouldn't have the same baggage we do."

"No, Michelle, this is my decision. It has nothing to do with you. They're my kids and they're going back to the city with me. Whatever it takes to raise them, I'll be the one to do it. I won't have them thinking I abandoned them."

My patience and good intentions could only go so far. "They already think that, Nicole. Your most recent loser boyfriend dumped them under my lilac bushes and drove away. They didn't even know who I was. Emma didn't speak for weeks. Jonah, your three-year-old son, had to comfort his big sister and now you decide you're ready to be Mother of the Year. Forget it! You're not taking those kids anywhere."

Nicole's blue eyes flashed. Part of me wished I could take my words back, the other part wished I had the nerve to say what I really thought.

"I'd let Children's Services have them before I'd ever come to you for help again," she shrieked. "You sanctimonious toad! What do you know about being a mother? What do you know about caring for anyone? You're the coldest, nastiest hag I've ever met. No wonder Grandma hated you. No wonder Mom couldn't stand the sight of you after Dad left. All you did was remind her of how much she had failed as a woman."

"How do you know? You can't remember what it was like back then. You don't know what I did for Mom. If it wasn't for me, Grandma and Aunt Wanda would've—"

"Would've what? Don't give me that, Michelle, I know all about it. Grandma told me everything. She told me how you babied Mom and talked to her late into the night after Dad left; how she always went to you for solace when life got too hard. She tried to lean on you and you failed her."

"I was fourteen. What was I supposed to do?"

"You were supposed to be there for her; to shut your mouth for once and just listen instead of trying to fix everything. You can't keep your mouth shut long enough for someone to tell you what they're really feeling. You assume you already know and belittle them for not being as perfect as you are. You've always been that way, Michelle, and no one can stand to be around you. I'll leave my kids in foster care before I let you poison them against me like you've been doing for the last eight months."

"Then why'd you leave them here in the first place?"

"Because I had no choice. But I know what I'm doing now, believe me, I won't make the same mistake twice."

I'd had it. Any reservations about taking her to court and ruining what remained of her reputation went out the window. "Then you better be prepared for a fight, sweetheart," I raged, "'cause I'm not letting you walk out of here with those kids. I'll hire the best lawyer in this county. No judge in his right mind would let you have them after what you've done."

Nicole smiled wickedly, "So, this is what it's come down to, my own sister taking me to court to get *my* kids?"

"You bet it is," I sneered back. "You don't deserve kids. I wouldn't trust you to take care of Gypsy and no one else in this county will either."

"I'm not a kid anymore, Michelle. You can't bully me around. I'm leaving here and I'm taking what's mine."

I couldn't seem to quit losing my temper, "Over my dead body."

"That won't be the hardest thing I've ever done," she challenged.

I wasn't behaving in a very Christian manner, but I couldn't get hold of myself. "Just go, Nicole. Go back to the city or whatever hole you crawled out of and leave us in peace. Your kids are happy and stable for the first time in their lives. Do them a favor and leave and don't come back. You won't be missed."

"Don't worry, when I leave you'll be the first to know."

Chapter Forty

I blew it, I blew it, I blew it! The situation couldn't have gone any worse if I had choreographed the entire thing with a Hollywood stunt team. Nicole would never speak to me again. She'd never listen to my advice. More importantly, she'd never agree to let me have the kids. I blew it.

I didn't want to take my sister to court. More than anything, I had wanted to solve this with love and compassion for the sake of her and the children. I wanted the best for everyone, even Dean, whom I knew did not really want the kids. He was only agreeing to it to shut Nicole up. But what would happen when there was trouble again and he no longer cared about making her happy. The kids would suffer, and it would all be my fault because my sister no longer had me to turn to.

As far as my Christianity was concerned, it had gone out the window at the first sign of trouble. I had prayed but then spoke in haste without waiting for the Father's voice to guide me. I understood more about the Christian charity that Grandma Catherine talked about. Enough to know I didn't have any. I was as guilty as Nicole, talking about the awful things that had happened to us as children, and then turning around and heaping the same disrespect on someone else.

I had to make things right, and that couldn't happen in a court-room.

❧

Nicole and I barely spoke. The county hospital called and said they were short-handed and wondered if I could work Saturday or Sunday.

I turned them down. I was terrified of going to work and then coming home to an empty house. I'd have to face that possibility on Monday, but wanted to put it off as long as possible. I didn't want to let her out of my sight for a minute.

She was still in bed Sunday morning when I got up and got ready for church. Emma woke while I was in the shower and left Nicole's bed to go to her own room to get dressed. That's where I found her when I padded down the hall to my room in my robe and slippers. "Is Jonah up yet?" I asked.

She shook her head. "He doesn't want to go to church today."

My first impulse was to go in there where he lay next to Nicole and drag him out of bed. *"In this house we go to church, young man,"* I could hear myself saying. Then I remembered all the times Grandma had said those exact words to me.

"He doesn't, huh?" I said instead. "When did he tell you that?"

"A little bit ago. I heard the shower running so I woke him up. He said he wanted to stay home with Mommy."

"What about you? Do you want to stay home with Mommy?"

She smiled innocently and shook her head. "No, I like church."

I tousled her hair. "Good; so do I."

�֍

"You're missing one today, aren't you?"

I turned and saw Angie moving through the crowd behind us after the service. Emma spotted her too, and rushed into her arms. "Angie!" she squealed. "I miss you. When can we come back to your house to play?"

Angie knelt down to return the hug and said, "Whenever you want, Doodle Bug. I miss you too. Where's Jonah?"

"He stayed home with Mommy."

"Oh." Angie looked at me.

Emma smiled bashfully at Angie's daughters. Even though she and the older girls got along famously, Emma was always shy when first seeing someone she hadn't seen in a while. Fear of acceptance into the group, I supposed.

"Hi, Emma," Molly, the oldest one, said.

Emma hung back until I gave her a gentle nudge. Molly reached out and took her hand. Katie took the other. The three of them moved off to the fellowship hall where the children usually romped while their parents visited with other members of the church.

"I take it things are a little difficult at home," Angie observed.

"Is it that obvious?" I asked.

She nodded. "Pretty much."

"I didn't want to fight with Jonah this morning about coming to church, especially since he was in bed with his mother. We are sort of fighting."

Angie took my elbow. "I'm sorry to hear that, Michelle."

"Yeah, me too; it looks like I'm going to have to hire an attorney."

"Oh, no." Angie turned and looked through the crowd. "There's Chris." She waved at her husband to get his attention and motioned for him to join us. "I've got a roast in the crock pot at home. Why don't you and Emma come home with us for dinner? We could talk there."

"No, thanks, I don't want to be an imposition and Nicole will be wondering where we are."

"You know it's no imposition. You can call her from the house. Come on, Michelle, Kyle's going too."

"Then I'm definitely not going."

I was sure she was matchmaking, but she looked truly perplexed. "Why? You need to talk to someone, Michelle, and who could offer better advice than a man of God?"

"Angie, this makes me really uncomfortable. I feel like all I'm doing lately is telling someone my woes. I'm sure people have better things to do."

"Nonsense."

Chris appeared at her side. "Michelle and Emma are joining us for dinner, honey. Isn't that nice?"

Chris grinned broadly. "The more the merrier. Let's go, I'm starved."

Nicole didn't answer the phone when I called from Angie's so I left a message on the machine, telling her where we could be reached. Surely she wouldn't take off without Emma. If she did…oh, I really would wring her neck. I comforted myself with a reminder that she liked to stay up late watching old movies and then sleep in. She probably hadn't rolled out of bed yet even though it was nearly one o'clock.

I was here to talk about what was bothering me with Angie, but my problems seemed distant seated around the table with Angie, Chris, their girls, Emma, and Kyle. The girls did most of the talking, telling us what had happened in Sunday School. We laughed, enjoyed the pot roast, and each other's company. After dinner and store bought apple pie the girls took Emma upstairs to play. "I can't be expected to do everything," Angie had said, when Chris made a teasing face at the bakery box.

"Let me help you with these dishes, Angie," I said, pushing my chair back.

"No, no. Chris can help me. You and Kyle go into the living room. You can talk in there."

From the smile on her face I wondered whether she was more interested in putting us together than for me to benefit from his counsel. "But I—"

"Just go." She put her hand on my shoulder and turned me toward the door. "I can't think of a better person to talk to when you're having problems, except my Chris here," she added with a wink, "but you can't have him. Now go. We'll be in after the dishes are finished."

"There's no use arguing with her, Michelle," Kyle said. "She's formidable once she gets something into her head."

"Tell me about it," Chris said laughing as he turned on the tap in the sink.

"Watch it, you two," Angie warned.

I followed Kyle into the seldom-used living room and sat down on the long, coffee-colored sofa. Kyle settled into an oversized recliner and put his hand on his stomach. "I think I overdid it in there," he said with a groan. "It isn't often I get such wonderful home cooking."

"Me either. I'm afraid most of mine comes out of a box." We relaxed into our seats and listened to the sounds of the house; we could hear dishes clink and soft laughter from the kitchen and muffled sounds of the girls playing upstairs.

"Angie says things aren't going so great at home with Nicole," Kyle said after a few moments of silence.

I nodded. No use keeping him in the dark since he mainly knew everything anyway. "That's the understatement of the year. We got into it pretty good the other day. I'm afraid I didn't handle things too well. I threatened Nicole with a lawyer."

"Ouch."

"I guess I have to follow through now. She is getting back together with her old boyfriend. He could show up to get them any day." I leaned forward and gazed at him earnestly. "I can't sit still and let her take the kids."

"I understand that."

"But what am I supposed to do? As mad as I am at Nicole right now, it doesn't seem right to alienate my own sister. I don't have much family to speak of. The only close relatives are Aunt Wanda and Uncle Jeb. Oh, Uncle Dewitt's right next-door, but he's been a stranger to his own brothers and sisters since the day he was born. I love Nicole. I hate to think I'll do something that will drive her away forever."

Kyle put his fingertips together like a teepee and rested his chin on them. "I don't envy the position you're in, Michelle. On one hand, if you fight her for the kids, you could be saving them from a life of pain. On the other hand, even if you win, you may drive a wedge between you and Nicole that her kids will someday resent you for. Really, it's only you who can make this decision."

"That's not what I wanted to hear, Kyle. I wanted you to say something wise and profound that would make all my problems go away. I almost wish I could go back to last year when none of this was my concern."

"You don't mean that."

"Sometimes I do," I admitted, instantly ashamed at putting my thoughts into words. "My life was so simple before all this happened, when all I had to worry about was me."

"Sometimes we're called to move out of our comfort zone for the sake of someone else; to sacrifice ourselves."

My temper flared. "You've got to be kidding. What do you think I've been doing for the past nine months? I've made nothing but sacrifices, and I haven't got anything back."

The patient, pious expression on his face only fueled my anger. "Do you have any idea how much money I've spent on those kids since they got here? I'm not begrudging them that," I hastened to add. "I want them to be safe and with people who care about them. Not like Nicole, who let them fend for themselves. They miss the neighbor lady more than they do their own mother. I would never do anything like that to them. But Kyle, come on. To imply that I haven't sacrificed is an insult. I've sacrificed everything. Money, time, independence—everything I have. And what have I gotten back for it?"

He still wasn't talking. His expression remained unchanged. I had half a mind to reach over and change it for him.

"Nothing," I practically shouted in response to my own question, "that's what— absolutely nothing! I give and give and give, and all I hear is how I should do more; that sacrifices have to be made."

I took a deep shuddering breath. I blinked tears away from my eyes and crossed my arms over my chest. I wouldn't cry. I wouldn't let him think his words had wounded me. They just showed his ignorance of the situation. Most of the time when people made barbing comments, they had no idea what they were talking about. Well, now he knew.

Kyle leaned back in his chair, but didn't take his eyes off my face. I wished he'd stop staring at me like that, as if he knew everything going on in my head. Just because he claimed to be a man of God, a counselor, didn't mean he could see into my soul.

Finally he spoke. "Do you really think you haven't received anything in return?"

I blinked. "What? What are you talking about?"

"I'm talking about everything you've received in the past nine months." He went on before I could protest. "I'm not suggesting you haven't given a lot to those kids. You've done more than most people would. You didn't have to accept them into your home that first day, and I commend you for doing it. But…you received a hundred times more than what you gave."

My anger boiled back to the surface. There he went again; making his ignorance apparent. I opened my mouth to give him a piece of my mind, and then clamped it shut again.

An image of Emma's face when she spotted the black chunky shoes on the store shelf flashed through my mind. It was followed in rapid succession by an image of Jonah standing on stage singing his heart out, the two of them running across the field in pursuit of Gypsy, and

Emma perched on a kitchen stool, a smear of flour across her nose, as she helped Aunt Wanda roll homemade noodles. I saw Emma and Jonah sitting on the bank with Uncle Jeb fishing. I could see them as plain as day in my mind's eye on Christmas morning when they came downstairs, and I remembered their squeals of delight and wonder when they spotted the packages under the tree.

Tears sprang to my eyes again, this time not out of anger or indignation. He reached out and took my hand. "Sometimes it's worth the risk of loving someone, Michelle."

I studied his face through the veil of tears, and tried to decipher if he was referring to the kids, God, or himself. Everything was so simple a year ago. I went to work everyday; was paid well for my efforts, took care of the farm and Gypsy. That was enough. I was happy, wasn't I? Wasn't I fulfilled? I didn't miss having anyone in my life, someone to come home to. I loved having my off time to myself. I didn't have to clear my schedule to make room for another's needs. I ate what I wanted. I stayed up late to watch old movies if I wanted. I slept in on my day's off and didn't have to worry about a little someone waking me up at seven demanding breakfast. The only wet towels I retrieved from the bathroom floor belonged to me. Compromise was not in my vocabulary.

That's how I liked it.

So why was I so miserable facing the possibility those things would go back to the way they were then?

"It's too hard," I admitted, my voice an unattractive croak. "It's easier never to have something than to try to get along without it once it's gone."

Kyle kneaded the back of my hand. I turned my hand over and curled my fingers around his. He was quiet for a long time. "If that's the way you want to live your life, Michelle, it's up to you," he said finally. "No one can tell you what you need to make you happy. You have a job you love. I know it brings you great satisfaction. The question is, is that all you want? Will that be enough when you look back on your life fifty years from now? For millions of people, it is. No one will judge you if you decide that's what makes you happy. But does it? Is there nothing more that you want?"

I pulled my hand away from his and pinched the bridge of my nose. "I never thought about it before," I replied honestly. "All I ever thought about as I was growing up was moving past whatever stage I was in at the time—getting it over with so I could move on to something else; hopefully something better. I never really enjoyed the moment I was in, no matter what I was doing. I didn't think about it. I never realized I wasn't enjoying myself. I wanted to be a nurse more than anything. Even nursing school, though I loved everything about it and met some really great and interesting people, was just another step I had to complete to move ahead. Then I got my first job. I thought after I had some experience, I could move up and earn more money. With more experience and education, I kept working toward higher seniority and better benefits. I never had that many expenses living on the farm, so my bank account kept growing. I remember thinking how cool it would be to save ten thousand dollars. That was my goal. It was such a big amount of money back then. I thought if I could save that much I'd be happy and secure—then it was twenty. When my savings and mutual funds reached fifty thousand, all I could think was, *"What good is fifty thousand dollars going to do a person in this economy?"* That was a pittance if something were to happen and I couldn't work till retirement."

I stopped talking and took a tissue out of a box on the end table. I looked into his kind face and smiled. "I never thought about having someone in my life. Relationships were so much work. Spouses, kids, mortgages who needed it? Whenever somebody would be bellyaching at work about their rotten marriage, credit card bills or whatever, I'd feel kind of superior, like, 'You should have thought of that before you got yourself into that mess. You should be more responsible like me.' Life was just plain easier back then."

"But were you happier?"

I shrugged. "I told you, I didn't think about it."

"I don't believe you."

"Why would I lie, Kyle?"

"I don't know; to protect yourself?"

"From what?"

"From opening your heart to someone."

I shook my head. He thought he had all the answers, but he didn't get it. "That's not it at all. I told you, I was too busy moving ahead with whatever I was doing at the time, I never gave myself a chance to entertain notions of a relationship."

"Is that what you did with us?"

"Huh?"

"In high school; you always held back. You never truly opened up to me. After we broke up and I joined the Air Force, I realized I really didn't know you at all. You gave just enough of yourself to let people know they shouldn't expect anything more. That's where it stopped. You didn't open up to me or Nicole or anyone. You cheated us, but you cheated yourself more."

My jaw clenched in anger. He sounded just like Nicole. I was sick of people telling me what a cold, unfeeling mess I was. I wasn't Grandma Catherine. I had feelings. I had love in my heart. I took care of strangers for a living. Hadn't I taken in my abandoned niece and nephew and given them everything their own mother withheld?

"If I held back, it was because no one, including you, ever made me feel like I could be myself. Any time I wanted to open up and show part of the real me, I was let know it wasn't a convenient time. I was always a burden to someone."

"Give the world a break, Michelle. You held back because you wanted to. You wanted to protect yourself, you said so yourself. You can keep on blaming the rest of us for what a rotten life you've had or you can make the best of what you've got left. You don't have to feel like you're a reed beaten down by the wind anymore. You have a choice. It isn't too late to let someone love you."

"Yes, it is," I insisted. "Yes, it is." I fell forward into his arms.

He pulled me against his chest and tilted my face up to meet his. "No. It's not."

My breath caught in my throat. Gazing into his eyes, I knew I could believe what he said. I didn't want him to let go of me. I forgot all about Angie and Chris in the kitchen and the girls playing upstairs. It was just the two of us. I prayed the moment wouldn't end.

"Michelle," he said, in his husky voice. He brushed his lips across my cheek and my nose. I wanted to tangle my fingers in his hair and force his mouth to mine but I didn't. What if he wasn't saying what I thought I saw in his eyes? I couldn't take the chance. I couldn't risk him rejecting me.

"Michelle," he repeated. He loosened his hold on me and looked down into my face. "I love you. I've never stopped, not in the last fifteen years. I realized it the first day you brought the kids to the preschool. I kept telling myself it was the memory of you that I loved; something lost in youth. It was easier dealing with that than accepting that there could never be anything between us."

My heart didn't know what to think. All my ears heard was, *"I love you,"* and *"There can never be anything between us."*

I pulled out of his arms and cleared my throat awkwardly. Emma? I needed to get her and get out of here. I needed to put some distance between Kyle Swann and me. He loved me. Now what? What good could possibly come of it? By his own admission, there could never be anything between us. I would have preferred he not even confess his feelings for me, knowing there was no hope for a relationship between us.

I took another tissue from the box and dabbed at my nose. "I—um, I need to find Emma…"

He grabbed me before I could finish my sentence. He pulled me against him and pressed his lips to mine. I could feel the barely suppressed passion in his embrace. There was nothing chaste and cautious this time. I melted into his arms in shock. My head was reeling by the time he released me.

"Kyle, I…"

He put a finger over my lips. "Shh, don't say anything. Except that you love me, too."

I put my hands against his chest and pushed him away. Tears sprang to my eyes. "Why? Why do you want me to say that? It's bad enough that you already have."

He pulled me back into his arms. His gaze was hard, almost angry. "Then tell me you don't. Say it. I want you to look into my eyes and tell me you don't love me."

I lowered my eyes and focused on his Adam's apple. He grabbed my chin and tilted it upward, "Either tell me you love me, or tell me you don't, but you have to say something."

"All right, I don't love you. Now, will you leave me alone?"

His gaze softened. "You're a terrible liar, Michelle," he whispered.

I jerked away from him, angry with myself this time. "All right, fine. You win. But what difference does it make? You said yourself there'll never be anything between us. We're two different people. Nothing'll change that."

He took a step toward me. I stepped back. My heels bumped against the sofa. He reached out and caught hold of my hand. "God has changed it. Remember? You're a new creature, old things have passed away, and all things have become new. I don't know what kind of future either of us have, but I believe we have a chance to pursue it, if you want to, that is."

I didn't know what to think. It couldn't be that easy; just apologize to God for denying him my entire life, and then "poof" my past was like it never happened. I couldn't be the woman God sent to Kyle. Surely there was someone else out there, more suitable, more holy. "Kyle, I don't know if I'm ready…"

"I don't know if I am either. All I know is how I feel right this moment."

When he pulled me into his arms again, I went willingly. I knew Angie and Chris were in the next room, their hands in the dishwater, within earshot of everything we said. And I didn't care.

⟨Chapter Forty-one

E mma had her car seat straps off her shoulders and unhooked before I got the car into park. She knew I didn't like for her to do that until the ignition was turned off. Today I didn't lecture. My mind was on other things.

She bounded out of the car as soon as I raised the back of my seat to let her out, and headed into the house. She had an exciting afternoon and couldn't wait to rub it in Jonah's nose about all the fun he'd missed. I gathered my purse and Bible from the passenger side of the front seat and followed her.

Emma had joined Nicole and Jonah in front of the television in the living room. Hamburger grease was congealing in a skillet on the stove. I dumped my things on the kitchen table and went straight to the sink to run dishwater. Nothing my sister said or did today, short of running off with *my* kids, could upset me. Kyle loved me. Nothing else mattered.

After the dishes in the sink were washed, I started working my way around the kitchen with a wet sponge. The stove and countertops were splattered with grease, fingerprints and everyday grime from a family who never took time to clean up as they messed up, which would have kept a small job from turning into a big one. By the time I got to the refrigerator, I decided now was as good a time as any to defrost the freezer in the twenty-year-old Kenmore.

I turned off the fridge and emptied the freezer's contents into the clean sink. Working here in Grandma's domain got me to thinking about her. What had happened to Catherine Barker in her youth that turned her into the woman we all knew? Was it her husband, my grandpa, who made her life so unbearable that she had to fight back to protect herself? Had it begun years before then? I never knew Grandma's parents and had never heard her talk about them. Were they poor? Did she have a hard, critical mother she couldn't please, no matter how hard she tried?

Something in Grandma's life must have contributed to her mean dislike for everyone and everything she came across. Even Aunt Wanda, who had seemed a mirror image of her when I was a kid, had been a source of great irritation. When Mom wasn't around to pick at, Grandma turned on Aunt Wanda. It was funny how I had overlooked it at the time, thinking Aunt Wanda deserved it. But no one deserved to be put down over things they couldn't change. Now that I thought about it, poor Violet took almost as much abuse and ridicule as I did. No wonder she had been so eager to marry Cliff and move away.

Actually Grandma's situation wasn't so far different from mine, although I loathed admitting it. Her husband had passed away. All of her children were raised and out of the house. For the first time in her life, her time was finally her own. Then the daughter, whom she already suspected of messing up her life with a loser, came home with no husband and two kids; two kids who ruined any hope she had for a peaceful old age. She didn't want to raise her grandkids. Even with Mom here, much of the responsibility for three people added to the household fell on Grandma's shoulders. I couldn't excuse the way she handled it, especially how she took out her frustration on me, but I could understand it a little.

I didn't say anything to Nicole about getting the kids up for school Monday morning. I left at my usual time with the three of them still asleep, hoping she'd do the right thing but not expecting much.

During my lunch break I went out to my car and called my case-worker's office. She wasn't in so I left a brief message telling her I needed to speak with her. I left my cell phone number and asked that she please not try to contact me at the house.

I thought about calling Kyle just to hear his voice. I called the pre-school instead and asked Miss Billie if the kids were there. Yes, they had arrived at eight-thirty and just finished their lunch. At least that phone call helped lift my spirits. I didn't know what to do. If only I knew what Nicole was planning. I wanted to enjoy thoughts of Kyle and our afternoon in Angie's living room, but I couldn't shake the eerie feeling that something terrible was brewing with Nicole and the kids.

I bowed my head over the steering wheel and prayed. *"God, you see what's going on down here. I don't know what to do. Nicole hates me. I don't want to fight her in court, but I don't see any alternative. I wish she would just go away and leave us alone but that probably isn't what You or the kids want. I know your perfect plan is for kids to be with their mother, but not when she's as lousy at motherhood as Nicole."*

It didn't seem like a very righteous prayer. I was only considering my needs and not the greater good of a family reunited. God probably wasn't listening out of spite. I was a failure as a sister, a failure as a prayer warrior. I wasn't even a good aunt these days. No, God was incapable of spite, but He wouldn't honor such a selfish request either. Still, if He could just work out things the way I wanted, it would make my life a whole lot easier.

❧

Nicole thrust a slip of paper into my hand when I came in from work. "Here, call this number."

I stared down at the paper. "Why? Who is it?"

"It's Mom. She wants to talk to you. She said she'd be home all night."

It took a moment to get over the shock. I hadn't talked to Mom in years; I had no idea where she was even living. How had Nicole found her? "Mom? Is everything all right? What does she want?"

"She's fine. She just wants to talk to you."

My concern turned to suspicion. "Why? What did you tell her?"

"I just told her what was going on around here."

"Why did you do that? It's none of her business. And how'd you even find her? As far as I knew, she'd dropped off the face of the earth. She hasn't had anything to do with this family for years."

Nicole raised her index finger into the air and said, "Not exactly true. She and I have been in touch for quite some time. We both have come to the point in our lives to let go of the past and move forward. I've tried to understand what Mom was going through when she left us here with Grandma. Sometimes you have to be the bigger person, Michelle, and forgive."

"Forgive?" I spat. "You were the one telling me the other day how you're life was so messed up because of her and Dad and how you can't hold a relationship together because of what they did. Now you're trying to tell me you've forgiven them."

"Michelle," she said patiently, "life is too short to harbor bad feelings toward our own family."

"I couldn't agree more. I just can't believe these words are coming out of your mouth."

She crossed her arms over her chest. "Are you going to call her or not?"

"No." I shoved the paper back into her hands. "I'm going to take a shower, and then I'm going to get something to eat. It's been a long day. Have the kids eaten?"

"Aunt Wanda sent over a meatloaf."

I started up the stairs. "She's going to be very upset if you don't call, Michelle," Nicole hollered after me. "You can't leave her waiting all evening."

"I don't care," I hollered back. "I waited for her for eighteen years." My conscience was immediately pricked at my attitude. I stomped that much harder to drown out the little voice in my head. I didn't want to hear the familiar lecture on Christian charity.

The instant the phone rang, I knew it would be her. It was nine-thirty; I was in my pajamas in the rocking chair in Grandma's old sewing room. Since I never sewed a stitch and had no inclination to start, I had converted the sunny room into a sort of study/retreat for myself, even though I liked to think of the entire house as a personal retreat...or at least I used to. I had given Grandma's old Singer to Aunt Wanda, but held onto the old pedal style one, much to the dismay of Uncle Bill's wife, Mabel. She swore only someone who actually liked sewing should have the antique machine. I disagreed, and since possession was nine-tenths of the law, I kept it. I cleaned it up and used it as a centerpiece for the room. I surrounded it with antique style lamps, doilies, and lace curtains. I threw an ivory, lace coverlet over the old rocking chair and set a porcelain doll in it when I wasn't occupying the spot. The room was the only one in the house that would make a robber think he had broken into a house that belonged to someone with style, grace, and a flair for decorating.

I closed the Bible in my lap and got up to answer the telephone in the hallway.

She got right to the point. "What's this I hear about you taking Nicole to court to get her kids?"

"Nice to hear from you too, Mom."

"Don't get smart with me, Michelle. Your sister called this morning all tore up over this. She said you're trying to steal her kids. You know her kids are all she has. If she lost them, she wouldn't have a reason to live."

"Kind of like you, Mom?"

"Michelle, why are you being this way? There's nothing to be gained by dredging up the past. All we need to worry about is the here and now. I want you to get off your sister's back and stop threatening her with court. Even after I left, your Grandma, God rest her soul; saw no need to take me to court. She just did what needed to be done and kept it in the family."

"Things aren't that simple anymore, Mom. Kids get sick but a doctor won't treat them if they can't get consent from the custodial parent. Emma starts school next year. I can't enroll her until I've done something legal. All I'm doing is trying to protect her and Jonah."

"Then let them go with their mother and mind your own business. Nicole told me Dean is coming to get her, and they're all getting a place in the city."

"Did she also tell you that Dean was the one who convinced her to dump the kids in my front yard in the middle of the night? Did she mention they didn't even have shoes on their feet? What about telling you how she was passed out drunk at the time and didn't know it had happened till she sobered up?"

"Stop being so melodramatic; everything worked out fine, didn't it? Now she's back and ready to accept her responsibilities."

"And what happens the next time she decides she isn't ready to be somebody's Mom, like you did? What if she's a thousand miles from here and it's too inconvenient to dump them off on me? Where is she going to take them then, or are you even worried about that? They're your grandchildren. I'd think you'd care about their well-being."

She sighed heavily. "I can see some things haven't changed. You're just like you've always been. I was hoping you'd mellowed with age, but I see that hasn't happened. You're still the one with all the answers; little Miss Doomsday. Why can't you leave Nicole be—to make her mistakes? That's how we grow up, Michelle."

For once I wished I didn't have to be the adult in every conversation. "We can't leave Nicole to her own devices, Mom," I growled into the phone. "She has two kids who depend on her. She's already proven she can't be trusted to put their needs in front of her own. I, for one, won't risk giving her another chance."

"Well, I've already decided to send her the money to defend herself. I'm not going to make her accept the help of some public defender when keeping her kids is at stake."

"Where are you even at, Mom? I didn't recognize the area code. For someone so interested in her daughter's life all of a sudden, you sure don't keep in touch."

"Because I can't talk to you, Michelle," she seethed. "I gave up on trying to be a mother to you long ago. You're so full of yourself and this grudge you won't let go of, I just can't take it."

I stared at the phone in my hand, incredulous. Surely I'd misunderstood. "You gave up trying to be my mother long ago? Nineteen years to be exact! You walked out on Nicole and me and never looked back, no explanation, no apologies just cowardice—just like Dad." I was so mad I wanted to throw something, preferably at her head.

I checked my anger and tried to calm down. If I told her right now that I wasn't the same, I'd been born again, I was a new creature, she would laugh in my face. And rightly so by the way I was acting.

"I'm not even going to dignify that with a response," she retorted. "What happened happened—period. If you want to spend your life eaten up with bitterness, that's your choice, but I won't let you drag your sister down with you. As far as the kids being better off with you, I'm not so sure about that. Nicole has her faults, but at least she can see them. You see nothing but what suits you. I feel sorry for you, Michelle."

Her end of the phone went dead. I couldn't believe she hung up on me.

ᗝChapter Forty-two

I heard a car outside and hurried to the window. It had been three days since my phone call from Mom. On the days I worked I couldn't get to the mailbox to see what came, but as far as I knew there had been no money sent yet. I finally got hold of my caseworker who suggested I get a lawyer. I had a good case, she assured me. It was only a matter of time before a judge awarded me custody. Sadly the wheels of justice moved slowly. Still, I couldn't shake the dread each time I thought of suing my own sister. I prayed every night for God to reveal to me if I was making the wrong move. I wasn't sure if God wasn't speaking or I wasn't hearing, but it still seemed to me that it had to be done. I just wished it were someone else doing it.

I slipped into my flip-flops and hurried to the road. I hoped Nicole wasn't watching from the window. I wanted time to sort through the mail before she accused me of invading her privacy, even though this was my house and all the mail thus far bore my name.

I flipped through the mail quickly; the electric bill, four pieces of junk mail for the kids to play with, and a letter addressed to Nicole Hurley. No return address but I recognized Mom's handwriting even after all this time. She obviously didn't want me to know where to find her, as if I wanted to.

Wrong. I did want to. That's why I looked for a return address. Even after everything we both said the other day on the telephone, part of me did want to know where my mother was; where to send a Christmas card or wedding invitation. Not that she'd come, of course.

Almost against my will, I turned the letter toward the sun to see what I could find out. The letter bore a faded Las Vegas postmark. That was one question answered. I squinted against the sunlight and made out the imprint of a personal check partially exposed between a fold of paper. I could imagine the quickly scrawled note wrapped around the check. *"You take this money, Nicole, and make your high and mighty sister eat her words. She thinks she can always get her way. We'll show her this time she doesn't rule the universe."*

How much money had Mom sent? Where did she get it? I didn't know if she was working, living with someone, or married again. I hadn't heard anything personal about her in years. I almost regretted not asking when I had her on the phone.

"So, Mom how's work? Anything good on the horizon? Do you have a special man in your life?" I could have asked those questions usually unnecessary when talking with one's own mother.

I tilted the envelope to one side and then the other. I could make out a scrawled signature. I glanced anxiously at the house and then tapped the envelope against my free hand to make the check slide out of the letter. Another quick peek and a few zeros were visible. I pinched the envelope between my finger and thumb with my right hand and tapped the opposite corner hard against my left hand. I glanced again at the house and then held the envelope above my head; a one then five slanted zeros—one thousand dollars. Wow! I'd never known my mother to have that kind of money at one time, especially money she could afford to give away.

Bitterness filled my heart. She could come up with a thousand dollars for Nicole to fight me in court, against the best intentions for her own grandchildren, but she couldn't send me one dime when I was struggling through nursing school. One time near the end of my final year when money was really tight, Mom showed up on the doorstep and stayed for a few weeks. It was the first time we'd heard from her in two and a half years. I was thrilled to have my mother back during a very stressful time in my life. Within hours though, I realized her presence was not going to alleviate any stress, but rather add to it. She was one more responsibility added to my already long list.

Besides paying for tuition, books, and living expenses, Grandma saw no reason why I should live here free of charge now that I was over eighteen. I had a licensing test coming up that was going to cost me an extra seventy-five dollars. At the time seventy-five dollars may as well have been seven thousand.

I got up my nerve and approached Mom. I sat her down and painted a bleak picture. I left out the part about how, if she thought about it, she'd realize she kind of owed me since she hadn't paid one nickel toward my rearing in five and a half years. It was implied. I wasn't through painting my picture when she saw what was coming and interrupted. By the time she was finished, I wished I had money to give her. I never asked for a dime again.

But somehow she managed to scrape together a thousand dollars for Nicole.

I headed through the house and out on the back porch where Nicole was reading a romance book she'd found on the bookshelves. I dropped the letter into her lap without a word and turned and went back into the house. Rude and childish, yes, but I couldn't bring myself to speak to her.

That night I heard her whispering on the telephone in the kitchen. When I walked in, she turned to face the wall and quickly ended the conversation. I saw the deer-in-the-headlights look on my sister's pretty face and was filled with remorse. I was over my aggravation at Mom for sending the money. Mom was simply being a mother; seeing what she wanted to see. She so desperately wanted to believe Nicole would get her life together and do the right thing by her kids that it was worth a thousand dollars to make it happen.

As far as Nicole was concerned, I imagined she saw things the same way. Her intentions were good. At this moment, she didn't plan on dumping her kids off again on an unsuspecting relative or friendly neighbor. Consequently it blew her away that I was being so hard on her when she wanted nothing more than her kids back.

"Nicole," I began gently, advancing into the room. "I don't want things to be this way. I don't want either of us to waste money arguing over your kids in a courtroom in front of a bunch of strangers. Why don't we forget this whole thing?"

Her eyes widened in surprise. She opened her mouth to speak. I could see she misunderstood me, so I hurried on. "You signed the kids over to me once. Do it again with my attorney. Only this time, let's make it permanent."

Her eyes narrowed and she clenched her jaw.

I kept talking. "You will always be Emma and Jonah's mother, but whether we want to admit it or not, they're better off living here. Just because I have permanent custody doesn't mean anything will change. You'll still be Mom and I'll be Aunt Michelle. You'll be welcome to come for holidays or to visit anytime you want. You'll still be their Mom; they'll just live with me. It doesn't have to get complicated. We need to put our egos aside and think of the kids."

There, I presented my case as well as I could. I wasn't sure how smart it was to offer open invitation to holidays and unannounced visits. I could see it causing all kinds of problems down the road but for the first time since deciding to keep the kids here, I felt a peace in my spirit. This is the way things were supposed to be. Not perfect, but doable.

This had to be what real Christian charity felt like. Not the ideal situation for myself but a sacrifice that put another's needs before my own. A sacrifice was when a person did something for someone else knowing there would be no recompense.

Nicole didn't see it that way. "What an ego you have, Michelle. It's a wonder you can fit through a doorway with that big head of yours. You are so sure a judge will take your side over mine. It hasn't even crossed your mind that he might actually think children are better off with their mother."

"Yes, it has. I know how…"

She raised her hand in front of her and cut me off, her anger building steam. "I can't believe you actually have the nerve to stand here and tell me you're doing this for the kids' own good, and even mine. We both know you'll do anything to prove how right you are and how wrong I am. I am their mother. Yes, I've made some mistakes, but I'm willing to try and do better. I'm not a drug addict. I've never been in jail. You won't have as easy of a time as you think you're going to have. I'm not saying I shouldn't have to pay some kind of penance for what I did, but I'm paying that everyday. I want my kids back. I'm ready to take care of them." She slumped into a kitchen chair, put her elbow on the table and held onto her forehead. "I'm going to do whatever it takes to get on with my life, which includes my kids."

My stomach tightened. Was I wrong? She looked so destitute, so defeated; had I judged her harshly all along? Just because I thought the kids would be better off here, didn't necessarily mean Nicole couldn't provide a decent life for them either.

She had a point. The kids had never actually been in danger when Dean left them under the lilac bushes. It was summertime. The farm was located down a quiet back road that saw little traffic. He knew Gypsy's barking would rouse me within minutes and I'd find the kids before any real harm came to them. It hadn't been the most responsible way to handle the situation, but not as bad as what other children went through everyday. Maybe the sacrifice God was calling me to make was to let the kids go.

"Is this what you want me to do, God?"

I went to her and put my hand on the back of her head. "Nicole, I never meant to hurt you."

She raised her head to look at me, her eyes hopeful. "I won't fight with you," I continued before I could change my mind. "Whatever you want to do, I'll help you out as best I can."

She gasped, "Do you mean it? Oh, Michelle!" She jumped up and wrapped her arms around me. She pulled me into a hard hug. When she drew back, both our eyes were filled with tears. "Thank you. You don't know what this means to me. That you actually believe in me, that's the best part."

I hugged her. "Nicole, I've always believed in you." I realized I didn't always believe in her. Thinking her own family considered her as a loser had to make her feel bad. No wonder she had no confidence in herself and allowed men to talk her into anything.

"I'm sorry," I murmured into her hair. I stepped back to look into her eyes. "I felt really put upon when the kids appeared out of the blue. I never thought about having kids, especially someone else's. It took a lot of time to realize they were a blessing instead of a curse." I dropped my arms and chuckled. "I had to learn in a hurry how to be somebody's mother. In the beginning I didn't want to learn. I wanted my freedom back. Then, the next thing I knew, I couldn't bear the thought of you coming to get them."

"I'm sorry, Michelle. I never should have put you through all that. You're right, you didn't want the headaches and I was wrong to put it on you with no warning or consideration for what it was like for you."

I lowered myself into a chair and she sat back down in the one she'd gotten out of.

"Nicole, can you forgive me? I was wrong. By the time you got back, I was so sure I knew what was going on in your head, I wasn't even willing to listen to what you were saying."

"It's all right, Michelle. I put you in a terrible position. It's my own fault that you didn't react the way I wanted you to."

"So, what do we do now?"

"Well, Mom sent me some money. I guess I should give it back to her since I don't have to hire a lawyer."

"That's between you and Mom," I said. "Whatever you decide to do is fine with me. I wish you would stay here long enough for Emma's preschool graduation in a couple weeks though."

"Well—" Her voice trailed off and she looked away. "I'd really love to see her graduate. I know she's put a lot of work into it and everything, but Dean is coming. I don't know exactly what he'll want."

I wanted to tell her Dean didn't deserve any say in the situation. This concerned the family in which he had no part. I bit my tongue. My perception of the man had nothing to do with whether Nicole wanted to include him in her life or not. While I saw nothing redeemable in the man, it wasn't my decision to make.

I needed to stay out of my sister's life. We began dinner together, chatting like old friends for the first time since she'd returned. I put my reservations to the back of my mind. I wanted Nicole to be happy. I needed to give her the chance to find happiness, even if it wasn't my version of happiness. It was her life. She could live it the way she wanted and I could get back to mine.

I thought of Kyle and the possible future we might have together. Without Emma and Jonah we would be free to pursue whatever we wanted.

Somehow, my freedom didn't hold the allure it once did.

I prayed I hadn't made a grave mistake.

Chapter Forty-three

I slept well that night for the first time since Nicole came home. Though I wasn't thrilled with the situation, I knew what was going on. Nicole was leaving with Dean, probably within a few days. I hated that Emma couldn't graduate from preschool; I didn't like it that they were leaving the preschool at all. They had grown so close to all the teachers and the women there had been such a help and blessing to me. Without Emma and Jonah, I would no longer see any of them except at church. I would suffer. But the kids would suffer most of all. I wondered if Nicole thought about enrolling them into a daycare wherever she ended up. Would she and Dean think their education was that important? Most counties had assistance for couples that couldn't afford daycare. I would have to tell Nicole before she left so the kids wouldn't be left with a neighbor again like before.

Saturday was my thirty-fourth birthday. If I had my way, I would have let it pass unnoticed like every other birthday. Nicole had other plans. The kids woke me up by bouncing on my bed and singing off key. Nicole stood in the doorway smiling. I gave her a nasty look. After breakfast she sent Jonah and me to the store for ice cream and hotdogs, the kids' menu, so she and Emma could bake a cake and decorate the house in honor of my getting older.

I ran a few errands while I was out and did the weekly grocery shopping. With Nicole in the house, we were consuming even more.

It seemed all I did was shop. But Jonah and I had a good morning together. I hadn't spent much time with him since his mother came back.

"There's Dean," Jonah said when I slowed down to turn into our driveway. I looked up in dismay to see the battered car sitting in my spot—already. What was he doing here so soon?

I kept my face impassive. "Do you like Dean?" I asked carefully as I climbed out of the car.

He shrugged, and I remembered the picture of how he used to look when he first got here, so tiny and uncertain. "Mommy does."

"Do you want to live with Mommy and Dean again?"

He twisted his mouth thoughtfully, before answering. "You mean Dean is going to live here?"

I couldn't believe Nicole hadn't discussed Dean's eminent return with the kids or the fact that they were all leaving. "No, you and Emma will go somewhere else to live with Mommy and Dean. I'll keep living here."

His eyes widened with worry. "What about Uncle Jeb?"

"Uncle Jeb will still live with Aunt Wanda. You can visit us whenever you want."

He chewed his bottom lip thoughtfully and then shook his head. "No, I'll just stay here," he declared. "When Mommy misses us again, she can come visit. I think that's the best idea."

My heart ached for him. I wanted to pull him into my arms and tell him I couldn't agree more. "Now you know, Jonah," I said instead, trying to keep the tremor out of my voice, "when Mommy decides to leave, you and Emma are going with her. She's your Mommy, and kids need to be with their Mommy."

He unbuckled himself and climbed through the seat I was holding open for him. "Not Emma and me. Remember, Aunt Shell? You promised. You said if Mommy wanted us to live with her that you'd tell her we wanted to stay here. You said she'd be okay, that you was the big sister and she had to do what you said. Don't you remember?"

Tears stung the backs of my eyelids. In all the confusion of the past few weeks, I had forgotten all about the promises I made on two different occasions; the first time last September when I found them

huddled in bed crying; and the second time when Emma was dis-
traught every time I left her side. Both times I had assumed they were
crying for Nicole when in actuality they were upset over the thought
of leaving the farm. I had promised them for all I was worth that I
would take care of it. I would make Mommy understand that they
wanted to live here on the farm with me. I promised I would make it
so she wasn't mad at them.

How could I have forgotten that promise?

Worse, how would I explain it to Nicole?

What about Jonah and Emma?

"Lord, help me make him understand this is for the best."

I closed the car door and squatted next to him. I smoothed my
hands on his arms. He was so beautiful. What would I do without him?
How could I get through one day without seeing his sweet face?

"I think Mommy and Dean are thinking about moving back to
the city," I began gently. "When they go, they want to take you and
Emma with them."

Jonah froze in place. His face was a mask of confusion. "Tell them
we don't wanna go, Aunt Shell. Tell them you promised. We can't miss
school. Miss Jennifer will be mad at me. We gotta stay here."

"Miss Jennifer won't mind, sweetheart. We can tell her when we
go to pick up all your stuff." I hated myself before the words were even
out of my mouth. I felt like such a rat.

"You mean we're not going back to preschool at all?"

"Not if Dean is here to take you, Emma, and Mommy back to
the city." I tried to smile. I rubbed his arms again. "You'll live there
with them."

He jerked away from me and stomped his foot. "That's not fair.
I don't wanna go. Uncle Jeb won't have anybody to help him in the
fields or go fishin' with," he finished quietly.

I reached for him again. "Oh, sweetie, don't worry about Uncle
Jeb. He'll be okay. All that's important is you and Emma…" My voice
trailed off at the sight of his expression.

He was staring at his feet. The toe of one shoe dug a hole in the
gravel driveway. Finally he looked back at me and asked in a small
voice; "Will you get another boy to stay in my room? Are you gonna
give him all my toys?"

"Of course not, Jonah, you're room will be here for when you come to visit."

"Nuh uh," he clenched his fists. "You're mad at me. That's why you're not keeping your promise. You're mad 'cause I wouldn't pick up my toys. Now Emma and me'll never come back. You'll find another boy."

I wrapped my arms around him. "Jonah, no, that's not it at all. I'm not mad at you. I love you. But your Mommy needs you with her now. I'll always keep a place here for you and Emma—forever. I'll leave your rooms just like they are now. You can come back whenever you want."

He lunged into my arms and clung to my neck. "Don't make me go, Aunt Shell. Please. I'll be good. I promise I will. I'll pick up my toys from now on as soon as you ask. I won't play on the kitchen floor and get in your way. Please don't make me leave."

I couldn't hold my own tears in check. They streamed freely down my cheeks. *"I'm doing the right thing,"* I said over and over in my head. *"I believe in my sister."*

I squeezed him tighter. I couldn't tell him this wasn't my idea; if I had my way he and Emma would live with me forever. Nor could I let him think I didn't want him anymore because he had been naughty. I never should have told him and Emma that I would make sure Nicole let them stay here. I never should have told Nicole I wouldn't take her to court and fight for them. But my biggest mistake was letting myself fall in love with them in the first place.

When his tears finally abated, I released him. He didn't look at me as he dragged his feet all the way into the house. I went around the car for the groceries and to pull myself together. As I popped the trunk lid, I thought I saw a face disappear behind the curtains. Had Nicole or Dean overheard our conversation? At this point, I didn't even care.

Chapter Forty-four

Gypsy's incessant barking woke me up Sunday morning. I raised my head from the pillow with a groan. Six fifteen. Ugh! That dog, every time I planned to sleep in she decided to bark her head off. I swung my feet over the edge of the bed and stumbled to the window. I hit the pane with the heel of my hand to get it to move upward. All the spring rain had caused the wood to swell, and it was even more resistant to the upward motion. One of these days I would get new windows. At a hundred and thirty dollars a pop, installed, it was something I always figured I'd put off until I was dead and buried. Let the next generation worry about it. But I was getting too old and impatient to keep banging away at wood windows. One of these days…

I couldn't see Gypsy from my window, but I could certainly hear her. She was directly below me on the porch where she'd spent the night. She liked to do that on nice nights when the weather cooperated.

Suddenly a vision of last summer, when the exact same scenario was played out, flashed through my mind. I jerked my head toward the driveway. I could barely see the backend of my Mazda from my vantage point. The only thing behind it was empty driveway. There should have been a car sitting there. That's where Dean parked last night after coming in from town and not speaking to anyone. Now his car was gone.

I forgot about Gypsy and the open window through which I was going to yell at her, and ran out of the room. My bare feet grew cold against the hardwood floor as I hurried across the hall. I eased opened the door to Emma's room. She and Jonah lay curled together in the double bed. I let out an audible sob of relief. "Thank you, God."

I moved to the next door. I rapped lightly with my knuckles and then pushed it open. I advanced into the room and gazed down at the empty bed, dumbfounded. I slid a couple of drawers open. Empty.

I ran downstairs and opened the front door. "Gypsy, get in here," I ordered. I didn't want her waking the kids, not until I found out what was going on. I turned on lights as I moved through the house, looking this way and that for a note or something. I was sure I'd find something in the kitchen. I didn't. Nicole was gone with no word as to her whereabouts.

How typical!

What was I going to tell the kids?

Monday morning the kids were back in preschool. I pulled Miss Gail aside and told her the latest development as Emma and Jonah trudged to the play area.

"I don't know how they'll do today," I told her. "They haven't said a whole lot since yesterday morning when I told them Nicole was gone. I don't know what they're thinking."

Gail shook her head. "I'm sure they think she's gone because of something they did."

"Maybe they're blaming me. Nicole and I exchanged words more than once. I know they overheard a lot and picked up on the tension."

She put her hand on my arm. "Honey, don't blame yourself. We all knew this would probably happen eventually. It's not very encouraging, but isn't it better that she left them with you before she took off. How much worse would it be if she moved them somewhere else, and then pulled a disappearing act?"

"There's nothing I can do, is there?" I said dismally.

"I wish I could say the kids'll bounce right back and you'll all live happily ever after. But even if you get permanent custody, Nicole will always be in your lives. She is their mother. She will most likely flit in and out of here whenever the mood strikes her, play Mommy for awhile, and then be gone again, leaving you to pick up the pieces."

I went to work with a heavy heart. It was a long twelve hours.

I picked up the kids at Angie's that evening and headed home. They still weren't talking. Emma was quiet. I noticed her fingers in her mouth several times. Jonah stared out the window the whole way home. Any questions from me were met with one-word responses. Here we go again. At least the kids knew me this time.

The phone rang just after dinner. Emma and Jonah were on their knees behind the coffee table watching television, an armload of coloring books in front of them. As soon as I heard Nicole's voice, I hurried from the room and out the back door.

I glanced over my shoulder to make sure I hadn't been followed. Then I growled into the phone, "Where are you? Didn't you learn anything from the last time?"

"I'm sorry, Michelle," she whined, although I heard no contrition in her voice. "I thought it would be better this way."

"How could it possibly be better?" I tightened my grip on the phone. I didn't want the kids to hear me but I wanted nothing more than to chew her out good and proper. "I can't believe you did it again, Nicole; just up and disappeared without a word. What do you think that's doing to your kids?"

"And what do you think it does to me to hear my own son cry and beg his aunt to let him stay with her so he won't have to go with his own mother?"

So Nicole had been the one listening at the window Saturday. I tried to imagine her pain, but it was getting harder and harder to do. "I'm sorry Nicole, but you really can't blame Jonah for that. All he knows is that living here isn't a constant struggle. He knows he'll wake up in the same bed he went to sleep in. Everything's the same; routine. Kids need that. They can't handle the alternative."

"Well, I can't give that to my kids right now, Michelle. I'm sorry but I can't." Her voice rang with self-righteous tears. "Dean and I are headed to Vegas. We're going to stay with Mom for a while till we get on our feet. I am going to use part of her money to have an attorney draft a permanent custody agreement for you. I'll send it and you can sign it and give a copy to your attorney, or however it works. I think that's best for everyone."

Tears came to my eyes. I couldn't stay mad at her. Whether she knew it or not, she couldn't have given me a better birthday present. There was no point in yelling at her. The deed was already done and nothing was going to make my sister feel the least bit responsible for the way things turned out. In her mind, things couldn't be peachier. She knew the kids were safe and cared for. She had Dean back and apparently, our Mother. I would take care of her kids. She could concentrate on getting her life figured out, which I had a sneaking suspicion would never completely happen. She was free and I...

I had come out the winner. It hadn't seemed that way last August. For the longest time, I thought God was punishing me for some terrible sin, much like Grandma Catherine had felt. But fortunately unlike Grandma, I realized before it was too late that Nicole's kids were the best things that could have happened to me. If they hadn't showed up under the lilac bushes, I never would've known how empty my life was. I never would have met Kyle again after fifteen years. More importantly, I may never have met my Heavenly Father.

Yes, I definitely won hands down.

"Nicole, I wish you and Dean all the best," I said sincerely.

"I know you do. I really appreciate everything you've done this past year, Michelle. I know I don't always act like it, but I do. You've always been the only person I could count on, no matter what."

"I'm your sister, Nicole."

"Well, I'm your sister, too, and I'm afraid I've been nothing but trouble."

"I'm not going to disagree with you, if that's what you're waiting for," I said with a chuckle.

"Michelle, I love you. Take care of my kids, will you?"

"You know I will."

"Tell them, I'll be back to visit them as soon as I get settled and then get some money together. Maybe you could keep Christmas open for us. We could bring Mom in for a visit. Wouldn't that be nice, the family together again?"

"Yeah, that'd be great," I said, both of us knowing it wasn't going to happen.

"Thanks for everything, Michelle."

"You too, Nicole; I mean that. Give Mom my love."

"I will. We'll see you in December."

I hung up the phone and wondered when and if I'd hear from my baby sister again.

Chapter Forty-five

"Hold your head still, sweet cheeks," I said, my teeth clenched around a mouthful of bobby pins. "I'm having a hard enough time getting this ponytail in the center of your head."

"Wait till Aunt Wanda gets here," Emma suggested patiently as I pulled her head into the angle I wanted. "She always gets it straight the first time."

I removed the bobby pins from my mouth. They were too big for her head anyway and they stood out against her blonde hair. Didn't these things come in white? "Oh, she does, does she?" I gave the ponytail a playful yank. "I think that'll do it. Yeah, that's better. Turn around and let me see."

Emma clutched the top of her head. "It's too tight. I can't close my eyes."

That was the least of her problems. The ponytail tilted crazily to the left. The delicate blonde tendrils I'd purposefully left down to frame her face looked scraggly and tangled. The angelic look I'd intended had somehow fallen short, so she looked more like a scarecrow at the end of summer. I grinned at my ineptitude. I spun her around, let the ponytail down and combed my fingers through her long hair. "How about we wait and let Aunt Wanda do it?"

"Yea!" she cheered. I agreed too much to be insulted by her enthusiasm.

"Is Pastor Kyle gonna be there to see me graduate?" she asked as I brushed out the damage I'd done.

My hands paused in their work for a moment. An image of Kyle's blue eyes looking at me from the pulpit yesterday evening while he read the part he had prepared for the graduation, flashed through my mind. "You know he is. Didn't he practice his speech last night at the dress rehearsal?"

"Yes."

"Then you know he'll be there."

I released her and she turned to face me. "I know. Do you think he'll come here after the graduation for our party?"

Heat rushed into my cheeks at the prospect. Even though I'd made it a point to help out last night at the dress rehearsal so I could see him, I still blushed at the thought of seeing him again. "I'm sure he'll be here."

"Does he like you, Aunt Shell?"

I smiled and tweaked her nose. "Why do you ask that?"

"I think he likes you. He looks at you an awful lot. Uncle Jeb said he looks like a puppy with a—with a—"

"A new bone?" I offered.

"Yeah, that's it, a puppy with a new bone."

"That sounds like Uncle Jeb. He shouldn't be talking like that in front of you. Don't forget Kyle is our pastor and we have to treat him with respect. Don't you go asking him any questions like that at our party tonight."

Emma's eyes grew wide. "Oh, I won't."

My reminder was unnecessary. As shy as she was, she wouldn't say anything to him or hardly any other adult in the room.

A party for a preschool graduation seemed a little pretentious to my old cynicism, but I couldn't resist. Emma was my preschooler, soon to be kindergartner, and I wanted to make a big deal of it. I took Aunt Wanda's advice to keep things simple and decided against the caterer. While I spent the day cleaning and hanging party decorations, Aunt Wanda had baked and whipped up hors-d-oeuvres to suit a five-year olds' palate. She, Jonah, and Uncle Jeb were due any minute to set things out and hopefully, to repair the damage I'd done to Emma's hair. At least she was clean; that was one maternal job I could handle.

I still couldn't believe the kids were mine, at least for now, until the next big blowup. Adoptions within a family were seldom uncomplicated. My caseworker warned me to expect disruptions from time to time until Emma and Jonah married—and even after. Nicole would never be completely out of their lives. She was their mother and I would always be Aunt Michelle. I wouldn't want it any other way, but down deep, I couldn't help wishing every now and then she would stay in Las Vegas with Mom.

"Yoo-hoo, where is everybody?"

"We're up here, Aunt Wanda." I reached for Emma to give her a kiss before our hectic evening began, but she was already gone.

"Aunt Wanda," she called on her way down the stairs. "Aunt Shell messed up my hair."

She reached the bottom of the stairs and headed toward the back of the house so I couldn't make out the rest of the complaint. I'm sure my ego was better off. I headed to my own room to finish getting ready. Emma would be fine now that the cavalry had arrived, and I could spend some time on myself. As Emma had pointed out, Kyle would be at the graduation and later, our party. Ever since our meeting at Angie's, we'd had barely more than a few moments together, and never alone. Kyle saw to that. I knew he didn't want to hurt his witness with people who might think the worst. I kind of liked being treated like a lady.

I didn't know where this relationship was headed and I wanted to enjoy every moment. I loved him too—enough to become a pastor's wife? I didn't know since I hadn't been asked yet, but I could think of worse things that could happen to a person. I smiled at myself in the medicine cabinet mirror. This time last year, I thought my future held nothing other than more of the present. Like Grandma, I imagined living here the rest of my days with Gypsy for company and my job and the garden to occupy my time. I couldn't have imagined how two little people under my lilac bushes could change everything.

They didn't deserve all the credit. I had a Heavenly Father up there with a sense of humor that knew exactly what I needed. Now I had everything I had sorely lacked: a house that knew the sound of children's laughter, a much-improved relationship with my family, and a man who loved me. More than that, I knew the Creator of it all loved me.

Even things with Nicole were better. She called when she and Dean got to Mom's house to let us know they had arrived in one piece. We were on friendly terms. For the time being, that was the best I could expect. I would continue to pray for her salvation and for our relationship to strengthen. I thought of Mom and wondered if she'd ever really come to visit. I didn't see it happening. Too much water had passed under the bridge. She never was strong; I couldn't see her facing Aunt Wanda and everyone else who thought she did wrong by leaving Nicole and me here nineteen years ago, and would have no qualms about telling her as much.

Maybe it was better just leaving things the way they were. Nicole wasn't completely wrong when she called me a control freak. I needed to work on that. Mom was who she was and so was Dad, wherever he was. I couldn't change the world, or even my little corner of it. But with the Lord's help, I could change myself and the way I saw the world.

Things would be fine. I had learned to open my heart. I had two beautiful children to get through each day. I didn't know what was in store for tomorrow, but for tonight, we were going to the church to see my little princess graduate from preschool. I wouldn't worry about tomorrow, the next day, kindergarten, or bullies in the schoolyard. Tonight was enough. I had people who loved me. People I loved back. There were some who looked up to me, and others who thought my life was a train wreck. That's what I'd concern myself with. Tomorrow was in the Lord's hands—tomorrow and the rest of my life.

I heard thundering feet on the stairs. "Aunt Shell, Jonah said I look like a grape in my purple dress."

"I did not. I said she looked 'great'."

I smiled again at the reflection in the mirror and opened the bathroom door. I wondered how many years it would be before I got an uninterrupted five minutes in the bathroom again. Funny, at this moment, it didn't matter.

❦ The End ❦

Teresa always enjoys hearing from her readers. You may contact her at: *teresa@teresaslack.com*

C oming soon from Teresa Slack... *The Ultimate Guide to Darcy Carter*

Darcy Carter is the Ultimate Guide Girl. She dropped out of school at nineteen to write the *Ultimate Guide to Writing a College Thesis* and hasn't come up for air since. She's written twenty books in just over ten years. Considered an expert in everything from parenting multiples and the NFL draft to online trading, she doubts she could guide herself out of a brown paper bag.

While her professional life is going better than she had ever dreamed it would, Darcy's personal life could use some work. Her relationship with God has fallen by the wayside at the same rate that her writing career has flourished. She's lost touch with her church friends and those with whom she went to school. Her nieces and nephew are growing up before her eyes, but she can't find the time to fulfill a simple promise she made years ago. Forget about time for a man in her life.

When her editor suggests she write *The Ultimate Guide to Finding Mr. Right*, Darcy balks. She wants no part in giving women false hope of finding a man she doesn't believe exists. To avoid Mr. Right, and hopefully discover where the discontentment with her life is coming from, she heads to North Carolina to research one last ultimate guidebook.

Unfortunately, North Carolina only amplifies the questions and doubts swirling around in her head rather than mollifying them. When did she start writing for money rather than the sheer love of the craft? Is she meant to do something else with her life? If she's no longer America's Ultimate Guide Girl, who is she? Can she trust her heart to recognize Mr. Right when he's standing before her, or should she continue to doubt his existence? Whom can the Ultimate Guide Girl trust to guide her; her Heavenly Father who gives wisdom to those who seek it, or herself, the woman with all the answers?

If you enjoyed this book and would like to pass one on to someone else or if you're interested in another Tsaba House title, please check with your local bookstore, online bookseller, or use this form:

Name_____

Address _____

City _____ State_____ Zip _____

Please send me:

_____ copies of *A Tender Reed* at $15.99 $ _____

_____ copies of *Nature Never Stops Talking* at $15.99 $ _____

_____ copies of *The Moody Pews* at $15.99 $ _____

_____ copies of *Streams of Mercy* at $15.99 $ _____

_____ copies of *The Payload* at $15.99 $ _____

_____ copies of *Your Rights to Riches* at $14.99 $ _____

_____ copies of *The Parenting Business* at $15.99 $ _____

California residents please add sales tax $ _____

Shipping*: $4.00 for the first copy and $2.00
for each additional copy $ _____

Total enclosed

Send order to:

    Tsaba House
    2252 12th Street
    Reedley, CA 93654

or visit our website at www.TsabaHouse.com
or call (toll free) 1-866-TSABA-HS (1-866-872-22

For more than 5 copies, please contact the publis
*International shipping costs extra. If shipping t
United States, please contact the publisher for rat